TILLY TENNANT

A Helping Hand
for the
VILLAGE
NURSE

Bookouture

Published by Bookouture in 2024

An imprint of Storyfire Ltd.
Carmelite House
50 Victoria Embankment
London EC4Y 0DZ

www.bookouture.com

ISBN: 978-1-83525-557-5
eBook ISBN: 978-1-83525-556-8

A Helping Hand
for the
VILLAGE NURSE

BOOKS BY TILLY TENNANT

To our nurses

CHAPTER ONE

Lunch was rushed. Lunch was always a rush; Ottilie was used to that. After bolting the last of her tuna salad, she snapped the lid on the sandwich box shut and was about to hurry back to the ward when her phone started to ring. Breaking into a smile as her gaze fell on the photo of a dark-haired, handsome man in a police uniform wearing a cheeky smile that she knew only too well, she swiped to answer.

'I've got thirty seconds,' she said, trying to sound stern but still smiling, 'so this had better be good.'

'It is. How do you feel about trying that new Thai restaurant later?'

'I thought it was all booked up?'

'It was, but I had to call there to give the premises the once-over after their alarm went off and I may have told them it was my tenth wedding anniversary and that we didn't have plans. As you can imagine, they were horrified.'

'And so they found you a table? Without you even having to ask?'

'OK, I may have asked. And I may have played a little on the fact that I'd just saved their business.'

'Had anyone actually broken in?'

'Well, no, but...'

Ottilie's smile spread further still. 'Some might see this as very dodgy behaviour, Constable Oakcroft.'

'They might. Or they might see a man who adores his beautiful wife so much that he'll move heaven and earth to give her a lovely night out at a restaurant he knows she's been dying to try for her anniversary. Especially as he feels so guilty for not having time to get anything else.'

'I told you I didn't need a gift.'

'You might not need one, but you deserve one. You deserve to be showered with gifts, but will a night at the Thai restaurant do for now?'

'I suppose I could eat some tom yum soup. And maybe some pad thai. Or a panang curry. Or—'

'We'll order the whole bloody menu if you want it.'

'Well, I wouldn't order the whole menu, because being too full is no good for any kind of physical exertion...'

'So salad it is then.'

Ottilie giggled. 'I could manage a bit more than that. It sounds amazing. Yes please. And then you can have your present when we get home.'

'Can't wait. I know sometimes it's hard living with me and sometimes I bring my work home, and sometimes I'm a pain in the arse, but I do love you more than life itself, Mrs Oakcroft, and can't tell you how grateful I am that you agreed to take me on. I'm a work in progress after all, and possibly a lifelong one at that.'

'Ditto to all that, Mr Oakcroft,' Ottilie replied, laughing again. 'I'll see you later for our hot date.'

'I'll be thinking of nothing else for the rest of the day.'

'Me too.'

Ottilie ended the call and went to the mirror in the staffroom to tidy her bun. She was still smiling as she smoothed a caramel strand of hair into a grip. Her thoughts went to the new restaurant she'd been desperate to try, to a well-deserved romantic dinner and to what might follow, and her tummy did a cartwheel. Already she was planning what she might wear. The black dress she'd picked up the previous week in a sale? Was it too much for a weeknight at quite a casual restaurant? But it showed her curves off in the most delicious way, which had been very apparent to her from Josh's face as she'd modelled it for him.

She'd never been what she'd class as slim; certainly she'd always been more solidly built than most of her friends growing up, but she'd always been comfortable with her curves. They were generous but firm, and her skin had always been clear and her blue eyes wide, and her hair had always naturally been a colour that others had paid a lot of money for. Josh had always said that, for him, it had been love at first sight.

For her, it hadn't been so much love as lust at first sight. She'd triaged him as a student nurse working in the accident unit, where he'd turned up with a cut on his hand from some barbed wire while on a public disorder call, and before the appointment was over he'd got her phone number. He'd told her afterwards he'd been so bowled over by her that he hadn't been able to help himself. He was the luckiest person on earth to have cut his hand that day, or so he'd said, but Ottilie knew different. She was the lucky one. Josh had made her who she was today.

She couldn't wait to give him his gift too. Not the saucy one they'd joked about – though he'd get that too – but the one she'd managed to keep a secret, even though it had half killed her. He'd always wanted to see the Northern Lights and she'd booked a cruise in Norway where they'd go out into the wilds to see them from the sea. She'd been saving for a couple of years, cutting her spending a little here and there: a cheaper shampoo or mascara, home-made lunches instead of the canteen, that sort of thing, subtle, so he wouldn't notice the money go from their joint account and she wouldn't be taking from the running of the house.

Their next week off was just over a fortnight away and she'd told him she was taking him to Blackpool. So he knew he was seeing some lights but not quite the ones he'd been expecting. And she was so excited to see his face when he finally worked it out that she could barely contain herself.

But she had a shift to finish, and about ten more after that before they could both hang up their uniforms and head off, and so she had to contain herself for that long at least.

The two hours since lunch had gone by in a blur. Some days work was busy but manageable, and some days the ward seemed to lurch from one crisis to another, each one dealt with in the nick of time, but it could be stressful on days like that. Today wasn't that yet, but Ottilie felt as if it might be heading that way. There had been some sort of commotion in Accident and Emergency. She didn't know what, but rumours had filtered up to the ward, a warning that they had to be ready to get very busy. For now, Ottilie was trying not to think about it. One patient at a time, she always told herself – she couldn't do any more than that if she was going to do her job properly, though it was sometimes very hard to stick to her own rule when there were so many demands on her time. She loved her job, but sometimes she wondered if she must be quite mad to do it.

'Nurse, when are you going to say yes? A man could die waiting...'

Ottilie's current patient coughed violently. She waited for him to finish with a tolerant half-smile.

'In fact,' he rasped as his breathing steadied, 'this one probably will.'

Her smile still in place, she took a note of his blood pressure. 'As I've told you every day since we admitted you, you're not going to die any time soon. At least, not as far as I can tell. Certainly not if I have anything to do with it.'

'I'm eighty-seven. It's only a matter of time.'

'It's only a matter of time for all of us. And with blood pressure this good you'll probably outlast me.'

Mr Pearson let out a theatrical sigh. 'If only I'd been born a few decades later, eh? Or you'd been born a few decades earlier...'

'I don't want any extra decades if you don't mind.' Ottilie undid the strap that she'd fastened around his arm to measure his blood pressure and wound it up.

'But you might have said yes, eh? A man can always have hope. I've got a bit in the bank, you know, if that helps to change your mind. And I'm on the way out so you wouldn't have long to wait for it...'

'Generous and tempting as that offer is, Mr Pearson, I think I'll stick with the husband I already have. He might not have quite as much in the bank as you do, but he's perfect.'

'Lucky bleeder too.'

Ottilie held a tumbler of water in front of his face. 'Drink. That jug is almost full, so you clearly haven't had enough today.'

'Will I have to go home later?'

'I don't see why not. Of course, the consultant will come and check everything, but as far as I can tell there's no reason to keep you here.'

'To my big empty house...' He gazed at the glass but made no move to take it.

Ottilie's smile slipped. Despite the jokes and banter, the man who'd been admitted to her ward a couple of days previously was perhaps really only here because he was lonely rather than any tangible illness that they could treat. She wished she could do something to change that – she wished it for all

patients like Mr Pearson, because he wasn't the first and she
was sure he wouldn't be the last. But no matter what she
wished, realistically there was only so much she could do. She
made a mental note to phone him once he was home to check
up, and so he'd have a friendly voice that might at least brighten
an hour of his day.

As she straightened his pillows, from the corner of her eye
she saw one of the ward clerks, Dawn, hurrying down the ward,
a look of panic on her face the likes of which Ottilie had never
seen in all the years they'd worked together. Dawn was so laid-
back everyone joked that she might well be doing her job in her
sleep for all the difference in her mood.

Before she was even within earshot she was talking. Ottilie
put a hand up as Dawn reached her. As far as Ottilie could see,
she'd only run the length of the ward, but for how out of breath
she was, perhaps she'd been running long before she'd
reached it.

'Start again! What on earth is wrong? What's happened?'

'Josh,' Dawn panted.

Ottilie's eyebrows drew together into an instant frown. 'My
Josh?'

Dawn nodded, dragging in breaths. 'Accident and Emergency just phoned... He's in there now... rushed in...'

'But I spoke to him... like a couple of hours ago! He
can't be!'

Dawn gave a vehement nod. 'They're asking for you. It
sounds...'

'Sounds what?'

The blood drained from Ottilie's face, suddenly ice-cold in
her veins. 'Dawn— What did they say?'

'Nothing. They said nothing at all.'

'They didn't say what had happened to him?'

Dawn shook her head and Ottilie knew, from that one small

detail, that it was bad. Dazed, she gestured vaguely at her patient. 'Can you...?'

Dawn wasn't medically qualified at all and there was little she'd be able to do for Mr Pearson, but in the panic that had seized her, that fact didn't even occur to Ottilie. All she knew was that she needed to get down to the emergency department as fast as possible.

Without another word, she raced from the ward. She could have phoned ahead, got the whole picture, but by the time she'd got through various members of staff to find out what was going on, it would be quicker to take the stairs that led from her ward to that department and see for herself.

She was shaking as she swiped her card to access the doors that separated her section of the hospital from the outpatient department. She had nothing to go on, no information, no reason to be afraid, and yet she was. Something in her heart told her to expect the worst.

CHAPTER TWO

As Ottilie drove over a pothole, the entire contents of her car boot rattled. Many of her most treasured possessions were in there – she'd decided to take them herself rather than trust them to the removal van. They seemed very conscientious, but you never knew. The way the whole lot had just been thrown into the air as she'd taken flight over a bump she hadn't seen until it was too late, she wondered now if that had been the wisest course.

The roads leading to the tiny Lake District village of Thimblebury were undoubtedly some of the most beautiful she'd ever driven, embraced by mist-wreathed hills and dizzying valleys of emerald green with the white dots of sheep clinging to their sides, but they were some of the most alarming too. They turned and twisted and narrowed into blind bends, or disappeared into dark tunnels of trees, and the potholes were something else. People complained about the roads back in Manchester, the rainy vista she'd left a couple of hours before, but they were nothing like this. It was lucky the views more than made up for some of the more... *rustic* surfaces.

Another jolt was met with another crash from the boot.

Ottilie grimaced and hoped that the tinkling sound she was convinced she'd heard wasn't her great-grandma's china tea service. It had survived the Blitz and several house moves before it had been passed down, and Ottilie didn't want to end up as the weak link in the chain. She tried not to recall how she'd hoped to pass it down herself some day, because that would mean recognising that she was childless and likely to remain that way now that Josh was gone, and so she turned up the radio to block the thoughts out.

She'd had six months to get used to her new status as widow. The word seemed old-fashioned and fusty whenever she thought of it, the preserve of old ladies, not someone like her. And yet, here she was, a widow, leaving her old life behind, searching for hope, clinging on to any tiny grain she could find.

Life without Josh had been unthinkable in the early days and weeks. Not just unthinkable, but not even real. She'd refused to believe he was gone. It was strange – in her job she'd seen more bereavement, more grieving and desolation than she could bring to mind, and she'd supported those families with sympathy and pity, yet she'd never really been able to imagine what it might be like. She couldn't have known how it would tear open a wound in her soul that felt as if it would never heal, how it would force a chasm between a new reality and a past she wasn't willing to let go of that might never be bridged. Every day that passed blurred the edges of the event a little, but that only made her want to fight harder to keep them sharp. She wanted to heal – so desperately sick of feeling bereft – and yet she couldn't let go of her grief, because it meant letting go of Josh and she would never do that.

It had happened so quickly and violently too, and in her more lucid moments she wondered whether that was part of the problem. Perhaps if there had been a creeping illness, a slow decline, some kind of warning, she'd have been prepared. But there hadn't. One minute he was on duty, fit and strong, looking forward to their wedding anniversary celebrations, as she was, and the next he was dead. Her Josh, her life, her light, the only man she'd ever loved – gone.

It had been a scuffle with a suspect gone wrong – someone had attacked him but they hadn't meant to kill him – at least, that was the official line – and that almost made it worse. It seemed like such a cruel twist, such a senseless end to a situation Josh had dealt with dozens of times before. She'd always had the vague, overarching worries that many other police wives had, but she'd never given them any serious consideration. Josh had always seemed so sensible, so instinctive, so good at his job that he could deal with anything. She'd never imagined for one second she'd be here, driving to a new life without him.

Glancing at the route on her phone screen, she held back a frown. The village ought to have been in sight by now, but she couldn't see any houses.

The road followed a gentle bend, and as Ottilie rounded it, she saw a man ahead, up on a grass verge. Dressed in green wellies and a fleece, it looked as if he was mending some fencing. Ottilie slowed as she drew closer then stopped and wound the window down. He looked around, a vague expression of surprise, his movements slow and measured. Ottilie would have had him at around his mid-seventies, maybe older, but although he was slow, she felt that the pace came from a place of care rather than ill health. In fact, judging by the tall-handled mallet he was wielding, he was still as strong as a man decades younger.

'Sorry to bother you,' she called across, choosing to kill the engine so she could hear his reply better.

'No bother.' The man's face crinkled into a smile. Ottilie decided that it would have been a handsome smile once, and it was quite winning, even now. 'You're lost?'

'A bit. I suppose you must get a lot of that round here, eh?'

He leaned on the handle of his mallet and regarded her

keenly. 'From time to time. Big towns are easy enough to find, tiny villages not so much. So where are you after?'

'Thimblebury. My directions say it's close, but I'm wondering if I've somehow missed it.'

'You've not missed it – it's over yonder. Road dips into a valley ahead. Thimblebury's there, nice and safe – at least it was last time I looked.' His gaze was keener still, and he seemed to study her intently. 'What do you want in Thimblebury?'

'I'm moving there. Do you know it well?'

She wanted to ask if it was a nice place to live, if she'd be happy – because many times over the past six months she'd felt as if she'd never be happy again – if she'd be welcomed, but perhaps that wasn't helpful in the current situation. If the answers to any of those questions were negative, it was a bit too late now. The house she'd shared with Josh in Manchester was gone, so there was no turning back.

'Ah!' He looked suddenly pleased with himself. 'I'll bet you're the new nurse.'

'I am,' Ottilie said, sensing a longer chat and getting out of the car to see him better. 'I'm Ottilie. How did you know?'

'Oh, there's been a bit of talk about who it might be. Gwen has been gone a couple of weeks; folks are impatient for someone new to take the job on. They'll be happy to see you. I'm Victor – pleased to meet you.'

'So you live in Thimblebury, Victor?'

'Not quite. My farm is on the hill. Close enough to be included when it suits though.'

'You've got a farm? I saw some sheep a way back – are they yours?'

'No, not mine. They'll belong to Hilltop. Used to keep sheep, but these days I have alpaca.'

Ottilie blinked. 'Alpaca? Sorry but I was not expecting that! Where are they?' She glanced up at the slopes behind him.

'They're fastened in for the time being, until I get this fence sorted.'

'So they're good business? I mean, better than sheep? Do you get more wool or something? Sorry but I know literally nothing about farming.'

'There's more money in the tourists that come to see them. I've got a little walking trail – families can take them for a stroll. Kids love it. It's still early in the season, a bit quiet yet – won't get going properly until July and August, but bookings are picking up.'

'I bet they do. I'd love it! I'll have to come up and see them before you get very busy. So you do that on your own? Sounds like a lot.'

He let out a chuckle. 'I know I look ancient, but I manage all right. I've got my daughters and their husbands too. I let them have bits of land for their houses, and they repay me by working the farm when I need help.'

'Sounds like a pretty good arrangement to me.' Ottilie smiled.

'So you'll be taking Wordsworth Cottage then?'

'Yes, right again.'

If Ottilie had come looking for anonymity, it seemed she wasn't going to find it. Village nurse was hardly the job for that anyway, but since Josh's death she'd spent so much time alone, the potential of being a part of a community again felt like it would be a welcome change.

Plenty of people had done their best to support her, of course – friends, family, colleagues – and so it was hardly their fault she'd felt so isolated in her grief. The simple fact was, many of them had only been a part of her life since Josh had been in it and, even if they hadn't, there was always some connection, something that made them remind her of him. And in the background was Ottilie's old people-pleasing instincts, despite her pain, not wanting to be the person who made others feel uncomfortable, not wanting to transmit her sorrow to anyone else, not wanting them to suffer because she was suffering. Her mum had seen it and told her to lean on those who wanted to help, because they did want to help, but Ottilie simply couldn't do it. In the end, there had been too much against her moving forward in Manchester. She didn't want to stay in the home she'd shared with Josh or work at the hospital where he'd died. And there were other complications too, fears she couldn't bring herself to say out loud, not even to her closest family.

'It's a nice size,' he said. 'Good for a family. Harold and Doreen managed to raise three there, no trouble.' He shook his head wonderingly. 'Their oldest went off to work in Exeter, you know, and they decided to go with him. Can't fathom it myself, at their age. You'd want to stay put. Anyway... you'll have plenty of room for your family.'

'That's good to know, but it's just me.'

Perhaps something of her inner pain showed in her face, because the man suddenly seemed unsure of himself, as if he felt he'd crossed a line he hadn't been aware had existed.

'Not married then?'

'I was,' Ottilie said bleakly. 'He died.'

'I'm sorry, I didn't mean to pry.'

'It's all right.' Ottilie tried to smile to reassure him, but the effort was too much. Josh's loss was still so raw for all the months that had passed since that horrendous day. She tried to move forward a little more every day, and she often convinced herself that she had, but the grief was always there, filling the dark spaces, showing itself whenever she dared to look. 'If you don't ask questions, then you don't learn anything about anyone, do you?'

Victor looked unconvinced. He sniffed and then shifted awkwardly to swap the hand that rested on the long handle of his mallet.

Ottilie tried harder to produce that smile, to reinforce her point. She was fine. Totally fine. People would ask – it was only natural – and she would tell them what happened because there was no point in hiding it. She would tell them how her soul mate, her one true love, her everything had been ripped from her life in the cruellest instant, and it would be fine. It wasn't her fault. It wasn't their fault. Did they deserve to be at the sharp end of the anger and resentment that sometimes took her in unguarded moments? Maybe it was down to the universe – whatever that was or meant, because people said the universe did this or that, but did it really? The only person she could get angry at was the man who'd attacked him on duty that day, but as they hadn't caught anyone yet, Ottilie didn't even have that.

'Got much to move in?' Victor asked. 'I could rally the troops if you need a hand.'

'I think I'll be all right. The removal van's following.'

'Ah, they'll do it for you?'

'The amount it cost to hire, I should hope so! But if you're looking for an excuse to come over, I'd love you and your family to visit so I can get to know you better. The kettle will be the first thing I unpack – can't survive without my tea.'

'You'll fit right in here then. I'm sure the wife will be itching to come over.'

'I'd like to meet her – I have a feeling I'll like her. I'm looking forward to getting to know everyone in time. Bring her over whenever you get a minute.'

'You might regret saying that.' Victor's smile was easier. 'Nobody in Thimblebury needs much of an invitation to come and nosy at you.'

'Honestly, that's sort of what I'm hoping for. This is all new to me – upping sticks and moving to the countryside – so a few friendly faces will be most welcome.'

'Oh, you'll get all that and more round here.'

Ottilie's reply was stolen by the rumble of a lorry coming down the road and heading in their direction.

'Looks like my removal van is going to beat me there,' she said as they watched it rattle past, a cloud of dust and fumes in its wake that seemed a crime as it climbed into the clear blue sky to dissipate above the valley. 'I suppose that means I ought to get a move on. I can't have them sitting outside waiting for me to open up.'

'Make them earn their money, eh?'

'I was thinking that they'd want a pot of tea, but you might have a point about that. The quicker my stuff's in, the quicker I can get settled.'

'Don't forget…' Victor nodded back at a house on a distant hill. It was squat and sturdy and made of stone as far as Ottilie could see from this distance, the sun glinting off slate tiles on the roof. 'Daffodil Farm – that's us. Anything you need, just knock. I'd give you a landline number, but I can never remember it, and the mobile phones I've lost in slurry and feed and such over the years, I don't see any point in having another. You can call the house though – there's always someone in.'

'Thank you,' Ottilie said. 'That's very kind.'

'Not at all. Least we can do.'

'What for?'

'For taking the job. You'll have your work cut out, let me tell you. Gwen never stopped – no wonder she chose not to live in the village – commuted in from Keswick, you know. If she'd lived here, she'd never have had a moment's peace. Half the village would still have her on duty if they could.'

'Well, I'm looking forward to starting.'

'You say that…'

Ottilie laughed at Victor's eyebrow raise. 'Honestly, a full schedule is exactly what I need. I love being busy. If anything, I'll be sticking my nose into things that probably don't need me, so I don't mind at all if I have a full appointment list every day.'

'Again, I have to say be careful what you wish for. I'll ask you if you still feel that way once you've done your first week. When do you start, by the way?'

'I'm taking a week of leave to get the house straight before I start and I have a bit of extra training to do, but if anyone needs me before then I'm happy to see them unofficially. I know you don't have a nurse at the moment, so I appreciate people are anxious about that.'

Victor scratched his head and then put his hat back on. 'I'm actually being serious now – I'd keep that to yourself. You'll have a queue at your front door before you can say hypochondriac. And don't forget we have a doctor.'

'Oh, yes.' Ottilie nodded slightly. 'I haven't met her yet in the flesh – only on Zoom. Dr Cheadle, isn't it? I'm planning to pop into the surgery later to introduce myself.'

'I'm surprised she didn't retire at the same time as Gwen. They've worked together for forty years and I know Dr Cheadle is right fond of her, and she's about the right age to finish too.'

'Well I'm glad she didn't. I'll be making full use of her local knowledge while I find my feet.' Ottilie glanced down the road to where the van had just gone. 'I'm sorry, I'm enjoying our chat but I really must...'

''Course. Don't let me keep you. Don't forget where I am if you need anything.'

'I won't. It was lovely to meet you, and I look forward to meeting the rest of your family. And your alpaca!'

Victor picked up his mallet as Ottilie got back into the driver's seat. 'And I expect you'll get more sense out of the alpaca than any of my lot.'

As Victor had promised, Thimblebury revealed itself like a sunrise gradually unveiling its glory as Ottilie drove into the hollow where it lay nestled. The housing market had been frantic that year and so, crazy as it seemed to her now, this would be the first time she'd visited in person. Desperate to make the move to secure the job, and with Wordsworth Cottage pretty much the only house for sale in such a tiny place, she'd made an offer on it without a physical viewing, from photos alone, almost the same day that the house had gone up for sale. It had been the only way, as far as she could see, and something in her heart simply told her that this village and this house was where she was meant to be at this point in her life. Risky, insane, foolhardy... her mum had many opinions on the matter, and to a point Ottilie could see why she might be alarmed on her behalf, but she'd spoken at length to the previous owners during the transfer, had trusted the surveys, and was now the keeper of a higgledy, ramshackle house that had been built over four hundred years before Ottilie had arrived on the planet. In her opinion, more decisions ought to be made this way, because far too often, life was too short to be cautious.

The houses of Thimblebury were scattered over the basin of the valley as if they'd been left by a child who'd finished playing with them. The narrow streets and lanes were random and chaotic but all the more charming for it. Ottilie was used to angular roads and avenues on the new estate she'd lived on with Josh, the houses precise and pristine and ordered. She'd been happy enough there, and she'd thought it pleasant and convenient and full of the trappings of modern life that she'd always wanted before, but since she'd lost Josh, she needed something completely different, something that wouldn't make her think of him every time she looked. She hoped Thimblebury, with its mismatched houses and wildflower verges, and swallows nesting in the eaves of thatches or gardens with bird boxes or bug hotels, and an antique red telephone box, and all manner of other little charms would be it.

The River Leven was relatively sedate at this point where it passed close to the village, and Ottilie had been delighted to cross it via an old stone bridge. She wasn't sure which bit of coast it ended at, but she did know that at some point it met nearby Lake Windermere and she looked forward to seeing for herself before too long. There were trees everywhere – tiny maples and magnolias in gardens, towering oaks and beech shading the churchyard and willows draped over the riverbanks. She'd never lived anywhere so vibrant and green. From the top of the valley, the village spread out like a living tapestry. It had looked pretty online, ideal for her new life, but up close it was breathtaking.

Ottilie was caught by a sudden wave of emotion at the sight and, from nowhere, tears filled her eyes.

'Josh...' she murmured. 'You'd have bloody loved this.'

Only she'd never know that for sure. Perhaps Josh would have loved it. Or perhaps he'd have been unmoved by the hedgerows where poppies and coltsfoot peeked from long grass while bees shuttled in and out, or the drystone walls where anemones and ivy thrived in the gaps, or the verdant fields that changed colour in the breeze like shoals of shining fish darting this way and that, or the cloud of starlings overhead or the rooks and crows standing sentry in the high branches of the trees, but he wasn't here to say.

Ottilie tried not to think of that as she continued into the village. Thimblebury was her new start and she had to be braver than this. She had to make it work, because the alternative was wallowing in her memories back in Manchester and, whatever else she was guessing at, she knew for certain Josh would never have wanted that.

The removal van was obscuring Wordsworth Cottage from view as Ottilie stopped the car. Two youths and a much older man were sitting on the stone wall of her front garden. The older man stubbed out a cigarette as he noted her arrival and came to greet her.

'Sorry,' she said as she got out of the car. 'I got a bit held up.'

'Not to worry; just that we couldn't do a lot until you got here.'

'No, of course. I'll open up now.'

'Lovely spot you've got here,' he said as he followed her to the gate.

For the first time, Ottilie's house was right there in front of her, in the flesh, and it was every bit as beautiful and welcoming as she'd hoped it would be. The front-facing wall was rendered a pristine white – it looked as if the sellers had painted it freshly for her, because it was gleaming in the sun. She made a mental note to email them to thank them. The gable wall was made of a sturdy dove-grey stone and the roof was heavy slate. The sash windows looked newly painted too, and the sage-green front door was dressed with a leafy garland hanging from an iron knocker, and a fragrant honeysuckle clinging to the surrounding trellis.

It was only May, and yet the garden was already a vibrant mass of summer colour: towering hollyhocks, rose bushes, poppies, marigolds, lavender, marguerites and many other varieties Ottilie had no name for. As she walked the path, they released bees and butterflies into the sky. In the shade of the house was a mossy-edged pond, a tiny water feature trickling into it and an *actual frog* sitting on the stones. It was like a house from a fairy tale, and standing in front of the entrance with a key in her hand, Ottilie could scarcely believe she owned it.

Suddenly aware of how long it was taking her to unlock the door and that, perhaps, she might look a bit nutty to her removal team as she stood and gazed at her house, she shook herself. There would be time later to come to terms with her new home and the life that would come with it, but there were more pressing matters to deal with. There was a lot to get inside and the day was already slipping away from them.

Ottilie turned the key in the lock and pushed the door open.

The smell was immediate, that strange smell that would smell like home once she got used to it but, for now, was unfamiliar. Different air, different rooms, different building materials, the products the previous owner used to clean, the food they ate regularly, even the places where the sun came in through the windows, all these things and more mashed together to create an individual aroma that every house had. This wasn't the same as the new build she'd shared with Josh in Manchester. This was somehow mellower, earthier, perhaps a note that told her she'd have to look out for damp during the winter months. But it was an old house and that was to be expected – it didn't worry her. There was something waxy in it, old wood and carbolic soap, and perhaps a hint of lavender and honeysuckle sneaking in from the clumps growing closest to the front door.

The layout was flat and broad. Ottilie had visited many houses – especially the old terraces where many of her family members had lived as she'd been growing up – where the house would look like nothing from the front but would reach back for what seemed like miles in the most deceiving way. But Wordsworth Cottage was honest about what lay beyond the entrance, the front door opening straight into a sitting room with stairs at one side and a parlour at the other, and the kitchen clearly visible beyond through an open door. It was all at once bright and yet cocooning, airy but cosy, felt very old but fitted with all the trappings of modernity.

On the shelf over the log burner stood a vase filled with pink carnations and an envelope tucked behind it. With the sounds of the removal men throwing open the truck behind her, Ottilie went over with a faint smile and opened it.

Hello Ottilie!

Just a note to welcome you to Thimblebury. We've left some local honey and teabags in the larder, a pint of milk and a block of butter from the dairy farm in Windermere in the fridge and some freshly baked bread in a crock on the kitchen counter. We thought it might be useful to start you off until you can get to the shops and you don't want to be worrying about any of that when you're trying to move in.

We hope your new life in Wordsworth Cottage will be everything you wish for. If you're half as happy here as we've been then it will be like heaven. Good luck with the villagers!

Fondest wishes,

Harold and Doreen

Ottilie gazed up at the carnations. She'd been feeling emotionally vulnerable as it was, but the kindness of Harold and Doreen was almost enough to push her over the edge. Sniffing hard, she went to the front door, still clutching the note, and called to the removal team.

'Anyone want a cup of tea?'

There was a chorus of approval, and while Ottilie went to her car to find her kettle, someone started whistling the tune to 'Jerusalem'.

She gazed up at the hills beyond her new home. In England's green and pleasant land... weren't they the words to that song? Well, she couldn't argue with that.

CHAPTER THREE

Ottilie opened her eyes as the sun streamed into the bedroom window. She'd been so tired the night before that she'd fallen into bed, not caring that she hadn't yet put curtains up and forgetting that dawn would wake her stupidly early without window coverings to keep it out.

As her eyes adjusted to her surroundings she let her gaze rove the room. There were still many so many boxes to unpack that she wondered if she'd be straight before the year was out. At least she could make use of the fact that she was up early to get started on that, she supposed.

Much as she already loved the cosiness of Wordsworth Cottage, the decor was far from her taste and she didn't think it would really feel like home until it was. The bedroom ceiling was papered with a delicate rose pattern – that was something she hadn't seen before, and not something she was entirely sure she was on board with. The fringed lightshade would have to go too.

In the corner of the room was a stack of boxes, still sealed. One of them contained a dozen or so glossy home interior magazines. She'd been buying them since she'd put in the offer on

Wordsworth Cottage. Planning the changes that would make it her own had given her something to focus on, something to take her mind off the nerves that twisted her gut every time she thought about the move, something to think about other than her grief. Because as much as she'd wanted to come here and as much as she'd understood how much she needed it, she'd been terrified. To come alone, to leave everyone she knew and loved behind, to start afresh in an unknown place, not certain if her own fragile mental state would be able to take it, had been scary. But she'd done it anyway and, despite the rest, was a little bit proud of herself for at least that, no matter how it turned out.

On a morning like this in the old days she'd have opened her eyes to find Josh already awake beside her, maybe reading the previous day's newspaper or scrolling through his phone. He'd turn and smile and he wouldn't need to ask what she wanted. Sometimes he'd say he was making a cup of tea but dash out to the café down the road and bring back breakfast bagels or muffins, to surprise her. Sometimes, he really was just making a cup of tea. Whichever way it went, Ottilie had been happy. But there was nobody to bring her tea in bed now, let alone any of the other stuff.

She lay for a few moments in quiet contemplation of the mad rose-patterned wallpaper on the ceiling and then let out a heavy sigh. Much as she would have liked to have gone back to sleep for another hour, there was too much to do and nobody else but her to do it, and so she swung herself out of bed and went downstairs to find something for breakfast.

The home-made bread and local butter Harold and Doreen had left for her had made a pretty fabulous breakfast. Ottilie had eaten it outside at a little mosaic and iron table they'd left in the back garden for her, listening to birdsong echo around the valley and not much else. It was so peaceful, the air so clean, she could barely believe places like this still existed. She and Josh had often tried to eat al fresco back in Manchester, but used to laugh that conversations over the roar of passing boy racers were more difficult than they were worth, so they often ended up back in the house.

Beyond the hedge that separated her garden from a fallow field were the crests of hills, black lines of shadowed valleys running between them. It was still early enough to see mist hanging there, though the day promised to be warm and it would soon dissipate. If she strained hard enough, she could just about make out the gurgling of the nearby river. Later, she'd go down and see it properly.

She reached for her mug, wrapping her hands around it and sighed as she gazed up at the majesty of those hills. Could she be happy here? If it didn't work out, it definitely wouldn't be the fault of the scenery, because this morning, with golden light and the mist and the birds singing to her and the scent of summer flowers in her head, this was just about the most beautiful place she'd ever seen.

Like everything else in Thimblebury – at least what she'd seen of it so far – the village shop-cum-post office was housed in a quirky stone-built cottage with a low wall and a front garden full of fragrant and slightly unruly flowers that lined either side of the path to the front door. As Ottilie pushed it open a little bell tinkled above the door frame and a man in his fifties shot up from beneath the counter looking faintly surprised to see her. Perhaps he didn't get many customers, because he certainly seemed to have been caught off guard by one entering.

'Oh!' he fumbled, blushing and slapping a book down on the counter, pressed open at the page he'd been – presumably – reading.

'Sorry...' Ottilie cast a glance around the interior as he

straightened his shirt. It was small, shelves crammed close together and right up to the ceiling, stocked with fairly basic stuff – teabags, instant coffee, sugar, tins of beans, bread... the usual. An open fridge contained milk and yoghurt and cheese that looked locally made – at least the packaging was quite rustic, and it was labelled Lake District Dairies. 'Didn't mean to disturb... You are open, right? Only the door was—'

'Open? Absolutely! I was just...' He let his gaze wander to the book he'd put down.

'Slow morning?' Ottilie asked as she looked at the title. '*The Shell Seekers*? That's an old one.'

'You've read it?'

'Ages ago. Please don't quiz me on it because I can't remember all that much about it now.'

'Did you like it?'

'Yes. At least, I think I did. What about you?'

He made an uncertain face. 'It's the book club read, but I can't say I'm sold on it so far. Give me a Jilly Cooper any day.'

Ottilie raised her eyebrows slightly. 'Jilly Cooper? Did not see that coming. I'd have said Lee Child, if you'd asked.'

'You like Lee Child?'

'No, I mean I would have had you down as a Lee Child sort of guy.'

The shopkeeper was pensive for a moment, as if the notion that he might look like a Lee Child reader demanded some consideration, but then he looked up as if he'd decided it didn't matter after all. 'What can I do for you?'

'I need a few odds and ends.' She went to the fridge and examined a glass bottle of milk. She couldn't remember the last time she'd bought milk in a glass bottle – it was always plastic when it came in the supermarket delivery. No supermarket delivery this week, though. She'd decided that buying locally would be a good way to get to know the village and would send a signal that she wanted to be part of it.

'On holiday?' he asked cheerfully. 'Picked a good week for it. Bit off the beaten track here, though. Where are you staying?'

'I've actually just moved into Wordsworth Cottage.'

'Ah! The new nurse!'

'One and the same. I'm Ottilie.'

'What-a-ley?'

'Ottilie Oakcroft. It's a mouthful, I know. Blame my mum. Well, for the Ottilie bit at least.'

'Ottilie... pleased to meet you. I'm Magnus.'

'And this is your shop? I mean, you own it?'

'With the other half. He's out at the cash and carry getting stock. He'll be sorry to have missed you.'

'I expect I'll run into him at some point soon. What's his name?'

'Geoff.'

'Geoff. I'll try to remember. So you've lived here all your life?'

'Geoff has; not me. I moved here from Iceland in the nineties.'

'Ah... I thought you had a slight accent but I didn't know what it was. You can hardly tell though... if you hadn't mentioned it to me, I wouldn't have known. So what brought you to England?'

'Geoff.' He gave a broad, soppy grin. Whatever charms Geoff had held back in the nineties clearly hadn't worn off, even all these years later.

'True love, eh? You could not ask for a more noble cause than that.'

Magnus's smile grew broader and brighter. '*The Princess Bride*! I love that film!'

'Me too,' Ottilie said. 'I watch it every Christmas. At least I used to...'

Her smile faltered as she recalled Christmases past, the ones she'd spent with Josh where they'd cuddled on the sofa beneath fleecy blankets with wine and crackers while they watched a movie they knew far too well but would put on every Christmas anyway.

'You know, if you're into movies we have a film club. Geoff converted one of the outbuildings here into a bijou and rather darling cinema. It's tiny, but plenty big enough for our little band. You're more than welcome to join us any time you like. We only show old stuff, but it's fun and you'd get to know a few of us.'

'Book club *and* film club? Thimblebury is already starting to sound like my sort of place. I'd love to.'

'A new member! Geoff will be so pleased; we haven't had a new member since… well, since me probably. We have a Facebook group where you can see what we're planning to show this month and you can make suggestions of your own if there's something you really want to watch. We don't put anything smutty on – Florence doesn't like that – and no gory stuff, because Geoff's not keen, but other than that we're all fairly open-minded.'

'Sounds good – I'll look you up when I get home.'

Magnus clapped his hands together looking very pleased with himself. Clearly he thought Ottilie's recruitment to the film club was something of a coup. 'And don't forget there's book club too if you'd like to join that.'

'I'll have to see how much time I have to read. It's far easier to spare an hour or so for a film than a week for a book. It might be that comes when I've settled in a bit and I know what my work schedule will be like. It does sound lovely, though and I will try. Who knew so much was going on in one tiny village?'

'Oh there's loads. We have a bunch of lake swimmers – I mean, why wouldn't we when we have so many beautiful lakes on the doorstep? Rani runs a cookery night once a month where she shows you how to make something or other – Geoff does that one, but I don't because I'm a terrible cook and there's really no hope for me. There's yoga and Zumba at the village hall. We used to have a mum and baby group, but sadly that's had to wind up.'

'Oh...?' Ottilie looked up from a block of cheese she was inspecting. 'Why's that?'

'Gwen – our old nurse – used to run it but she's gone now and nobody else has the time.'

'Hmm... seems like a thing you'd need though. Were there many mums using it?'

'Maybe a dozen. Some travelled in from neighbouring villages. Used to run every Tuesday morning.'

Ottilie was thoughtful for a moment. She couldn't promise to be free every Tuesday to take on a new group herself; she couldn't guarantee she'd be free once a week without fail because her nursing duties would eat into her time and there would undoubtedly be emergencies to attend, but perhaps she could organise a new group and get someone else to deputise for her when she couldn't make it. After all, Gwen seemed to make it work and she had nursing duties too. Perhaps Ottilie would ask Dr Cheadle about it. A parent and child group seemed like a very important thing to have in a place this remote.

She'd seen many patients during her career, and often the thing they needed as much as care for their physical health was consideration of their mental well-being. Becoming a parent could be isolating and even a once-a-week place to go and chat to others who understood the pressures was often a lifesaver. Out of all the clubs and societies that Thimblebury seemed to have, that one felt like the one they couldn't afford to lose.

'I'll have to see what I can do about that,' she said, more to herself than to Magnus.

'People would definitely use it. Especially as we've got a couple of youngsters in the village ready to give birth any time now. Of course, when I say youngsters, I mean they're younger than me, which could be anything under the age of fifty.'

Ottilie smiled. 'I'm sure I'll meet them at some point then.'

'I'm sure you will. In fact, Geoff's niece is about to pop.' Magnus lowered his voice and cast a wary glance around the shop, despite it being empty apart from the two of them, as if he was about to share something scandalous. 'Not quite eighteen yet. Poor thing got caught out by a proper scally on his holidays. He's skipped off back to Lancashire and left her quite literally holding the baby. At least, when it comes she will be.'

'Ah. Who's that? Should I go and visit her?'

'I'm sure they wouldn't mind if you called to say hello. Stacey – that's Geoff's sister – lives at Watersmeet Cottage. She's still got Chloe at home with her so she'll be easy enough to find.'

'Chloe is her daughter? So that's who's pregnant?'

Magnus nodded.

'Right,' Ottilie replied thoughtfully. 'I expect she's already under the care of a midwife, but I don't think it hurts for her to have a second point of contact, just in case she needs it. If you think it's all right, I'll pop over later. Perhaps you'd give them a call for me to warn them I might visit, if you don't mind. Nobody wants a random stranger turning up on their doorstep.'

'Not at all, though Stacey won't mind. She's very sociable and a bit lonely, quite honestly. Her husband left her for another woman when Chloe was eight, and she finds it very hard to be single.'

Ottilie nodded. Although Stacey's situation was clearly a source of sadness, at least it would be common ground between them. And she didn't doubt that she'd come across more stories like theirs, and it would be good for her to be faced with the knowledge that she wasn't alone in loneliness or grief, and that people everywhere were living their lives through those hardships. Anything that could shake Ottilie out of her self-pity had to be good for her.

She paused. Magnus seemed to know a lot about the village

and was keen to share. Perhaps he'd be a mine of information, and it never hurt to be armed with some foreknowledge. But perhaps it wasn't very professional of her to dig for personal information about people she'd potentially be treating at some point. Foreknowledge could be useful, but it could also create prejudice and she certainly didn't want to be guilty of judging someone before she'd even had a chance to get to know them.

'So that's the film and book clubs I've got to look out for, yoga and lake swimming if I fancy them, and a playgroup to organise. Well that ought to keep me busy enough! I'm so glad I came in for milk!'

Magnus tapped the side of his nose with a cheeky grin. 'You'll always get more than you came in for here. Whatever you need to know about anyone or anything usually comes through this shop eventually. Geoff says I'm a terrible gossip, but I make no apologies for it.'

'Well, like I was saying to someone yesterday, how do you find out about anything unless you ask?'

'Hmm. So what secrets do I need to know about you?'

'Oh, there's nothing. I've led a very boring life.'

'I don't believe that for a minute. Nobody – even the people who think they have – have led boring lives. Everyone's got a story.'

'I'm afraid mine would put you to sleep. I qualified as a nurse after I left college and I've worked as a nurse ever since. Married, house, one holiday abroad a year... all the usual stuff.'

'And how is your other half finding Thimblebury so far?'

'It's just me. He died at the end of last year.'

Magnus looked so utterly mortified at her reply that Ottilie wanted to lean over the counter to hug him and tell him it was really fine and that she was really fine and there was no need to worry. But she could only give a tight smile. It wasn't true. Perhaps she was on the right path to fine, but there was a way to go yet.

'I'm so sorry,' he said. 'I had no idea.'

'Of course you didn't. Like we said, if you don't ask, you don't know. It was hard, but I'm getting better every day. That's kind of what the move here is about. New start and all that.'

'I can only imagine. I'd be inconsolable if anything happened to my Geoff. If there's ever anything we can do to help, anything at all, you only need to ask.'

'That's so kind of you; thank you. And the same goes for you. If you need any help or advice and it's out of surgery hours, please call at the cottage. I can't promise to be as knowledgeable as Dr Cheadle, but if I can help I will. I'm really looking forward to getting involved in some of the village clubs too; it'll be nice to get to know everyone.'

'You might regret saying that,' Magnus replied with a low chuckle.

'I don't think so. I have a very good feeling about Thimble-bury already.'

CHAPTER FOUR

When Ottilie had said she fancied walking the long way home to explore the village, Magnus had burst out laughing.

'There is no long way around Thimblebury! It's so tiny; I'm not sure if that's where the name comes from, but there's definitely no more than a thimbleful of houses!'

'Oh, it doesn't look that small.'

'Perhaps I make it sound worse than it is – Geoff always says so. Sometimes it feels it. Sometimes I long for a bit of culture and civilisation. That's really why we started the film club. It's about as close as we're going to get to a cinema in Thimblebury and I used to love going to the cinema in Iceland.'

'Well, I'm looking forward to getting to know what the village has to offer and definitely look forward to the film club.'

'And we'll be very happy to see you there.'

Ottilie had thanked him for his brief description of the village's layout and, loaded with milk, cheese and a few other locally produced goodies, had left the shop determined to see for herself just how big her new home was.

Ottilie's mum hadn't been keen on the move for her daughter. While she understood Ottilie's desire for a fresh start, and the attractions of the beautiful Lake District, she couldn't fathom why Ottilie would choose such a small village. Yes, the perfect house had gone up for sale, and yes, there was a job there, ready and waiting, but surely Ottilie ought to be in one of the bigger towns like Keswick or Bowness where there would be more going on. Surely they had perfect houses and ready-made jobs in places like that, and surely Ottilie wouldn't be so isolated living next to one of the big lakes in the more popu-lated towns? If she was lonely without Josh, surely moving somewhere so small out in the sticks would make that worse, not better? And when it came down to it, Ottilie's mum couldn't see why her daughter had to move away from Manchester at all. There were plenty of suburbs and nearby villages where Ottilie could have that new start, all pretty, all with good houses and job prospects, and all within striking distance of Ottilie's childhood home so that her mum didn't have to go so far to visit.

Ottilie had tried to explain how hard it would be to live in the same house – even the same city – she'd lived in with Josh, working at the hospital where she'd been on shift the day he'd died, and how nervous knowing his attacker still walked the streets there made her, but her mum had been unconvinced. She'd fully admitted, however, that she'd wanted Ottilie to stay for selfish reasons, and Ottilie understood that too, but as soon as she'd seen the job in Thimblebury it had felt like the right job for her, and when she'd seen Wordsworth Cottage up for sale, it had looked so perfect that it had really felt as if the two opportu-nities combined was the universe trying to tell her something.

The early mist had lifted from the hollows and now the green slopes surrounding the village were drenched in sunlight, the light and shade trickling down tree-lined slopes and clumps of vibrant wildflowers and tall grasses making the scene like something out of an impressionist painting. Ottilie drank it in as she sat on a painted wooden bench that someone had placed on a quiet lane, very helpfully facing the hills as the perfect viewing point.

To her right was a swinging wooden sign proclaiming that the house behind it sold honey from their own hives, and to her left was an old red telephone box, still complete with a phone. Ottilie presumed it still worked or it wouldn't be there, but she couldn't recall the last time she'd seen an old phone box that contained an actual phone. They stood in people's gardens as ornaments or were used as tourist curiosities in the bigger cities, some had started to house emergency defibrillators (which, in her nursing capacity, she wholeheartedly approved of) and she'd even seen one or two repurposed into miniature libraries or honesty boxes selling home-grown vegetables… but a working phone? It had to be years, probably before Ottilie had become an adult. Who used such a thing nowadays? Even the old people she'd treated in Manchester had mobile phones. Everyone had mobile phones, didn't they? But then she recalled Victor saying he didn't. Although, she also recalled with a smile, according to him there were half a dozen of his old mobiles languishing at the bottom of slurry pits.

She'd been sitting for some five minutes or so, lost in her thoughts as she admired the scenery, when she noticed the old lady. She was hunched and her steps were slow, but somehow she didn't look frail. If anything, she looked a little bit glamorous, with unexpectedly thick, dark hair cut short and neat, and bright inquisitive eyes. Her smock was a pretty checked fabric, layered over nylon trousers, and the wicker basket she carried looked heavy. Ottilie watched for a moment and wondered whether to ask if she needed help.

As her gaze fell on Ottilie, she gave a cheerful nod. 'Good morning.'

'Good morning!' Ottilie nodded at the basket. 'Looks heavy.'

'Aye, it is.'

'Do you have far to go? I could—'

'Not far.' The lady stopped and held Ottilie in a keen gaze for a moment. 'Mancunian?'

'My accent is that strong?' Ottilie asked with a smile.

'No, but my grandson is living there so I recognise it well enough. So if you're from Manchester and you're sitting in Thimblebury with a bag full of shopping from Geoff's, I'm assuming you're the new nurse?'

'Blimey you're good!'

'Word gets round here fast, especially when you've been chatting to Magnus.'

'Ah. To be fair, he did warn me that he liked to gossip.'

'Says you're on your own. Lost your husband. That right?'

Ottilie nodded and the lady gave a sharp tut.

'I am sorry to hear that,' she said, shaking her head. 'Young woman like you shouldn't be widowed like that.'

'Thank you,' Ottilie said. 'But these things happen, don't they?'

'They do.'

Ottilie got up. She didn't want to disappear into the crack of darkness the mention of Josh always opened up and she didn't want to make this lady feel uncomfortable by exposing her sorrow, so she did the only thing she could do – she turned it around, made herself useful. 'Want me to help carry that basket?'

'You saying I look like a six-stone weakling?'

'No, but you did say it was heavy.'

'Never did me any harm carrying it before, and I've been carrying it for a lot of years. More than you've been around.'

'But there's nothing wrong with accepting a bit of help every now and again.'

'That's true, but if you take this from me I'll go all off balance and tip over. Best if I keep hold of it.'

Ottilie let out an unexpectedly genuine giggle. 'If you put it like that. Maybe I can walk a bit with you? I don't know the village well so I'd appreciate you pointing out the landmarks.'

'Hill there. Hill there. Another hill there… there you go – all the landmarks.'

Ottilie laughed again. 'I suppose I was asking for that. Have you always lived here?'

'Born and bred. Makes me sound boring, doesn't it? But there are worse places to spend your days.'

'I'm beginning to see that already. It's beautiful here.'

'A bit different from Manchester, I imagine.'

'Very.'

'It'll take some getting used to; might be a bit quiet for you.'

'Different from Manchester is what I want right now, and I'll take a side of quiet if it's on offer.'

The lady began to walk and Ottilie took that as an invitation to fall into step with her.

'I'm Ottilie, by the way.'

'Pleased to meet you. I'm Florence. Most call me Flo.'

'Pleased to meet you, Flo.'

'Didn't say you could call me Flo, did I?'

Ottilie gave her a sharp look but then relaxed as she caught the corners of Flo's mouth turn up in a secret smile. Flo, as she was learning fast, was dry and quick-witted, and it would take a little time to get the measure of her humour.

'So you said your grandson lives in Manchester. Whereabouts?'

'Oh, don't ask me – Manchester's all the same as far as I can tell.'

'You don't go to visit?'

'I've been a couple of times, but he mostly comes here to see me. I don't care for big cities and I'm too old to get into the habit of visiting them.'

'Was he born here like you?'

'Born, but his parents moved away from the village when he was five or six. Can't exactly remember.'

'They left the village? You must have been gutted.'

''Tis what it is. His mother said there were no prospects, and I suppose she might have been right.'

'Do they visit a lot?'

'From time to time. Heath's thirty-five, so he mostly pops over for the odd hour by himself. Haven't seen much of him the last year or so... messy divorce. I could see that coming – the girl was a nightmare. I tried to warn him, but... Not that anyone listens to me. You'd think over eighty years of life experience would count for something, but apparently not.'

'I suppose when you're in love with someone you don't want to see trouble ahead, even when people are warning you.'

'True enough. I suppose you must think a divorce is a terrible waste.'

'Why do you say that?'

'Your husband was taken from you; didn't get a choice. He was a good one?'

'The best.'

'That's like me. We had fifty happy years but it was all over in an instant. I'm used to being alone now, but that doesn't mean I don't miss him still.'

'I don't think I'll ever stop missing Josh.'

'I don't suppose I can tell you much you don't already know about it, but if you ever want to talk, I'd be all ears.'

'Thank you. I really just want to get stuck into my work here and fill my days, you know? It helps to be busy.'

'That's what I did. I wasn't working – I'd already retired by then – but I kept myself occupied as much as I could. It's too easy to wither away and follow them sooner than you'd like, especially at my age.'

Ottilie could understand that better than Flo could ever imagine. She was much younger, but the temptation to simply give up had been there for her too, only she'd been determined not to go down that path. Her being in Thimblebury was a huge step towards that aim. 'Sadly I've seen a lot of that during my time nursing; people so affected by their loss that they simply give up. I'm glad you didn't do that.'

'I had my family to think of, didn't I?'

'You did, and I'm sure they're glad too.'

Flo sniffed hard. 'You'd think, wouldn't you? Not that my feckless son and his wife have ever shown any gratitude. I hardly see them these days.'

'At least your grandson visits.'

Flo broke into a slow smile. 'Bless him.' She threw a sideways look at Ottilie. 'But not enough these days. How old are you?'

'Thirty-five. Why do you ask?'

'No reason...'

Ottilie held back a frown but then gave a mental shrug. It was probably best to leave it at that, because she had a suspicion that Flo had a reason she wasn't ready to divulge as yet, and it probably involved cooking up some kind of match with her grandson. She was sure Flo's grandson was a perfectly nice man, but she had no desire to get involved. She didn't want to get involved with any man, certainly not now, and perhaps not ever. As far as she was concerned, Josh was the love of her life and she didn't see how she could ever love anyone like that again. She didn't *want* to love anyone like that again, because the risk of losing them was too terrifying to contemplate. What she'd gone through these past months was something she didn't have the strength to ever go through again. This time she'd come through it and was moving on, but there wasn't going to be a next time. This was it, a one-time deal.

As these thoughts went through her head, they continued to walk, but after a few moments, Ottilie realised that Flo had stopped and reached out for a nearby gatepost to steady herself. She suddenly looked pale and clammy. Ottilie dashed over.

'Blasted blood pressure...' Flo rasped. 'Be all right... give me a...'

'You don't look all right.'

Ottilie's instincts took over. She led Flo to a nearby bench and then proceeded to check her vitals, keeping a close eye on Flo's responses as she did.

'You know where you are?' she asked.

'Of course I do,' Flo said, managing a withering look despite being so obviously unwell.

'Don't be cross – I'm not trying to insult you; I'm just making sure you're all right.'

'If I was all right we wouldn't be here on this bench, would we?' Flo put a hand to her head and closed her eyes. 'I need a moment and I'll be good again. That's what usually happens.'

'You get this a lot?'

'Sometimes.'

'And the doctor has seen you about it? Are you on medication?'

'Don't need it, and Dr Cheadle is busy enough without a silly old lady complaining about the odd dizzy spell. It will pass; it always does. There's nothing wrong with me except age, and Dr Cheadle can't do anything about that. If she could, there'd be a queue outside her door day and night.'

'Still, I think you ought to get checked. How do you know it's your blood pressure?'

'I googled it.'

Ottilie bit back a smile. 'I suppose that's one place to start.'

Flo opened her eyes. 'Just because I'm old doesn't mean I don't know how to use a computer. Heath bought me one last year and showed me how to use it.'

'I didn't mean that. I only meant it's a logical place to start. And without trying to sound patronising, because I can see you're a smart woman, the results you get when you google symptoms aren't always reliable. I'd be happier if you saw Dr Cheadle when you can. We could go now, if you like.'

'You're trained – can't you just tell me what it is, save us the bother?'

'I could have a go, but I'm not trained in the way she is. I mean, I could take some educated guesses and I might be right, but you might need to see a consultant and have tests and that's all way above my pay grade.'

'Hmm...'

Flo tried to push herself off the bench, though she still looked ashen and there was a thin sheen of sweat on her forehead.

'There's no rush,' Ottilie said. 'Sit until you feel able to walk. And like it or not, I think we should go straight to the surgery and get you seen.'

'I don't have an appointment.'

'I'm sure when I explain she'll make five minutes to see you.'

'This is ridiculous...'

Flo looked annoyed, but behind the impatient grimace, Ottilie could see fear. She'd seen it often enough to recognise it. Many of her patients had been like this over the years, unwilling to admit they needed help when deep down they knew the truth, unwilling to recognise their own increasing frailty. It was easier to ignore it, to pretend it wasn't happening, because the alternative was terrifying.

'You're right,' Ottilie said gently. 'It will more than likely be nothing to worry about, but I'd feel better if we went along and got Dr Cheadle's opinion. So could you put up with the imposition as a kindness to me? I won't sleep tonight if we don't go to see her.'

'I suppose it wouldn't hurt. But if she's busy we're not going to add to her burden...'

'Of course not.'

'And I'll need a minute.'

'Take whatever you need. Is there someone we ought to call?'

'Call who you like, they won't have time to come.'

'Not even the grandson you're so fond of?'

'Oh...' Flo waved a dismissive hand. 'He's got enough on his plate without racing up and down after me.'

'Maybe after we've been to the surgery you can give them a call and fill them in? At least they'll know something's going on. Might persuade them to make time to visit a bit more often, mightn't it?'

Flo was silent for a moment. Then she gave a slow nod. 'I suppose that's true. Right... I'll have a go at walking now.'

Ottilie took the basket and offered her free arm for Flo to take hold of.

'You'll have to direct me,' she said.

'Thought I might.'

Ottilie grinned. She'd met her match here.

The receptionist at the surgery looked up from a computer with a weary greeting as Ottilie approached, Flo leaning on her arm.

'Hello, Flo. What brings you here?' she asked, glancing with some curiosity at Ottilie.

Flo nodded at her support. 'I've been told to come by the new nurse, who's decided to start work straight away.'

'Oh!' The receptionist stood up, looking suddenly brighter. 'You're the new nurse?'

'Ottilie...' She gave her best and most disarming smile. It was prudent to get along with the reception team right from the start if she was going to get anything useful done. Besides, Ottilie liked to build good relationships with her colleagues. As far as she was concerned, people spent far too long at work to make enemies of their co-workers. It wasn't productive and it wasn't nice.

'I'm Lavender. Nobody told me you were coming in today or I'd have tidied your office...'

'Lavender... what a lovely name. And don't worry, I'm not coming in officially. I've only brought Flo because I think Dr Cheadle might need to take a look at her. Would that be possible?'

Lavender looked doubtful. 'I can ask, but she has a full clinic.'

'I said it would be a waste of time.' Flo gave Ottilie a look of triumph. 'I said she'd be too busy.'

'Yes,' Ottilie replied, unperturbed. 'And Lavender said she could ask. She hasn't asked yet. You never know – we might get lucky.'

Lavender gave the room a quick sweep. There were four people in the waiting area: a woman with a teenage girl, another in her sixties and a man who was perhaps late thirties to early forties at a wild guess. Without waiting to hear more, Flo disengaged herself from Ottilie's supporting grip and went to sit next to the lone woman.

'Oooh, Janet... How are your migraines?' she asked.

As they launched into a conversation about Janet's ailments, Ottilie gave Lavender a secret smile.

'Yes,' Lavender said quietly. 'She's always like this.'

'Well, I really think she needs to be seen, even if she doesn't, so I'd really appreciate you having a word with the doctor. I mean, I could see her and explain, if it helps.'

'I could take you through when she's finished with this patient if it's urgent—'

'That's all right – we can wait. There are people here with appointments, and as Flo seems to be getting back to herself, I don't suppose there's any rush. As long as we see her before the end of surgery, I think that would be fine. Are the people here the last appointments?'

'For this morning, yes. Afternoon surgery is in a couple of hours. Dr Cheadle needs to have lunch and write up her notes and all that sort of thing before we get the next lot in.'

'I understand. But if she could spare five minutes that would be great. I'd like to introduce myself before I officially begin work anyway, and as I'm here, there's no time like the present.'

Lavender nodded. 'I'm sure that would be all right.'

Ottilie glanced back at the waiting area to see that Flo had finished her enquiries after Janet's migraines and had moved on to the woman who was waiting with the teenager. Ottilie took a wild guess that this might be Geoff's sister and her daughter, and this was confirmed as Flo greeted her.

'Hello, Stacey. How's Geoff?' She nodded at the younger woman. 'Here for a check-up, love?'

'I'm here for Mum,' the girl said. 'I'm all right, just getting fatter every day.'

'Oh...' Flo looked at Stacey. 'What's wrong with you then?'

'I...'

Stacey looked helplessly at her daughter. Ottilie knew a good moment for an intervention when she saw one. She bounded over.

'Did I hear you say Stacey?' she asked Flo very deliberately before turning to the woman in question. 'I've just met Magnus and he told me you were sort of related to him. I wanted to come and say hello, so it's lucky I've bumped into you here.'

Stacey gave a blank look, and Ottilie sat on the bench next to her.

'I'm the new nurse – Ottilie. I'm thinking of restarting the mother and baby group...' She turned to Chloe and smiled. 'Magnus told me you were expecting, so I thought it might be good to ask what sort of thing would be useful to you. I mean, what would you like from a playgroup? Is there any other sort of support group or social group you might like to see in Thimblebury?'

Chloe shrugged. 'Is there one where they take the baby and bring them back when they're earning?'

'Chloe!' Stacey gasped.

'No, I'm sorry...' Chloe looked suitably mortified. 'I'm having a bad day, that's all.'

'Hormones, I expect,' Ottilie said. 'Totally understandable. You're allowed to feel a bit crabby every now and again in your situation; don't worry about it.'

'You mean the situation right now, or the one where my life is ruined?'

Ottilie offered the most sympathetic look she could. It was true that she'd never experienced pregnancy, let alone one that was so fraught with external issues, and so while she couldn't empathise with Chloe at all, she wanted to understand how it might feel, and she wished she could say something to make it better. She doubted there was anything but at the same time felt confident that time would make things better. There wasn't really a way to make her see that either, she supposed. But it looked as if she had good support in the form of her mum and wider family, and that the community would also rally around her, and that had to be worth a lot.

'But what's wrong with you, Stacey?' Flo asked, completely ignoring any other discussion. 'You're all right, aren't you?'

'I could ask the same of you,' Stacey said with a shrewd look that made Ottilie give an internal round of applause. Nicely sidestepped.

'I had one of my turns,' Flo replied with a sour look Ottilie's way. 'And the nurse said I had to come to see Dr Cheadle. Honestly, it's a complete waste of time.'

'It's never a waste of time,' Ottilie said with superhuman patience.

'Nurse...'

Ottilie looked round to see the receptionist beckon her back to the desk.

'Doctor says she'll take a quick look at Flo. Do you want to go in with her? You said you wanted to talk to Doctor.'

'If I could, that would be great. Might as well fill her in on what happened—'

'Which was nothing,' Flo cut in.

'And introduce myself at the same time,' Ottilie said with a faint smile. She turned to Stacey and Chloe. 'If you don't mind, perhaps I can catch you another time for that chat?'

Chloe shrugged, while Stacey looked more enthused. 'That would be nice.'

'Perhaps we could grab coffee somewhere.'

'In Thimblebury?' Chloe gave a scornful look. 'You'd be lucky – we don't even have a coffee shop.'

'There must be a café or something?' Ottilie asked.

'Nope. There's a kiosk where you can get something to take away, like if you're driving through, but you can't sit in there and meet friends. Honestly, you'll find there's nothing in this village. If not for this baby, I'd be getting out, and if you had any sense you'd get out while there's still time.'

'Really? I like it so far; it's lovely.'

Chloe shrugged again. 'You were warned.'

Ottilie wondered how to answer that, and then decided there wasn't a way. Instead, she smiled again before following Flo, who was already grumbling her way to the reception desk to be shown into the GP's consulting room.

'What can I do for you?' Dr Cheadle asked as Flo and Ottilie were shown in.

'I didn't want to come,' Flo said, taking a seat at the other side of the GP's desk anyway.

'I persuaded her to come,' Ottilie said. 'And I'm very sorry for asking you to see us at such short notice—'

'Not a problem...' Dr Cheadle waved away the apology. 'If my nurse thinks I ought to take a look at someone, then that's good enough for me. Pleased to meet you in person, Ottilie, by the way...' She gave a wry smile. 'Nice to see you getting straight down to work even though your first shift isn't until next week.'

'I hope you don't think I'm one of those nurses who can't do a thing unless you tell me what to do first. And I don't make a habit of this, just so you know. But I was concerned about Flo's funny turn. She says she's had something like it before. I thought hypotension but... well, I'll let you examine her; you know much more than I do.'

'I love the phrase *funny turn*,' Dr Cheadle said, going round the desk with her stethoscope at the ready. 'It's very much all-encompassing, isn't it? Anything that's not quite right, it's a funny turn. Although it sounds vague, you know straight away that it means something quite significant; you just have to get to the bottom of what that is.'

She warmed the end of her stethoscope and nodded at Flo. 'Right, let's have a listen.'

Flo looked far from happy but sat quietly as Dr Cheadle listened to her heart. She looked equally put out when her blood pressure was measured and her pulse taken.

'Any nausea?'

Flo shook her head. 'A bit dizzy, I suppose.'

'A lot dizzy from where I was standing,' Ottilie put in. 'Pale too. And clammy.'

'Hmmm.' Dr Cheadle was thoughtful for a moment. Then she sat down at her computer and began to type. 'Blood pressure's not what I'd like it to be. Heart sounds a bit sticky too. I think I'll send you for some scans.'

'At the hospital?' Flo asked, looking as if someone had offered to punch her in the face.

'Yes,' Dr Cheadle said.

'But that means I have to get there! It's all the way out at Kendal!'

'Generally it is quite useful for the subject of a scan to be there, yes.'

Flo folded her arms stubbornly. 'I can't get to the hospital.'

'Come, Florence,' Dr Cheadle said. 'If I didn't know better, I'd say you were being deliberately stubborn because you don't want to go.'

'Isn't there anyone who could take you?' Ottilie asked.

'Plenty of people,' Dr Cheadle said in a sceptical tone.

'Everyone's busy,' Flo replied.

'I'm not,' Ottilie said brightly. 'If it means you go, then I'll take you.'

'You don't even know me!'

'What, so I can't drive someone I don't know to a place? However do taxi drivers manage? And bus drivers must have a nervous breakdown every time they look at the passengers queuing at a stop.'

Ottilie shot Florence a challenging look. She could give as good as she got, and Flo was going to find that out.

'I've put the request in,' Dr Cheadle said. 'You'll get an appointment in the post in the next few days, Florence. I'm sure you'll find a way to get there.'

Looking like a sulky teenager, Flo nodded nonetheless. Ottilie didn't care how much she complained as long as she went for the tests, and she'd say so too. She'd start as she meant to go on – she was the local nurse, which meant she was everyone's nurse, including Florence, and she took that responsibility seriously. If that meant annoying one or two people to keep them safe, then she'd deal with the fallout.

She turned to Dr Cheadle. 'If you have time, I'd love to run some ideas by you. I know it's early days and I haven't even started work yet, but—'

'I was going to suggest a working supper,' Dr Cheadle said. 'I was meaning to contact you before next week anyway, so it's good that you've come to see me. When are you free? I expect you haven't had much time to unpack and shop and such, so how about a spot of something to eat at my house? You're not vegan, are you?'

'No...' Ottilie gave a bemused smile. There was no messing about with her new boss, it seemed. Direct – the way she liked it. She was already beginning to feel that they would work well together. She also felt she was going to like her very much on a personal level. For a start, in all her years nursing in Manchester, she'd never been invited to one of the doctors' houses, so that was new and not unwelcome. 'And I'm not allergic to anything either. Supper sounds lovely. As you can imagine, right now my diary is very sad-looking.'

'How about tonight then? I've got a leg of local lamb on order at the farm shop and there's always leftovers, so plenty to feed one more mouth. Shall we say seven? And don't fuss about bringing anything; I have plenty. Just yourself is all that's required.'

'That's...' Ottilie blinked. She liked direct, but this was another level. 'Sounds great!'

CHAPTER FIVE

'Make yourself at home. There's wine in the fridge... glasses are on the shelf over in the corner. And for God's sake, stop calling me Dr Cheadle – it's Fliss!'

Fliss turned from the stove where she'd gone to check on the meal after letting Ottilie in. The air of her cosy, rustic kitchen was warm and humid, filled with the aromas of delicately spiced lamb and rich gravy. She flung open a window to let out some steam, inviting in a cooling breeze from the garden. A bee wandered in for a moment, and then bumbled back outside to settle on the honeysuckle that hugged the window frame. 'You do drink wine? Because I probably have a bottle of cordial or something collecting dust if you don't. I couldn't tell you where it is, though.'

'Oh, that's OK. I drink wine. As a GP, you might decide I drink too much.'

'I can assure you that none of my medical opinions on your wine consumption will be aired tonight,' Fliss said with a light laugh. 'I drink little else and definitely too much. But I always say if it was good enough for the Romans then it's good enough for me.'

Ottilie went to the fridge. 'Any particular wine?' she asked, scanning a rack of half a dozen bottles of assorted grape and vintage.

'Take your pick. I'll drink all of them eventually, so I don't mind which I sink first.'

Ottilie selected a Merlot, the label of which boasted a handsome wine with notes of black cherry and vanilla. It was odd to find a red in the fridge perhaps, but she'd already decided from their brief interactions that Fliss Cheadle was a woman who did things her way and didn't care what anyone else had to say about it. She obviously just liked her red wine chilled in the same way that white was, and it didn't bother Ottilie anyway.

'My other half did mention joining us, but I thought it might be easier if he stayed out of the way for our first getting-to-know-you supper,' Fliss said as Ottilie reached for two glasses from an open shelf.

'I wouldn't have minded him being here.'

'I would!'

'Well I hope you didn't kick the poor fella out of his own house on my account. Where's he gone? The pub? I saw it earlier. It looked a bit small but cosy. The... I've forgotten what it's called.'

'The Mousehole.'

'Oh, that's it! I thought it sounded cute. Is it nice? Do the locals go in there much?'

'Yes. I can't walk in there without it turning into an impromptu surgery, so I don't bother. If I were you I'd avoid it for the same reason. You'll be ordering a gin at the bar one minute and inspecting someone's piles the next. No, don't worry, he's at home. I think he's got a box set of something or other to catch up on anyway. I'm sure you'll meet him sooner or later.'

'At home?' Ottilie smoothed a frown. Had she heard correctly?

'Yes, his place. We don't live together,' Fliss said. 'God, we'd have killed each other long before now if we did.'

'But you're married?'

'Oh yes!' Fliss tapped her spoon on the side of the saucepan she was tending. 'A good marriage too – better than most, I'd say. I'm very fond of him, especially at a distance. We meet up most nights for an hour or two, either at his or at mine, and then we go our separate ways.'

'That's...' Ottilie fought that frown again.

'Novel?' Fliss turned to her with a wry smile. 'Or perhaps weird is the word you were really looking for? Don't worry, I've heard it all before so it doesn't bother me which one you use. It's our marriage and we like it this way, and the opinions of others on it don't matter to us.'

'I don't have an opinion – well, nothing negative anyway. I suppose I'm just surprised and curious as to how it works. Like on a purely practical level; doesn't it cost you loads to run two households, for example?'

'Worth every penny for the space we get from each other. Lucky, also, that we bought our homes when the village – the country in general – was much more affordable.'

'So you don't have children? I mean...'

'God no!' Fliss laughed as she poured the gravy into a boat. 'Little horrors! Don't get me wrong, other people's children are fine in small doses, but I don't have a maternal bone in my body – never have – and it's too late for that to change.' She aimed a shrewd look at Ottilie. 'I know some of your background but not all. I know, for instance, that you don't have children either and that you're widowed, but not much else. I'd be interested to hear more if you're up to sharing. If nothing else, it seems a good idea to avail myself of some details, because it might make it easier for our working relationship.'

'Oh...' Ottilie poured the wine and took a sip from her own

glass. She didn't know much about wine, but this tasted expensive. 'Well, I qualified in—'

'No, I don't want your professional résumé,' Fliss interrupted in a very deliberate tone. 'I know all that, and quite frankly you wouldn't be here if I hadn't approved of it. I'm talking about your story... your background, your personal history, not your training. You came to Thimblebury because your husband died. No children... I'm right about that much? But still, why leave Manchester? There was no reason to stay close to other family members, particularly in your circumstances? Wouldn't having family close by have helped you through your loss? For me that would have been the obvious choice.'

Ottilie gave a vague shrug. 'I just wanted a new start.'

'Wanted or needed?'

'A bit of both, I suppose...' Ottilie sighed as she set down her glass. 'There was stuff happening. It was complicated.'

'Complicated how?' Fliss switched off the stove and turned to give Ottilie her full concentration. 'I imagine the loss of a spouse is complicated in and of itself. There were other things?'

Ottilie hesitated. There were things she still felt uncomfortable sharing, even here, away from the dangers she'd left behind in Manchester – however real or imagined they'd been. She let out another deep sigh. Surely here, with Fliss, there was no danger in sharing. And it felt right, somehow, perhaps for the first time since Josh's death, to open up and be honest with someone, and who better than the GP she'd soon be working closely with? She hoped for open and honest from Fliss after all, so the least she could offer was the same.

'Josh was killed on duty,' she began slowly, trying to find the words that would least feel like blades cutting her anew. 'He got too close to something, got involved where others didn't dare.'

'Like what?' Fliss folded her arms, paying close attention.

'There was... is a notorious local family. Criminals, you

know, fingers in every pie, but nobody can ever catch them out. Mostly clueless little runts, petty crimes, and nobody ever really saw them as inherently dangerous before... Josh used to laugh about them – all his team did. But then something changed. He found something that might have changed that. His colleagues all told him to step away, that it would end badly, that he ought to turn a blind eye because they were so lawless but also so stupid – which sounds like a terrible thing for a police officer to do. Now I wish he had.'

At this point Fliss's mouth fell open. She reached for her wine and seemed to have forgotten all about her cooking as she took a seat at the table. 'You think he was murdered? I mean, that's what I'm getting from what you're saying.'

'I suppose, if you want to put it like that,' Ottilie said, a familiar sick chill creeping over her. Whenever she thought about what Josh had gone through before his death, the reasons for it, and whether he might have been saved on a different day, she wanted to collapse, to cry out, to weep until there was nothing of her left but tears. But none of that would change what was, and so she didn't. Instead, she did the only thing she could, the thing she was certain Josh would have wanted her to do – she soldiered on. She put all that out of her mind and tried to focus on the future, on making a positive impact where she could, on restoring the balance of kindness to a world that too often felt like it was built on pure evil. 'I don't know if his attacker meant to kill him, but he... she... they... I don't know. It happened. He died from his injuries.'

'You make it sound as if nobody has been caught for it.'

'That's the thing. His superiors think they know – hell, everyone knows who did it and why – but there's no evidence as yet, so nobody has been convicted. Nobody's even been arrested without being released straight after, because there wasn't enough to link them to the attack.'

'That's shocking! No wonder you wanted to leave

Manchester! To walk down the street and look your husband's killer in the face and not know it! I can't imagine...'

'Yes, there was that. But rightly or wrongly, and maybe I was being paranoid, but I was scared too. They were still out there and... I don't know; I'm sure it wasn't the case at all but... I was scared they'd come for me. Pathetic, I suppose, because why would they care about me? They'd already got rid of Josh, so what threat was I? But still...'

'Ottilie...' Fliss reached across the table and gave Ottilie's hand a reassuring squeeze. 'That's completely understandable. You shouldn't be beating yourself up for a reaction that almost any sane person would have. It all sounds dreadful, and nobody can fix what's past or replace what you lost, but I hope you find the peace you're looking for here in Thimblebury. We're all rooting for you. Anything you want, anything you need, you only have to ask.'

'Thank you.' Ottilie sniffed away her tears. She hated how they made her feel like a victim. To cry almost felt like she'd gifted Josh's attackers another victory, and despite her promises to herself to make the world better, she had no intention of making it better in any way for them. She let her shoulders drop and relaxed. The truths she'd needed to share without realising it had been told, and perhaps it would mark a turning point she hadn't realised was on the horizon. 'I'd rather people didn't know all that stuff. You know, about Josh and—'

'Of course! Nobody will hear it from me, I can promise you that.'

It was like an unspoken pact had been made between the two women. Ottilie offered no more information about Josh's death and the circumstances that had led to it, and Fliss didn't ask. Instead, talk turned to more manageable topics, like the work-load at the surgery, what Ottilie might expect during her first week as their nurse, the extra training Fliss wanted her to undertake so she could help prescribe medicines and perform more complex procedures, how tourism affected (or didn't) the village, who Ottilie might want to look out for and how feasible any plans for new community projects might be.

'This lamb is incredible!' Ottilie gushed as the first mouthful went in. 'How do you get it so tender?'

'Ah, that would be telling! I can't have you making it yourself, otherwise you won't want to come over for supper again.'

'That's where you're wrong – if someone else is cooking I'm always there.'

'You don't like cooking?'

'I love cooking, but that doesn't mean I don't appreciate it being done by someone else every now and again. I think... actually, I don't think it's cooking I love so much as eating!'

Fliss smiled as she spooned some more potatoes onto her plate. 'There's something we definitely agree on. Speaking as a GP, I absolutely drink too much, and I probably eat too much as well... and almost certainly I eat the wrong foods. Just don't tell any of the patients, or I'll never be able to look them in the eye and offer nutritional advice ever again!'

'Especially if they're as stubborn as Flo.'

'Florence...' Fliss's smile broadened. 'She's one in a million, that lady. Keeps me on my toes. Not as a GP – she's fit as a flea and will outlast us all – but as a neighbour.'

'But you sent her for tests?' Ottilie frowned. 'So maybe not so fit and healthy?'

'To make you happy,' Fliss said. 'And, I suppose, to cover my own backside a bit. It never hurts to be sure, does it? And I have to confess that her dizzy spells are a little concerning. But we're not going to talk shop all night, are we?'

'We might talk shop a bit. I thought that was why you invited me over.'

'I invited you over to get to know you. And to give you the

heads-up on the village. If you're going to live in Thimblebury, I think it's only fair to warn you about the quirks and idiosyncrasies that the vast majority of the residents seem to be blessed with.'

'Fair enough!' Ottilie put another forkful of lamb in her mouth and chewed. She almost sighed at how good it was. 'So what do I need to look out for?'

'You mean *who* do you need to look out for? Florence, for a start – but you already know that by now. Don't listen to a word of Geoff at the store's gossip. Magnus is as bad. By the time something has got to them, it's already been exaggerated way out of proportion. I mean, their gossip is fun, but...' Fliss shot Ottilie a mischievous grin. 'Who else? Let me see...'

'Maybe I ought to find out everyone's quirks for myself.'

'It would certainly be more entertaining for me that way,' Fliss replied with a light laugh. 'I'd love to be a fly on the wall for some of your first meetings with the people around here. Who have you met so far?'

'Well, Flo of course. And Magnus. I called in at the shop. And yes, he was very keen to give me the gossip! I met Victor, who has the alpaca.'

Fliss nodded. 'Lovely man. Lovely family too. And despite the alpaca breeding, probably the most normal family you're likely to find around these parts.'

'I had a quick chat with your receptionist before we came in to see you.'

'Lavender? I'm glad you got a chance to meet her. You'll soon find she's totally indispensable – I dread to think how the surgery will cope when she retires.'

'That's good; I'm sure I'll need someone who knows the ropes to help me a lot at first. I also met a lady named Stacey and her daughter.'

'Chloe, yes. A bit of a troubled young woman, and I think

the family have their work cut out trying to keep her head above water.'

'Troubled how? I don't want to pry, but if I'm going to be seeing her as a nurse... I mean, I suppose she has a midwife, but is that someone local?'

'No, she travels in from Keswick. Pregnancies are rare when the majority of your population is over fifty, as they are in Thimblebury. I know we have a few but not really enough to warrant having a midwife based here.'

'I can see why Chloe was so negative about it then. Even the few minutes I managed to chat to them I could see she's unhappy living here.'

'And yet she'd struggle if she left – at least in my humble opinion. Especially now, with a baby on the way and the prospect of being a single mum, she needs her family and this community around her more than ever. But she's that age, isn't she? Where we all think we know everything and nobody can tell us any different. She'll have to make her mistakes and figure out how to fix them, just like we all did.'

'There's no mother and baby group, so I'm told.'

'Like I said, there aren't many mothers with young children. I mean, there are a few, but the local authorities didn't see enough of a need for it with the numbers we have, so they pulled the funding.'

'But if there's a venue it's possible to run it from in the community? As a project we take on ourselves and manage with volunteers?'

Fliss sat back and regarded Ottilie with some humour. 'And that's something you're looking to oversee? You don't mess about, do you? You've barely opened your suitcase and you want to get stuck in. Don't get me wrong, I like it. I certainly like the energy. I think you and I are going to get on very well.'

'I just want to be a part of the community, and I think there's no better or faster way to do that than to *be* a part of the community. Like, play an active role, get to know people, get to know their lives, be involved in them. And' – she shrugged – 'I like being busy.'

Fliss continued to regard Ottilie with that same humour, only now she was silent. Ottilie reached for her glass and took a gulp. Suddenly, she wasn't sure she liked the scrutiny. Could Fliss see motives other than the ones Ottilie had mentioned? Because Ottilie couldn't deny that there were far deeper motives for her actions than simply becoming a part of the community. If she was busy, she couldn't think about Josh, and if she couldn't think about Josh, then she couldn't grieve, and if she couldn't grieve then she didn't have to admit that he was gone. She could pretend, just for a while, that the only reason she hadn't seen him was that she'd been far too busy with other things, like it had once been when they'd both worked opposite shifts and missed each other for days on end.

'I'm sure you realise,' Fliss began finally, 'that you'll be plenty busy enough doing your nursing duties.'

'Of course, but in a way, I think that this is all part of the same duty of care. I'm a nurse during the day when I'm paid to care, but I don't stop caring when I get home. I'm a nurse and a human being too.'

'No, that's true,' Fliss said, taking up her cutlery again. 'I think any health professional can relate to that. Well, if you want to take on some community projects, I'm sure there are plenty to sink your teeth into. In fact, I happen to know there's a low-key sort of soup kitchen run by Janet Ainsley that takes meals round to those who're a bit worse off. People around here – especially the older generation who've always been self-suffi- cient – want to keep their dignity. Janet and a couple of helpers take them food, but they do it very much on the quiet, so you won't hear about it in the village like you do other things. I'm sure they'd always be happy for an extra cook in the kitchen or an extra pair of hands on delivery, and you have the added advantage of being the nurse, so nobody would question you calling at someone's home.'

'That sound like a brilliant idea. I'd love to get involved in that. I think I'll talk to Chloe again about the mother and baby group, and maybe some of the other mums before I do anything there.'

'And if you're looking for fun things to get involved in, Magnus runs a group for film buffs.'

'Oh, yes, he did mention that when I went in the shop.'

'And there's a book club who meet in the village hall once a month. If you read, that is.'

'To be honest, I don't read as much as I'd like to, so meeting up to talk about a book might give me the push to get it finished and to read more in general. Sounds good. Who runs that?'

'Nobody really runs it; we sort of take it in turns to shout up about a book to read and when to meet next. There's a Facebook group for it; I'll send you the link.'

'You go to the meetings?'

'When I can. Like you, it forces me to stop thinking about work and read more, and that can't be a bad thing.'

'Sounds brilliant. Loads to do already! Maybe too much, but I don't mind that – it's what I was after.'

'Make sure to leave enough time for your actual job,' Fliss said.

'Yes. I must warn you, I haven't done community work since my nurse training. I've mostly worked on hospital wards since then.'

'If that's the case, I think you've chosen the perfect place to start. It's rather lovely that we have such a small community here, so you'll become well acquainted with your patients. I know in big cities that almost never happens. Makes your job a lot easier as you get used to what everyone needs and already know their medical history when they walk in the door. I'm sure you'll pick it up in no time.'

'I hope so.'

'So, how are you finding Thimblebury so far?'

'I love it.'

'Good...' Fliss lifted her glass in a toast. 'I was hoping you'd say that. To a long and fruitful partnership.'

Ottilie clinked her glass against Fliss's and smiled. It was exactly what she'd been hoping for too.

CHAPTER SIX

It was early summer and the weather was still unpredictable at times. Today had started out fine, but as Ottilie had sat in Fliss's kitchen, the weather had taken a sudden turn. By the time she got back to Wordsworth Cottage, darkness had fallen, bringing with it heavy rain and violent gusts. Fliss had informed Ottilie that there was no taxi service in Thimblebury and that the nearest taxi company was two villages away, so nobody ever bothered to order one just to get from A to B within Thimblebury itself, and she apologised that she'd had too much to drink to drive Ottilie home. She'd offered to get her husband from his house to do it, but Ottilie had insisted that she was perfectly happy to walk. It wasn't so far, after all, and seemed like a waste of petrol – not to mention the inconvenience.

Some of the lanes of Thimblebury were narrow, and what was quaint and pretty during the day seemed more foreboding at night. Perhaps it was the rain lashing her face as she marched towards home, or the wind trying to blow her hood off, or the fact that the streets were poorly lit and she lost her way more than once, or any combination of these things, but Ottilie had left her relaxing, cordial evening with Fliss behind and was now on edge. Almost as soon as she'd left the GP's house she'd sobered – which was perhaps a good thing in the circumstances. Her walk would eventually take her close to the river, and on a night like this even the most sedate body of water was a potential deathtrap.

Or perhaps the danger was all in her imagination. It wouldn't be the first time since Josh's death that she'd heard footsteps close behind only to turn and find nobody there, or to sense a breath on her neck, or to jump at the shadow of someone passing by the glass front door of her old house.

Before she'd decided to move away from Manchester she'd had a state-of-the-art security system installed and she'd virtually stopped leaving the house after dark. Josh's colleagues had done their best to reassure her, had told her they'd be on constant lookout for her well-being, that they'd bring Josh's attackers to justice soon enough, but it wasn't enough for her to feel safe. And she felt stupid for not feeling safe, and she wondered if they all secretly thought she was stupid too. Stupid, and a burden, because didn't they all have enough to do without watching over a neurotic widow with an overactive imagination? Of course nobody was coming to get Ottilie because, in the scheme of things, she was unimportant – in her more pragmatic moments she knew this – but that didn't help when the fear took hold.

As she'd looked forward to the move to Thimblebury, she'd imagined – or perhaps hoped was a better word for it – that she'd feel safe in the countryside. In a tiny village with the cutest houses she'd ever seen and a sweeping landscape that was full of poetry and magic she couldn't feel anything else, surely? But tonight, in the rain and the wind, with the wrong turns, she was seized again by a vague sense of panic that she couldn't quite name. There was no reason for it, and yet she felt it.

More than once she turned, convinced someone was following her, to find nobody there. Even the welcoming glow of lights at windows did nothing to make it better. She considered, for the wildest moment, knocking at one of them and asking to be let in until the dawn came and everything looked safe and cute again, but she reminded herself that she was the new nurse here, and if anyone was going to take a single thing she said or did seriously then that was a very bad idea. At the very least she'd look like a wuss, and at worst she'd seem completely mad. It wasn't the first impression she was keen to give, either way. So she put her head down and hurried on, almost crying out with relief when, finally, the gabled roof of Wordsworth Cottage, slick with rain, came into view.

She went through the gate and hurried to the door, opening up with a shove and tumbling over the threshold to slam it shut behind her again. Resting her head against it as she tried to get her breathing under control, she closed her eyes and took a lungful of that air, with its unfamiliar scents that – she hoped – would soon smell like home. Right now, the best she could hope for was a sanctuary, away from the night, where she could lock the door and lock out the things that would make her scared, even if they didn't really exist and it was only the action of locking the door that made her feel safe.

After a moment she shrugged off her dripping jacket and hung it on the balustrade at the bottom of the stairs to dry. Her shoes followed, landing in a heap by the door where she kicked them off, and then she went through to the kitchen to put the kettle on, the room flooded with light when she located the switch. Before she did anything else she went to the window to close the curtains. It wouldn't stop anything out there getting to her, but perhaps she'd rather not know it was coming.

Above the gurgle of the kettle boiling she could hear the trees creaking in the garden as the wind pushed them from side to side, and the door of the summerhouse rattling in its frame, and a plant pot that must have been blown over rolling around on the patio. She wasn't about to go outside for any of them, and as she massaged her temples, trying to convince herself that she was a total idiot, she wished it would all stop. More than that, more than anything, she wished Josh were here. She'd go to sleep tonight, dreaming of his arms around her, keeping her safe, and she'd wake in the morning and he wouldn't be there, just like all the other times she'd dreamed of him since his death, and her world would come crashing down around her, as always, at the awful realisation that she would never lie in his arms again.

He'd never tickle under her chin and tell her not to be daft, or push his fingers through her hair and tell her how he hated to see her cry, or hold her hand, or curl that reassuring arm at the small of her back, just close enough so she felt he'd catch her if she ever fell, or grin that silly grin they'd share when they were both thinking the same thing about a person or situation that was unkind to say out loud but still funny to both of them, or leave her little notes in the tea caddy before he went to work on an early shift, knowing she'd find it when she came downstairs for her breakfast. There would be no more flowers to say sorry for finishing later than he'd promised, no more uniform strewn across the floor when she'd woken to find he'd crawled into bed beside her at some point during the night... No more any of the many things she'd loved about their lives together.

No more Josh.

The sound of the kettle turning itself off snapped her out of the spiral of misery she was being dragged into. At least getting dry and warmed again would give her something to do to take her mind off how wretched she was feeling, so she busied herself making a hot drink and then went to find her hairdryer and a warm sweatshirt. She considered for a moment lighting a fire, but it was summer and it seemed a bit wasteful, and besides, she wasn't entirely sure where all the things she'd need to light a fire were, only that the previous owner had left some for her, and so decided it would wait for another day.

It was gone eleven by the time she'd started to feel human again, and thoughts had turned to bed. Despite how it had ended, the day had been a good one. It had been productive and she'd learned a lot about her new home already. Her phone sat on the dressing table next to her as she took off her make-up and moisturised, and she almost jumped out of her chair when it began to ring with an unknown number. For a moment she thought about ignoring it, but the notion of it being someone in need was too much to shrug off. It might well be nothing at all – a scam, a poorly timed sales call from a foreign call centre, a wrong number – but it might also be someone who wanted her help.

'Hello?'

'Hi...' The voice at the other end of the line was brisk. 'Is that the nurse?'

Ottilie frowned. 'Who is this? I haven't actually started... Has something happened to someone?'

'I'm Heath Reynolds. You've been treating my grandmother, Florence. She said I could ring you; she said if I had any questions about her condition, I could speak to you.'

Not only did he sound brisk, he sounded stressed. Still, it was a hell of a time to phone somebody just to ask about his grandmother's funny turn, and Ottilie quickly decided that it was quite inconsiderate.

'I wouldn't go so far as to call it a condition but...' Ottilie held back a sigh of impatience. 'What do you need to know?'

'How long has she got?'

Ottilie blinked. 'What?'

'How long? She's dying, right? So how long? Should we prepare for the worst sooner—'

'We only ordered her tests today! Where have you had this

information from?' Ottilie asked, although it was pretty obvious where he'd had it from. What was less obvious was why Florence had told him she was dying. As far as Ottilie was aware, no such event was remotely imminent. And if you asked Fliss Cheadle, it wasn't likely to happen for many years.

'There's something wrong with her heart – that's what she said. Said you were sending her to the consultant as a matter of urgency. Tests, scans, all that, but she said you feared the worst.'

Ottilie tried not to smile. She had a feeling she might know what Flo was up to. *Little minx...*

'She did have a moment today that caused me some concern, and I did take her to see the doctor and we did order tests, and yes, there could be a problem with her heart, but that's one of the less likely explanations based on the checks we did today. More likely is... Look, I'm sorry, but I don't think I can discuss this with you.'

'But Gran said—'

'I know, but I'm sorry – I have a duty of confidentiality and I can't discuss it with you.'

His reply sounded exasperated. Ottilie wondered whether he was close to losing his temper, because it certainly sounded that way. 'Can you at least tell me whether I have to come to Thimblebury?'

'I don't know. If you feel you want to see her that's up to you, but—'

'That's not what I'm asking. Should I be worried enough that I *need* to see her?'

Ottilie paused. 'I suspect she wants to see you, which is why you've had this phone call from her. I could be wrong, but I'm guessing this is her way of telling you she misses you.'

'If that was the case, she'd surely just say so.'

'Perhaps she feels she can't. She knows you're busy and your life is elsewhere and really complicated, so perhaps she feels that, in the scheme of things, she isn't high on your list of priorities. She probably misses you but doesn't feel able to say so because she thinks she ought to wait until you have time for her.'

'What's that supposed to mean? And what do you mean by my complicated life? What's she been saying?'

Ottilie knew then she'd already said too much on the subject of his personal life. Right now, she wished she hadn't been told. The best approach was to pretend she hadn't heard that particular enquiry. 'It's none of my business, but I would say that she won't always be around and maybe you should make the most of the opportunities you have to see her while she is. One day it will be too late and you'll wish you had.'

'I do!' he shot back, and there was real offence in his tone.

Yep, Ottilie decided, definitely about to lose it.

'Like I said, it's none of my business. I'm not trying to tell you what to do; I'm only offering an explanation as to why she might have called you and said what she did because you asked me. But I suppose it might not have been that at all. She might just as easily have got muddled up over what we told her at the surgery. She hadn't been well, after all.'

'She doesn't get muddled up; she's always been sharp. There's definitely an agenda, but it's not what you're saying. You obviously don't know her – she's never been one of these needy types – and if you want to project your own needs onto someone, maybe pick someone other than my gran.'

Ottilie's hackles rose at his dig, but she wasn't going to get dragged into a slanging match. 'Look,' she said stiffly, 'I really don't know what to say, only that I'm sorry but I can't discuss this any further with you.'

'But I'm family.'

'How do I know that? I only have your word for it.'

'Who else would care enough to phone you? Why would someone ring pretending to be me? For fun?'

'I don't know. I'm just telling you how it is. It's the law, and that's that.'

'Then why tell her to give me your number if you had no intention of giving me any information?'

'As I've explained, I didn't.'

'Then where did she get that idea? And you must have given her your phone number for something.'

'In case she needed me! It was for her to call in an emergency and nothing else, and I don't appreciate you using it to call and insult me! I can assure you that in no universe would I ever give her this number to inform you of her impending demise or otherwise. It would never have happened before, but now that we've had a conversation I'm more certain of that than ever! So, Mr Reynolds, as I'm not currently on shift, and as it's incredibly late, I'd appreciate it if you could leave me alone!'

Ottilie was about to end the call when she caught his heavy sigh.

One more chance, she supposed – everyone deserved one more chance to prove they weren't a total arse.

'I'm sorry,' he said. 'It's no excuse, but I've had a hell of a week and this was the icing on the cake. Just so you know, I don't make a habit of this sort of thing. Quite honestly, I didn't realise how late it was. I've been stewing on what she said and I needed to hear more detail and...'

'I get it. I understand why you might worry about her, and being so far away it's not so easy to pop over and check in on her. If it helps ease your mind, I really don't think you need to worry – not for her physical well-being in any case.'

'But I ought to worry about her mental state? I don't get it; she's always been so... well, tough. Nothing gets to her.'

'Perhaps emotional well-being covers it better than mental state. And as for her being tough, even the strongest of us sometimes needs someone to lean on, right?'

'Right... I guess... I'm sorry to have bothered you.'

'Forget it. Don't get angry with your grandmother, will you?'

'Of course not. I could never do that; she means too much to me. And you're right, I've probably been neglecting her. Actually, definitely been neglecting her. Like she told you, things have been complicated in my life, and people who matter have taken second place. But I'm working hard to change that.'

'Again, it's not my place to comment.'

'No, I hear you. No comment, as any good newspaper journalist will tell you, is telling enough. I'll let you get back to your evening.'

'I—'

Before Ottilie could say anything else, he'd ended the call.

Well, that was… interesting.

As she went back to her skincare and highlights of the conversation began to drift through her mind, she wondered if she'd been too harsh. Clearly his ill-timed and brusque phone call had come from a place of worry. Had she come across as judgy and sanctimonious? Had she been unfair? If she'd been given the same information by a loved one, she might have reacted in exactly the same way. But even as she went over it, she wondered why it mattered anyway. She didn't know him and he didn't know her, and perhaps they'd meet at some point during one of his visits to Flo, but it was hardly going to be an encounter that would make any difference to her life.

She did, however, wonder if she ought to check in on Florence. Her new friend struck her as far more astute than to be under the erroneous impression that she was about to fall off her perch, and judging by what Fliss had said, that was hardly likely to be a threat for the foreseeable future. But something was wrong – why else would she have told her grandson that? She seemed indomitable, but Ottilie knew only too well how people with hidden pain often went to great lengths to keep it hidden. And if there was something wrong, if there was something troubling Flo, Ottilie wanted to help. Even if she couldn't do anything practical, at least Flo would know someone was there for her.

As she flicked her phone to silent mode and slid into bed, she made a plan of action. First stop tomorrow was Flo's house.

CHAPTER SEVEN

Ottilie's planned visit to Florence's house got waylaid but in the nicest possible way – at least, it had started out that way. At the village store-cum-post office, as she was asking Magnus which cottage belonged to Florence, Victor came to pay his newspaper bill. Apparently, Thimblebury's shop-cum-post office was also their newsagent. Ottilie wondered what else they sold – she wouldn't have been surprised to find a fashion boutique in the back room.

'Nurse!' He smiled broadly as she turned to see him walk in.

'Ottilie,' she reminded him. 'Call me Ottilie.'

'Ah yes, knew it was something a bit funny. How are you settling in?'

'Great,' Ottilie said, ignoring the observation on her name. It was unusual, she supposed, and it wouldn't be the first time someone had said what Victor had just said about it. 'Slowly but surely I'm getting my bearings. Thought I might have a walk around the area today, take in a bit of the scenery, you know. If I'm living in such a beautiful place I might as well make the most of it.'

'True enough that tourists pay a pretty penny to come and see it.' Victor rubbed at his neck as if he was suddenly struck by a bout of shyness. 'I suppose we take it for granted living here and seeing it all the time. If you're at a loose end... Ah, I'm sure you're too busy.'

'For what? Do you need help with something? I haven't started work yet but I'm happy enough to offer a bit of neighbourly advice if something is bothering you.'

'Not me... the missus. She's got this thing... Well, she says it's a rash, but...'

Ottilie glanced and saw Magnus raise his eyebrows. She had been warned by Fliss that this might happen, but really, she didn't mind. Even Victor had joked about it the day they'd first met. But as a new arrival into Thimblebury, whatever she could do to endear herself to the locals was a bonus as far as she was concerned.

'I mean,' Victor continued, 'if you're not too busy and you don't mind. Happen it's nothing but she's a bit of a worrier, so...'

'I'd be more than happy to look. I can come up to the farm now if you like.'

'Could you? That would be grand! I'm going straight back up after I'm done here so you could hop in the Land Rover with me if you like.'

'I thought you were going to see Florence,' Magnus cut in.

'I can see her later. She's not expecting me anyway so it doesn't really matter what time I show up there.'

Ten minutes later, Ottilie was in the passenger seat of a Land Rover she could scarcely believe was still on the roads. There was more rust than metal, the exhaust backfired every few minutes and the suspension – even though one would expect that the roads were bumpy out here – was non-existent. Victor shouted conversation over the roar of the engine and gears that ground alarmingly as he changed them.

The experience wasn't dissimilar to a ride she'd been on in the desert with Josh, where they'd been flung around in a buggy going up and down sand dunes on holiday in Egypt. It was one of the rare holidays they'd managed to get during their years together – one of them always seemed to be working when the other was off. From nowhere, Ottilie found herself giggling as they went over a particularly rough patch of road, and she was shaken from side to side like she was on a cheap fairground ride.

'You all right?' Victor asked, clearly not getting the joke.

'Yes, it's just a bit mad coming up here, isn't it?'

'Not the best roads, I'll grant you. Old Banger can cope with it, though.'

'Old Banger? That's what you named your car?'

Victor grinned. 'Well, that's what she is, right? But you can keep your fancy cars; I wouldn't swap her for anything.'

'They do say if it ain't broke, don't fix it.'

'She breaks almost every week, so that's got nothing to do with it,' Victor said with a chuckle. 'Lucky I know a thing or two about fixing her.'

After another violent jolt that set Ottilie off again, a rambling house came into view. When she'd first seen it from a distance, it had appeared to be quite compact, but on closer inspection there seemed to be extensions coming off every-where from the main building, and all of them looked as if they'd been added at different times and in different styles.

'Is that yours?' Ottilie asked. She wanted to find a compli-ment of some kind – people liked to be told their house was lovely – but nothing came to mind. It was... something. Messy, she'd call it, chaotic, perhaps a bit dated, but there was a certain homely charm to the net curtains in the windows, the floral linen swinging from the washing line and the array of old coal scuttles and sinks and tin baths and other oddities that had been set out in the front garden and filled with plants. As Victor pulled up outside the gate, Ottilie could also see a large vegetable patch and a gathering of fruit trees shading part of it. The house was set in grassland that stretched for miles, with rolling hills and low cloud a dramatic backdrop, and in a distant field she could see a collection of sheds.

'Is that where the alpaca live?' she asked, pointing to them as they got out of the car.

'It is. We could pop up to see them later if you like.'

'I'd love that!' Ottilie said. 'Never seen any up close before. Are they friendly?'

'Good as gold. Even better if you've got a handful of oats for them.'

Ottilie's gaze went out to the landscape again. It was then she noticed two more houses. They were next door to each other and looked small – though it was hard to tell at this distance. She recalled that Victor had gifted his married daughters some land. Were they his daughters' houses then?

'Corrine's got the kettle on.' Victor pushed open the gate and nodded for Ottilie to go through. 'I recall you said you liked the odd cup of tea.'

'More than the odd cup,' Ottilie said. 'I think I might need addiction services.'

'You'll fit in well with us then,' Victor replied as he followed her to the front door. 'Don't bother knocking; door's open. I've got to scrape my boots here or my life won't be worth living, but you go on in.'

The front door opened directly into a large kitchen with a low ceiling and stone floors. It was filled with freestanding solid wooden cabinets – not a flatpack unit in sight – and a large scrubbed and whitewashed dining table took up the remaining space. Under the window was a cracked ceramic sink and an old-fashioned kettle with a whistle was sitting on a wide stove.

As Ottilie walked in, a lady came from another door and broke into a smile.

'You must be the new nurse! Vic said he'd bring you over, but I didn't expect you to be so fast!'

'So you must be Corrine?'

The lady nodded, her smile spreading. 'I am.'

If someone had asked Ottilie to pick out the woman married to Victor in a random line-up, this lady was the one she'd have gone for, no messing. Somehow, they seemed to suit each other. She was trim and petite, down-to-earth and practical in her dress, and she looked strong and capable despite her advanced years, just as Victor did. And she had such quick warmth and kindness in her eyes that Ottilie immediately loved her.

'Ottilie...' she said, breaking into a wide smile herself. 'I do prefer it to Nurse.'

'I can imagine!' Corrine gestured to a seat. 'Take a load off; kettle's almost boiled. Do you like fruit cake? I've got the neck end of one in the cupboard somewhere...'

Without waiting for Ottilie to confirm whether she liked fruit cake or not, Corrine had pulled a tin that had once contained Christmas biscuits from one of the cupboards and opened it up. Inside, Ottilie could see a stout-looking slab of dense cake, heavy with fruit.

'I can't remember the last time I ate it, but, yes, I am partial to a bit of fruit cake,' she said as Corrine cut into it. 'So, Victor said you wanted to ask me about a problem—'

'At least have some tea and cake first!' Corrine said. 'And I am sorry he mentioned it to you – I told him not to.'

'And I did warn you that you'd get pestered by everyone about every little thing that ails them,' Victor said from the door as he walked in. 'I never said we wouldn't do any of the pestering, but you did say you didn't mind.'

'See you here, or see you in the surgery – I'd see you eventually,' Ottilie said. 'And if it's too big to deal with easily out of hours, I'll just ask you to make a proper appointment. And besides, if I get tea and cake into the bargain then I'll consider it a fair deal.'

'And alpaca, don't forget.' Victor winked.

'Oh...' Corrine poured boiling water into a brown teapot. 'You're going to see the girls, are you?'

'They're all girls?' Ottilie asked.

'Easier that way,' Victor said.

Ottilie wondered why it was easier, but he didn't offer any more information. Perhaps they were more docile than the males – if he was using them to entertain tourists, then she supposed that made sense.

Instead, he took the conversation in a surprising direction. 'Has Heath Reynolds been bothering you?'

Ottilie stared at him – she couldn't help it. 'How did you...?'

Victor looked at Corrine, who suddenly seemed more ill at ease than she had on Ottilie's arrival.

'He phoned here this morning and asked if I could look in on Flo from time to time,' Corrine said. 'He said you'd told him she might be lonely but that he can't get to Thimblebury often, and that his mum and dad can't either. But I know what he can be like.'

'What can he be like?' Ottilie asked.

'He's one of them – moves out of the village and forgets how things work around here. Thinks he can click his fingers and folks will jump to his commands. He's used to people doing what he tells them.'

'He certainly won't find me doing what he tells me,' Ottilie replied, perhaps too tartly because Corrine shot a furtive glance at Victor as if worried she'd offended their guest. 'I've got a certain amount of patience, and I'm happy to help anyone, but I won't be taken for a mug. He did phone me and, to be honest, it didn't bother me that much, because if I'd been in his position

I'd have probably phoned too. I put him straight, though – don't worry on that score.'

'I told him I do check on Flo – we all do. Is she all right?'

'You know I really can't say anything about her, right?'

'Yes, yes...' Victor said quickly. 'Of course... Wouldn't be right.'

'But you don't need to worry about her,' Ottilie added. 'At least, I've no reason to think so at the moment. I think she would probably appreciate a visit from her grandson, but there's not a lot I can do about that. I did think I'd go and see her after I've been here.'

'I could come with you, if you like,' Corrine said.

'That would be nice.' Ottilie took the cup Corrine handed to her and added some milk from a jug. 'I'm sure it would cheer her up.'

'You think she's down? She never says so.'

'I don't know, but there's a reason her grandson was concerned. I mean, there must be.'

'He used to visit a lot more than he does now,' Corrine said.

'He's busier than he used to be,' Victor said. 'And that ex-wife of his... Well, I don't gossip, but I don't know how he hasn't taken a stick to her.'

'Victor!' Corrine shot an apologetic look at Ottilie and then a warning one at her husband. 'You can't say things like that!'

'All I'm saying is she sounds like a piece of work and he must have the patience of Job. Everyone knows it. The day they got married everyone could see how that was going to turn out. Florence tried to warn him, but they say love is blind – in this case it was deaf too.'

'Is she from Thimblebury?'

'No.' Corrine poured herself a top-up from the teapot. 'To be fair, neither is Heath... well, born here but not raised here. His mother wasn't from the village and she never settled, even after the wedding and Heath's birth. They moved when Heath was quite young, but he's always been very good about visiting his grandmother in the past.'

'Not now?' Ottilie asked, sipping her tea.

'None of my business really,' Corrine said briskly. 'I know how I'd feel if my family stopped visiting me so often, though.'

'It sounds like he's had a lot on his plate. Perhaps when things settle he'll be able to see more of her again. She seems very fond of him – was singing his praises when I last spoke to her.'

'Oh, she won't have a bad word said about him – thinks he's made of gold,' Corrine said.

'He's not so bad.' Victor reached for the teapot. 'Sometimes a bit impatient, but I expect that's the city boy in him. Things move at a different pace here and it's not always easy to wait when you have to.'

'I've noticed that already,' Ottilie said. 'I like it, though. Sort of what I've come for.'

Corrine gave her a look of such profound sympathy that Ottilie almost didn't know what to do with it. Her gaze went down to her cup.

'Victor told me about your loss,' Corrine said. 'I really am very sorry to hear it.'

Ottilie gave a stiff nod, hardly daring to look up because her eyes were filling with tears and she didn't want to show them. She had to be better and stronger than this. How was she going to be any use to the people of Thimblebury if she couldn't even have a conversation about loss without bursting into tears?

During her career as a nurse she'd learned to be practical and resilient, that death is an inevitable part of life, that everyone loses someone eventually and that the only way to deal with that is to accept it and try to move forward. She'd lost count of how many people she'd guided gently to their ends, holding their hands in the final moments when those dearer to them couldn't be there, easing their pain, assuaging their fears.

She knew how this worked, and yet she didn't seem to be able to use any of the wisdom she'd amassed over those years to help herself. She couldn't accept Josh's death and move forward in the way she'd helped so many others do.

If it had always been this hard for all those families over the years, then what was worse was the realisation that, perhaps, Ottilie had expected too much of them and that she'd somehow treated them with cruelty and not the kindness she'd been trying to offer. What if there had never been any accepting and moving on? What if that was a myth she'd invented to enable her to do her job, so that she could keep moving on to the next patient? What if everything she'd strived for was wrong?

Victor started to whisper, and when Ottilie finally managed to sniff back her tears and look up, he was trying to communicate something to Corrine, clearly not wanting Ottilie to know what it was. At the sight of Ottilie's renewed attention, both turned to her with smiles that were far too bright. Perhaps they'd been trying to decide what to do about her distress, because, no matter how hard Ottilie had tried to cover it up, it must have been obvious.

'Yum...' she said in a bid to rescue the mood. 'This cake is lovely. Did you make it, Corrine?'

Corrine nodded.

'She can make them with her eyes shut,' Victor said.

'I've made so many of them,' Corrine agreed. 'Same cake, week in, week out, because old guzzle-guts here can't get enough of it.'

'I don't blame him,' Ottilie said, cramming some more into her mouth.

Corrine looked pleased but waved away the compliment anyway. 'It's easy enough to make – anyone could do it.'

'Not this well I'm sure,' Ottilie said.

'I'll give you some to take home if you like.'

'That would be lovely, if you could spare it.'

'There's another tinful in the pantry – always is, always enough to spare.'

'When you're done,' Victor said, 'we can go up and see the girls if you like.'

Ottilie turned to Corrine. 'Don't you want to talk to me about your problem first?'

'Oh, that'll wait. I'm sure it's nothing anyway. You go up and see the girls while I finish cleaning in here, then I'll take five minutes of your time. That's if you'd like to and you're not too busy.'

Ottilie laughed. 'How can I say no to a morning with a bunch of cute alpaca? It's a deal.'

There was a little kick of excitement as Ottilie spotted Victor's 'girls'. She felt like a kid again, being taken to a petting zoo.

'Oh they're so cute!' she cried.

'They're pretty all right,' Victor replied with obvious pride. 'Good girls too, all of them.'

As one, they seemed to spot him and ambled over. The humans and alpaca reached the gate that separated them at the same time.

'They know this is who brings them the food,' he said, chuckling as he rubbed the nose of a black-and-white, dainty-featured girl. 'All right, Alice,' he said. 'Morning, Mabel. Daisy, Jemima, Dorothy, Maggie, Lizzie... Now, now, Bettina, there's no need to shove... Kitty, you daft thing.' Victor nudged a biscuit-furred alpaca away as she tried to nibble his sleeve. 'I don't keep your treats up there, do I?'

Undoing the gate, he motioned for Ottilie to follow him. She hurried in and closed it behind her, careful not to let anyone make a break for it. She needn't have worried – they were all more concerned with following Victor to the barn than what she was doing. Victor got a bag from a locked cupboard and opened it up.

'This is what they're after. Watch – they'll go mad in a minute. It's like catnip to them.'

He gave Ottilie a handful of dried brown pellets then got some out for himself, the alpaca crowding around them, looking about as excited as docile, woolly alpaca could look.

'There you go,' he said, holding out his hand.

Ottilie followed his lead and got just as much attention. They didn't care who was doing the feeding, as long as they got some.

Ottilie laughed. 'God, I think I'm in love,' she said, lost in the moment. Right now, there was only the creatures, adorable, friendly, bringing purer joy than she'd felt in a long time. 'They do go mad for this stuff – what is it?'

'Nothing as special as you'd think. They love eating is what it is.'

Ottilie's palm was empty in no time, and then the alpaca looked up at her with huge brown expectant eyes.

'Can they have more?' she asked.

'I expect so. Only a bit, though – have to be careful not to overfeed them. Little and often, and they need to forage for their own or they get bored.'

Victor held out the bag. Two of the alpaca tried to go directly to source but Victor swiped it out of their way.

'Patience, Gertie, Astrid, you little thieves.'

'How do you remember who's who?' Ottilie asked.

'You get used to them. They all have different markings, which helps, but they all have their own personality too. Even if the markings didn't separate them that would. It doesn't take long to work them all out.'

'They all seem very much motivated by food.' Ottilie laughed as Alice licked the last treat from her hand.

'Aren't we all?' Victor said, in a tone that was so weirdly profound that Ottilie had to laugh again.

'Does Corrine come up here to feed them?' she asked.

'Not as much as she'd like to. She's busy with house stuff.'

'Ah, old-fashioned, is it? Men in the fields, women in the kitchen?'

Victor grinned. 'I think the answer might disappoint you. I can cook well enough but she doesn't let me near the stove. She likes to do it and she's not so keen on muddy boots, so...'

'I suppose that's fair enough. You seem like a pretty good team to me either way.'

'I wouldn't survive without her, I know that much.'

He fastened the bag up and locked it away again. They spent a few more minutes petting, but when they realised they were getting no more treats, most of the girls wandered off.

'Fickle,' he said.

'Yes,' Ottilie agreed with a laugh. 'How ungrateful.'

'Well,' he added briskly, starting towards the gate, 'no point in waiting around here when they've lost interest. Might as well get back for another pot of tea.'

Ottilie's cheeks were flushed when she and Victor arrived back at the farmhouse. Her smile was so wide it was almost hurting her face, but she couldn't help it. There was nothing quite like a fresh, sunny day surrounded by the most glorious scenery and the cutest, woolliest, daftest creatures on earth, she decided, to lift a person's mood so completely they might as well be a different person altogether.

'I see you took to the girls well enough,' Corrine said, laughing, as they walked back into the kitchen, bringing the freshness of the hillsides with them.

Already, Ottilie had noticed that the air of the lakes and peaks of her new home seemed to cling to jackets and trousers and weave itself into her hair so that whenever she went from outside to in, she carried it with her.

'They're sweethearts, aren't they? Soft as old cushions and daft as brushes the lot of them.'

'Oh, I'm in love with them. Victor says I can adopt them if I like, save him the job of mucking out their sheds every day.'

'He says that, but he'd never part with them – like pets to him they are.' Corrine smiled at Victor. 'Isn't that right?'

'No,' he said but was holding back a grin as he sat at the table and reached for the teapot, giving it a rub before clearly deciding it was warm enough to drink whatever was in there and pouring some out into a cup that was still standing on the table from earlier.

'Let me make a fresh pot,' Corrine said, taking it from him and picking up the cups. 'Haven't had a minute to clear all this away since you went out – been stripping the beds.'

'That's all right,' Ottilie said. 'If it's all the same to you, though I'd love to stay a while longer, I really do need to go and see Florence. Perhaps I'll get a cup of tea another time? I can take a quick look at your little problem and then I'll be on my way, if that's all right.'

'Aww...' Corrine flapped and fussed and seemed not to know what to do with herself as she came over to Ottilie and flashed a section of neck by pulling her collar out of the way so briefly that Ottilie barely saw what she was meant to be looking at. 'It's a spot, see – nothing really to worry about.'

'Looks funny to me,' Victor said, and in such a deadly serious tone that Ottilie knew he'd seen something that had alarmed him.

Ottilie nodded at a chair. 'Corrine, take a seat for a minute and let me have a closer look. I'm sure you're right – nothing to worry about – but it was hard to tell from what you just showed me.'

Corrine looked as if she wanted to argue but then did as she was asked. Ottilie pulled her collar gently away to reveal an angry-looking patch of skin. Strangely coloured and oddly shaped.

'Not so much a rash as a bit of a lesion,' she said quietly as she pondered it.

She didn't like the look of it at all, but she didn't want to alarm Corrine and Victor.

'What is it?' Victor asked.

'It's not bothering me that much,' Corrine said. 'I'm sure it just needs a bit of antiseptic cream or something.'

'Still...' Ottilie put her collar back and forced a smile. 'I'm going to ask Dr Cheadle to see you. It'll probably be something and nothing, like you say, but we'd all be happier if she confirmed that. How long did you say you've had it?'

'Couldn't really say. Only noticed it a few weeks ago. Thought it would heal but...' Corrine shrugged. 'Doesn't seem to be. What do you think it might be?'

'Hmm...' Ottilie didn't want to say, but everything she heard from Corrine made her slightly more alarmed. She didn't know what it was, but she didn't like the possibilities that were forming in her mind. 'It doesn't hurt to get a second opinion.'

Victor and Corrine exchanged a worried look.

'Look, why don't you phone the surgery and make an appointment that suits you? In the meantime I'll speak to Dr Cheadle and give her the heads-up; that way she might bring it forward and see you quicker.'

'Is there a need to see me quick?' Corrine asked, and immediately Ottilie realised she'd said the wrong thing.

'Not especially, but the sooner we get to the bottom of it, the sooner your mind's put at rest, right? I don't think it can hurt to get it sorted. As you say, a bit of antibiotic cream or something and I'm sure it will be right in no time.'

'I'll get on to the surgery,' Victor said.

'Are you quite flexible?' Ottilie asked. 'Able to attend any time, I mean?'

'Yes,' Corrine said. 'Nobody's schedule to worry about but our own.'

'In that case, maybe I'll give Lavender a call and see whether she has anything free for this afternoon. Give me a second...'

Ottilie took her phone out into the front garden. She wanted a better signal, but she also didn't want to alarm Corrine or Victor unnecessarily.

'Hi... is that Lavender?' she asked as the call was answered.

'It is. Who is...?'

'Sorry, it's Ottilie – your new nurse. We met yesterday when I came in with—'

'Flo, yes, I remember. What can I do for you?'

'I was wondering if Dr Cheadle has any slots spare this afternoon. I'm up at Daffodil Farm just taking a look at Corrine and I could do with Doctor's help.'

'You do realise you haven't started working for us yet,' Lavender said in a dry tone. 'But you seem to be finding plenty to do anyway.'

'And making plenty of work for you, yes, I know. I'm sorry about that. But if you could do something just this once I'd be really grateful.'

Lavender was silent for a moment. Ottilie imagined she was looking at the appointment schedule or something. 'What should I tell Doctor is the problem? Just to give her a bit to go on before she sees Corrine.'

'It's probably nothing...' Ottilie glanced back at the house and lowered her voice. 'There's a little lesion that I don't like the look of. I can't be certain, but I wonder if it ought to be biopsied.'

'In that case, I'm sure she'd want me to force an appointment into the clinic schedule whether we have space or not.

Tell Corrine to come down at five. She can have the overtime slot.'

'There's an overtime slot on the clinic?'

'No, I just invented it. But I know Fliss wouldn't want to leave this.'

'Thanks, Lavender – I owe you one.'

'Two, if you count Flo.'

'Two.' Ottilie smiled. 'I'll try not to make a habit of it.'

'Please do,' Lavender said with that tone of vague humour again, and then ended the call.

CHAPTER EIGHT

Ottilie was beginning to think she ought to have forgone the week of leave she'd given herself before she started her new job and just jumped right in. Since she'd arrived in Thimblebury she'd more or less been doing it anyway, even if it was in a very informal and ad hoc way. But then, she wondered if she'd have ever been told about Corrine's worrying lesion, or seen Florence have one of her funny turns if she hadn't been out and about, talking to them socially. She felt both women were the sort of people who'd ignore symptoms, file them under something to worry about another day and get on with the demands of their lives. Ottilie had seen plenty of patients during her career who were like that, who'd left something that should have been an early warning until it was too late, simply because they'd felt to bring attention to it was to cause an unnecessary fuss. And if that was the case with Corrine or Flo, she was glad that she'd been there to help.

Flo was very much on her mind as she walked the path down the hill from Daffodil Farm. Victor had wanted to give her a lift back, but beside the fact that she didn't think her bones would stand any more rattling in his mad old Land Rover, Ottilie decided that they had things to talk about and that she'd enjoy the walk. So she left them to it.

Outside on the hillside there was a stiff breeze, but the sun was bright and warm when the wind dropped. Set out before her, like an emerald quilt, were the hills and valleys of her new home, the ribbon of the river shining in the distance as it cut through the land. From here she could just pick out a sliver of blue that must have belonged to Lake Windermere, though she wasn't entirely sure. She hadn't yet got the lie of the land, but that was something she was keen to rectify. At least she knew where Flo's house was, sort of. Once she was back in the village proper, she was sure it wouldn't take long to locate it.

Ottilie's hand went to her pocket. Corrine had insisted that she wrap the last slice of fruit cake and sent her away with it – 'in case you get hungry on the walk down'. Ottilie had to smile as her fingers traced the outline of the carefully wrapped pack-age. It was so endearingly old-fashioned, the notion that she'd need to eat something simply because she'd walked down a hill. It was the sort of thing her great-grandma would have done – a woman who'd died when Ottilie had been in her early teens but a woman who'd had a profound impact on Ottilie nonetheless.

It had been her great-grandma Matilda who had first made Ottilie think about nursing as a career. She'd tell stories of her own exploits, during and after the war where she'd cared for soldiers injured in battle, and Ottilie had been transfixed by them, in awe of her bravery and compassion. Though she'd never consciously acknowledged it at the time, those stories would come to shape Ottilie's own life, her choices, her desire to do good.

A sudden gust swept across the hillside, rustling through the long grasses, rattling the trees and whipping Ottilie's hair around her face. She gathered it into her hand to hold it as she walked, at least until the wind had died down again. How different a place could look in the bright light of day. Looking around now, she could barely believe she'd been so afraid the night before. There was nothing to fear here. Nobody was coming to find her, and the hills and grass and sky held such beauty that surely this was heaven? It didn't change just because darkness fell over it – the same hills and grass and sky were still there, even when she couldn't see them.

With a faint smile, she shook her head, inwardly scolding herself. These random moments of panic and anxiety – they weren't her. They had to stop; she couldn't go on being afraid of everything.

The fact that Magnus's directions had been very precise, coupled with the fact that you could walk the entire length of Thimblebury in about ten minutes, meant it didn't take long for Ottilie to find Florence's house. It was exactly as Ottilie would have imagined if you'd asked her: a house full of contradictions, from the outside at least.

It was built in the traditional stone of many others around these parts, but Flo had painted it a pastel green, which made it stick out. Ottilie could imagine that most of her neighbours hated it, but perhaps nobody said anything because she was such a longstanding and valued member of the community. There were plenty of other places where she would have been told in no uncertain terms what everyone thought of her decor and asked to change it. The garden was filled with trees and shrubs and there was a scarecrow wearing an incongruous studded leather jacket and hat. It looked so strange with straw sticking out of the sleeves and a cloth face poking out from beneath the cap that Ottilie almost burst out laughing at the sight of it. And there were other little oddities – a water feature made from a child's plastic paddling pool and a bird bath made from bits of an old car – that spoke of Florence being someone who did things her own way and had slightly unexpected tastes for a woman of her age.

Ottilie took it all in as she made her way up the path to the front door and then knocked.

'Oh...'

The door flew open almost immediately, and Ottilie had to wonder if Florence had been waiting behind it.

'Is it about my tests?'

'I thought I'd pop by,' Ottilie said with a smile, deciding not to point out that Florence hadn't even had her tests yet. 'We never really got to finish our chat, did we?'

'I thought we had. Was there something else you needed to say?'

'Nothing in particular. General stuff. But it seemed as if we were cut off.'

'Didn't seem that way to me.'

'Is it a bad time?' Ottilie asked. 'I could come back. Or, you know, see you around. I didn't mean to disturb you; just trying to be neighbourly. I am new here after all, and as I said to you yesterday, I feel I need to make an effort to get to know people.'

Florence paused, but then she seemed to brighten. 'You've come at a good time actually. Yes, come in and have a cup of tea. I do have company already, but if that doesn't bother you, there's always room for one more.'

Ottilie followed Florence through a cramped hallway to an equally cramped living room. Every surface was covered in odd ornaments, mismatched and with seemingly no trends or taste to speak of, only a random magpie collection of trinkets. Some were old, some were modern, some traditional and tasteful, some tacky. Ottilie felt sure that each one must have a history that granted it a place amongst Flo's belongings, and maybe one day she'd ask about it.

There were photos nestled in between them – Ottilie presumed they were of family – some black and white, some sepia, some faded colours. Every inch of wall space was filled with old watercolours and tapestries and yet more photos. There was a glass display case crammed with bone china all belonging to perhaps half a dozen different tea services – again, none of it particularly matched in tone or taste – and a bookcase stuffed with tatty books.

The many questions Ottilie had about the vast collection of stuff were forced out of her head when she noticed a man was sitting on a sofa draped in crocheted blankets and embroidered throws, balancing a cup and saucer on his knee. He looked up at Ottilie's arrival in some confusion.

'This is the nurse,' Florence announced.

His frown gave way to a look of understanding, and then something like annoyance.

'I'm Ottilie...' She stuck out her hand. 'And you must be...?'

She wasn't certain but wondered if this might be the famous grandson. If so, he hadn't wasted any time coming to visit. Whether it had been prompted by guilt or concern didn't matter; Ottilie approved. At least he cared enough to drive straight over either way.

'Heath,' he said, shaking her hand stiffly. He looked even more annoyed when he let go than he had before.

'Hello, Heath. It's nice to meet you in person.'

'Is it?'

'Of course!' Ottilie said, taken aback by the brusqueness. Hadn't they sorted out their misunderstanding on the phone the previous night?

'I've been telling Ottilie all about you,' Flo said, showing Ottilie where to sit. Right next to Heath, as it happened, and Ottilie was certain that was no coincidence because there were plenty of other spots available. But she sat down anyway, body folded in tight, not anxious, exactly, but perhaps a little guarded.

'I'm sure you have,' Heath said flatly.

'Good things,' Ottilie replied.

He put his cup and saucer down on a side table and stood. 'I expect you two need to talk, so I'll clear off.'

'Already?' Flo looked crestfallen.

'You don't need to go on my account,' Ottilie said.

'You only just got here!' Flo added.

Heath turned to her. 'I've been here two hours, Gran.'

'So you can only spare two hours for me nowadays, can you?' Florence pouted. 'On a meter, am I?'

'Of course not, but I've got things to do. I'm sorry...' He bent to kiss her on the cheek.

Ottilie noticed suddenly how tall he was. Florence wasn't exactly huge, but he towered over her. He had to be at least six feet tall, maybe more. His hair was a thick chestnut, longer on top and cropped at the back, his eyes a dark brown. The notion that he was actually quite handsome was a vague one in the back of Ottilie's mind. There was too much else going on for her to really acknowledge it. Like why was he suddenly leaving? Was it because she'd arrived? A quick glance at the table revealed that he hadn't even finished his cup of tea.

'I'll call over next week,' he added.

'Don't say it and not mean it.' Florence looked like a disappointed toddler. 'I know you: out of sight, out of mind.'

'That's not fair, Gran. I visit when I can.'

Florence glanced at Ottilie before she turned back to him, but Ottilie couldn't read it. Was there some silent message there for her, a cue, something she was meant to do or say at this point? If there was, Ottilie hadn't got it.

'Right you are then,' Flo said, seemingly content to leave things at that. 'Next week? I'll bake.'

'Sounds good.'

Heath kissed her once again and then nodded shortly at Ottilie before striding out. A moment later the sound of the front door slamming shut echoed around Florence's tiny house.

Well, that wasn't weird at all.

CHAPTER NINE

If Ottilie imagined that her dealings with Florence and Corrine were going to be indicative of her dealings with all her patients in Thimblebury, she was to be disappointed. As much as those two ladies had welcomed her care and expertise, some of the other village residents were less than enthusiastic about their new nurse. She wondered, as she battled mistrust and doubt from every appointment, if her first day on the job had, perhaps, been an unfortunate fluke, a clinic filled with patients who wished she was Gwen, their previous nurse. But her second day on the job had so far brought more of the same and she began to wonder if she was ever going to win these people over. It didn't matter what she did or what she said, at the end of the day she wasn't Gwen.

'You're not going to put extra tape on?' Mr Hodgkins, her three fifteen, stared down at the wound Ottilie had just cleaned and re-dressed. 'Gwen always puts extra tape on.'

'I promise, it will be secure as it is,' Ottilie said with all the patience she had left – which wasn't much after two days of hearing about how much better Gwen was at everything. Gwen was faster, Gwen took her time, Gwen explained everything better, Gwen didn't insult their intelligence by explaining too much, Gwen always went to fetch them from reception rather than calling for them at the doorway, Gwen always checked with Dr Cheadle, Gwen never needed to check with Dr Cheadle, Gwen was gentler, Gwen tied her bandages tight enough, Gwen didn't tie them so tight they cut off the patient's circulation, Gwen knew what was wrong with them as soon as they walked into the room and didn't need to ask endless questions.

Of course, Gwen had also been their nurse for over forty years; she was bound to know each of them and their medical needs intimately. Gwen was bloody perfect – it was a wonder she hadn't been declared a saint and a statue of her erected in the village square. Ottilie had no personal grudge, but she was only human, and she was getting sick of being told how much better her predecessor was. She felt like pointing out that Gwen had abandoned them by selfishly and unhelpfully retiring and that, like it or not, they were stuck with Ottilie, and if they didn't like it, they were welcome to leave Thimblebury for a town where the nurse was more like Gwen.

She didn't, of course. She only smiled and explained that she was sure Gwen's way was great, and that she'd bear their comments in mind, but that she also had her own ways of doing things and she was sure they were just as effective, and that everyone would get used to the change in time.

In fairness to Gwen, she did sound like she'd been a great nurse and Ottilie could understand why everyone had become so attached to her. There were people who'd been cared for by Gwen their whole lives, who now had kids of their own who'd also been cared for by Gwen. There were many villagers who'd never known any other nurse, and for the rest, the previous one was so far back in the memory she might as well have never existed. Ottilie wasn't so green not to realise that patients always felt safer in hands they knew well and trusted with anything. One day, perhaps, they'd trust Ottilie like that too. But that day seemed a long way off.

'And if there's a problem,' she continued, 'I'm only at the end of a phone. I can see you and fix it in a jiffy.'

'Because Gwen said that it was very important not to let anything get in there.'

'Nothing will get in there – it's very well covered.'

'But I can see a gap...' Mr Hodgkins frowned at Ottilie's handiwork and began to pull at the bandage. 'See? There!'

There wasn't a gap until you started messing...

With a sigh, Ottilie tore off another strip of surgical tape and tightened up the dressing.

'Better?' she asked, looking up.

With an expression that was far from convinced, he gave a sullen nod. 'I suppose it will probably hold.'

'Good. So I'll see you next week. Shall I book you in for Tuesday again?'

'God willing I'm still here next Tuesday.'

'Why, where are you going?'

'Well, I'm old, aren't I? At my age you never know.'

What was it about this village that everyone seemed to be obsessed with their expected imminent demise?

'Let's book you in on the off-chance you do survive another week, eh?' she said cheerfully as she pulled up her diary page on her laptop.

Before she'd given him a time, he began to leave the room.

'Wait, I haven't—' Ottilie jumped up to stop him. 'I haven't given you an appointment card.'

'I don't need one.'

'But I haven't given you the appointment!'

'Gwen gave me the same time every week.'

Ottilie held back another sigh. 'Hang on... let me change this...'

She went back to her laptop to find the identical slot a week on, but Mr Hodgkins didn't wait to find out whether it was still available. He hobbled out, letting the door slam behind him. Ottilie considered running after him for a moment, and then decided she'd simply have to see him when he turned up. That had the potential to mess up the schedule, because she realised very quickly that she'd already given his slot away, but there wasn't a lot she could do about it. More to the point, she didn't see what she'd gain by trying to make him aware that she needed him to take a different slot, because he'd only grumble about how Gwen would never make him do that and probably turn up for his usual anyway.

She twisted the cap from a bottle of water, took a sip and then squeezed her eyes shut for a moment to collect herself. She wasn't used to this. Things had always run far more efficiently at the hospital in Manchester where she'd worked before. Well, perhaps efficient wasn't the word for it – at times it could be as chaotic as anywhere else – but at least there were systems in place that everyone tried to stick to. And at least she wasn't constantly being compared to the nurse who'd been on shift the day before her. She supposed, as she opened her eyes and stared out at the honeysuckle growing around her office window, it was one more thing about Thimblebury she'd have to get used to.

Her laptop pinged a notification, and she flicked screens to see that her next patient had arrived in the clinic, having been checked in by Lavender on reception.

Here we go again...

A quick stride down the short corridor that led from her treatment room-slash-office brought her to the reception area. Sticking her head around the door, she called out, 'Mrs Icke...'

There was no answer. There were three women in reception, so she looked at them and called out again. One of them had to be Mrs Icke. Then one of the ladies nudged another, who was engrossed in a gardening magazine.

'She's a bit deaf,' she said to Ottilie. 'You have to come and get her usually because she won't hear you call.'

'Oh...'

Mrs Icke looked up, saw Ottilie waiting, and then pushed herself painstakingly from her seat. She gave Ottilie a very obvious once-over. 'I didn't think you'd be so young.'

Ottilie smiled. 'I wish. I can assure you, I'm older than you think.'

'What?'

'I said I'm not young.'

'All right! No need to shout! Why didn't you come and get me?' Mrs Icke began to totter after Ottilie, who held open the door for her. 'Gwen always came to get me. I could have been sitting there all day!'

'I'm sorry – I didn't know. I'll remember next time.'

'Speak up! Don't mumble! Gwen didn't mumble... honestly, youngsters today...'

'I wish I was a youngster,' Ottilie replied as she led the way. 'I'm thirty-five. Hardly a youngster, though I appreciate the compliment.'

'You're still mumbling!'

'Never mind – it wasn't important anyway. I'll be sure to come and get you next time.'

'That's what Gwen always did.'

'Yes, I know.'

'There's no point in leaving me sat there all day.'

In the treatment room, Ottilie gestured for Mrs Icke to take a seat.

'How have you been?' she asked as she logged into the patient records.

'Surely you know that,' Mrs Icke said, looking surprised and faintly disapproving.

'It was a polite— Never mind.' Ottilie held in yet another

sigh of resignation, mixed with some mounting frustration. 'Blood pressure check is it?'

'Don't you know that either?'

Don't you know what a rhetorical question is?

Ottilie looked for her equipment. 'Come on then – left arm. Let's have a look at you.'

Mrs Icke slapped her arm onto the desk, sleeve already rolled up. At least this appointment would be quick, Ottilie thought as she folded the cuff around it.

'It's a bit high,' Ottilie said as she watched the numbers.

'No it's not.'

'Only a touch,' Ottilie added.

'Gwen said it was fine.'

'It might have been fine last time Gwen took it. It's a little high today, though.'

'It can't be.'

'Have you noticed any symptoms?'

'No.'

'Been doing anything you think might have made the difference? Hang on, where's your list of medication...'

Ottilie began to search her computer for the medical records, only to be distracted by a thump on the desk.

'Well this is a pretty picture, isn't it!' fumed Mrs Icke. 'You mean to say you don't know?'

'Not off the top of my head, no, but the list is—'

'Gwen could tell you in her sleep!'

'I'm sure she could, and even if I could I'd check anyway in case something had changed that I didn't know about.'

'If something had changed, Gwen always knew.'

'Hmm...' Ottilie said, going back to her screen, trying very hard to hold a sarcastic reply – and she had many to choose from. What was that Fliss had told her about enjoying community nursing?

. . .

One thing Ottilie could get used to very quickly was lunch at the surgery. In her previous job at the hospital it was always something of an afterthought – a hurried sandwich or a mug of instant soup, just to make sure she didn't keel over mid-shift – and then back to work. There was no time to taste, let alone savour what she was eating, and very little time to catch up with colleagues.

But here at Thimblebury's tiny surgery, Dr Cheadle – or Fliss, as she insisted her colleagues call her, although Lavender often called her Doctor, no matter what she said – had always made a point of closing the doors and, unforeseen emergencies notwithstanding, gathered her staff to take their breaks around the same table and to talk through their day, or anything else that was on their mind, together. They'd all bring food to share. Ottilie hadn't realised that this ritual was in place on her first day in the job, but as this was her second and she now knew the drill, she'd made a pomegranate, feta and couscous salad, while Fliss had brought chicken drumsticks to go with it, and Lavender had made a pie with cherries from her own garden for afterwards.

'I don't think I'll ever get used to this,' Ottilie said as she helped herself to a second slice of Lavender's pie, the remains of her chicken littering a plate in front of her.

'The pie?' Fliss asked with a note of humour. 'It's very good, but really...'

Ottilie laughed. 'This whole downing tools thing and taking a proper lunch. I've spent my entire career so far grabbing what I can and working with indigestion. This is very new for me.'

'As far as I'm concerned, none of us works to our full potential if we don't take time to recharge. When you're tired, hungry, rushed, stressed... then you make mistakes. I see this time as an investment in good patient care. This afternoon we'll be refreshed and at our best and we'll have had a moment to connect, which I hope makes for good mental health and good working relationships.'

'Gwen used to say—' Lavender began but then stopped. The expression of exasperation Ottilie had hoped to keep from her face had obviously shown itself anyway.

'Cheer up,' Fliss said to her, laughing again. 'I know everyone's going on about Gwen – the whole village adored her. But they'll get used to you quicker than you imagine.'

'We had some patients come into the surgery crying, begging her not to retire. Said they wouldn't be able to cope without her,' Lavender told her.

'That doesn't surprise me one bit,' Ottilie said. 'Pretty much everyone I've seen in surgery this last couple of days seems annoyed that I'm not Gwen. I realise change is tough on some of the older ones, but it's hardly encouraging. She doesn't live in the village, I gather.'

'No,' Lavender said. 'She wasn't daft. As you've found out already, people don't leave you alone if they know where to find you; she didn't want to be pestered when she wasn't on shift.'

'Like I said,' Fliss put in, 'the patients will come round. I don't think they were all that keen on me when I first took over, but I don't doubt there will be a fuss when I retire too. They like who they know – it's nothing personal.'

'Please don't retire yet!' Ottilie replied. 'I don't think I could cope, let alone the patients! Please give me a few more years, at least until they get their head around me!'

'In a few weeks they'll have forgotten all about Gwen and they'll love you,' Lavender said.

'And I've no plans to retire yet,' Fliss added. 'I'd be bored to death, for a start.'

'Good!' Ottilie turned to Lavender. 'How long have you been here?'

'At the surgery?'

Ottilie nodded and Lavender blew out a breath. 'I honestly

can't remember. My youngest had just started nursery school, so...' She did some counting in her head for a moment – at least Ottilie thought so, because she looked as if she was trying to work it out. 'I'd say about twenty-five years,' she said finally.

'So you must like your job then.'

'I do.' She looked at Fliss and grinned. 'It's absolutely nothing to do with the fact that there are hardly any other jobs in Thimblebury at all...'

'I've told you before,' Fliss said as she poured cream onto the slice of cherry pie she'd dished up for herself, 'you know where the door is when you've had enough.'

'Well' – Lavender's grin widened – 'that's my problem, isn't it: I don't seem to know when I've had enough.'

'I could put you in touch with a good counsellor about that.'

Both women started to laugh. Ottilie watched, already fond of them despite only spending a short time working alongside them. She loved that they felt so comfortable around each other. Too many of her colleagues at the hospital dared not even speak to the senior doctors, let alone banter with them. It spoke of a good working relationship, of mutual respect and a deep affection that came from years of cooperation. Fliss clearly trusted Lavender with the administration of the surgery, which meant she could devote all her time and energy to her patients without distraction. Ottilie looked forward to the day when she'd slot in as well, where she'd have complete and total trust in the people around her, comfortable enough to be able to say anything to them. She'd already had a preview of that day, when she'd gone to supper at Fliss's house, and she liked the way it looked.

'Corrine already loves you,' Lavender said, turning to Ottilie, and though she was smiling there was something more serious in her tone. 'Singing your praises when she came in to see us.'

'And I don't blame her,' Fliss said, also looking more serious. 'I suspect you may have saved her life.'

Ottilie shook her head. 'I didn't do anything special. Victor was the one who asked me to take a look, and I didn't really know what I was looking at. That's the only reason I sent her down to see you.'

'But you did send her down, and that's what counts. You could just as easily have assumed it was something and nothing and told her to fetch lotion from the pharmacy.'

'Nobody in my shoes would have done that.'

Fliss raised her eyebrows. 'I've worked with the odd one over the years who would.'

'I couldn't live with myself if I had,' Ottilie said firmly. 'I hope she's going to be all right.'

'If the biopsy comes back positive, I feel confident that she'll still be all right. I think we caught it early enough for a very good outcome.' Fliss dug her fork into her pie and smiled at Ottilie. 'That was a good day's work.'

'Let's hope we can get a good outcome for Florence too,' Ottilie said. 'I popped in to see her, to check how she was doing... What's the deal with the grandson?'

'You mean the golden boy Heath?' Lavender said with a grin. 'Sun shines out of somewhere it ought not to be able to, if you ask Flo.'

'I get that impression,' Ottilie said. 'He was there when I went to see her, but as soon as I sat down he rushed off. Said he'd got stuff to do, but I felt as if I was the reason.'

'I wouldn't take it personally,' Lavender said. 'I don't know much about it, but from what I can tell, his divorce messed him up quite badly. He's probably terrified he might fancy you. From what Flo says, I wouldn't blame the poor boy if he was put off women for good.'

'She was that bad?' Ottilie asked.

'I only met her a couple of times, but I didn't warm to her at all.'

'We don't know what went on there,' Fliss cut in. 'No point

in speculating, especially now it's over.'

'I'm only saying I think it was a very bad divorce, and I think she put him through the wringer.'

'As long as he's there for Flo, I suppose we ought to give him the benefit of the doubt,' Ottilie said thoughtfully. 'Does she have much in the way of family?'

'Not local,' Fliss said. 'It could present a problem if she needs hospital visits over the next few weeks and months.'

'We have a community ambulance service, right?'

'A very sporadic one,' Lavender said. 'Spaces on that are like gold dust round here. One ambulance serving about half a dozen villages. A nightmare trying to book someone onto it.'

'Has she got something coming up?' Ottilie asked.

'I'm going to request an echo and some scans. Perhaps if we can work some magic and get them all on the same day, it might only need one hospital trip.'

'If you pass it on to me, I'll see what I can do,' Lavender said.

Fliss gave a grateful nod.

'If all else fails and she has no transport, I'll drive her to the hospital,' Ottilie said.

'Oh, she'd love that,' Lavender said drily. 'Chauffer service! Careful, you might have her thinking she's someone special.'

'That's not such a bad thing. I don't think she's feeling very special these days. I think she's lonely more than anything.'

Ottilie was silent for a moment. Despite Flo's tendency to be abrasive and her moods a little unpredictable, she liked her. She hated the idea of her being so lonely that it might be affecting her physical health. Perhaps she needed to speak to the grandson again, see if she could get to the bottom of the family situation and see if anyone there could spare more time to pop in on a more regular basis. And she could see about them getting her to the hospital for tests too, saving her the need to fight for a spot in the community ambulance.

A muffled ringtone interrupted her train of thought.

'I think that's mine,' she said, rifling through the handbag at her feet. 'Sorry...' Frowning at the screen, she barely looked up as she rose from her chair. 'I think I should take this...'

Hurrying from the kitchen, she answered the call. 'Faith, hi.'

'Hi. How have you been? Sorry I haven't been in touch for a while but—'

'God, no, don't apologise; it's fine. I get you're busy. How are you? How's everything at the station?'

'Still weird without Josh really. I mean, we have a new guy, as you can imagine... Well, not new really, is he? Been with us a few months. And he's good but, you know, Josh... he had a way. Well, you'd know that. He made the working day a whole lot better just because he was there.'

Ottilie gave a tight smile. She'd had plenty of these conversations with Faith and other colleagues of Josh since his death, but they never got any easier. 'He used to say the same about you. So... not that I mind you calling, but is there anything in particular you wanted to talk about? Of course, I appreciate you checking in on me like you do, but it's kind of awkward as I'm at work. I can call you back later if you want to chat.'

'I wanted to see how you were, but I also wanted to tell you something before it got to you through the official channels. Those guys aren't always blessed with tact.'

Ottilie's forehead creased into a frown. 'Tell me what?'

There was a pause, barely a second long, and yet so loaded it could have been an hour's worth. 'We've arrested someone.'

Ottilie didn't need to ask who they'd arrested or what for. Specifically who, she didn't know, but the mere fact that Faith was phoning her at all with this information told her all she needed to know. There was no other arrest that would mean anything to her.

Taking the phone outside, she perched against a low wall in

the tiny garden at the back of the surgery. Thimblebury's surgery building had once been a house, and still retained many of the original features, including the garden, which Fliss tended herself despite not living there. A snowy butterfly with delicate green markings landed close by, and Ottilie watched its wings tick-tock open and closed with a detached sort of fascination as she tried to absorb fully what Faith was telling her.

'Is it—' She cleared her throat and started again. 'Is it who we thought it might be?'

'Yes. I don't want you to get your hopes up because they're a slippery bunch, but between you and me, it's a promising development.'

'So we might finally get our justice?'

'We can hope so. But be prepared: it could go either way – and often does.'

'Hmm.' Ottilie watched as the butterfly took off and landed again on the next shrub along. 'You don't need anything from me, do you? I don't have to come and give a statement or anything?'

'Not yet. Perhaps an impact statement if it gets that far. Don't worry – I'll keep you posted. As soon as I hear anything, I'll let you know.'

'Thanks.'

'Don't mention it.'

'No, really, I mean thanks for everything. I know you all want to catch Josh's killer as much as I want you to. I appreciate all that you're doing.'

'It's our job.' There was another brief but loaded pause. 'Are you OK?'

Faith sounded concerned, and Ottilie could imagine the uncertainty in her own voice that might have triggered such concern. But she wasn't OK and she didn't suppose she could hide it. How was she meant to feel about these new developments?

On the one hand, justice might finally be served, but that wouldn't bring Josh back. What it would do was rake up all the emotions Ottilie had battled so hard to move past during the six months since his death, reopen wounds that had been healing, sharpen pain that had dulled with time. And what if this wasn't the justice she'd craved? What if it was a false hope, another dead end? She wasn't sure she could take being flung back to the beginning of the nightmare. She wasn't sure shc had the strength to walk that path again to get back to where she was now.

'Of course,' she said, forcing brightness to her voice. 'This is good news.'

'Are you sure? Because if you need someone to talk to, I can get—'

'Not the liaison guys, not again. I know they do good work but don't waste your precious resources on me. I've had six months to get my head around it and... well, this has thrown me a bit, but I'll be OK.'

'I was going to say I'd get a day off and come out to see you. Where is it you've moved to? Somewhere in the Lakes, right?'

That familiar, groundless fear swept over Ottilie again. She didn't want to say where she was, not even to Faith, whom she ought to trust above anyone else, the colleague Josh had valued. He'd always called her his 'work wife'. They were close friends, but Faith was also too close to the case, too close to people who might discover her location, even if Faith never meant it to happen, even if she never meant to let it slip, she might.

It was silly – ridiculous even – and yet Ottilie couldn't shake the doubts.

'Honestly, I'm fine,' she said briskly. 'When I get a free day, I'll come to see you. It'd be nice to catch up if you have time – and I'm already starting to miss Manchester.'

'Sure, I'd like that. Text me when you have a day off and we'll grab coffee. There's a new place near Piccadilly station, supposed to be nice. If you wanted to come in on the train it means we could grab a couple of proper drinks too.'

'That sounds good. Sorry, but I... Thanks for calling, Faith. I really appreciate you keeping me up to date.'

'No problem. You take care, right?'

'You too. Bye.'

Ottilie watched the screen go dark as the call came to an end. Then she grasped the phone tight in both hands and stared into space. Another butterfly landed close by, this one scarlet and black, as delicate and ethereal as the first, but she hardly noticed it.

'Ottilie...'

She turned to see Lavender at the back door.

'Are you all right?'

'Um... sure... sorry – someone from back home.'

'Are you sure you're all right? You look—'

'I'm fine. Did you need me?'

'I'm about to open the doors for the afternoon surgery. You've missed the last cup of tea, but I could bring one through to the treatment room for you...'

Ottilie pushed herself up from the wall and forced a smile. She seemed to be doing so much of that these past few months she did it with barely a conscious thought.

'You're an angel,' she said. 'Thank you. I'll go and get set up.'

'Full clinic again,' Lavender said as Ottilie followed her inside. 'Doesn't look too bad, though. Quite a lot of routine stuff.'

'That's good,' Ottilie said, hardly registering what Lavender was saying. Her thoughts were all over the place, but she was going to have to pull herself together – and quick – if she was going to function the rest of the afternoon.

CHAPTER TEN

Throughout her working life, Ottilie had done shifts. As a student nurse she'd often been given the worst: long nights and stupidly early mornings, bank holidays and weekends and basically the times that nobody else wanted to do. Sometimes she worked two back to back, and they were the worst – her legs would throb and her back would ache, and she'd knock off feeling as if she'd never slept in her life. It was part and parcel of the job; people didn't get ill on demand and certainly didn't wait until it was convenient for the medical staff, but sometimes it could be draining. Despite this, she'd loved her job at the hospital so much that she'd never really questioned the need. Coming here to Thimblebury, working in a surgery with clearly defined hours (apart from emergencies, but Fliss mostly dealt with those) was a novelty. Being home every evening was certainly a novelty, one she'd looked forward to enjoying when she'd been working her notice in Manchester.

But tonight, once again, her fears were getting the better of her. The phone call from Josh's police colleague, Faith, had rattled her. She'd found it difficult to think of anything else all afternoon, and though she was quite sure she hadn't made any mistakes during afternoon surgery, she couldn't honestly say for sure.

Tonight was also her first film club at Magnus and Geoff's home-built cinema. She'd been so looking forward to it, but now, with her mood through the floor, she wondered whether she ought to make an excuse not to go.

Josh would never have done that of course. Josh would have picked himself up, defied those who might ruin his life and gone out just to make a point. He'd have wanted Ottilie to do the same, and so, despite how miserable she was, she decided that not only would she go for that reason, but also because she wanted to make friends and settle into Thimblebury quickly. Only then would these moments of sadness and fear start to lessen until they stopped completely. At least she hoped so. And the best way to do that was to get involved in everything the village had to offer.

While she had a few hours until the screening was due to start, she decided to make dips to go with the boxes of crackers and breadsticks she'd bought online to take and share. Nothing fancy but something to take her mind off her anxieties. The cheeriest playlist she had blasted out from her music dock and she forced herself to sing along as she chopped cucumber and garlic, coriander and mint. She might look quite mad to anyone who happened to peer in through the window at that moment – a face of misery, singing at the top of her lungs anyway, but if it banished the wretchedness she'd be as mad as it took. She'd heard it said that to make a happy face was halfway to being happy, but so far it was taking some effort.

She wondered who might attend the film club. Magnus said that it could be anywhere up to twenty of them, but that depended on what the film was. Tonight they were watching *Chicago*, chosen by Magnus and Geoff. Ottilie liked a good musical, but they weren't for everyone. Because she didn't know how many to cater for, she'd phoned the shop to ask Magnus, but he didn't really know either. He'd got rough numbers from people he'd asked, but he said that even people who confirmed attendance earlier in the day didn't always turn up.

Once the dips were all finished and packaged up, Ottilie went to get changed into something a bit more presentable than her old joggers. She settled on a pair of flared jeans and a floral gypsy top, gathered her hair into a clip and refreshed the minimal make-up she'd worn that day. With a last look in the mirror, fairly content with what she saw, she gathered her offerings and headed out.

It was still warm, and the jacket Ottilie had put on soon felt like too much. But she was laden with the snacks she'd made for the other film club members and had no arms free to take it off, and so had to suffer and hope that she wasn't too sweaty by the time she got to the shop. She knew from Magnus that Geoff had built the cinema himself in one of the outbuildings. It wasn't visible from the front and Ottilie was curious to see what he'd done. She'd heard of people building home cinemas, but she'd never actually been in one.

There was a closed sign on the door of the shop. Ottilie wondered if someone would hear her knock anyway, but when she did so and waited for a few moments, only to get no answer, she decided to try and find a way around to the back of the building. There was a side gate, hidden behind dense shrubs, and she called as she pushed it open.

'Anyone home?'

Magnus's voice came from somewhere she couldn't immediately see. 'Ottilie? Hang on one minute...'

Then Magnus himself appeared and led her down the narrow opening between the shop and the neighbouring building into a small but pretty garden formed into a sort of makeshift quadrangle by two timber annexes, the back of the shop and a fence. The garden was kitted out with wooden furniture, a swing seat, a water feature, a fire pit and what looked like a swanky pizza oven. Clearly Magnus and Geoff enjoyed their outdoor space. Ottilie turned her attention to the other buildings. One had wide windows that revealed a fitted kitchen.

'Is that where you live?' Ottilie asked. 'I thought you might live above the shop.'

'Oh, no, we came into a bit of money so we built ourselves somewhere more private.'

'It's gorgeous!'

'Thank you!' Magnus said, clearly delighted with the compliment. 'That's the cinema, next to it.'

The building that stood alongside was in the same wood panelling but didn't have any windows. It didn't look very big, but perhaps the outside was deceiving. Ottilie had to wonder how much money they'd come into, because she didn't imagine running a village shop would pay enough for all this, but she'd been brought up better than to ask. Perhaps the facts would come to light as she got to know them, but for now she had to admit to being wild with curiosity. Even with the very good pension Josh had left her, her wages and the money she'd made from selling the house in Manchester, she could never have dreamed of being able to afford anything like this. She had to wonder how they'd managed to get planning permission too. Perhaps one of them had connections, because this seemed like a lot for any local authority to approve.

'Let me take some of that from you.' Magnus held out his hands. 'What have you been up to? You didn't need to bring food; we've got plenty!'

'Yes, but I couldn't very well turn up empty-handed, could I? You'd think I was a freeloader and never invite me again.'

Magnus chuckled as he took the tray from her. 'As if! Of course, I say we have plenty of food, but nobody's ever complained about having more.'

'It's only some dips and crackers and things. Nibbly bits.'

'Nibbly bits are the best.'

'Josh always used to say that. He loved a good wedding buffet.' Ottilie tried not to let her sudden sadness show.

'You're a bit early,' Magnus said, clearly uncertain whether he was meant to address her comment about Josh or whether he would only make her sadder if he did. 'We'll have a drink in the house while we wait for everyone else if you like. Geoff's just making a jug of sangria.'

'Sangria?' Ottilie smiled. 'God, it's years since I had any of that.'

'It's such a kitsch drink, but we can't get enough of it. What can you do when the taste is missing, eh?'

'Oh, there's nothing wrong with a nice cold glass of sangria,' Ottilie said as she followed him into the wooden building they called home.

Inside, she gazed at the ultra-modern interiors. If she'd have hazarded a guess at Magnus and Geoff's taste, it would have been some miles from this, and it seemed strange to find something so cutting edge in such a sleepy village. The kitchen was all gloss and chrome, with high ceilings and glass fittings, while the glimpse she got of the living room through an open door was white and grey. It was more like a slick Manchester loft conversion than a Lakeland home – totally at odds with the cramped and homey shop they ran from the front cottage. In fact, it was very like the sort of interior that Josh would often lust over whenever they went shopping to kit out their home. He'd say, 'Next year, when I've saved a bit more,' but next year never came. They'd spend their money on holidays or meals out or theatre trips and the savings would never grow. Ottilie never minded – she'd rather spend it on time together anyway.

A man who had to be Geoff looked up from stirring a jug. He broke into a delighted smile. 'You must be Ottilie!'

She nodded, and he leaped forward to grab her by both shoulders and kiss her lightly on each cheek.

'How lovely to finally meet you!'

Ottilie smiled back, and she could see immediately why Magnus had fallen for him. While he wasn't exactly handsome, there was such a softness, such a gentle kindness to him that it made him look handsome. His hair was white now but still thick, swept up into a quiff, grey eyes full of fun, a face that looked as if it was smiling even when he wasn't. He was broader than Magnus, but it looked good on him. Ottilie would have put him in his mid to late fifties perhaps, older than Magnus – although she didn't know for sure how old Magnus was. And she was notoriously bad at guessing ages – something Josh had often teased her about.

'It's so good to finally meet you too,' she said. 'Every time I've been in the shop I've missed you.'

'Oh, love, there's never a down moment with that shop. Not that I'm complaining – business is business and we can't afford to sniff at it, can we? Come... sit down. What would you like to drink?'

'Well, I was promised sangria.'

'Sangria coming right up!'

'Oh!' Magnus hurried towards the entrance. 'Stacey!' he called as he went.

Ottilie looked to see her at the window, waving to be let in. Chloe wasn't with her, and Ottilie was almost glad about that. Chloe had seemed like quite a negative girl when they'd met briefly in the waiting room of the surgery, and although Ottilie understood she was having a rough time with a pregnancy she hadn't wanted, it wasn't what Ottilie needed right now. Stacey, if Ottilie recalled her information correctly, was Geoff's sister, and looking at her after meeting him, she could see the resemblance. Stacey seemed more upbeat, like her brother.

'Hello!' she said, beaming at everyone in the room as

Magnus showed her in. She held a bottle out to Geoff. 'Brought wine.'

'Oh, you needn't have – we've got loads.'

'I know, but I can't turn up empty-handed.'

'That's what Ottilie said.' Geoff smiled. 'Thank you; we'll have it later.'

'This is all very civilised,' Ottilie said. 'It might be the first time I've sat in a cinema with wine and dips. It's usually watered-down Fanta and some crusty popcorn.'

'There's no point in having your own cinema if you can't make it as swanky as you like,' Geoff said.

'Magnus says you built it.' Ottilie accepted the glass she'd been offered. 'That's pretty amazing.'

'Well, when I say *built* it,' Magnus put in, 'I mean he gave the specs to a builder, who put it all together.'

'Perhaps dreamed it is a better way of putting it,' Geoff said. 'And if you can dream it, you can always find someone to build it, if you know where to look.'

Geoff handed Stacey a glass of sangria.

'So' – she turned to Ottilie after a nod of acknowledgement to her brother – 'how are you settling in?'

'Good, I think. There are things I'm still not used to – silence outside at night for a start. Where I lived before there was traffic noise pretty much twenty-four-seven. The most I get here is the odd sheep bleating.'

'It's quiet, that's for sure,' Stacey agreed. 'Too quiet, if you ask my Chloe.'

'You can't blame her. I suppose at her age she wants night-clubs and bars and excitement.'

'Oh, I think she's had enough excitement for one year,' Stacey said, shooting her brother a wry look. 'I think all the excitement is what got her in her current predicament.'

'How is she coping with that?' Ottilie asked. 'She didn't seem too happy last time I saw you.'

'She was having a bad day. She's up and down – some days she can cope, some days she can't. I think some days she pretends it's not happening, and others she's terrified.'

'But she wants to keep the baby?'

'That changes, depending what day you catch her. But I've said all along that if she can't cope, I'll take over. There's no way I'm letting that baby be taken from our family, and I think if it happened, Chloe would live to regret it.'

'Totally,' Geoff agreed. 'We'll all rally around her if we need to. I'm looking forward to babysitting quite honestly.' He looked at Magnus and smiled. 'I think we both are, aren't we?'

'I can't wait!' Magnus took the cling film from a bowl of tzatziki Ottilie had made. 'It'll be brilliant.'

'I'm sure Chloe won't be standing in your way,' Stacey said. 'I'm sure she'll let you babysit every night, if you want to. But I do think she needs to get used to the idea of motherhood, because there won't always be a queue of people to take the baby off her hands.'

'But it sounds like she's going to have a good support network,' Ottilie said. 'And if I can get the mother and baby group up and running again, that will be another outlet that I hope will help.'

'I'm not sure she'd go, if I'm honest,' Stacey said doubtfully. 'She's not really a mixer in that way. I think she'd find the idea of sitting with other mums a bit...'

'Uncool?' Magnus offered.

Stacey nodded. 'Something like that.'

'Well, it's not even organised yet, so it's something for her to think about. Perhaps she'll change her mind when the baby comes and she feels it might be good to talk to women who are going through similar things.'

There was a tap at the window, and they looked round to see Florence there. Magnus went to let her in and returned a few moments later. She nodded acknowledgement to everyone in the room.

'I can't say I'm very keen on your pick this time,' she told Geoff. 'But I suppose it's watch that or sit on my own in the house.'

'Have you seen it before?' Ottilie asked.

'No.'

'You might have a pleasant surprise if you give it a chance,' Magnus said. 'It's a brilliant film.'

'Lavender says it's a bit racy.'

Geoff laughed. 'Oh, there's nothing that you wouldn't mind the vicar seeing. Is Lavender coming?'

Florence shook her head.

'Oh.' Ottilie frowned. 'She told me she was going to try to make it.'

'Told me she'd seen it before,' Florence insisted.

'We've seen most of them before, but it's never stopped us showing them again,' Magnus said.

Ottilie put her glass down. 'Shall I text her to see what she's doing?'

'If you don't mind,' Geoff said. He turned to Magnus. 'Who else are we waiting for?'

'Rani and Harji said they'd most likely come. Victor's girls said they'd come too.'

Ottilie waited for him to give more names, but it seemed that was it. She'd been expecting more of a turnout but wasn't sure if this was a good showing or not. Nobody seemed to think it wasn't, so perhaps the numbers were always more or less what they were this evening. Either way, she was looking forward to seeing Geoff's little cinema for herself, and it was a film she'd seen before and was happy to see again, and she liked who was here so far, so all in all, it promised to be a lovely event.

Ottilie tapped out a message to Lavender.

'What time do you usually wind things up?' she asked, looking up from her phone.

'Why? Have you had enough already?' Magnus asked.

Ottilie laughed 'No. I just wondered if the proper party started after the film.'

'I wish,' Geoff said. 'But at my age, after the film there's more likely to be cocoa and then bed.'

'You're not that old.'

Geoff looked suitably flattered but shook his head. 'Sixty this year – November actually.'

'Oh, a big one? Doing anything nice?'

Geoff looked at Magnus. 'Are we? I don't think we've decided yet, have we?'

Magnus tapped the side of his nose. 'Don't worry, I have some ideas.'

Ottilie sipped at her sangria and was about to ask what those ideas might be when the sound of a text coming through on her phone stopped her.

'Lavender says she's coming,' Ottilie said, reading the message. 'Only she might be late. Can we leave the side gate open for her and not to bother waiting, just start the film.'

'The gate's always open – she knows that,' Magnus said. He looked around the room. 'We'll give it five more minutes for everyone else and then we'll start.'

Magnus was still humming 'All That Jazz' as he prised a cork out of yet another bottle of wine.

'I'd forgotten how much I love *Chicago*,' he said, and Geoff nodded agreement.

'We ought to do a few more musicals.'

'*Greatest Showman*?'

'Yes!' Geoff yelped, and Florence rolled her eyes.

'I don't think I'm going to like that.'

'Have you ever seen it?' Geoff demanded.

'No, but—'

'Florence,' he said sternly. 'Don't be a Debbie Downer. If you gave some of this stuff a chance you might find you do like it. You enjoyed *Chicago*, didn't you?'

'Not really,' Florence said, and Ottilie, who'd been given a glass of red by Magnus, couldn't help but grin. Every time she'd looked Flo's way, the old lady had been tapping her toes or fingers like mad.

Perhaps because Geoff was right and she didn't want to admit it, Florence turned to Ottilie. 'A little bird tells me you've been up and down the village like some sort of Florence Nightingale. Telling everyone to go and see Dr Cheadle for this or that. Can't you get enough drama at work?'

Ottilie blinked. She wasn't quite sure what to make of Flo's statement. Was it praise or criticism? And what Ottilie had done off duty was hardly up and down like Florence Nightingale. More like she'd lent a helping hand to a couple of new neighbours.

'What's this?' Magnus asked.

'Victor told me that if Ottilie hadn't sent Corrine straight to Dr Cheadle there might have been trouble,' Stacey put in.

'I only asked her to make an appointment as a precaution,' Ottilie said. 'It was nothing.'

'Not what Victor says. He says Dr Cheadle has organised an urgent appointment at the hospital with an oncologist so she must think you've seen something bad too. And if it turns out to be cancer and they catch it early, like Dr Cheadle says to him, then you'd have saved Corrine's life.'

'It really isn't like that at all,' Ottilie said. 'I was only doing my job.'

'Ah, but you weren't doing your job,' Florence said. 'Nobody asked you to go and look at Corrine, did they?'

'Actually, Victor did. It just so happened I hadn't officially started work yet, but I didn't see what difference that made.'

'Exactly!' Florence said triumphantly.

Ottilie was still confused over whether Flo was in favour of off-duty nursing or not, but she simply shrugged.

'I've got to have a scan at the hospital,' Florence continued. 'But it's pointless sending me letters for scans because I can't get there. Might as well give the appointment to someone who can go. And it will probably be a waste of time, even if I do go. I shall phone them and tell them so. I can't be doing with all that fuss.'

'I think you ought to go,' Ottilie said.

'So you do think I'm ill!'

'No, but I think we ought to rule anything sinister out.'

Ottilie glanced at the assembled neighbours and new friends and wondered if she ought to be having this discussion with them there. There were rules about this sort of thing and she didn't want to fall foul of them. What little she'd confirmed about Corrine was probably too much.

'Flo,' she said, lowering her voice, 'you really must go for those scans. If you're stuck for transport, then I'll take you, like I said I would.'

'I don't think so,' she said flatly.

'Could you do it for me if not for any other reason?'

'What do you want to go for?'

'Well,' Ottilie began, reaching for a decent excuse, 'I don't know the area very well, and I expect I'll end up going to the hospital for my job every now and then, so you can show me where it is. You've been before, right?'

'Yes,' Florence said slowly. 'I do. I'll have to sleep on it.'

'You do that,' Ottilie said and was convinced that Florence wouldn't be able to resist the offer in the end.

CHAPTER ELEVEN

Florence was warming to her, Ottilie could tell. During their drive to the hospital a few days after the film club meeting she'd opened up about her past, her family and she (almost) admitted that she felt somewhat abandoned by them. She laughed at a couple of Ottilie's jokes and didn't make nearly as much fuss about having to go to the hospital as Ottilie had imagined she would, even when they finally arrived at the outpatient department and were directed to a very long wait in the clinic.

The tests and scans went smoothly enough, and before they made their way back to Thimblebury they decided, on a whim, to drive into Kendal for a cup of tea and a scone and so that Flo could get some 'proper' mint cake, not that 'tourist rubbish' from a shop she hadn't been to in years. If Ottilie hadn't known better, she'd almost say Flo was enjoying their afternoon out, despite being adamant that she didn't want to go.

Before the light started to fade they took a drive along the shores of Windermere. Ottilie was driving and so couldn't look properly but still marvelled as she stole the odd glimpse.

'My God!' she exclaimed. 'It's huge!'

It glowed aquamarine in the afternoon sun, tranquil and

vibrant and totally unexpected. It could have been one of the glamorous Italian lakes, apart from the darker, lusher greens of the hills that surrounded it and the quintessentially English houses that peppered the view, and the patchwork of hedgerows that criss-crossed the hills.

'There's boats and everything on it,' Florence said. 'Big boats, you know. You should take a trip.'

'Do you want to take a trip? We could go now?'

'I've done it all before,' she said in a practical tone, folding her hands into her lap. 'I can wait for you if you want to.'

Ottilie paused for a moment and then shook her head. 'It's getting late, and it's not like the lake's going anywhere. I'll come another day.'

As they drove on, following the contours of the lake and then eventually leaving it behind, Flo suddenly stiffened in her seat, more animated than Ottilie had ever seen her.

'Stop the car!'

Ottilie twisted to look sharply at her. 'What's wrong?'

'There's a place I want to see.'

'What place?'

'I haven't been there in years. I'd love to see it again, and I'm sure it's around here.'

Ottilie found a place to pull in off the road and killed the engine. Whatever this place was, to get Flo this excited it had to be good, and she was curious herself.

Flo clambered out of the car and began to march up a steep path that wound its way up a hill, beneath the shadow of which they were parked. Ottilie jogged after her, quite surprised at the gradient – which was tougher than it looked – and at how Flo seemed to be managing it better than she was, despite the huge age difference. Perhaps she was going at it with a bit too much enthusiasm, however, because after a few minutes she had to stop and get her breath, and Ottilie was only too glad to join her. She started again, and stopped again half a dozen more times as the landscape fell away, trees and shrubs and the car getting smaller and smaller, the vista of the lake sparkling in the evening sun.

'Are you sure this is a good idea?' Ottilie asked.

'I'm not dead yet, no matter what the hospital says.'

That wasn't what Florence had told Heath, but Ottilie decided not to mention that. It seemed Flo said whatever suited her at any given moment in time, depending on what she wanted to get out of it.

'How much further?' Ottilie panted, the muscles in her legs screaming for mercy. She didn't consider herself unfit, but this hill seemed to have other ideas.

'Not much. It'll be worth the climb, I promise.'

'It had better be!' Ottilie said drily, and Flo gave a breathless laugh. 'How are you managing this? I'm shattered! Are you secretly a mountain goat?'

'I've lived here all my life; I'm used to hills.'

Ottilie stopped short of reminding her that she was also a lot older these days, because it didn't seem helpful and would probably offend her anyway. She supposed a life of walking the hills and valleys of this beautiful part of the world must do something to keep one sprightlier in their senior years and left it at that.

The breeze was stiffer up here, the hillside more exposed, dotted with hardy shrubs and lichen-stained rocks standing proud of wild grass. The ground was scarred with a past of ice and sun and centuries of farming and soil erosion, and the further up they got, the more precarious their footing was.

Ottilie searched her pocket for a hairband to keep her hair from her face, and marvelled at how Flo didn't seem to miss a step, where she herself scrabbled to stay on her feet as the looser scree gave way.

Eventually the path levelled out to reveal a sort of grassy plateau that had been hidden from view until they were on top of it. And snuggled in a crevice in the hillside was a roaring waterfall bubbling into a sort of rocky cauldron, perhaps eight to ten feet in diameter.

'Wow!' Ottilie stared at it, the rush of the waterfall in her ears, the blues and lilacs of a late-afternoon sky behind her, the sun low in the sky and the water a frothing white, bouncing from the rocks that formed the natural pool below. 'This is amazing!'

'I told you so.' Flo looked at it with pride and with some wistfulness. Ottilie didn't know the ever practical and acerbic Florence could be wistful, but there was no mistaking the look. This place was gorgeous, incredible, and yet, for all that, it had taken a real effort to get up here to see. Ottilie had to wonder if it held more significance for Flo than just a pretty feature she'd wanted to share with her new friend. 'I used to swim in there.'

Ottilie glanced at her and then back at the pool. 'It looks cold.'

'Freezing, yes, it can be. But on a hot day the best thing ever. Me and my friends back in the day, we used to come up here all the time. This was our local swimming pool. We'd bring sandwiches, bottles of cider we'd stolen from our dads, one of us would bring a radio we'd play until the batteries died. You could be entertained for hours up here, and only people who lived hereabouts knew it, so there were no tourists getting in the way of everything.'

'And people still don't know about it? Tourists, I mean.'

'There's only you and me, isn't there?'

'That really surprises me. What with Instagram and whatever, you'd think someone would have posted about it and brought everyone flocking. I'm sure there must be loads of people who'd want to come here if they knew about it.'

'God forbid!' Flo blurted, the old brusqueness back. 'Imagine! People are so stupid, always looking for the next thing –

some would go to a burning tyre dump if someone told them it was good!'

Ottilie had to laugh. 'Not quite. But I sort of see what you mean, and that's why I'm even more surprised this place is still such a secret.'

'Let's hope it stays that way. It's ours.'

'Ours? I like that it's not overrun, but isn't the countryside supposed to be for everyone?'

'If you want everyone to come then it will be ruined. If people knew this was here there'd be pop bottles and crisp packets everywhere. When people learn respect, then they can come, but I'm sure I'll be cold in the ground by the time that happens.'

'Someone other than you and your old friends must know it's here.'

'Only locals, and we all like to keep it that way.'

Ottilie had to smile again at the notion that Flo must consider her enough of a local now to bring her here. 'So you came here a lot?'

'In the summer we practically lived up here. And this is where I met Eric.'

'Eric was your husband?'

Flo nodded slowly. 'He was up here one day with his mates and I was with mine. I fancied him like mad the minute I laid eyes on him. He asked me to meet him afterwards and that was that. We used to come up here all the time when we were courting.'

'That sounds kind of heavenly.'

'It was.'

Florence was silent for a moment as she gazed into the pool, as if it were a portal to a perfect past of long summers and young love, a past that was simpler and happier than her present could ever be.

'You know,' she began after a few moments, 'I could go for a dip right now.'

'In there?' Ottilie stared at Flo, who nodded shortly. 'No. As your nurse I have to say I'm strictly against you getting into that freezing-cold water.'

'You're not on duty at the moment, are you, Nurse? So are you anyone's nurse at all today?'

'Florence,' Ottilie replied, making her tone as stern as she could manage, 'it's far too cold. You'll have a heart attack!'

'Don't be daft. The sun's out, it's summer and no colder than it ever was when I used to come up here. I know what I'm doing; I've been in a million times before.'

'When you were—'

'Young?' Flo raised her eyebrows. 'Yes, I do realise I'm no spring chicken. All the more reason to take a dip, as far as I can tell. I'm not getting any younger, and for all we know I could be gone tomorrow. Might as well live for today.'

'You can't be serious?'

'Perfectly.'

'But...' Ottilie cast around for something to put her off. 'You don't have anything to swim in!'

'Don't need anything.'

'Of course you do!'

Florence rested impatient hands on her hips and regarded Ottilie as if she felt sorry for her. 'You mean to tell me you've never skinny-dipped?'

'Never!' Ottilie said, uncertain that she liked the way Flo was looking at her – as if she thought her a bit of a wet weekend. 'Certainly not on a hillside in England!'

'All the more reason to do it. What's life if we don't live it to the full?'

Along with the pity for Ottilie, Florence had a strange sort of spark in her eyes, and for a startling instant Ottilie saw the woman she'd once been: fearless, daring, greedy for life, a woman miles ahead of the conservative times she'd been born into. For all her disapproval, had she been a young woman she'd have been a social-media influencer, off having adventures around the world and broadcasting them to an army of admirers who had their own adventures vicariously through her, who would be just like her if only they dared. She'd have been skydiving and swimming with sharks and cutting her way through rainforests and anything else that came her way. Ottilie also saw that she really wasn't joking, and her fears were confirmed when Flo perched on a rock and began to take off her shoes.

'Paddle!' Ottilie said helplessly, knowing already that she'd lost the battle. 'Dangle your feet in and that's it.'

'Too deep to paddle. It's all or nothing.'

'Flo, please... we've just been to the hospital and we've no idea what those scans might uncover—'

'If my heart's going to give out then I can't think of a better way to go. If you're so worried, come in with me. That way you can save me if I have a funny turn. You swim, don't you?'

'Yes, but—'

By now, Flo was unbuttoning her blouse. Ottilie desperately scanned the hillside. It was deserted, but surely Florence wasn't going to take everything off?

'You'll have to go home in sopping underwear,' she said, grasping for something else that might put Flo off.

'Which is why I'm going to take it off,' Flo replied with such obvious practicality that Ottilie felt quite stupid for even suggesting she might keep her undies on.

'Are you mad?'

'Possibly,' Flo said with a half-smile. 'I am old after all. You get a bit mad as you get older, don't you?'

'I thought you were supposed to get more sensible.'

'Sensible!' Flo snorted. She had the slightly manic look again that Ottilie found unnerving. Whenever Ottilie felt she was beginning to work her out, Flo would do or say something that took her back to square one. The more she knew Flo, the less she felt she knew her. But she couldn't deny that there was something about her she rather liked, something that drew her in. She'd never met anyone like Flo before, and she only wished she'd known her in her youth, because she would have been dazzling. But her next sentence knocked the wind from her sails.

'I'll leave sensible to you, Nurse Ottilie.'

The comment cut her to the quick. Worry, intrigue, admiration – all the things she'd felt for Flo a second before was replaced by offence.

'What's that supposed to mean?'

'What I said. You're far too sensible.'

'Why does it feel as if sensible is code for boring?'

'I didn't say boring – you did.'

'You think I'm boring?'

'I think you're cautious.'

'I have reasons for being cautious... And there's nothing wrong with cautious.'

'No one ever had fun being cautious, did they?' Flo said with a grin as she shrugged off her blouse. 'So are you coming in or not?'

Ottilie stared at her, torn. Was she really boring? Was that how Flo saw her? Was that how everyone saw her?

'You say you came to the Lakes for a change,' Flo said, 'so change. You want to be a local, then be a local. This is what we do.'

Ottilie narrowed her eyes. Was this mind games? Was this reverse psychology to get Ottilie to join in?

'I'm pretty sure that's not true,' she said, folding her arms. 'I've never heard Magnus say he's off up the mountain to skinny-dip.'

'Ah, but Magnus isn't a true local.'

'Yes he is. At least, he's more local than me. This won't work. I'm not getting in, and I don't think you should either.'

'Two minutes – come on, I dare you. Two minutes is nothing. I'm old; if I can do it, so can you.'

'Florence, I hate to break it to you, but you *are* old, and that's what worries me.'

'That's it, insult me. Ageist.'

'There's nowhere to get in safely. And even if you do somehow get in, there's nowhere I can see to get out again.'

'How do you think we got in all those years ago? We jumped in.'

'Absolutely not!' Ottilie yelped. 'Your bloody heart will stop!'

To her annoyance, Flo only laughed. 'Joking – your face! The stones over there make a step below the water.' She pointed, and Ottilie could make out a rock beneath the surface a few feet away. 'I'm going to get in there. If you're scared you could just sit on there and dip your legs in.'

'I thought you said it had to be all or nothing.'

'If you're Lakeland born and bred, it is. We're a bit hardier around here.'

Ottilie's arms folded tighter. 'When was the last time you swam here?'

Flo pulled down her skirt and shrugged vaguely. 'I don't know... a few years. Heath brought me up.'

'Heath?' Ottilie's forehead creased into a deep frown. 'Heath brought you up here and let you swim? How long ago was this?'

'I told you, I don't recall. Before he married that witch but after his grandad died. We packed our costumes and towels one morning and came up here.'

'Whose idea was that?'

'I don't remember.'

Ottilie suspected that Flo had nagged Heath to bring her

here, as she was nagging Ottilie to let her swim. But she couldn't rule out the notion that Heath may have suggested it, and if that were the case, it made him pretty stupid as far as she could see. As if she needed any more reason to think that this guy was bad news. For what it was worth – probably very little – she decided to say so.

'Well, that was irresponsible of him.'

Flo didn't reply. Instead, she lowered herself into the water. Ottilie was relieved to see that at least she hadn't followed through on her threat to go naked and had kept her underwear on.

As Flo struck out across the pool, she smiled, a picture of absolute joy. Her breathing was raspy already, and Ottilie could tell that the water was very cold, but Flo didn't seem to be hampered all that much. She looked so happy, so confident, the ghost of the teenager she'd once been breaking through, that as Ottilie watched her, she couldn't help but replay her words. Did she really think Ottilie boring? Staid and sensible and far too predictable? Ottilie reflected on her own life experiences and had to admit that she'd never done anything remotely as daring as this. She'd never swum in a river or a lake, she'd never hiked a mountain, she'd never ridden a horse or a motorbike or paraglided on a foreign holiday or been down in a cave or... Now that she thought about it, she wondered if she'd spent her entire life in cotton-wrapped safety. Until Josh's death, of course, but that had been a whole other sort of danger and not one she'd asked for.

Ottilie watched, and she saw how Flo was loving her life at this minute, and part of her desperately wanted to join her, but something held her back even as she recognised in her own soul a lack of an adventurous spirit. She looked at the water, depths unknown, captured by the rocks, more tumbling down from the waterfall above, and it didn't look inviting to her; it looked cold and unforgiving. Stunning as the spot was – and there was no denying it – and as much as Ottilie wanted to prove to Flo and herself that she could be spontaneous and daring, she couldn't bring herself to get in.

Aware, suddenly, that Flo seemed to be slowing up, and that she also seemed to be shivering slightly, Ottilie pointed to her watch.

'I really think we ought to get back to the car before it gets too dark to see our way down the hillside.'

For once, perhaps because she was starting to feel what Ottilie could see, Flo didn't argue. She swam with more obvious effort towards the stone step and tried to haul herself out. Ottilie saw immediately that she wasn't going to be able to.

'Perhaps it's a good thing you didn't get in,' Flo said a bit sheepishly. 'I'm afraid I might need a bit of a hand here.'

Ottilie bent and pulled. She was worried she might catch Flo's legs on a sharp rock, but there were bigger worries than that, so she put it out of her mind.

With a grunt and a shower of cold water, Flo emerged and fell into her arms. She'd been heavier than Ottilie had imagined, and she was only glad her strength hadn't failed her, because they might have been really stuck. Her own clothes were wet too, but there was no time to think about that, because she could see that Flo had been in the water too long. Ottilie cursed herself for not being sterner as Flo shivered, her face paler and her lips almost blue.

'You need to get your clothes back on and quick.'

'I'm going to get my undies off first.'

'No time. You need layers on now.'

Flo's coordination seemed to have gone out of the window with her body heat, so Ottilie dried her as best she could with her own jacket and then helped her into her skirt and cardigan before putting on her socks and shoes for her. She was still damp, despite Ottilie's efforts, and her clothes probably weren't keeping her as warm as they needed to.

'I'm a silly old woman, aren't I?' she asked, as meek now as she'd been defiant half an hour earlier.

Despite the fact that it was hardly dry, Ottilie wrapped her jacket around Flo's shoulders and gave her a patient smile. 'Of course not. Perhaps you overestimated what you're still capable of though.'

'I just wanted to try it one more time. I wanted to feel young again. You understand, don't you?'

'I do.'

'I just wanted to do what I might never get to do again, I thought it might be the last time I'd ever be up here.'

'I know – I get it. I don't want to say I told you so, but it was a bloody daft idea, even if I understand why you wanted to do it.'

Florence gave a weak laugh. 'Aren't all the most fun things only fun because they're daft ideas?'

'I'm not sure I'd call hypothermia fun.'

'I haven't got hypothermia – it's summer.'

'You can still get too cold if you dunk yourself in an ice-cold mountain pool, summer or not. Come on... somehow we've got to get back to the car.'

They'd taken no more than half a dozen steps when Ottilie realised Flo was in no state to negotiate a steep, rocky, downhill path. It had been hard enough going up, but down was always more treacherous, and that was without the added complication of Flo being frailer. Above them, the blue of the sky was fading as the sun hovered at the horizon. They had maybe an hour at most until it was too dark to see. Flo was shivering, a bit confused, and Ottilie, staring down at their path, was gripped by a mounting panic. They were going to be stuck up here if they didn't get moving, and yet, she could see that Florence was going to need a lot more assistance than what she could give.

She was wondering who was best to call for help when Flo's own phone started to ring from inside her handbag.

Florence waved a vague hand. 'Not now, whoever you are.'

Ottilie could see that she didn't really want to ignore the call, and that she was probably too weak and disoriented to get it.

'Let me,' she said, sitting Flo on a boulder and shoving a hand into her bag.

Flo's phone was an old analogue brick with buttons. It took Ottilie a second to figure out how to answer it.

'Hello, Gran. I'm at your place but... where are you?'

Ottilie immediately recognised the voice of Flo's grandson. 'Heath? Is that you?'

'Who's this?'

'It's Ottilie... the nurse. Don't worry – your gran's with me. You're in Thimblebury?'

'Yes. Where are you?'

'Um...' Ottilie scanned the landscape. 'I don't actually know, but we're kind of stuck.'

'Stuck how?'

'We're up a hill somewhere. Your gran wanted to show me a —' Ottilie suddenly recalled that Heath had brought Flo swimming up here before. 'The pool! You know it, right? The rock swimming pool with the waterfall?'

'I know it,' he said tersely. 'What the hell are you doing up there?'

'It's a long story and I don't have time at the moment. Your gran's not well and I can't get her down. I'm sorry, but could you—'

'I'm on my way.'

The line went dead. Ottilie glanced at Flo, who, despite her current state, seemed annoyed by the turn of events.

'Sorry,' Ottilie said. 'I can guess what you're going to say, but we'd be up here all night without help.'

'Yes, but I'll never hear the end of it.'

'Of course you will. Heath will want you to be safe and he

won't have time to lecture you. He's your favourite grandson for a reason, isn't he?'

'He's my only grandson, and yes, he'll find time to lecture me. I'd rather him not have to come up here to get me.'

'We don't have a choice I'm afraid.' Ottilie gave an encouraging smile. 'But on the bright side, he was at your house. That would have been a nice surprise if you'd been home, wouldn't it?'

'If I'd been home it would have been, but I wasn't at home, was I? I was at a stupid hospital appointment.'

'Erm, I think being up this hill is the issue, not your tests,' Ottilie said, and she couldn't help a small laugh. She perched on the boulder next to Flo and wrapped an arm around her, rubbing her shoulders in a bid to warm her up.

'I hope he's not long,' Flo said, and Ottilie knew from that small statement that Flo wasn't feeling quite as bullish as she'd have her believe. She was unwell, perhaps a little scared and, if she was being honest, Ottilie was a bit scared too. Scared that something bad would happen up here and she wouldn't be able to stop it. Not scared for herself – and that made a change considering her life right now – but scared for Flo.

'He said he was coming straight here.'

'I feel so stupid,' Flo said after a pause.

'You're not stupid.'

'That's not what you really think. Heath will think the same as you.'

'It's not, and I'm sure it's not what he'll think either. And even if we did think that, would you care? Take comfort in the fact that you're living your life. You said it yourself – I'm boring.'

'I never said that; I said cautious.'

Ottilie gave a tight smile. At least Flo was still lucid enough to recall their exact conversation from earlier – that was a good sign.

'Try as I might,' she began slowly after another pause, 'I feel as if my life stopped when Josh died. Whenever I try to get back in the game, something...' She gave a helpless shrug. 'Something stops me.'

'What?'

Ottilie's thoughts went to the clouds that obscured the clear skies of any future she might try to build for herself. Without Josh, yes, but she could have done it if perhaps the manner of his death had been different, if the repercussions of that weren't still hanging over her. If she didn't see fear and uncertainty at every turn. If only there was a resolution for that, at least she might not feel so stuck. And she was trying, so, so hard. She was here in Thimblebury, she'd thrown everything she had into making her new life here work, and yet, it was never quite right.

'I wish I knew,' she said with a sigh. The real reasons she knew only too well, but they weren't for Flo to hear, not here and not now – if ever. 'It's like a locked door. I can see the rest of my life on the other side, but the key's gone missing and I can't get through. So I'm stuck here, watching it drift away from me, further and further the longer I stall.'

'You feel all that because you didn't get in the pool?' Flo asked with some incredulity in her voice, and perhaps a little wryness.

Ottilie shot her a sideways glance. She was definitely starting to feel better.

'I didn't get in the pool because of all that. It's like I feel guilty for having a life at all, even though I know being miserable or denying myself the right to move on won't bring Josh back. I just don't know how to stop feeling this way.'

'You don't seem miserable to me.'

'It's inside, hidden deep. You must know how that is?' Ottilie glanced again at Flo, who nodded shortly. 'Nobody can see it – I make certain of that – but I know it's there. You must have been the same when you lost Eric. I don't want to forget Josh or pretend I never had him, but...'

'You don't need to explain. I understand. I'm glad we had this chance to talk, even if it did mean getting stuck up here,' Flo said. 'You can always talk to me. I know what it's like to lose a husband after all.'

It wasn't the same, though it very much was, but Ottilie only forced another smile and rubbed Flo's arm a bit harder.

'I ought to phone Heath and ask him to bring blankets. I never gave it a thought.'

'He'll be on his way.'

'Probably too late, yes.'

'I might try to walk a bit. We might even get down to the bottom before he starts to climb.'

'I don't think that's a good idea. The light's fading and you're still not well. We'd end up falling and in a worse state than we are now. Best to wait.'

'See... cautious,' Flo said, and Ottilie's smile grew.

'Boring.'

'I suppose sometimes cautious is good. I suppose it's very good in your line of work.'

'I suppose it must be. Never really thought about it.'

'Thank you for looking after me.'

'I couldn't very well leave you to freeze.'

'No, I mean all the other times. You didn't have to take me to the hospital. You didn't have to go into Kendal with me and have tea. You didn't have to stop the car for me to come up here. You've been lovely to me since you arrived, and I know I can be a daft, stubborn old sod at times.'

'Maybe I like daft and stubborn.'

'You must do.'

'Maybe I like spending time with you.'

'I don't know why. Nobody else seems to.'

Ottilie raised her eyebrows. 'Is that really true? Because it seems to me that most everyone in Thimblebury loves you.'

Flo laughed. 'Where did you get that idea? Now I know you're just trying to make me feel better! Everyone in Thimblebury thinks I'm a pain in the arse and even you must know that!'

'Never,' Ottilie said.

The conversation died, and the two women gazed out onto the valley below them, the hills beyond, the lake shining in the last of the sunlight, each lost in their own thoughts. At least, Ottilie knew she was and she supposed, from Flo's silence, that she must be too. A quick glance reassured her that nothing more sinister had halted her chatter, and then her thoughts turned back to the swirling mist of problems that always seemed to plague her waking thoughts.

Uppermost, apart from her immediate difficulty, was the arrest of a suspect for Josh's attack. Faith had kept her informed, and knowing that the perpetrator was most likely in custody ought to have eased Ottilie's mind. But it didn't, for so many reasons, but mostly because they couldn't be sure that this was the right person, or that they'd been in it alone, and for those reasons she was still anxious in the dark, still nervous when she was alone. She'd told herself a million times that there was no need to feel that way because they didn't know who she was, and they certainly didn't have any reason to come after her, and yet she did. Perhaps, now that Josh was gone, she'd never feel safe again. He had always been her net, her comfort, her security, and now he was gone, leaving her alone, trying her best to navigate the world, and, as yet, she still didn't seem to have figured out the direction of the wind let alone set any kind of course.

But perhaps she was being hard on herself. Perhaps coming to Thimblebury – though it had been a knee-jerk reaction of sorts – was already a course. Perhaps she'd set it without realising.

The sounds of falling scree shook her from her musings. A moment later, Heath was standing in front of them, his chestnut hair damp at the fringe from the exertion of the climb, dark eyes looking from one to the other with an expression somewhere at the centre of annoyance, humour, exasperation and distrust. Ottilie wasn't sure which of those were being directed at her, and she wasn't about to waste time asking. She supposed the situation wasn't showing her in a very good light, but perhaps there'd be time later to inform him of the facts, and then he might not judge her so harshly. However he felt about her, all she required of him was that he helped her to get Flo down to safety. The rest could wait.

'I'm not even going to ask,' he said coolly.

'I'm sorry,' Flo said as he went over to offer his arm. 'I feel like such an old fool.'

'You're nothing of the sort,' Ottilie said, fuelled by a sudden need to defend her. From what, she wasn't sure, but she supposed it must be from her grandson's criticism.

Heath shook his head and clearly wanted to disagree. 'God knows how you managed to get up here.'

'We've been up here before,' Flo said. 'You and me, remember?'

'Yes, but that was years ago.'

'I'm not totally infirm yet.'

Heath looked as if he had a counterpoint to make there too but seemed to have at least the tact not to air it.

'We were fine,' Ottilie said. 'But then Flo got a bit cold, that's all. Anyone who got a bit cold would struggle, no matter how much younger.'

'And I suppose she got cold in there...' He hooked a thumb at the pool, water still rushing in their ears as it dropped from the hillside above to fill it over and over. 'So that was a brilliant idea, wasn't it?' He looked Ottilie up and down. 'I suppose you persuaded her it would be all right?'

'Of course I didn't! I didn't even go in!'

'But you thought it was all right to let my gran get in? I thought you were a nurse. Remind me never to get ill in Thimblebury.'

Flo might not have been at her best, but at this her hand shot out to slap his arm. His look of shock gave Ottilie a childish sort of satisfaction, but she was going to enjoy it nonetheless.

'Apologise!' Flo snapped.

'For what?' he asked with a note of offence. 'I didn't do anything wrong!'

'I'm not in a wheelchair yet, and it's not Ottilie's doing if I decide to take a dip. I do have some free will, you know, even at my age.'

'That's not what I meant—'

'It doesn't matter,' Ottilie cut in.

'It does!' Flo insisted. 'I have my own silly self to blame for this mess and I won't have you insulted. And, Heath, you're better than that.'

Heath didn't apologise and, despite her chastisement, Flo didn't push it. Perhaps she was still a bit too weak for that, but she'd made her point. Ottilie didn't see a reason to chase the topic any further either, so she turned her thoughts to their descent.

'Right,' she said briskly. 'Are we going to do this or what?'

CHAPTER TWELVE

What would have been a difficult, if not impossible, journey down the hillside was made a lot easier with Heath's help, even though Ottilie accepted it grudgingly. It was clear from his monosyllabic responses to pretty much everything that was said to him that he was annoyed. Why, Ottilie didn't know and didn't care to ask, though she could probably guess at many reasons. Because he'd been called out of his way, because he'd been asked to do something that was tricky, because he was a busy man who didn't have time for this sort of nonsense, because he really didn't like Ottilie. There might have been many more, but they weren't her concern. At least, she told herself they weren't her concern, but for reasons she couldn't quite put her finger on, she did find herself caring. But what did it matter to her whether Flo's selfish grandson liked her or not?

OK, perhaps not selfish but certainly self-absorbed as far as Ottilie could see. His life wasn't going so well and it seemed to mean that he didn't have time to consider that others might not be faring so well either. Flo wasn't getting any younger, and yet he was making his displeasure at the inconvenience of having to get her down this hill very evident, like she was a knot in a shoelace he was trying to tie when he had somewhere to be, or a puncture in a tyre on his way to work, or a phone glitch that meant he couldn't get online.

They drove back to Thimblebury – Heath in his car with Flo, and Ottilie in her own, following. She'd wanted to have Flo in with her so she could keep an eye on her condition, but Heath hadn't given her a choice – he'd ushered his gran into his own and sped off before she'd been able to voice her opinion. So she'd driven back reflecting on what an arse Flo's grandson was and marvelling that Flo had thought for even half a second that she and Heath might be a good match. Had she been looking for a man, Heath would be at the very bottom of any list of potentials... even if he was quite good-looking. And anyway, looks were superficial.

Even if Ottilie did think he was attractive – which she definitely did not – it didn't matter. Even if he might actually be angry with her only because he was worried for his gran, and even if that was a tiny bit attractive – and Ottilie definitely did not find it attractive in his case at all – she wasn't interested. And perhaps she might be able to see that he'd been damaged by his previous marriage – if it was anything like as tumultuous as people said – but that didn't give him the right to go around being rude, and it definitely did not make him attractive. He was absolutely, categorically not attractive. Only on the surface and only to others but definitely not to Ottilie. So that was final. No looking at Heath and thinking that the rudest, brusquest man she'd ever met was a tiny bit attractive. And anyway, she'd lost the most perfect man there had ever been, so how could she even look at anyone else?

Ottilie could have driven straight to Wordsworth Cottage and let Heath and Flo get on with things, but there was no way she could leave Flo without checking her over and giving some advice. And so she pulled up outside Flo's cottage just as they were going inside. It bristled that he hadn't thought to wait for her, closing the door behind him as she got out of the car. And so she marched up to the front door and hammered on it.

It was opened immediately.

'Oh,' Heath said. 'Sorry...' He didn't sound sorry at all. 'I thought you'd be heading home.'

'I wanted to check on Flo first.'

'She's fine. I'll make her a cuppa and she'll warm up.'

'Still, I'd rather see for myself. She might look all right, but she might not be.'

'We'll phone the doctor's if she's not.'

'I'm here – surely it's easier to let me look her over and save the bother.' She stared him down. 'What are you worried about? Why's it such an issue?'

'It's not.' He moved back from the door to let her in. 'Go on then – knock yourself out.'

Florence was sitting on the sofa. Ottilie pulled one of the throws from a nearby chair and wrapped it around her.

'I'm all right,' Flo grumbled, but secretly Ottilie wondered if she was quite enjoying the attention. Now she had her new friend and her grandson fussing over her, and as someone who'd told Ottilie she was lonely, that must have been nice.

'I'll get you a hot drink,' Ottilie said, but as she straightened up to go to the kitchen, Heath gestured for her to sit down.

'I said I was going to make her a cuppa and I will.'

'Do you want one, Ottilie?' Flo asked. 'Make Ottilie one too!' she called after Heath without waiting for Ottilie's reply. And then she glanced back with a faint smile. 'You never say no to tea, if memory serves me correctly.'

'Too right,' Ottilie said, although tea with a sulky Heath wasn't her idea of a friendly cuppa. 'Thank you. I'll stay for a quick one, then I'll leave you to your visitor.'

'Oh, Heath doesn't mind you being here. It's someone his

own age to talk to after all, instead of having to listen to his old gran go on about her ailments.'

Ottilie narrowed her eyes. 'I thought you said you don't have any ailments. And you're no dull old gran – far from it.'

'I think I'll have some biscuits,' Flo said. 'I don't suppose you could go to the kitchen and ask Heath to bring some in when he brings the tea?'

Ottilie wasn't fooled by Flo's sudden weak-old-lady act. Something was cooking here. At least it meant Flo was getting back to her old self. Perhaps she hadn't been as ill as Ottilie had supposed on the hillside. Perhaps she'd known Heath would be at her cottage, and perhaps she'd deliberately engineered the need for a rescue to bring him out to them.

Ottilie dismissed the idea. Surely nobody was that manipulative. And she didn't want to contemplate the reasons why Flo might do this, but if there was any grain of truth in it, well, Ottilie would have to subtly disabuse her of the possibility of any kind of success. She wouldn't be pushed towards anyone, and she was quite sure Heath would feel the same.

She got up and went to the kitchen. Heath was standing next to the window, staring out as the kettle boiled beside him. As she spoke, he whipped round, as if she'd startled him from thoughts that had taken him far away. His brown eyes were almost soft, and for a moment Ottilie was thrown by them. There was more kindness in there than she'd ever seen before. So he was capable of looking less than angry – well there was a revelation. But it was gone in an instant and his expression was cold and distrustful again.

'Your gran wants some biscuits,' she said. 'I can take them if you show me which cupboard they're in.'

'I'm surprised you don't already know.'

'How would I know?'

'Well, you seem to be making yourself very at home here.'

Ottilie stared at him. 'What's that supposed to mean?'

He seemed to size her up, and she felt herself shrink from it, even though she didn't want to. 'Why are you so interested in my gran?'

'I like her. I'm new here and she's been nice to me. I'm her nurse... I mean, why do I need a reason? Is there a problem with being interested in your gran?'

'Depends on why.'

'I don't think it's any of your business.'

'And yet you seem to be making her very much your business. Why were you out with her today? Don't have any mates your own age?'

'I was taking her to the hospital, if you must know. She needed to go for tests and she had nobody to take her.'

'I would have taken her. Nobody asked me.'

'Perhaps she didn't ask because you're always so busy with that terribly important job you have – whatever it is – she assumed you wouldn't have time.'

'I'm a management consultant and I would have had time.'

'That's not how Flo saw it.'

'And so you had to do it? There was nobody else?'

'Does it matter as long as someone does it?'

'I don't know.'

'Never mind,' Ottilie said, her patience on the edge. 'Forget the tea. I'll find the biscuits myself and then I'll get out of your hair.'

She opened and closed a few cupboards while he watched her, silent. She could feel his eyes on her the whole time, and it wasn't pleasant. Once she'd grabbed a pack of creams, she spun round, unable to contain herself any longer.

'Whatever it is you clearly think I'm up to, you're wrong. I don't know what it was that happened between you and your ex, but perhaps you'd like to bear in mind that not every woman is her.'

His mouth fell open, and at least he had the decency to look slightly ashamed at her words. 'What did you say?'

'You heard me. Believe what you want, but I have your gran's best interests at heart, nothing more and nothing less. I took her to have her tests today for that reason. I followed her up that hill because it seemed important to her that she go, and I asked for your help to get her down because I wanted her to be safe and well and at home again. It's clear to me that you don't like me, and let me be clear that I don't really like you, but if we can get along for her sake then I'd say that's a win – wouldn't you? So why don't we try? Because she seems very keen that we do.'

He gave a short nod. 'I'm sorry,' he said quietly. 'I guess that was uncalled for.'

'Completely uncalled for,' she replied stiffly. 'But thank you for acknowledging it.'

'You can see, surely, how I might get the idea... well, you're always here.'

'You're not, so I don't see how you could know that.'

'I come as often as I can,' he said, his tone offended.

'I'm sure you do.'

Without another word, Ottilie went back into the living room and handed the biscuits to Flo. 'I'm sorry, but I have to go.'

'Already? You haven't had your tea.'

'I really need to get back – it's already later than I'd meant to be home.'

'But you never say no to tea! And I thought you wanted to check me over!'

Ottilie gave a faint smile. 'I think you're all right. If there's anything to worry about, I'm sure Heath will come and get me. And I have tea at home, so...' Ottilie's smile grew into something more genuine. 'I've had a very... *interesting* afternoon. Nice – bits of it at least. Bits not so much. Definitely eventful. Thank you.'

'Thank you,' Flo said. 'Very much.'

'Well,' Ottilie added briskly, 'I'm sure I'll see you at the surgery in the next couple of weeks to go over your test results – unless Dr Cheadle wants to, that is – but I'll still be around for you to talk to if you need me.'

CHAPTER THIRTEEN

Ottilie staggered under the weight of the box in her arms as she stood outside the front door of the cottage where Stacey and her daughter Chloe lived. She'd seriously underestimated what she could carry and how long she could keep hold of it, and if someone didn't answer the door in the next ten seconds she was convinced she'd drop it.

Thankfully, the door opened in less than ten, and Ottilie peered over the top of the box to see a surprised-looking Stacey.

'I wondered if you and Chloe could find a home for any of this baby stuff,' Ottilie said. She nodded at the threshold. 'Can I...?'

'Oh yes! Come in!' Stacey stepped back. 'Sorry for being so slow, I wasn't expecting... Sorry, the house is a mess and—'

'If I had a pound for every house call I've done where they've apologised for a non-existent mess, I'm sure I could retire. I would have phoned ahead but I forgot to get your number from Geoff and I thought it would be just as easy to pop round. My friend in Manchester was getting rid of this and I said I knew just the person who might appreciate it.'

Sometimes it was kinder and less humiliating to tell a little white lie. Ottilie had gone searching for donations after Geoff and Magnus (mostly Magnus, whom, Ottilie was learning, didn't know when to shut up) had told her how Stacey and Chloe were struggling to afford equipment for the baby and were running out of time. But Ottilie didn't want to make Stacey feel like a charity case. She wanted it to feel to them like they were doing the favour by taking unwanted items off someone's hands. Pride was a funny thing, Ottilie had learned from many years of doing her job, and it often stopped people taking help that they needed and sometimes caused more pain than the need itself.

'Let me take it,' Stacey said.

'Careful,' Ottilie warned, desperate to dump the box but uncertain whether Stacey could cope with the weight any better than her. She was only tiny after all, a good four or five inches shorter than Ottilie's average height and slender with it. 'It's heavy – heavier than it looks.'

'So am I,' Stacey said with a laugh.

'Well, if you grab one end and I keep hold of the other and you can lead me to where you want me to put it down.'

Between them, they took it through to the kitchen.

'Obviously there's no obligation to take any of it,' Ottilie said as they navigated a narrow hallway. 'And what you don't want I'm sure we'll find a home for somewhere else. Might come in handy for the new mum and baby group – if we ever get that off the ground, that is.'

With a thump, both women let the box drop onto the table. Chloe was in there, the remains of a meal in front of her, studying something on her phone.

At the commotion, she looked up. 'What's in there?'

'Hello, Ottilie,' Stacey said wryly. 'How lovely to see you. How are you?'

'Yeah,' Chloe said with the briefest, most perfunctory smile. 'Hi, Ottilie. So what's in the box?'

'Hopefully stuff you can make use of,' Ottilie said.

At this, Chloe seemed more interested. She put down her phone and got up to look inside the box.

As far as Ottilie was aware, her pregnancy was about four months along, but you'd never know to look at her. Like her mum, she was petite – perhaps an inch or so taller but not much – and unless you knew what to look for, her bump didn't show much at all. In fact, she looked to be still wearing her own pre-pregnancy jeans – the button undone at the waist where there was a little swelling, but other than that, pretty much fitting as they would always have done.

Her gaze went back to the plate of uneaten food – there looked to be a lot left. Of course, she couldn't know how much had been put out for her in the first place, but still...

Ottilie's gaze went briefly to the kitchen. It was tidy and modern, with glossy fitted cupboards and patterned blinds at the window – far more contemporary than the outside of the cottage had suggested she'd find inside. The walls were painted biscuit with a row of mint-green tiles along the worktops.

As Stacey cleared away her plate, Chloe dug a hand into the box and pulled out a teething ring. She looked unimpressed.

'Don't worry,' Ottilie said. 'All those sorts of things can be disinfected and sterilised and will be perfectly safe to use.'

'And beggars can't be choosers,' Stacey added.

'I can afford a plastic rattle,' Chloe fired back. 'I'm not that broke.'

'It's a teething ring,' Stacey began but then let out a sigh. She turned to Ottilie. 'Can I get you a drink?'

'Oh, I didn't want to disturb your evening. I only came by because—'

'It's the least we can do since you brought us all this stuff,' Stacey said.

Ottilie smiled. 'That'd be nice. Actually' – she glanced at

Chloe then back at Stacey – 'if you have time, I'd like to pick your brains.'

'Well,' Stacey said, brushing crumbs from a chair and indicating to Ottilie that she could sit, 'there's not much else going on.'

'Never is,' Chloe added.

Stacey ignored her daughter's jibe. 'What would you like to drink?' she asked Ottilie. 'I've got tea, coffee, hot chocolate... I think. Or maybe something stronger? I could crack open a nice bottle of white I've had in for a while and nobody to share it with.'

'I'll have whatever you're having.' Ottilie took the seat Stacey had wiped over for her.

'Right then.' Stacey went to the fridge. 'Wine it is!'

'I'll have a glass,' Chloe called over.

Stacey spun to face her with a deep frown.

'Kidding,' Chloe said. 'Obviously. I'll go upstairs and get out of your way.'

'No, stay,' Ottilie said. 'It's about the mum and baby group I want to restart, so I really need your opinion more than anyone's.'

'I'm not a mum.'

'But you will be soon, and I hope you'll use the group when you are.'

Chloe pursed her lips slightly. 'I don't think sitting in a church hall watching a load of babies drool and pinch each other is really my scene. Sorry.'

'You don't think it would be beneficial at all?' Ottilie asked.

'I don't know, maybe for some, just not me. For a start, I won't have anything in common with any of the other women.'

'Of course you will,' Stacey said. 'You're all local and will all have young kids.'

'Wow,' Chloe said caustically. 'Why didn't I think of all that? Obviously, we'll all be friends for life.'

Ottilie wasn't about to let Chloe's lack of enthusiasm put her off. Perhaps Chloe couldn't see the point now, but when the baby came she might feel differently. Ottilie was convinced that a support network of others going through the same ups and downs of new motherhood, or the experience of those who'd done it more than once, would be good for her to have. And even if she never went to the group, others would use it. One of the first things she'd been told on her arrival in Thimblebury was how the community was missing groups like that. And it was something for Ottilie herself to focus on – and God knew she needed things to keep her occupied.

'Maybe you could give it a try once or twice,' she said. 'If only to make up the numbers until it gets established. We need to get funding from the council and they're more likely to chip in if they see there are lots of people wanting to use it. If you get nothing out of it, then there's no pressure to keep coming.'

'But I bet,' Stacey called over from where she was twisting a corkscrew to open the wine, 'you'll be surprised how much you enjoy it.'

Chloe looked unconvinced but said no more about it. Instead, she put her hand into the box again, this time pulling out a stack of bibs. There was a tiny, secret smile, Ottilie was sure, as Chloe looked at the colourful designs. She might tell everyone that the prospect of motherhood was unwelcome, that she was bored and inconvenienced by the whole thing, but Ottilie could see that somewhere, deep inside, a small part of her, as yet unacknowledged, was looking forward to meeting her baby.

'Oh, they're cute!' Stacey brought two glasses of wine to the table. 'Always good to have spare bibs – you'll get through loads of them.'

Chloe dug in again and needed two hands to pull out an activity centre, complete with buttons and levers that made various sounds, and panels with different textures and brightly coloured illustrations on them. Her smile was more obvious this time.

'Seems a bit soon for this,' she said, already losing the battle to appear disinterested.

'You'll need it sooner than you think,' Stacey said. 'Especially if they're a clever baby like you were.'

Then Chloe pulled out a plastic cone and frowned at her mum as she held it up.

'Part of a breast pump, I imagine,' Stacey said in answer to Chloe's wordless question.

With a grimace, Chloe let it fall back into the box. 'I don't think so.'

Stacey chuckled. 'There's plenty of time to come round to that idea.'

Chloe shot a sour look at Ottilie. 'I suppose you're one of the *breast is best* brigade. Going to tell me why I shouldn't be using bottles.'

'I'm going to do no such thing,' Ottilie said. 'Firstly, I'm not your midwife. Secondly, I have no experience – no kids of my own – and thirdly, in the end, the choice is one that has to suit you and your needs. As I say, I'm not your midwife, but if I was qualified to give advice, I'd say don't get bullied into anything you don't want to do. Bottle, breast... I'm sure baby will do fine with either.'

'I couldn't have put it better myself.' Stacey said.

'It's going to be bottles,' Chloe said emphatically. 'No argument.'

'Then it's bottles,' Ottilie said. 'What's your midwife say?'

'She keeps giving me all of those stupid leaflets. I don't need to read those leaflets to know what I want.'

Ottilie was quite sure nobody could tell Chloe what she did and didn't want, no matter what evidence they might try to put in front of her. In a way, she liked that about her. Ottilie herself had always been more of a people pleaser, often doing what she thought others wanted of her rather than what she felt was right for her. But that was who she was, and at her age, it was unlikely to change.

It was perhaps inch by inch, but Ottilie felt she had made progress with Chloe. They'd had a meaningful conversation of sorts, and Chloe had opened up, in a fashion, and if that was all Ottilie got that evening, she'd still consider it a success.

Stacey, on the other hand, was far more willing to chat. She'd hinted at what Magnus had already told Ottilie – that she was lonely, desperate for a relationship that might last but unable to find the right man, and now even further away from that as she did her best to support Chloe through a pregnancy she'd never wanted. It seemed so sad to Ottilie that both women had been let down by bad men, and sadder that she herself had been blessed with a perfect man who'd been taken from her all too soon. There was a disconnect sometimes, in the world, in life, that seemed more than unfair – it seemed downright cruel.

She'd got so absorbed in getting to know both women that she hadn't realised how late it was until Chloe announced she was heading to bed.

'Is that the time?' Ottilie said, looking at her watch and then noting darkness beyond the windows of the kitchen.

'You can stay for one more drink, can't you?' Stacey asked Ottilie as Chloe left them with a brief thanks for the baby equipment.

Emboldened by the drinks she'd already had and enjoying Stacey's company, Ottilie was tempted. Even as she said yes, she wondered if she'd already stayed out too late. She would have to walk home in the dark because she'd had too much to drive, which might well prompt one of her panic attacks, but at the same time, perhaps one more drink would give her that little bit extra Dutch courage.

The decision was taken out of her hands when, with a laugh, Stacey went to pour more wine, only to find the bottle was empty.

'We really went at that!'

'That's OK,' Ottilie said. 'I really ought to get back home anyway – work tomorrow, and I won't be much use if I'm tired and hungover.'

'Want me to walk with you?'

Ottilie shook her head. 'Don't be daft; there's no need. It's not that far.'

She'd have loved nothing more than to have Stacey's company for the walk, but she wasn't about to let Stacey take her home and then have to walk back to her own house alone, no matter how safe Thimblebury might be at night.

'OK.' Stacey took the empty bottle to a recycling bin. 'If you're sure.'

'Positive.' Ottilie collected her things and followed Stacey to the front door.

'Thank you for calling round,' Stacey said with a broad smile. 'And for the box of baby stuff. It's been lovely chatting. Promise you won't be a stranger – come round whenever you like.'

'That's an offer I don't need making twice!' Ottilie said. 'Thanks for the wine.'

Head down, Ottilie hurried along the deserted lanes of the village. It was a calm, mild night, and yet the trees still seemed to creak in a way that felt threatening as she passed them, and in the distance a howl rang out across the hillsides. A fox perhaps, but it did nothing to settle Ottilie's nerves. If only she could shake these ridiculous, nameless, baseless fears that seemed to attack her from nowhere and for no reason when she most needed to have a clear head. But even after weeks of living in

Thimblebury, of getting to know the charming and welcoming village, she couldn't. While other aspects of her life were going in the right direction, there were things that felt as if they would be a part of her forever – the loneliness, the fears, the doubts and anxieties that had come since Josh's death.

Perhaps once a conviction had been secured and Josh's murderer had been brought to justice, perhaps then things would change. For now, that situation still hung over her – not exactly a cloud above her own patch of sky, but a dark mass on the horizon, always threatening to blow her way. Perhaps if that was gone, things might brighten in her life again. As her steps quickened, she decided she'd call Faith in the morning for an update. There might not be any news, but at least it would feel good to be doing something about it.

She'd just passed Flo's house and noted that the lights were still on when the creak of a gate made her spin round. A man was leaving. He looked at her at the same time as Ottilie turned.

'All right?' he asked.

It was Heath. Ottilie didn't know whether to breathe a sigh of relief or be annoyed that the one person she'd met when she was so jittery was Flo's sullen grandson.

'Yes, thanks.'

Ottilie turned to hurry away, but then he called her back.

'Hey... hang on a minute.'

She turned back to see him jog over.

'Listen, I just... about the other day... I owe you an apology.'

'Sure,' Ottilie said, not entirely certain what he was apologising for. Maybe it was a general sort of apology for being an arse. 'Whatever – it doesn't matter.'

She glanced back at the road to her house. Was that it? Could she go now?

'Are you OK?' he asked, studying her.

'Yes, why wouldn't I be?'

'I don't know. You seem... Have you got far to go?'

'Not really.'

'You're heading home?'

'Yes.'

'Maybe I could walk with you.'

Ottilie stared at him. 'What for?'

'I don't know...' he said lamely, seeming to be taken aback by her question. 'Because... well, it seems like a good thing to do. It's dark.'

'And it's also Thimblebury,' Ottilie said, torn because she desperately wanted company for her walk home, but why did it have to be him? He was the one person she didn't want to show weakness to. 'Nothing's going to happen to me here.'

'I know,' he said, looking at her like he didn't believe she believed that at all. 'Maybe I'm just a man whose gran taught him to be chivalrous. And maybe I'm trying to get brownie points, in case she's watching from the window.'

Ottilie glanced at Flo's cottage and immediately noticed the curtain fall back across the window. At this, despite everything, she had to smile. And as she looked back at Heath, he was smiling, and it was surprisingly warm.

'Nothing gets past your gran, does it?'

'And God knows I've tried to get plenty past her over the years. So could you help a guy out?'

'Since you put it like that, I don't suppose I can refuse.'

'You could, but I'm sure you must have worked out by now how much grief that would cause me.'

'Go on then – just this once. And only to save your neck. It's really not far, though. By the time we've both thought of the right kind of small talk to make we'll be at my door.'

'I don't really do small talk, so that's all right. I meant it earlier, though. I'm not so pig-headed that I don't realise I owe you an apology.'

'For what?'

'For the way I spoke to you when I came to help you get

Gran down the hill. I was having a bad— It doesn't matter. Whatever kind of day I was having doesn't excuse it; I realise that now.'

'Do you?' Ottilie shot him a sideways glance. 'Or did you only realise when Flo told you off?'

'OK.' He chuckled softly. 'That too. She rules with a rod of iron, does my gran.'

'I guessed that. You're close; you and her?'

'We used to be. Maybe not as close these days, and I feel guilty about that. My gran and grandad were always more... well, let's just say that sometimes they felt more like parents than my parents did.'

'When you say used to, what's changed?'

He gave a vague shrug. 'Life. I'm not proud of the fact that I often let other things get in the way. I ought to see her more but...'

Ottilie nodded slowly. At least he recognised that.

'How did the tests go?' he asked.

'At the hospital?'

He gave a short nod.

'OK,' Ottilie said. 'Pretty much as you'd expect.'

'When will you have the results?'

'They'll go straight to Dr Cheadle. I'll only know what's in them if she needs to let me know. Like if I need to be a part of Flo's care.'

'So you think there'll be something in them that means she needs care?'

'I didn't say that. None of us know what's going to come back at this point. I only mean that I won't find out unless I have to be involved.'

'But you could find out if you chose to, regardless?'

'Well, yes.'

'Could you find out and let me know?'

Ottilie frowned.

'I know,' he said, with some humour in his tone again. 'Patient confidentiality. Could you at least give me a clue?'

'Sorry,' she said, 'unless your gran chooses to share what she knows, I really can't. I'd be breaking about a million rules and if I got found out—'

'I wouldn't tell anyone.'

'I'm sure you wouldn't, but that's not how it works and that's all I can say about it. I really am sorry. If it helps, she seems fit enough to me. I don't think I could have stood even one minute in that pool, let alone the time she swam about in it, so she's probably healthier than I am.'

'She looks well enough to me, but I'm not sure she's so convinced.'

Ottilie recalled the very first conversation she'd had with Heath, over the phone, him in a state of panic because of something Flo had told him about her health. It was encouraging to see him care so much about his gran. It made her stop and re-evaluate. Whenever she decided he was an impatient, annoying man who found it convenient to forget about his old gran living in an obscure village in the Lake District, that fact alone showed those assumptions were wrong. She supposed that what everyone said about his failed marriage and what he himself had just told her about bad days must be true and must certainly have some bearing on his behaviour. While it didn't justify it, perhaps she could cut him some slack.

'I think,' she began slowly, 'that ageing can be scary. The most robust, most resilient of us can be unnerved by age. Things don't work quite as well as they used to, you're not as strong, you wobble, you get tired and ill more easily, your confidence gets knocked. I don't really know your gran, I have no idea what she was like in years gone by, but I can guess that she was someone who took no prisoners. It's easy to forget for us, who haven't yet got to that stage in our lives, that your body starting to fail you is frightening. And for someone like Flo, realising that, increasingly, you have to rely on others is even more so.'

'You sound like someone who's seen a lot of it.'

'I've been nursing for a long time – I've seen plenty.'

He didn't reply, and evidence of his lack of small talk was clear as they fell to silence, the only sounds their footsteps and the nocturnal landscape beyond the village. They walked like this for a few minutes, until he finally spoke again.

'She's lucky.'

'Your gran?'

'Yes. She's lucky that you've come here.'

'Oh...' Ottilie waved away the compliment. 'They had Gwen, and apparently she was brilliant.'

'I'm sure she was, but my gran never needed Gwen like she seems to need you, so I can't say either way. I don't think Gwen would have driven her halfway across the county for hospital appointments and then taken her for tea and Kendal mint cake and then followed her up a hill so she could take a look at one of her favourite places.'

Ottilie smiled. It seemed Flo had recounted their afternoon in quite a lot of detail.

'I just wanted you to know that I do appreciate what you do for her. I know what I've done or said might not have given that impression, but I do.'

'It's no problem.'

'She's not loaded you know,' he said after another pause.

Ottilie looked sharply at him. 'I didn't think for a minute she was.'

'Well, I just wanted to clear that up. Because it might look as if she is – owning outright a house in the Lake District and having Grandad's pension.'

Ottilie stopped dead on the path and stared him down, her face burning. 'Do you think I'm after her money?'

'No, I...'

'I'm fine from here,' she said coldly. 'You can go.'

'I'm sorry, I don't know why I said that; it's just I've had experience of—'

'I don't care what your experience is! How dare you accuse me of only caring because I think there's money in it!'

'That's not what I said!'

'That's exactly what you said! Goodnight, Heath. Thanks for the escort, but I can manage from here.'

'Ottilie, I'm sorry!'

'Go away!'

Ottilie turned and marched towards her house. At least it was within sight. She was so furious, so hurt, so humiliated by his accusation that she couldn't even turn to see whether he was following. Was that really how it looked? Did everyone think that? Did people think she was after Flo's money? She couldn't bear the thought, and as she pushed her key into the front door, angry tears burned in her eyes. Much as it went against everything she was, relations with everyone in the village would have to be strictly professional from now on, and that applied to Florence most of all.

CHAPTER FOURTEEN

'You look awful.'

Lavender gave a look of sympathy as Ottilie walked into the reception area of the surgery to start her shift.

'I've been better,' she replied. 'Didn't sleep very well. What's on this morning?'

'Sorry, but if you were hoping for an easy one then I'm going to have to disappoint you. It's rammed. If you're really not well I can call some of them to see if I can reschedule.'

'No.' Ottilie shrugged off her jacket. 'I can manage.'

'Are you really all right?' Lavender asked, looking more closely at Ottilie. 'It's only a bad night's sleep and nothing more serious?'

'I hardly got a wink, but don't worry, I'm OK.'

Ottilie gave a strained smile in a bid to reassure their receptionist. A bad night's sleep was perhaps an understatement. She'd spent hours tossing and turning and thinking about what Heath had said to her before she'd stormed off. Why did it matter? She'd told herself not to take any notice, that nobody else in the village was thinking such awful things of her, but still she couldn't get it out of her head. She wanted – *needed* – to settle here; she'd wanted to fit in, to find a home and a new start, and the notion of having to leave because people didn't trust her or like her was one that filled her with trepidation and pained her more than she could say. Her whole working life – her life before that – had been a journey to be the very best she could be, to care for others, to make a difference where she could. To have anyone suspect that her motives were less than pure cut deep. Then she got to wondering if Heath had aired those suspicions to anyone. Had he mentioned them to Flo herself? It didn't seem likely – at least, Flo had given her no cause to think so – but she couldn't discount the possibility.

'I'll bring you a coffee through. A two-scoop Lavender special. Just ask Dr Cheadle – one of my two-scoop specials would bring the dead back to life, so it ought to keep you awake for the morning surgery.'

'Thanks,' Ottilie said, trying to smile again, this time at Lavender's joke, but failing to produce anything that looked convincing.

As she went through to the treatment room that also served as her office, Ottilie could hear the first of the morning's patients being greeted by Lavender. Mr Hodgkins and his dressings. She couldn't help but let out a groan. If there was one day where she didn't need him and his complaining, this would be it.

Morning surgery had been every bit as trying as Ottilie had feared, but she'd got through it at last and made her way to the kitchen for the daily lunch get-together. Lavender was unwrapping a plate of what looked like mini pies while Fliss was sitting at the table bent over a printout.

'Change of plan – I know I said I was going to bring quiche, but I saw these ham-and-egg pies in the bakery and they looked too good to leave behind.' Lavender turned to Ottilie as she came in. 'Fliss has brought some leafy stuff – did you bring the potato salad?'

'I'm sorry,' Ottilie said wearily. 'Totally forgot it this morning – meant to say something but haven't had a chance. Do you want me to run home and get it?'

'I'm sure we can do without. We can have it tomorrow.'

Fliss looked up at Ottilie and frowned. 'Lavender says you didn't sleep well. You look like someone who hasn't slept well.'

'I'll survive,' Ottilie said, flopping into a seat.

'Should we reduce this afternoon's clinic for you?'

'God no, it will only make it worse for another day. Honestly, I can cope. What's that?' Ottilie added as she caught sight of a name on the printout Fliss had been reading.

'Corrine's biopsy results.' Fliss held the page out and Ottilie took it, her breath catching in her throat as she read the summary.

'At least we've caught it early,' Fliss said grimly. 'Gold star to you for that.'

'Poor Corrine.' Lavender brought the plated pies to the table and sat down. 'And poor Victor. Corrine's his life – he'll be worried to death.'

Fliss turned to the receptionist. 'Could you do the necessary? Get them down to see me as quick as you can.'

'Isn't the usual course to refer them to the consultant to go through diagnosis and treatment options?' Ottilie asked.

'I'd rather talk to them first,' Fliss said. 'I feel a personal obligation, and that's the way I like to do it. The consultant will be a stranger to them – it's much easier to hear this kind of news from a trusted face.'

'In that case, could I continue to be involved somehow?' Ottilie asked, completely forgetting that only a few hours before she'd vowed to keep out of any business in the village except that which she'd been employed to get involved in.

Fliss nodded. 'I think that would be welcome. I know

they're very fond of you already and it might be good for you to see them every now and again and keep their spirits up, perhaps provide reassurance or explain things they don't understand or that are worrying them. We all know how hard it is to get answers from the consultant sometimes, so I don't want to leave them at the mercy of an overstretched department.'

'I'll make sure I keep an eye on them,' Ottilie said. 'By the way, have we had anything back for Florence yet?'

'Not yet,' Fliss said.

'Want me to chase it?' Lavender asked.

'If you get time.' Fliss took a pie and added it to a plate that already contained a mountain of salad. 'Though I'm not overly worried about her at the moment.'

Being in a converted house, the surgery still had a working doorbell, and it rang through into the kitchen.

Lavender frowned. 'I'm not getting that – everyone knows we close at lunch.'

Fliss gave a vague shrug and reached for some salad dressing, and Ottilie was about to load her plate with greens when it rang again.

Lavender's frown deepened and she folded her arms tight.

'Absolutely not. They can come back when surgery restarts.'

'It might be a delivery or something?' Ottilie suggested.

'We're not expecting one.'

It dinged a third time and Ottilie got up. 'I'll see who it is.'

'No, I'd better—' Lavender cut in, perhaps worried that Ottilie going to do her job might make her look bad, but Ottilie smiled tightly.

'Don't worry, I'll tell them to bog off for you.'

At the door was a woman in overalls holding a bouquet. 'This is the surgery, isn't it?'

Ottilie would have thought it obvious from the sign on the door where they were standing, but she simply nodded.

'Great.' The woman handed the flowers over. 'See ya.'

A few seconds later the delivery van had gone and Ottilie was still standing on the doorstep holding the flowers. *Someone's been lucky*, she thought, wondering if Fliss or Lavender were celebrating some anniversary or event that they'd neglected to mention. But as she took the flowers inside and began to look for a card, she quickly realised that the flowers weren't meant for Fliss or Lavender – they were for her. The message on the card was neatly typed. Clearly the order had been phoned in or placed online, the shop transcribing their words for them.

To Ottilie

Please accept my apologies for what I said. It was totally out of order.

Heath

Putting the card back, she swept into the kitchen and dumped the bouquet in the sink.

'Who's the lucky girl?' Lavender asked, going to look.

Ottilie snatched the card out from the flowers again and put it in her pocket. 'Me, but they're not wanted.' She looked at Lavender. 'Take them home if you like.'

'Why would you not want them?' Lavender asked, her curiosity clearly in overdrive. 'Who are they from? An unwelcome secret admirer? A not-so-secret admirer?'

'An arse,' Ottilie replied shortly. 'Someone who thinks a bunch of wilted flowers will put the most hurtful thing anyone's ever said—' She shook her head. 'I don't know why I even care.'

'Put them out in reception if Ottilie doesn't want them,' Fliss said, obviously just as curious but with more tact than Lavender. 'It'll brighten the place up a bit.'

Ottilie sat down to resume her lunch, though her appetite was gone. What was wrong with that man? She didn't have a clue what to make of him; she only knew he seemed to blow hot and cold and didn't have a consistent opinion about anything or anyone. One thing was certain: she wasn't going to mention this to Florence – there was no need to give her ideas. She only hoped that Lavender wouldn't either. Fliss wouldn't gossip, but Lavender might let it slip.

Ottilie could outright ask her not to tell anyone, but then that might be counterproductive, because if Lavender thought there was some drama there, some story to tell, she might be more tempted to tell it. Besides, she didn't want to discuss it with Lavender or Fliss. She didn't want to have to repeat the thing Heath had accused her of. She didn't want to think about it, but it was more than that; a part of her was afraid that others did think it and by bringing it to their attention she might somehow force them to examine the idea further. And they might come to the same conclusion that Heath had done.

It was silly, like her fears about Josh's attacker coming for her were silly, and yet she was held hostage by these things that she knew weren't true, that she knew wouldn't happen, unable to shake the notion that in some way, however unlikely, they would.

'By the way,' Lavender said, paying Ottilie closer attention than her next sentence would suggest, 'Magnus asked me to ask you what you fancy for the next film-club screening. He said it was your turn to choose and you haven't DM'd him. He says anything as long as it's in the rules and something he can get hold of easily enough.'

'Um...' Ottilie stabbed a quartered tomato. 'I'll have to think. When does he need to know by?'

'End of the week I should think.'

'Fine,' Ottilie said, her mind a whirl of thoughts, and not one of them dedicated to choosing a movie for film club.

CHAPTER FIFTEEN

Ottilie had been in Thimblebury for just over a month. In some ways her new home got more familiar every day, but in others it was always changing. The weather had warmed and the tourist season had started in earnest. It didn't impact Thimblebury directly – the village was far too small to attract holidaymakers – but it did mean that the district in general was busier, the streets of the nearby towns buzzing with visitors and the bright dots of hikers on the hills a regular sight. From time to time a group would wander through Thimblebury and stop to look around, and once or twice Ottilie had been engaged in a pleasant chat with someone from out of the area asking for recommendations.

A week of boiling-hot weather had finally broken – the first real heatwave Ottilie had experienced here, and as she walked the steep path up to Daffodil Farm, the air was heavy with rain. It was still humid, and her clothes were damp, her hair sticking to the back of her neck, and she very much hoped that Corrine and Victor's kitchen would be cooler than the air outside.

As she reached the gate, the front door opened and Corrine emerged, beaming at her.

'I saw you coming across the field. I said to Victor it looked like you, and it was!'

'I hope it's all right to call.'

'Of course it's all right! Come in... Have you got time for a cup of tea?'

'Always,' Ottilie said with a smile, glad to see that Corrine looked bright, despite getting her skin cancer diagnosis only days before.

'We were planning to pop down to see you,' Corrine continued as she waved Ottilie in. 'So it's lucky that you're here.'

'Oh? For anything in particular?'

'Only to say thank you. If you hadn't taken a look at my neck... well, all I can say is I'm glad you called up to the farm that day.'

Ottilie sat at the table.

A moment later, Victor came through from the hallway with a wrapped box in his hand. 'Hello – we saw you come up across the field,' he said, repeating what Corrine had told her. Then he put the box on the table in front of her. 'It's not much. We didn't know what you'd like but we wanted to show our appreciation.'

Ottilie looked up at him, bemused. 'You didn't need to get anything at all. I was only doing my job.'

'You hadn't even started your job,' Corrine chided as she put the kettle on the stove to boil. 'Don't come over all modest. You damn near saved my life as soon as you set foot in the village, and what a lucky day it was for me when you came.'

Ottilie unwrapped the parcel to find a huge box of chocolates inside.

'Aww, thank you. I'll take these to share with Dr Cheadle and Lavender, if that's all right.'

'No need – we got some for them too,' Victor said. 'You keep those to yourself.'

'Was there something you needed to say?' Corrine asked.

Ottilie turned to see her spooning loose tea into a pot.

'No, I just wanted to see how you were doing. And... maybe sneak a little visit to your alpaca.'

Victor laughed. 'Ho! That's the real reason, I'll bet! Nobody ever comes to see just us; they always want half an hour with the girls.'

Ottilie had really come to see them, but she didn't want them to think she was overdoing it, so she'd seized on seeing the alpaca too as a way to put them off the scent. In reality, she'd been worried how they were coping after getting Corrine's diagnosis and wanted to see for herself. She realised she needn't have worried. Corrine and Victor were old school, practical and pragmatic as they came, and they'd weather any storm as long as they had each other. And, for now, Ottilie was in no doubt that Corrine, getting early treatment, would live to fight another day and they would have each other for a lot longer.

'I'd say wait until you've had your tea,' Corrine said, going to the window and looking out, 'but I think it's going to rain in the next hour or so and you might want to go over before the field gets too boggy.'

'I don't mind that,' Ottilie said.

'You don't mind at the moment, but you might when the mud sucks away your favourite shoes,' Victor said with a grin. 'Come on, lass. Let's go and say hello – Corrine can keep the pot warm for when we get back.'

The rain held off long enough for them to reach the stables where Victor kept his 'girls'. As they'd done the last time, at the sight of him opening the gate they all moved as a herd towards him. It was funny, so sweet that Ottilie couldn't help but break into a broad smile.

'They love you,' she said.

'Greedy little buggers,' Victor said, but there was real affection in his tone.

A moment later they were in the field with the gate safely closed again, Victor clicking and fussing at his girls as they crowded around him, all woolly faces and huge eyes. One or two sniffed a bit curiously at Ottilie, but mostly they only had eyes for Victor.

'All right there, Alice...' he said as the black-and-white one nudged her nose into the palm of his hand. 'I know what you're after.'

Ottilie and all the girls followed him to the barn and watched expectantly as he produced the sack of pellets they seemed to like so much. He offered Ottilie a handful, as he'd done before, and then took some out himself.

Ottilie's smile grew as they crowded her, tickling her palm as they hoovered it clean. It didn't take long for it all to be gone.

'Are they allowed any more?' Ottilie asked.

Victor gave her one more handful. 'That'll do,' he said.

Ottilie tried to reach the ones who hadn't had the first treats, but some of them still went for seconds despite her efforts.

Then Victor fastened up the sack and wiped his hands.

'This cancer business...' he said, turning to Ottilie, his eyes glazing as he rubbed his hand over Daisy's head.

It pained her to see that amiable, avuncular old face so sad. It was the first face she'd met on her arrival in Thimblebury, and he'd made her so welcome she'd never stop being grateful.

'We've caught it in good time and the survival rates in cases like Corrine's are really good. Treatment will be fast and brilliant, and she'll be well in no time.'

'Can you promise that?'

'Nobody can promise anything in this world, but if I was asked to bet I'd put my house on it.'

At this he seemed to brighten. 'Don't mind me; silly old bugger. I've just got used to having her around, you know.'

'There's nothing silly about worrying for her. You know, if you need to ask questions or you feel as if you need to talk something through that's bothering you, you only have to come and find me. And don't think you're a bother, because it won't be any bother at all.'

Victor brightened further still, and then a mischievous look crossed his face. 'You know what... I think you're all right.'

Ottilie laughed. 'Thanks.'

'Better than that old Gwen. I know everyone falls down worshipping her, but she were always a bit bossy for my liking.'

'Oh, I can be bossy.'

'But you're kinder with it. We won't forget any of what you've done for us. Not ever, as long as any of us lives.'

Ottilie laughed again, but with a lump forming in her throat this time. 'Don't start getting all sentimental. You'll start me off, and you don't want that.'

'Aye...' Victor drew in a breath and reached into the sack of treats. 'One more for the road, girls, and then that's enough for today. You're going to bankrupt me with all you eat.'

The rain was coming down properly and Ottilie was soaked through by the time they got back to the farmhouse. Corrine tutted as she put the kettle on to boil.

'Let me get a hairdryer for you,' she said to Ottilie, taking her jacket to hang it over a chair near the stove.

'It's only a bit of damp. It'll be dry by the time I'm ready to go.'

'Victor will run you down the hill. Can't be walking in this – you'll be soaked to the bone.'

A low rumble of thunder ripped across the sky. Corrine's hands went to her hips. 'Well that's settled it. No argument – we'll take you home in the Land Rover. I'm not having you get struck by lightning.'

Ottilie could see that when Corrine said no argument, she meant it, and so nodded agreement to the plan. 'Thank you.'

'It's the least we could do as you came up to see us. Now, are you having cake with this tea?' she asked, putting a slab of fruit cake out and setting it in front of Ottilie before she'd had an answer.

Looks like it, Ottilie thought, trying to hold back a grin.

'Have you got some sandbags at your place?' Victor asked as he pulled off his wellies at the back door.

Ottilie turned to him. 'Sandbags?'

'Rain looks set to last a while. It's always better to be safe than sorry.'

She stared at him. 'You think it will rain that much? Wouldn't bad rain be more likely in the winter?'

'Forecast says it will be a good drenching. Unusually high rainfall for this time of the year, they said. Climate change and all that. We'll see.'

'You can always come up to us if your kitchen gets a bit of water in it,' Corrine said mildly. 'Nice and high up here – we never get flooding.'

Ottilie looked from one to the other. How could they both be so calm at the prospect of weather bad enough to flood homes? It could only mean that it was a common occurrence in the area, but nobody had ever mentioned it to her, certainly not when she'd been buying Wordsworth Cottage. Would it have put her off if they had? Time would tell, and she tried to quell the building panic by noting that if Victor and Corrine were calm about it, perhaps it was never as bad as the forecasters might have people believe.

Actually, now that she came to think of it, how many times had she seen cataclysmic forecasts on the TV warning everyone not to venture out, only to be disappointed by a dribble of rain and a wind barely strong enough to lift her hair? She tried to be positive.

But the sandbags...? *Sandbags?* Did she really need those?

'Nice cup of tea while you dry out,' Corrine said, breaking into her thoughts.

Ottilie gave a distracted nod as she looked to the windows, where the rain was beating hard enough to stir that sense of panic up again.

As Corrine poured her tea, she pulled her phone from her soggy bag and checked the weather app. Rain for the rest of the day, according to that, but when had it ever been accurate? It used to be a standing joke between her and Josh; they'd decided the people who updated it must stick their heads out of the window hourly to see what the weather was doing right then, and make that their forecast for the rest of the day.

We'll see, Victor had said. A bit like the app then.

An hour later Ottilie was back in the village. Victor dropped her off with a cheery wave and had seemingly forgotten all about his warning that she might need sandbags. But Ottilie hadn't. Instead of going home, she pulled up her hood – for what use it was – and headed to the shop. If anyone knew what she needed – and might possibly be able to provide some – it would be Magnus and Geoff.

Her anxiety was building, her thoughts muddled. She'd had panic attacks before, but they'd always been over things that weren't real – at least, her logical mind knew they weren't. But this was an actual threat. Wordsworth Cottage was all she had in the world and she had to protect it. Did that make it worse or better than the imaginary dangers that sometimes gripped her? Did that make it any easier to cope with? At least she had the power to take practical action here, and surely that had to be worth something. Surely that must give her a sense of agency, something that she often felt had drifted away from her reach. Here, at least, she could take steps to prevent disaster.

. . .

Magnus looked up from his book. Whenever Ottilie went in he had a book open at the counter. Usually she'd ask what he was reading, but today that didn't feature in her thoughts at all.

'Ottilie!' Magnus smiled. 'Good weather for the ducks, right?'

'Yes.' Ottilie was dimly aware of the fact that her coat was dripping onto the shop floor. Ordinarily she'd apologise for it, but her manners seemed to have gone from her thoughts too. 'I don't suppose you have sandbags?'

Magnus closed his book and looked surprised. 'What would you want those for?'

'Well, Victor said...' Ottilie's panic burst like an overfilled balloon. 'Victor thought...' she continued, feeling a bit silly, 'it might rain a lot.'

'It probably will, but I don't think it will rain enough to come into your house.'

'No...' Ottilie grabbed a deep breath. 'I suppose so. I... Well, he asked if I had sandbags. And I don't think I do – at least, I haven't seen any when I've been pottering around, so...'

'Ah.' Magnus gave a sage nod. 'I suppose your cellar may trap some water. If it does, we can help you find someone with a pump to get it out. I'm not sure sandbags will really stop that from happening – it's down below, you see.'

'I don't think I have a cellar,' Ottilie said.

'Well then, you don't need to worry. I thought you did – lots of houses here do.'

'So you've never been flooded? Since you've been in Thimblebury it's never happened?'

'Some of the houses right by the river once, I think.'

'I'm not so close to the river, am I?'

Magnus shook his head. 'I don't think so. I'm sure yours has never flooded.'

The last bit of tension drained from Ottilie, her whole posture softening. 'You know what – bless Victor and Corrine for looking out for me, but they didn't half put the fear of God in me earlier,' she said with a shaky laugh. 'I thought I was going to have to buy a boat.'

'They were perhaps thinking your house is closer to the river. It's easy to get mixed up.'

'And their farm isn't even in the village proper, and I don't think they come down all that often.'

'Exactly.' Magnus smiled. 'So did you think of a film for movie night? Maybe not *The Day After Tomorrow*,' he added with a quick grin.

'And definitely nothing to do with Noah's ark,' Ottilie replied, smiling herself now. 'I was thinking maybe *A Knight's Tale* or something like that? Something a bit swashbuckling and romantic.'

'Ah, you're in the mood for romance?'

'I'm in the mood for a bit of Heath... *Ledger*,' she added quickly, suddenly aware of her face burning. What was that about?

'A very good choice,' Magnus said. 'I second that – a very beautiful man. Such a shame he went too soon.'

In an instant, Ottilie's embarrassment had turned to melancholy. She knew all about beautiful men gone before their time. She tried to shake it – the rollercoaster of emotions she'd been through this afternoon couldn't be good for her.

'I'm sure it will be easy enough to get hold of that film,' Magnus said, thankfully oblivious to her spiralling mood. At least he didn't show that he'd noticed, even if he had.

'I'd better take some milk and bread while I'm here,' Ottilie said. 'At least then if the weather gets worse I won't starve.'

Ottilie went to the stand where the bread was usually stored to see that the choice was a lot smaller than usual – though it wasn't always massive anyway.

'I think everyone's had the same idea,' Magnus said apologetically. 'There's not much left.'

'That's all right.' Ottilie chose a couple of baguettes before going to the fridge for a bottle of locally farmed milk. 'I can make do with what you have.'

Magnus rang up the bill and Ottilie paid, feeling easier than she had when she'd arrived. Then she headed back out into the storm, ready to lock herself into her little cottage with blankets and tea and wait for it to be over.

CHAPTER SIXTEEN

Ottilie found herself in sudden darkness. With a twitch and a click, the TV, the lights and everything else in the house went off. The storm had been lashing Wordsworth Cottage for hours, beating at the windows, shaking the trees and shrubs in the garden so that they scraped against the house as if to be let in, water running from the guttering in a steady stream where it must have overwhelmed the narrower channels.

Fumbling on the coffee table, her fingers finally found the shape of her phone and she grabbed it to flick on the torch. She had a vague idea where the fuse box was but had never needed to visit it, so it was vague at best. Magnus had thought her house had a cellar and had said that many of the ones locally did. She'd never asked when she'd bought the house whether they had one that had been filled in and she'd probably taken less notice of the plans than she ought to have done. Would that be a problem? Or might it be her saving? At least she didn't have to go down into a damp, musty basement for her fuse box, like they did in horror films. If that had been the case, she might well have taken to her bed and hidden under the covers until morning, even though it was only just gone nine.

The problem wasn't the fuse box, as Ottilie quickly gathered after flicking the switches a few times and getting no response. It was then that she looked out of the window and realised she couldn't see any lights on in the village – at least, not in the closest houses. So it was a bigger power fault? Perhaps the storm had brought down a cable. How long would she be without electricity? Without it, was there any point in staying up after all? It was far too early to go to bed, but there was no light to read by and no television.

She could continue to use her phone, but not knowing how long she'd be without power to charge it and thinking she might need it in an emergency, perhaps that wasn't such a good idea. She supposed she could go and find some company in the village – perhaps Stacey or Magnus and Geoff would be OK with her calling on them and spending the evening there – if only because she was getting increasingly unnerved being alone in the dark like this.

She dialled Stacey's number first.

'Hello?'

'Hi, Stacey. Sorry to bother you but my power's gone off. I was wondering if yours was on.'

'No, nothing here either. I'm guessing the storm's taken it out.'

'That's what I thought. How are you coping there?'

'Oh, we're fine. I've got solar lanterns in the garden – I've brought them inside – and we've got a cupboard full of candles, thanks to endless Christmases where my aunt buys me a smelly one every year that I never use. Are you all right there?'

'Well, I wish I'd thought about a candle supply before now. I don't have solar lanterns either.'

'You can have some of our candles if you want to brave the storm to come and get them. Or you could always stay over,' Stacey added, perhaps sensing the anxiety in Ottilie's voice.

'We've got a sofa bed we can flip out for you, and it would be nice to have company.'

'Chloe's not there tonight?'

Stacey laughed. 'Oh, she's here – no company though. Too busy on her phone.'

'I'd really like that,' Ottilie said.

'Come over. Want me to meet you halfway?'

'No, no... that's OK – wouldn't want to get you out in this. I'll be with you in half an hour or so.'

'Great. See you then.'

Ottilie could hear the rushing currents of the nearby river even from here, though it was too dark to see it. There were closer houses than Wordsworth Cottage, but it sounded so much more aggressive than it usually did, and Ottilie couldn't help but wonder if her home might still be in danger, despite Magnus's efforts to reassure her earlier. The rain was heavier than ever – though the thunder and lightning seemed to have calmed, which was a relief.

The wind had done some damage – in her path were smashed roof tiles, ripped-off branches and bits of fence panel, and an entire tree lying across the road at one point. Not a very big one, granted, but big enough to cause a problem for anyone who might need to pass and, with the lack of street lighting, practically invisible until you were right on top of it. Lower-lying sections of road were already waterlogged too, huge puddles that more than once she almost landed in. Ottilie picked her way around the fallen tree and wondered who she could call to make it safe. Perhaps when she got to Stacey's house they could google the most appropriate organisation and let them know.

Passing Flo's house, she wondered whether to call and see how she was doing. But as she drew closer, she saw the light from some flickering candles in one of the upstairs windows and wondered if Flo had done what she'd considered doing and gone to bed to hunker down until this was all over. If that was the case and she might be sleeping, then she didn't want to wake her. Ottilie had to wonder if that would have been best after all, and whether she was a bit crazy walking out in this, but the die was cast and so she marched on, the wind whipping around her and rain stinging her skin as it slapped her face.

Stacey's living room was bathed in warm, low light. Ottilie had hung her wet coat on a peg by the front door and taken off her boots, and even though it was summer, she was chilled from her pummelling by the wind and rain.

'You look like a drowned rat,' Stacey said. 'If I'd realised how bad the rain was, I'd have come for you in the car.'

'You wouldn't have got through,' Ottilie said, taking Stacey's offer of a seat on the sofa. 'There's a tree blocking the road. We probably ought to call someone about that. Not sure who.'

'Me neither. I bet there's an emergency helpline somewhere. We'll have a look while I make us a drink. Do you need a towel?'

'I might feel a bit warmer once I'm dry,' Ottilie admitted.

'You can borrow my hairdryer if... ah...' Stacey started to laugh. 'No electricity. Maybe not the hairdryer then.'

'You don't realise how much you rely on it every day without thinking about it until it's not there, do you?'

'I'm sure we can say that about a lot of things. Travel back in time – no thank you, not even to marry a handsome prince. I like my mod cons.'

Stacey disappeared and came back a few moments later with a fluffy towel. 'Here you go. I'll bring some drinks through. Had to boil some water on the hob in a pan, so not sure how nice it will be.'

'It's warm, that's the main thing.' Ottilie smiled, grateful for the drink and the towel and a house with light, but more than anything, grateful for company. She could face this now; here with Stacey the storm didn't seem nearly so threatening. 'Where's Chloe?'

'Upstairs. Moping probably.'

'She's struggling a bit?' Ottilie asked, following Stacey into a kitchen lit by solar lights that had been brought in from the garden. It was still quite dim, but she could make out the mugs sitting on the worktop and the pan on the stove, steam wreathing from it as the water came to a boil. The air felt clearer in here – Ottilie had been struck immediately by the smell in the living room of different scented candles all clashing with one another.

'She'll come round,' Stacey said mildly. 'She just doesn't want to admit to herself that this baby is coming. She's in for a shock when she goes into labour, but she won't have any real discussion about what we're going to do and what to expect. She won't even do antenatal classes. I can't say I blame her, but as my mum used to say, if you're old enough to do the dance, got to expect the bunions when it's over.'

Ottilie burst into laughter. 'I've never heard that saying!'

'Well, that was my mum for you. Had her own unique take on the world. Half the stuff she said only made sense to her.'

'Oh, I think that makes sense; I've just never heard it before. So you don't have your mum now?'

Stacey shook her head. 'There are times when I bloody well wish I did, though. I miss her every day.'

'Yeah, I know how that feels.'

Stacey glanced up, her expression one of profound sympathy as she poured water from the pan into the mugs. 'Must have been hard.'

'Losing Josh? It was. Still is. It feels as if it gets further away

– the event itself – but it never seems to get any easier, like people keep telling me it will.'

'The people who tell you that are often the people who've never experienced it. And even if they have, your loss is your loss, and it's not like theirs. Nobody grieves in exactly the same way as someone else – at least, I don't think they do.'

'I think you might be right.'

'There are some blankets in the chest in the living room if you're still cold.'

'I'm feeling a bit better now,' Ottilie said as she wrapped her hands around the mug Stacey had given her. 'I wonder how long this power is going to be out.'

'I don't think a tiny place like Thimblebury is a massive priority to get back on. Could be hours, could be the rest of the night maybe. I don't suppose the electricity company wants to send workers out to repair in weather like this. Perhaps if it's out in one of the bigger towns as well they might – more people to complain about it if they don't.'

'Does it happen often?'

'No, only twice as far as I can remember. I mean, we lose the electricity on occasion, like everywhere, but it's never normally for this long. You can stay over if you want to, you know. It's no bother, and I imagine it's a bit scary sitting in your house alone with all this going on.'

'I haven't brought anything with me.'

'We've got a spare toothbrush and you can borrow some of my pyjamas if you like. It's really no hassle.'

It was tempting, and although Ottilie didn't want to impose on Stacey, certain that she was only offering out of courtesy, it would be good to know that there was someone in the house with her. It had been so long since she'd gone to bed feeling anything other than lonely she'd almost forgotten what it was like to feel safe, to know that support and company was on hand.

'Honestly,' Stacey said, seeming to read her thoughts. 'It'll be company for me as well as you. I'm more than happy to sit up and chat a while anyway, and it's likely to rain for the rest of the night so you'll only be getting wet again on the way back to your place.'

Ottilie nodded. 'That sounds nice. As long as it's not putting you out.'

'Not one bit.' Stacey smiled. 'It'll make a nice change from flicking through the channels on the telly. And an actual conversation with an interested person and not the top of some-one's head while they look at their phone – how can I say no to that?'

CHAPTER SEVENTEEN

It was only an old sofa bed, with springs where they shouldn't be, worn in places and creaking even over the roar of the wind outside every time Ottilie turned over, and yet Ottilie had slept better than she'd imagined she would. There was plenty to keep her awake – not least the worry about her house, and yet she'd managed to drop off at some point. When Stacey came downstairs and woke her, the living room was in bright daylight.

Ottilie pushed herself up and looked up at the clock over the mantelpiece. 'I should get back – need to get my stuff for work.'

'I can run you over if you want to stay for breakfast.'

'That's really kind of you, but I think I'd like to go and check the house over before I do anything else. I can get breakfast at work between patients. Is the power back?'

Stacey flicked a switch, filling the room with yellow light. 'Looks like it.'

'That's one good thing, but now I'm hoping I didn't leave anything daft plugged in overnight – I did rush out in a bit of a panic.'

Ottilie collected her clothes from where she'd left them on a nearby chair and hurried to the bathroom to wash and get changed. Chloe's bedroom door was closed, and Ottilie supposed she must still be sleeping – if she had no reason to get up this early, she wouldn't either. But then she heard Chloe's voice. It was muffled, so Ottilie couldn't tell what she was saying, but she sounded angry.

None of her business, she reminded herself, though her interest was piqued. Who could have upset her that much? Perhaps the father of her child? Stacey was under the impression he'd done a disappearing act, but perhaps Chloe had tracked him down and for whatever reason wasn't telling Stacey that? It was pure conjecture, but for someone who loved people as much as Ottilie did, the notion was one that would probably bother her all day.

As soon as she'd closed Stacey's garden gate behind her and started to walk away from the house, Ottilie knew something was wrong. The ground was sodden, a layer of surface water that didn't seem to have drained away swirling around her boots. And as she made her way down the lane, past the fallen tree, into the subtle hollow where Wordsworth Cottage was nestled, it got deeper.

Ottilie's blood seemed to turn to concrete. The water was up to her ankles now, and she wasn't even at the bottom of a dip that she'd never really taken much notice of before. It hadn't seemed to matter – not while the weather had been kind and clement – but as she went further and further, dread in her heart, it suddenly mattered very much.

As her own cottage came into sight the water was above her ankles, and at the gate it was lapping around her calves. Fighting back tears, she waded through it to her front door.

The unthinkable had happened, the thing that Victor had warned her about but that everyone else had assured her wouldn't. The water was in her hallway, in her living room, in her kitchen... brown and silty, swirling around the ground floor in eddies that carried her belongings on them like a ship broken up on a stormy sea. Her breath caught at the sight of a wedding photo she'd had on the hearth, the wooden frame acting as a float, her and Josh smiling up from it as it drifted past her legs. Ottilie stared, standing like a statue in the water, unable to process what she was seeing, even less able to act. Numb, she backed out of the house again, shutting the door as if she could shut away the damage.

When she heard her name being called she could barely focus enough to respond, still staring at the house, her brain refusing to function.

'Ottilie!'

Eventually, she turned to see Magnus and Geoff hurrying towards her, both in wellington boots and raincoats – though the rain had stopped. Magnus looked as if he was more likely to burst into tears than Ottilie right now – it was certainly going to be a close-run thing.

'Oh!' he said, his gaze going to her waterlogged garden. 'I'm so sorry!'

'You didn't do it,' Ottilie said in a dull voice.

'But I told you not to worry! I thought—'

Geoff put an arm around him and pulled him close. 'It's not your fault, love. It's nobody's fault; nobody could have seen it coming.'

'Victor did,' Ottilie said.

At this Magnus did start to cry. 'I feel so responsible!'

'We'll help you to put it right,' Geoff said to Ottilie. 'What can we do? And you have insurance, right? You can call them first of all, and then we'll see about getting the water out.'

'How do you even get this much water out?' Ottilie asked, struggling to see through her own tears.

'Stay with us at our place while it dries out,' Geoff added. 'And don't make excuses – we insist.'

Ottilie really didn't want to. It wasn't that she didn't appreciate the kindness of him, and of his sister Stacey, but she wanted her own house. Lonely as it might be, unfamiliar and anxiety-triggering, it was still hers. Everything she needed was there: her life, her history, her past and future were all there. It was where she needed to be, especially now.

'I have to get to work,' she said, her voice curiously calm, as if the events of the day thus far belonged to someone else's life. But she didn't know what else to do, how else to react when nothing about this would compute.

'You can't go to work today. Nobody will be getting to the surgery today anyway.'

'Fliss will be expecting me. I have to go.'

Ottilie looked down at herself. She was going to have to go inside again to get her uniform, but at least that was upstairs in the bedroom. She could wade through the water in the hallway, do what she needed to do and get out again. She had to get to work; she couldn't let Fliss down and, besides, it was easier to bury herself in her job and not think about what she had waiting at home. Perhaps she'd return to find the water had receded, and then all she'd have to do is wait for it to dry and then clean up. Was that how it worked? She'd seen endless news reports about flooded families over the years, but apart from a tut of sympathy she'd never really taken a lot of notice. She certainly hadn't considered how to deal with the same happening to her – she'd never needed to.

Geoff and Magnus watched as she went back down the path. One of them called to her, but she wasn't listening.

With a splash, she dashed through the water at the foot of the stairs and then ran up them, soaking the carpet along the landing as she went. Into the bedroom, grabbed her uniform from a hanger and back down with it bundled in her arms. She glanced at her car – there was probably no point in trying to take that, looking at the roads, it might be easier to walk than run the risk of deeper water flooding her engine. So she shut the door and, for what it was worth, locked it, and then gave Magnus and Geoff a tight smile.

'It's fine. I'm fine. You don't need to worry. I'll sort it all out later when I've finished work.'

She was far from fine, but what else could she say?

'Ottilie!' Lavender was at the door of the surgery when she arrived. They hadn't yet opened up. 'We didn't think you'd be coming in.'

'Why not?'

Lavender shot her a look of pure disbelief, glanced down at where water sloshed around their feet, and then back at her. 'The whole village is under water and your house is in a dip.'

'It's under water too, but what's the point in me being there? I can't do anything about it; I might as well be working.'

'I'm not sure we're going to be able to run clinics today,' Lavender said. 'I'm just about to see what the damage is.'

'Has Fliss been flooded too?'

'Her house is a bit higher; I don't think she's fared too badly compared to some. Garden's waterlogged and it's come through the kitchen floor a bit, but she thinks it will dry out. Cellar's taken the brunt of it, but she says they're designed to do that so she's not worried.'

'I never thought about that.' Ottilie wondered whether she'd been too quick to celebrate the fact she didn't have a cellar. If that had taken all the floodwater, as it had in Fliss's case, she might have been better off. But there was no point in dwelling on that now.

Lavender pushed the door open, creating a slight current. The water was in here but only as deep as the soles of Ottilie's boots, so perhaps they'd be able to siphon it out somehow during the course of the day, as long as there was no more rain, that was, and as long as the river started to recede enough so it could swallow back some of what it had spat out.

'What are we going to do about the patients?' Ottilie asked.

'Fliss is on her way in. We'll have an emergency meeting and decide what to do when she's assessed the damage. It might be that we can somehow soldier on.'

'We could move people upstairs and see them?'

'We could, though it's not very well equipped and we'd have to move some of the stuff we store up there. Might be a bit musty too, seeing as we don't use that floor all that much.'

'It would mean we don't have to turn people away.'

'Let's see what Fliss says when she gets here.'

Ottilie and Lavender went through to the surgery kitchen, water sploshing around their feet. Ottilie was getting sick of the smell – the same here as at her house, of silt and mud and old, rotting vegetation. It seemed to hang in the air like a cloud, thick enough to chop through.

'Weren't there any warnings about this?' Ottilie asked as she bent to pick up some soggy paperwork floating on the surface of the water and spread it out on the table.

'No. Wouldn't be the first time the environment agency has been caught on the back foot, but I think there'll be hell to pay this time. Fliss, for one thing, won't be letting this go without saying something to someone in charge. If she gets her way, heads will roll.' Lavender gave Ottilie a pained look. 'Is it very bad at your place?'

'Bad enough.' Ottilie was exhausted already, simply from looking around at what seemed like an endless mess that they had no prospect of ever getting clean. So much for a refreshing sleep on Stacey's sofa. Where did they start? The village as a whole, not just her; where did they even begin getting back to normal? And everyone seemed so matter-of-fact about it, where she felt as if what had been left of her world was caving in.

'Victor's bringing a pump down,' Lavender said. 'We could get him to do your house first.'

'What's the point? The water isn't low enough around there – it will come back in as quick as he sucks it up. Best to do here, where there's a fighting chance of getting it dry. And we need this place to be clear for the patients.'

Lavender started to fish objects out of the water that had been lifted clear from low shelves in the deluge. Ottilie was about to help when her phone rang. With some impatience she pulled it out of her coat pocket and frowned at the screen.

'Faith, hi.'

'Can you talk?'

Ottilie glanced at Lavender. It wasn't the best time and she would have said so, but something in Faith's voice stopped her.

'I've got a few minutes. It's kind of hectic here at the moment. We've had some flooding.'

'Oh,' Faith said, 'sorry.'

She didn't sound all that sorry, but Ottilie wouldn't expect her to. After all, she couldn't know how bad things were here, and she clearly had something else on her mind. Ottilie's own thoughts flicked to Josh and the efforts to bring his killer to justice. Something had gone wrong – she knew it in an instant, and Faith confirmed her fears in her next sentence.

'We've had to let him go, Ott.'

'Right,' Ottilie replied slowly, as if Magnus had just told her he was out of milk. She was numb enough this morning, over-whelmed by events here, and there was only so much she could process at once.

'There wasn't enough evidence to bring it to trial. It's possible witnesses were got to – we don't know for sure – but what we have is too circumstantial. I'm sorry, Ottilie; we're back to square one. I wanted to let you know as soon as I could.'

'Thank you.'

'Ott... are you all right? Do you need me to come—'

'No. There's no point. I get the picture and there's a lot going on here. Like I said, the village is flooded.'

'OK. Well, if you change your mind, you know where I am. And if there's anything you don't understand or you want to ask about...'

'Yes, I know. Thanks, Faith. It was good of you to call.'

'I'm sorry it wasn't with better news.'

A lot of people seemed to be telling Ottilie how sorry they were today. But none of this was any of their fault. None of it was anyone's fault, so why did Ottilie suddenly feel a rush of anger breaking through the numbness? Suddenly, she wanted to scream at the world, but she swallowed it back. Screaming wasn't going to make any of this go away.

As she locked and pocketed her phone, she could feel Lavender's eyes on her.

'It's nothing,' she said, though Lavender hadn't asked.

'Didn't sound like nothing.'

'It's nothing I can do anything about.'

'We all have to deal with lots of those things, but that doesn't mean it won't help to talk about it.'

'It won't achieve anything, even if it helps. And we're busy with this. I don't want to start, because I might not be able to stop.'

Lavender didn't push it. Perhaps Ottilie secretly wished she would. On some level she recognised that Lavender was right, that it would be healthier to share her fears and disappointments rather than bottle them up, but she couldn't bring herself to face it, let alone speak any of it out loud. She needed time to process it all and there wasn't any – not now, not while there was all this chaos in front of her.

.   .   .

Ottilie was working on autopilot. She knew it, and there was nothing she could do about it, and she only hoped that she wouldn't make any mistakes. Luckily, nobody arrived in her clinic with anything too difficult to deal with. Some patients rescheduled, having been hit by the flooding in their own homes and deciding that was the more pressing matter. The ones who came were so preoccupied with the state of the village, their neighbours' houses or their own, or where the water level was at the river, or how long the clean-up might take that they were barely interested in Ottilie's ministering anyway.

Downstairs, she could hear Victor and his sons-in-law trying to clear up the ground floor of the surgery. Fliss was using an old bedroom to see her most urgent cases, but it was far from ideal and she'd asked Lavender to put as many off as she could for that day at least, and possibly for the following few if she could get away with it. Poor Lavender was left ankle-deep in water downstairs, having to greet the patients who did make it and showing them what the new temporary arrangement was.

Lunchtime arrived. If she hadn't been still so shell-shocked by the day's events, Ottilie might have missed their usual get-together around the table in the old kitchen. Nobody had brought food and nobody was in the mood to sit and chat, even if they could have made use of the kitchen, which was still as soggy as everywhere else, despite Victor's best efforts.

'I could pop over to the shop and get us something to snack on,' Lavender offered from the doorway of Ottilie's makeshift treatment room.

'I'm not really hungry,' Ottilie replied.

'You must want something – even if you don't fancy it, you need a bit of fuel inside you. How about I see if they have a pasty or something? I'm sure Magnus would warm it for you in his microwave.'

Ottilie nodded, though she wasn't bothered either way. At least it seemed to make Lavender happy.

'I'll be back in a tick,' she said, hurrying towards the stairs.

Ottilie could hear Fliss talking in the next room. It sounded like a one-sided conversation, as if she might be on the phone. Ottilie pulled out her own and scrolled through some old emails, looking for the phone number of her home insurance. It was probably a good idea for her to make some phone calls too, and that was perhaps the most important one.

Twenty minutes later, Ottilie's phone call had ended. She'd been staring into space in the five minutes since, and it was only the sound of Lavender knocking on her door that snapped her out of it.

'Magnus didn't have any pasties so I got—' Lavender strode to the desk and dropped a white paper bag onto it. 'Ottilie... What on earth is the matter?'

'I'm fine.'

Lavender clicked her tongue against the roof of her mouth and frowned. 'Seriously? This is what fine looks like for you? I can see you're not fine. What's wrong? I mean, apart from the obvious. Has something else happened today? Because I know it's been a stressful one, but you weren't like this first thing.'

Ottilie wondered whether she'd simply been hiding it better first thing. But first thing she hadn't had a conversation with her home insurers that had ended in her being told that she wasn't covered for flooding. First thing she hadn't been staring down the fact that her home was conceivably damaged beyond what she could afford to fix, and first thing she wasn't contemplating the idea that she had no plan B. All her money, everything Josh had left her, had been sunk into the gorgeous cottage that was meant to be her new forever home, somewhere she could feel safe and start again without him. But what now? Now it was under water, and even when that was resolved – as it would naturally be, she supposed – what was she to do about the inevitable damage?

She tried to see it logically. She didn't yet know how much damage there was and it might not be so bad. But she was buckling already under the weight of everything that had gone before, and this was the final straw that everyone talked about, the one that would break her back.

'You should go home,' Lavender said. 'Let me ring round and cancel your appointments. It's bound to be on your mind and I'm sure Fliss will agree that you need to be on site, doing the necessary.'

'But there's nothing I can do, is there? Until the water goes, what is there to do?'

'I don't know, but there's no point in you being here.'

'You and Fliss are here, and you had flooding too.'

'Fliss has her other half on hand to deal with that, and so do I. You have—'

Lavender stopped mid-sentence, but it didn't matter, because Ottilie knew what she was about to say and it was true – she had nobody to help her. The thought of going home to face that mess alone seemed so overwhelming that she suddenly wanted to burst into tears. But she wouldn't allow that to happen.

'At least there's no more rain in the forecast, so with a bit of luck the levels will go down quickly,' Lavender added. 'That's a silver lining, isn't it?'

Fliss appeared at the doorway and looked pointedly at Ottilie. 'Are you still here? Surely none of your patients are so urgent they can't wait? You must want to go home and start sorting out?'

Ottilie fought harder to keep the tears at bay as she shook her head. 'I don't want to look at it. I don't know where to start. At least here I feel useful; I know what I'm doing. There... I feel so helpless.'

'Have you called your insurers?' Fliss asked.

'Yes.'

'Good, at least that's one thing you've dealt with. I can give you the number of a professional who might be able to help with the clean-up, and I'm sure Victor will bring his pump round as soon as he can. Everyone's in this together and we'll all help each other out. Chin up, Ottilie. It seems hopeless now, but in a few weeks we'll be dried out and decorated again and it will be like it never happened.'

Ottilie nodded, her throat tightening. She wanted to give words of appreciation, to thank Fliss for her encouragement, but she couldn't. Instead, her throat narrowed and her heart started to pound and the room began to spin around her, and though she pulled and pulled she couldn't get any air into her lungs. She knew what was happening to her and she knew how to stop it – she was a nurse after all – but she couldn't. It was like she'd left her body to drive itself, looking helplessly on from the side-lines as she gasped for air and her heart beat at twice the speed it was meant to.

And then Fliss's face was close to hers, calm and sure. 'Breathe... that's it, grab a hold of it and breathe...'

Ottilie wanted to, she really did, but she could only stare at Fliss, hearing her words but barely comprehending them.

'Ottilie!'

Fliss's hands were on her shoulders. She twisted to look at Lavender. 'Top drawer of my desk... little bottle of rescue drops. Nip and get them, would you?'

Lavender rushed off while Fliss turned back to Ottilie. She was in total control, her words calm, her tone measured. 'It'll pass in a minute, I promise. Try to breathe for me – I know it's hard, but try anyway.'

Ottilie closed her eyes. What was happening to her? She'd been anxious before, but never like this. And in the background there was shame. Whatever else was going on here, she didn't want Fliss to see her like this. She didn't want anyone to see her like this. She fought harder for control, trying to concentrate on slowing her breathing.

Lavender appeared a minute or so later and handed Fliss a tiny bottle.

'Open wide,' Fliss said to Ottilie before tipping a couple of drops of something on her tongue. 'Right, give it a minute. You'll be fine once it gets to work.'

Ottilie nodded, tears leaking from her eyes. She could hear Lavender tell Fliss she was going to make some calls. Perhaps they were going to cancel Ottilie's clinic after all. And much as she hated the idea, Ottilie had to admit she was in no state to see patients. She squeezed her eyes shut. Perhaps this was a terrible dream, and when she opened them again she'd wake and it would be over.

But when she opened them, Fliss was still studying her with real concern, and they were still upstairs in the makeshift treatment room because downstairs was too waterlogged, and she hadn't been dreaming at all.

CHAPTER EIGHTEEN

In truth, it was a sort of delay tactic. Ottilie knew that Stacey and Chloe's house had been spared from the floodwater because she'd spent the night there. And she knew that the village shop was safe, and that Victor and Corrine were out of the way up on their hill, and she knew that Lavender and Fliss – though affected – were more than capable of dealing with it. But as far as she knew, nobody had looked in on Flo. She needed to get back to her own house, especially as Fliss had gifted her a cut afternoon clinic so she could leave early to inspect the damage more fully, but she couldn't face it. Out of sight wasn't exactly out of mind, but she could pretend, just a little, that the problem wasn't waiting there for her, so she went home via Flo's house, wading through floodwater of differing levels depending on the terrain of that section of village, to see whether she was safe.

Flo had sandbags at the front door of her cottage. The water didn't look too high here either, so perhaps her foresight had spared her. Ottilie reflected ruefully on the fact that she hadn't taken Victor's advice more seriously and got some sandbags herself, although she hadn't a clue where she'd have got them from, and perhaps the water would have been too high for them to save Wordsworth Cottage anyway – the levels certainly seemed lower here than what she'd seen at her own house that morning.

Leaning over the sandbags, she knocked and called through the letterbox. 'Flo... are you home? It's Ottilie.'

Flo appeared a moment later holding a mop and looking about as disgruntled as Ottilie had ever seen her.

'I suppose you're another person who thinks I can't manage. People have been knocking all day. Honestly, I've been through worse than this and I'd clean it up a lot faster if you'd all leave me to it instead of bothering me every five minutes.'

'Sorry,' Ottilie said. 'I just wanted to know how bad it was and...' Her sentence tailed off. She'd been about to say she'd offer help, but Flo had made it very clear that she didn't want it, even if she might need it. Stubborn and independent to the end, even when her body told her differently; that was Flo – as Ottilie was fast learning.

'I would have thought you've got clearing up to do of your own,' Flo said, leaning on her mop and eyeing Ottilie critically. 'What are you bothering me for when your own place must be under water?'

'It is,' Ottilie said. 'At least, it was when I left it this morning.'

Flo stared at her. 'You haven't been there?'

'No, I had to work.'

'And Dr Cheadle made you stay? Well, I—'

'We still have patients who need care,' Ottilie said. 'It's not her fault. And there didn't seem any point being home anyway; not a lot I could do, because the water was just... well, just sitting there.' She glanced into the hallway behind Flo and could see that it was wet, but it looked as if the sandbag defences had kept the worst out, while Flo was mopping up the rest. 'Will your floors be ruined?'

'Might be. I'm hoping they'll dry out without too much damage. Lucky it was only a puddle here really. I would think it's worse where you are, closer to the river.'

Ottilie nodded. 'A bit.'

'Then I suggest you go home and see what's to be done. You've got insurance?'

Ottilie nodded but stopped short of telling Flo that it was absolutely no use in this case.

'At least it'll pay for any damage then. I haven't got any. My own stupid fault, but I couldn't afford it and couldn't see the point. Doubt it would have covered me for flooding anyway.'

If only Ottilie had checked more thoroughly. Now that she considered it, Wordsworth Cottage was so close to the river, it was obviously at risk, and obvious that no insurer would want to cover it for flooding. She'd been so eager, so desperate to make the move she'd hardly looked at any paperwork at all. For all she knew, she might not actually own Wordsworth Cottage.

'I think I'll have to wait for the water to recede at my place before I can clean up,' Ottilie said. 'So I might as well be giving you a hand here.'

'It won't go away just because you can't see it,' Flo said with a shrewd look.

'I know, but I might not feel so helpless if I can't see it. At least I can do something useful here – at my place, I'd be wading around with not a clue where to start.'

Flo was thoughtful for a moment, and then nodded. 'Come in. There's a spare mop in the cupboard under the stairs and I haven't managed to get the kitchen dry yet.'

Flo had been missing for ten minutes or so before Ottilie realised it. She went through from the kitchen to the hallway, wondering if she'd be finishing, but there was no sign of her. And then she noticed Flo's boots on the bottom stair, and heard muffled tones coming from the floor above. Flo must have been on the phone to someone. Perhaps she was trying to recruit more help after all. Maybe it was Heath – it seemed a safe bet. As far as Ottilie had seen, he was the only member of Flo's family she could rely on.

It was good – Ottilie was glad she was finally admitting to needing help, and at her age she needed to keep the stress to a minimum. She wondered how others in the village were managing – especially older or more vulnerable residents. Perhaps she ought to form some sort of village task force – if it hadn't been done already – to see how they could help those people. She was certain Victor and his family would help, Magnus and Geoff too, perhaps Fliss and her husband if they could spare the time from clearing their own places.

Ottilie went back to the kitchen. Maybe it would be useful to get Flo's thoughts on her plan when she came back downstairs.

'Cup of tea, I think,' Flo said as she returned.

Ottilie was closing the back door, having tipped a sludge-filled bucket down a drain, despite the fact that the drain was as waterlogged as the rest of the garden. But she couldn't tip it down the sink for fear of blocking it, and there didn't seem anywhere else remotely sensible to dispose of it.

'Let's have a break.'

Ottilie leaned on the mop and looked around. The floor was silt-covered, and though a lot of the water had been cleared, there was still much to do. If Flo's place looked like this after her working on it all day, Ottilie could only imagine how much it was going to take to do her own. And then she wished she hadn't thought about it, because it was still there, waiting for her when she left here, and she wanted to cry at how overwhelming the prospect was. If someone had offered to take Wordsworth

Cottage off her hands this minute, a straight swap for a nice house in a dry suburb of Manchester, like the one she'd lived in with Josh, she'd be sorely tempted to take it. Right now, Wordsworth Cottage didn't feel like her home; it only felt like a huge mess that she could do without.

'I think,' Ottilie said slowly, drawing a breath and looking up at Flo, 'that you're on your way to being a bit straight here, and you're right. I need to go and see what the damage is at my house. There's no point in putting it off any longer. I can come back later if you still need me?'

'Don't be daft – I didn't need you in the first place. I only let you stay because I could tell you didn't want to go home. But you ought to.'

'Will there be others in the village who might need help? I was thinking of getting together a little team of us to—'

'For once will you look to your own needs? Anyone who needs help will get it... and that includes you.'

'I don't need—'

'If you're about to say you don't need help, I'm going to thump you around the head with that mop you're holding. Now go. There must be a million things to sort out at your house.'

'Mostly where all the water is going to go.'

Flo nodded. 'If it's any consolation, I think the levels are going down already. If it stays dry the rest of the night and tomorrow it might go down enough. The house will still be damp but you'll have a better idea of what needs to be ripped out and binned and what you can save.'

Flo's tone was so practical Ottilie could hardly believe she was talking about a home. But perhaps practical was the only way anyone could be in this situation. And perhaps if Ottilie hadn't been sent a bombshell in the form of Faith's phone call that morning, she might have felt more practical about things too. As it was, she didn't know how much more of this she could take.

. . .

Ottilie dried her eyes as a second knock echoed through the house. She'd have been better off staying at Flo's because she'd been next to useless here at home. Never in her life had she looked at a situation and felt so utterly powerless to change it – except, perhaps, when she'd lost Josh, but even then it wasn't the same, because she hadn't been expected to do anything to change that.

She got up from the chair at the kitchen table, where she'd sat, water swirling around her boots, staring at the mess and – to her great annoyance – sobbing. It made her angry that she was crying, but it was one more thing that she was powerless to stop. It was like she was two different people – the Ottilie who could see that nothing was going to be fixed without facing her problems head-on, and the Ottilie who was wrung out like an old dishcloth, who had nothing left to give and was really past caring.

Wading to the front door, doing her best to look presentable, she noted the tidemarks along the base of the wall. There was a stripe of discoloured plaster, and that had to mean the water had receded enough to expose that, didn't it? Surely that was a good thing? She tried to be encouraged, because that would at least help to improve her mood to face whoever had called. She supposed it might be someone from the village coming to see if she needed assistance – perhaps Victor or Fliss or even Flo.

Her mouth must have dropped open as she answered the door, because Heath frowned slightly at the sight of her.

'Gran told me you might need some sandbags,' he said, nodding to a van.

'I didn't know you had a van,' she said, immediately feeling stupid for it.

'Borrowed it,' he replied, as if he thought it might not be the most obvious observation in the circumstances either. 'Can't get many sandbags in my car.'

'That's really kind of you, but I'm not sure they're much good now. The water's already in.'

'True,' he said, with more patience than Ottilie suspected he had, 'but if we can keep it at bay outside the house, we might stand a chance of clearing inside your house. Gran says Victor has a pump. So if we stop the outside water getting in we can pump out inside. It might be better than waiting for it to clear on its own – the longer everything is submerged, the more damage there's going to be. At least, that's how I see it.'

'Oh...' Ottilie glanced at the van and then looked back at him. Was that a grain of hope, taking root in her heart? There was certainly genuine concern in his face, unlike anything she'd seen there before; even when he'd come to rescue her and Flo from the hillside that time he hadn't looked so worried. 'Shall I help you get them from the van then?'

'I can do it.'

'No, I want to—'

'You must be exhausted. Sit in the van if you like while I sort it. It's dry and warm – put the radio on or something.'

'I can't do that.'

'Why not?'

'I wouldn't feel right watching you work and me sitting there. It is my house after all.'

He didn't argue – and on another occasion Ottilie might have found the easy loss of any chivalry quite amusing. He simply nodded towards the van. 'Come on then – let's get them down before the light goes.'

'I can't believe you drove all the way up from Manchester to bring these,' she said as she followed him down the path – more like a muddy stream right now. The water feature in her garden was probably about the driest bit.

'Neither can I,' he said. 'I'm missing a match for this.'

As he turned to her, she detected a hidden smile.

'Who's playing?'

'United.'

'Ah, not missing much then.'

His smile grew, clear and warm. Ottilie liked it. Perhaps it had something to do with him feeling like her saviour, but the idea had come from nowhere – she more than liked it. It might not be such a hardship to see a lot more of it.

'City fan then?'

'Of course.'

'Right. Is that only since they got good, or were you there for all the years of rubbish?'

'It's a family thing – it's in our DNA, so I can't help it.'

'Like an inherited illness, you mean?'

'Oi!'

For the first time that day Ottilie smiled. It was almost like her muscles had forgotten how, because it felt stiff and wrong, but it was there all the same.

The bags were heavy and Ottilie's feet were cold from hours inside wellies surrounded by water, but doing something useful made her feel brighter. Heath's company was helping too. Since their first meeting she hadn't known what to make of him – and she still didn't – but she felt as if she was starting to get some answers. He was a man who clearly answered a call for help. He was a hard worker and he put others first, and he would do anything for his gran, including driving from Manchester to the Lake District and missing a football match to help a woman he didn't really know, just because Flo had asked him to.

He'd gone to the trouble of borrowing a van and sourcing sandbags too at very short notice. She had to be impressed and a little touched by all that. Whatever else she discovered him to be, he seemed like a good man. She was getting attuned to his sense of humour too. She'd assumed he didn't have one until now, but today, as they worked together with the goal of securing her house, she realised that wasn't the case. He had a sense of humour; it just took work to understand. It was dry, like Flo's, and sometimes it was easy to miss when a comment was said with seriousness or when it was said as a joke.

They piled their defences high at both the front and back door, and there were some left over that Heath used to stopper sections where he thought water might creep back in again, such as low air bricks. By the time they were done, twilight was moving in.

'I can't thank you enough,' Ottilie said.

'What about inside?' Heath asked.

'I suppose I'd better start trying to bail it out. At least now I can do that with some hope that it might actually stay out. And I think the levels have been dropping anyway over the last few hours.'

'What about the pump from Daffodil Farm?'

Ottilie shook her head. 'I don't think it's fair to ask Victor to bring it at this hour. He's been up and down all day as it is, helping everyone else. I'll do what I can myself and then perhaps ask him tomorrow if I still need it.'

Heath looked past her into the hallway of Wordsworth Cottage. 'There's no way you can clear all that yourself tonight. I'll give you a hand.'

'You've done enough. I couldn't—'

'The longer it sits, the worse the damage will be. I know you think you can't, but you're going to have to swallow your pride. It makes no sense to send me away – we've already got this far; what's the point in any of this' – he kicked a sandbag – 'if you're going to leave the inside under water? We might as well not have bothered.'

Ottilie couldn't argue with his logic, but it wasn't in her nature to take advantage of people's kindness, and she said so.

'It's hardly taking advantage,' he said tersely. 'I offered. And besides' – he paused, looking embarrassed – 'I think I owe you the favour.'

'You don't owe me anything – you've done more than enough.'

'All right then, perhaps favour is the wrong word. It's more...' He shook his head. 'I don't know what the word is. I only know I got you wrong and I feel bad about it.'

'That's all forgotten – you don't need to worry about it.'

It hadn't been forgotten, but he'd more than made up for anything insensitive he'd said previously by being here today. For this, she was willing to forgive if not forget, but it didn't seem as if he could move past it quite as easily.

'Sometimes we get people wrong – that's how it is,' she said. 'As long as we're open to seeing them differently if we've got it wrong, so that we get it right... that's all that matters.'

'Still, I want to stay and help.'

'It's going to be a long night.'

'Well, that promise has never been made lacking so much fun before.'

Ottilie gave a small laugh. 'I'll bet. I won't lie; I'd appreciate a bit of help. Maybe I'll let you stay an hour or so.'

'Spoil me, why don't you?'

She gave a tired smile. There wasn't a lot to smile about, but his presence was making her feel she could manage the odd one. Glancing around, she could see there was still much to do, but with Heath there, for the first time that day, she was beginning to feel she could manage it.

CHAPTER NINETEEN

No matter how she'd looked at the problem, there didn't seem to be a solution. Nothing that was obvious to Ottilie, at any rate. It was quickly becoming apparent, even without a professional opinion, that the house was more damaged than she could afford to repair.

Way more.

There were cosmetic things, like sodden, discoloured wallpaper and paintwork and ruined carpets, but there were also things that looked more ominous, like crumbling plaster, warped woodwork and waterlogged floorboards. And that was just the obvious stuff. There were bound to be things she couldn't see or didn't understand. What about her wiring – was that safe? What about the foundations – were they compromised in some way?

She could remortgage, she supposed, or take a loan of some kind, and that wouldn't be so bad if the sums involved weren't potentially huge enough to terrify her. She'd started to hear gossip in the village, reports of what others were having to find to fix their own flood damage, and some were running into tens of thousands. And what if she went through all that, found the money, fixed the house, only to be flooded again? What then? There was only so much money she could borrow.

She'd gone to film club that evening despite everything, because it was better than moping in her stinking, silt-stained house, but she'd struggled to enjoy it. Nobody seemed to have noticed, however, and she was glad of that much. As for the others, spirits were remarkably high, given that many of them were dealing with the aftermath of the floods too. Maybe they had more of a plan than she had, or maybe they were all pretending just like her.

Magnus and Geoff, as they always did, had opened a couple of bottles of wine and laid out nibbles. Ottilie had apologised for not contributing, but Magnus had simply thrown his arms around her in a tight hug.

'My goodness! You don't need to apologise for anything! I'm glad you're here.'

Poor Magnus. He'd spent most of the evening overcompensating, telling her how sorry he was for his flippantly delivered and disastrous advice the day she'd come to see him about sandbags. She'd told him every time that it wasn't his fault, but she could see that he didn't believe that for a minute. It was obvious he suspected that, on some level, she did blame him, and it didn't matter how many times she reassured him otherwise, he'd probably always believe that. Ottilie got it; she'd have blamed herself too had the tables been turned.

Lavender shot her a glance of understanding as Magnus came over for the fifth or sixth time since the film had finished and they'd all got together to discuss it with their drinks and nibbles, to see if she was all right and if she needed more food or more drink, but really, just to keep the subtext going.

Lavender had warned her this would happen. Lavender had already warned her that Magnus had been up and down the village telling anyone who'd listen how bad he felt, as if he'd somehow ordered the river to overfill. At this point, Ottilie was so tired of thinking about the flood she was almost sick of hearing Magnus's apologies. She didn't want or need them – she only wanted to find a way out of the situation it had left her in.

She'd confided this to Lavender – not that it was a secret of any sort – but she hadn't been able to bring herself to admit that she wasn't covered on her house insurance and that it was completely her fault. She felt stupid for not checking, and she was certain everyone else would think her stupid too. And she hadn't yet told anyone how desperate her finances were now that she had to find so much money to fix the damage, and that she was increasingly of the opinion that her only option was to cut her losses and sell Wordsworth Cottage. It would have to be at a knockdown price, because the new owners would have to spend all the money she couldn't on making it habitable again, and with the proceeds, Ottilie doubted she'd get another suitable house in the Lakes. She'd have to go where she could afford to live but felt certain it would be closer to Manchester, and would mean leaving Thimblebury and her job as their village nurse behind.

It felt like a bitter prospect after she'd worked so hard to settle here, but she'd learned that life was often like that and there was no use in complaining about it. At least, that was what she told herself. The reality she had to deny every morning was that to leave Thimblebury, just when she'd started to feel like she belonged, might break her. She'd lost too much already to lose this. She'd grown to love this quirky, time-trapped, sometimes silly little village, the glorious rolling hills surrounding it, the glittering lakes on her doorstep, the cottage gardens stuffed with flowers. Even the river that had caused so much damage was a beautiful, meandering current, lined with reeds and willows and yellow marsh flowers and wildlife the likes of which Ottilie had never seen.

She loved her new friends, her job – and she'd grown weirdly fond of hearing how great the previous nurse, Gwen, was, because she hoped it meant that one day they'd all be telling her replacement how great she was. Not because she was great, but because she saw that when Thimblebury took you in, it really took you in. Being a part of this village was to have the maddest extended family, a bunch of people who would do anything for you and love you to the end. She'd never known community like this before and she doubted she would again. They'd found her when she'd needed them most, and how could she leave them now?

Stacey came with her drink. 'How are you doing there?' she asked gently.

Ottilie forced a smile, pushing her melancholy to one side. There would be a time for misery later, when she was alone, not now amongst people who were trying so hard to be there for her. 'The film cheered me up.'

'Did it?' Stacey looked cynical, and at this, Ottilie couldn't help a short laugh.

'OK, you got me. It took my mind off things, at least.'

'I don't believe that either.'

'OK, then while I was here looking at that I couldn't be at home looking at the tidemarks on my walls – that do you?'

'That's what I thought.' Stacey patted a hand on Ottilie's arm. 'Have you had anyone in to quote yet?'

Ottilie reached for a tortilla chip from a bowl – not because she wanted it, but because she wanted to pretend this wasn't bothering her as much as it was. At home she was barely eating for the worry, but she didn't want anyone else to know that. 'You mean someone to give me a cost for the flood damage?'

Stacey nodded.

'I don't even know who to get in.' Ottilie nibbled on the chip. 'How do I know who to call until I can see what needs doing?'

'Have your insurers sent round an assessor yet? Surely they'd be able to tell you what needs doing. Sometimes they can send the appropriate people to you as well – I'm pretty sure they have approved tradesmen on their books for this sort of thing.'

'Is that what they do? I've never had to get one in before. I suppose it'll get sorted one way or another,' she added carefully. 'It's not really dry yet.'

'Isn't it?' Stacey gave a grimace of sympathy. 'It must have been bad at your place then. Almost everyone else seems to be drying out.'

Ottilie shrugged. 'It still smells musty, so I assumed it was still wet. I've never been flooded before, so I don't know how it works.'

'Why don't I come round tomorrow and—'

'It's fine,' Ottilie said, perhaps too testily, because Stacey looked taken aback. If she was puzzled by Ottilie's reaction she didn't say so, and Ottilie instantly regretted her tone. 'I'm sorry. It's just been stressful, you know? And I realise it's been stressful for everyone and I'm not a special case or anything. I know you're trying to help but...'

Where did she begin? Of course it had been stressful for everyone else, so how come it seemed to Ottilie that everyone else was coping so much better than she was? She could blame it on the added burdens in her life, but that didn't seem fair. Didn't everyone have added burdens that weren't always apparent to their friends and neighbours? That was life, wasn't it?

'We all want to help, if you'll let us,' Stacey said.

Ottilie shook her head. 'People have got enough going on in their own lives without worrying about mine.'

'Is that how it was in Manchester?'

'That's how it is the world over, isn't it?'

'I don't know much about the rest of the world, but that's not how we do things here.'

'Maybe, but I've got it covered.'

Stacey's look of scepticism grew. Again, she looked as if she wanted to air her doubts, but if she truly had them, she didn't.

'OK then,' she replied instead. 'That's good then. Just know that if you need help you only have to ask.'

'I've had so much help already. Even Flo's grandson has been round helping me to clean.'

Stacey's eyes lit up and Ottilie could have sworn she saw mischief there. 'Not you as well,' she groaned.

'What?' Stacey painted on a look of innocence. 'No clue what you're talking about.'

'Flo seems intent on matching us up. I can do without the rest of you joining in.'

'But he is good-looking.'

'Yes, I haven't failed to notice that.'

'I mean, you'd have to be dead not to notice that. And he's single.'

'Newly single and very messed up from it, as far as I can tell.'

'Why, what's he said?'

'It's more what everyone else says. Victor said his wife was a nightmare; Flo had a few choice words too. And you can tell how untrusting he is – you know he accused me of being after Flo's money?'

'Jesus!'

'I couldn't have put it better myself.'

'I know his wife was a bit of a gold digger, but even so. You're right – does sound like there are some whopping trust issues there.'

'And I might feel sorry for him if she was, but I don't have the time or energy to go down that particular rabbit hole.'

Stacey smiled slowly. 'I still think you might be exactly the person he needs.'

Ottilie's laugh was louder than she'd intended and a few people turned to look her way with some confusion. But Stacey's suggestion had thrown her a curveball. There were people who might be able to help banish Heath's demons, but certainly not her. She had plenty of demons of her own – very different from Heath's, she'd imagine, but there all the same. The last thing she needed was to add another heap of angst to her own.

She straightened her face and looked at Stacey. 'Have you ever had a conversation with him?'

'A bit of one – I don't suppose anything more than ten minutes, when he's been visiting Flo. Why?'

'If you had, you'd realise what hard work he is. I mean, don't get me wrong, I'm grateful that he came to help me out of a tight spot, and his company wasn't completely awful, but small doses is a phrase I'd definitely apply to him. I don't know if he was always like that but, if not, his ex-wife did a real number on him. And if he was, then I can sort of see why the marriage ended.'

'It was her fault.'

'So Flo says...' Ottilie lowered her voice. Even though Florence had elected to give this film-club meeting a miss, she still didn't want her words to get back to her via someone else. 'But she's going to say that, isn't she? She's always going to side with him because she dotes on him. Wouldn't any grandmother side with her grandson?'

'Flo's not like that; she calls a spade a spade.'

'I'd be inclined to agree, but even the most pragmatic people can have a blind spot when it comes to family. Anyway, it doesn't matter who did what. I'm not interested in the slightest.'

'I would be.'

Ottilie could have mentioned that Stacey had been alone for a long time and that she'd made no secret of her loneliness, or the fact that she would welcome some romance in her life, but she didn't. And the fact remained that Ottilie herself was nowhere near that stage in her own life yet. For her, a forced single life was still very new and painful, and she was in no emotional state to think about starting anew with anyone else, least of all someone who seemed as damaged as Florence's dour and difficult grandson. Her situation was very different from Stacey's, and so perhaps that was why Stacey didn't seem to understand it.

'Well, good luck if you decide to go there.'

'If only he was interested in me. I'm far too old for him, for a start.'

'Stacey, you're gorgeous and funny and he'd be lucky if you looked at him twice. As for too old, you're what...? About forty?'

Stacey laughed. 'Forty-nine and far too old.'

'Forty-nine is still sexy.'

'Try telling that to the men of Tinder.'

'I'm not talking about Tinder – I don't need to go on there to be sure it's full of arseholes. I'm talking about real life. The love of your life is waiting out there for you... and definitely not on Tinder.'

Stacey grinned. 'Even Chloe says that and her generation are all about Tinder, aren't they?'

'How is she, by the way?'

'Still in denial but getting bigger by the day – big enough to tell now. It seems to have happened all at once.'

'I bet she's thrilled by that.'

Stacey laughed. 'Absolutely. I suppose that's one thing about me not having a man – at least I'll have time to be a proper nan to the little one. And Chloe will need me to be there for her.'

'She's lucky to have you.'

'Try telling her that.'

'Before or after I've told the men of Tinder?'

Stacey nudged her. 'I'm glad you moved here. I know it wasn't a good reason that brought you, but I like you being here.'

Ottilie gave a pained smile. That might soon change, and Stacey's words would make her inevitable decision harder than ever.

CHAPTER TWENTY

Fliss let the letter drop onto Ottilie's desk. 'What's this?'

Ottilie looked up to see Fliss looking visibly upset. She'd never seen her like that in all the time she'd been working with her.

'Why?' Fliss demanded.

'Um...' Ottilie was thrown by Fliss's tone. 'I didn't think... well, I haven't even worked my trial period yet and...'

'You don't like the job?'

'I love the job, but I didn't think my resignation would be a problem.'

'Of course it's a problem, but that isn't the issue. If you love the job, then what?'

'I want to go home.'

'I thought Thimblebury was home. I thought you liked it here.'

'I do.'

'Then I don't understand. You like the job, you like the place. So what's going on?'

'Nothing. It's just...' Ottilie floundered.

'So all that stuff you said when you first arrived about

wanting a new start and being determined to make this one work was...'

'I meant it and I tried, but I just don't think it's working out.'

Fliss paused, and Ottilie could see her resetting her emotions. 'Is this to do with the floods?'

'A bit.'

'So you're going to let a freak storm drive you away?'

'It's not like that.'

'Then explain it please. I don't want to lose you, Ottilie, so if you explain it to me, perhaps I can help.'

'You'll get another nurse soon—'

'I don't want another nurse. We work well together, don't we? Brilliantly, in fact. I'd say so – wouldn't you?'

'I've hoped so, yes.'

'Then why would I want a new nurse? There has to be more than what you're telling me, because this' – she flung a hand at the letter – 'makes no sense.'

'I can't stay, even if I want to, that's all.'

'Can't or won't?'

'Can't. I want to; I really do.'

Fliss studied her for a moment. She glanced at the letter and then back at Ottilie with something like betrayal in her eyes. Ottilie had never imagined this would bother her boss as much as it seemed to.

'I'm not going to accept this without a better reason than anything you've given me so far. And let me tell you people round here will be devastated. They won't forgive you. They've just come round to you being a replacement for Gwen. You've worked so hard towards that; I can't believe you'd throw it all away.'

'I know.'

Everything Fliss was saying made sense – it was how Ottilie felt too. But this was the way things had to be. She couldn't saddle herself with the kind of debt fixing Wordsworth Cottage would create so the only option she could see was to accept the kind offer of moving in with her aunt in Manchester until she found a cheaper place. There were towns in Cheshire that were far more affordable, some with big hospitals desperate for nurses, and though the prospect didn't thrill her, a move to one of those seemed like the most sensible solution. It would leave her debt-free and enable her to swallow the losses she was bound to suffer from the sale of an imperfect house here.

She looked up at Fliss. 'What do you want me to say?'

'I don't know, but I'm not accepting your resignation.'

'You have to, because I'm leaving.'

'Then we have a problem, because I won't.'

Fliss swept out of the office without letting Ottilie get another word in. Not that there was any point – they'd reached a stalemate anyway and Fliss didn't seem in the mood to back down. What the hell had just happened? Ottilie had imagined that Fliss might be a bit put out, annoyed perhaps that she'd have to begin another recruitment process when she'd not long got Ottilie in post, but she'd imagined that resigning would be a lot simpler than this.

Almost as soon as Fliss had left, Lavender knocked and, without waiting for a reply, walked in. She dropped a wad of correspondence onto the desk next to where Fliss had left Ottilie's resignation letter.

'Thanks for putting her in such an excellent mood,' she said flatly. 'You might have warned me you were planning to land that on her.'

'I didn't think she'd take it so badly.'

'Then you haven't been paying attention.'

'I don't know why; it's nothing personal. People leave their jobs all the time.'

'She likes you and she was hoping she'd be able to work with you until her retirement. She trusts you as much as she trusted Gwen, and that's hard to find.'

'But I was never guaranteed to stay that long.'

'Buying a house here was a fairly good indicator as far as Fliss is concerned.'

'But work isn't like that, is it? People come and go; that's how it is.'

'Not in Thimblebury they don't – at least not as often as that. Fliss doesn't like change very much. Why do you think a doctor as good as she is still works here in this tiny surgery after all these years? Because she likes to feel settled and she likes what she knows. She likes you and she wants to keep you, and she doesn't want all the hassle of recruiting again.' Lavender folded her arms, studying Ottilie. She shook her head slowly. 'I don't get it. I thought you liked it here.'

Ottilie tried not to sigh. Hadn't she just had this conversation with Fliss? 'I do like it.'

'Then why are you going? If it's the flood, then you have to understand that's not normal for round here—'

'But it happened. Who's to say it won't happen again? It doesn't matter whether it ever happened before, because it might. I know now that it *can*.'

'It won't!'

The sigh Ottilie had been holding on to came out. She didn't want to end her time here in a cloud of animosity, but that was what she seemed to be building. Time for the truth? It was the only way to make people understand, even if telling it was going to be awkward.

'I can't afford to stay. My house insurance doesn't cover flood damage and I don't have enough money to repair it even if I knew where to start – which I don't. The sensible thing – really my only option, as far as I can see – is to sell up. And as I won't get what I paid for the house because of the damage, I won't be able get anything like it close by,. So I have to look further afield.'

'Further afield? Such as?'

'I don't know where exactly. There might be parts of Manchester I can afford. Perhaps bits of Cheshire or Staffordshire. That's something I need to figure out.'

'Then why give your notice in so soon?'

'Because...' Ottilie swallowed a tidal wave of emotion that had sprung suddenly from nowhere. 'Because the longer I leave it, the worse it will be. It's hard enough to go as it is, without prolonging the agony. So I'm going to go and stay with my aunt in Manchester for a while. She's got a spare room I can have until I've sold Wordsworth Cottage and found a new place.'

'Hmm.'

While Lavender was silent, deep in thought, Ottilie felt the weight of her secret lift. It had been a silly, pointless secret – she realised how silly now that she'd said it. There was no shame in what had happened – even though some might say she had only her lack of attention to blame, because it was true that if she'd read the small print of her insurance policy she wouldn't be in this predicament – but she was certain she wasn't the first person to be guilty of not reading something properly. And she supposed if she had read it, she might have thought twice about buying Wordsworth Cottage, and for all the hardship the flood had brought, she wouldn't swap her time here in Thimblebury for anything.

'What if we could fix it?' Lavender asked finally.

'Fix what? The house?'

Lavender nodded. 'You'd stay then?'

'Of course I would! But I've already told you—'

'I know – you don't have the money. I still think there has to be a way around it. There has to be a better solution than you moving away. If you want to stay, like you say you do, then we need to find a way to help you do that.'

'It's going to cost a fortune.'

'There might be a way to do it that doesn't. How much, realistically, do you think you have to spare?'

Ottilie was thoughtful for a moment. 'I don't honestly know. But I don't imagine it would be enough, and I couldn't accept money from any of you.'

'We wouldn't expect you to. But we might be able to call in favours. If you won't accept money, would you be able to accept time, expertise and assistance?'

'People have their own repairs to look to – they don't have time for mine.'

'We'll see,' Lavender said, eyeing the resignation letter on the desk. And then, just like Fliss, she flounced out without giving Ottilie a chance to pursue the conversation any further.

Ottilie's own gaze went to the letter, lying open on the desk, the words she'd chosen so carefully that morning typed neatly on the page. Not knowing what else to do with it, for the time being at least, she decided to fold it up and put it in a drawer. She'd have to choose another moment – a better one, when Fliss might be more receptive – to try again. Perhaps when she'd had time to come round to the idea that Ottilie would be leaving. Fliss knew now that it was on her mind, so she'd be ready when Ottilie presented the letter to her again. And Ottilie would be more forceful too. Much as she loved the idea of Lavender's plan, it wasn't realistic. As she'd just told her colleague, people had their own worries; they weren't about to get involved with Ottilie's, no matter how much they wanted her to stay.

'I've got a bone to pick with you.' Flo sat across from Ottilie and plonked her basket on the desk.

'I know your test results have been a bit longer than I thought they—'

'Not that,' Flo cut in. 'What's this about you selling up?'

'Oh, that...' Ottilie had to be impressed at how fast word got round, even if she was taken aback by Flo's sudden confrontation. She would have asked who'd told Flo, but there didn't seem a lot of point. Half the village would know from one source or another, and the other half would know by teatime. 'Can we talk about that later? Like maybe not in clinic time?'

'Why isn't Dr Cheadle giving me my results?'

'She really only sees you about tests if there's anything to worry about.'

'You said there was.'

'That's not exactly what I said. I said I wanted to be certain.'

'And?'

'Well, the ones you've had so far haven't shown anything that concerns us. So that's good, right? You'll be able to put your family's minds at rest.'

'Like they'd care,' Flo sniffed.

'I think Heath might,' Ottilie said patiently.

'Right.' Flo seemed to soften at the mention of her grandson. 'So it's true?'

'What is?'

'You're moving away?'

'Yes,' Ottilie said, not seeing the point in trying to hide it any longer.

'Fat lot of good it was getting to know you then. If you'd said you were only going to be here for five minutes I wouldn't have bothered. Total waste of time – and I don't have much of that left at my age. We're not that bad, are we?'

'Of course not!'

'I don't know what's so good in Manchester that you're pining to go back. I don't know why anyone would pine to live there. Heath is all in love with the place too. Dirty Manchester. Wouldn't catch me living there.'

'When did you last go to Manchester?' Ottilie asked, trying not to laugh.

'1979. Didn't like it at all.'

'I think it might have changed a bit since then.'

'Yes, well, a leopard never changes its spots.'

Ottilie was fairly certain that proverb was aimed at people rather than cities, but there was probably no point in telling Flo that.

Flo sniffed again. 'It's always the way. Everyone leaves in the end.'

'I don't want to leave, and I'll stay in touch.'

'No you won't. Everyone says that and they don't.'

'I promise I will.'

Flo got up. 'So I don't need to bother with any more tests?'

'I don't know. Are you still having your funny turns?'

Flo opened her mouth but then paused. 'I am.'

'Oh.' Ottilie gestured for her to sit down again, but Flo picked up her basket. 'I need more from you than that if we're going to do something about them.'

'What's the point? You won't be here to take me to the hospital.'

'Someone will take you.'

'What do you care either way? You won't be here. No... if I'm going to fall off my perch, then so be it. I'm old anyway – bound to happen sooner rather than later. Perhaps people will realise they miss me when I'm gone.'

'Flo, please...' Ottilie began, but Florence swept out of the room in much the same way as Fliss and Lavender had done earlier that morning. Déjà vu didn't even begin to cover today, and it was only eleven thirty. Who else might be queuing up to tell her how disappointed they were that she was leaving? She'd never imagined there'd be so much fuss; it wasn't like she was Thimblebury born and bred or anything. People would move away from the street she'd lived in with Josh in Manchester and she'd hardly notice they'd gone. If anything, all this fuss made it harder still. This was precisely what she'd come to Thimblebury looking for, and here she was, thinking of leaving it all behind. She began to wonder if she might be persuaded to listen to Lavender's plans to keep her there after all.

CHAPTER TWENTY-ONE

Corrine wasn't taking no for an answer, and Victor was backing her the whole way. Ottilie had used every excuse she had not to accept their offer. Deep down, she wanted to. Despite feeling overwhelmed by their generosity and undeserving of such kindness, she wanted to accept all the offers that had been made since Flo and Lavender had galvanised the entire village into action. It was a way out she hadn't seen coming.

The socially acceptable thing was to thank people for their kind offers but refuse them anyway. But Ottilie realised that the time for socially acceptable was gone. Desperate circumstances called for desperately impolite measures. She could stay with Corrine and Victor at Daffodil Farm – they seemed keen enough, and she knew how indebted they felt to her. She could allow spare hands to rip out all that was rotten and waterlogged from Wordsworth Cottage and replace it with new – it would cost, of course, but it would cost an amount she might be able to stretch to, rather than something that would bankrupt her. She could do all that and her problems would be solved, but she didn't know how she could live with the sense of obligation afterwards. She'd owe everyone so much, a debt that she could never repay. She'd never been one for that sort of thing, always making her own way where she could. Accepting help didn't come easily.

'The way I see it,' Corrine said, putting a cup of tea down in front of Ottilie, 'it's silly to say no. It's not just that we don't want you to leave – I have a selfish reason too.'

Ottilie didn't imagine Corrine having a selfish bone in her, but she simply gave a tense smile as she reached for the teacup.

'You know all about my cancer,' Corrine said. 'If we had a new nurse, I'd have to start from scratch with them.'

'They'd only have to read your notes to be up to speed,' Ottilie said. 'And quite honestly, I won't be that involved in your treatment anyway from here on in. Most of it will be at the hospital.'

'But you'll be looking in to check on my cuts?' Corrine took a seat across from her.

'Cuts?'

'You know, when they cut this damned spot out and patch me up. Someone will have to check on me to make sure it's not infected or anything, won't they?'

'Any competent nurse will be able to do that.'

Corrine shot a look at Victor.

'Corrine would feel better if it was you,' he put in, seemingly at her bidding, though she was perfectly able to say so herself.

'You found my spot after all,' Corrine added.

'You found your spot,' Ottilie said. 'I only advised you to do what I'm sure you would have done eventually anyway, which was to go and see Dr Cheadle. Much as I'd love to take credit for it, I can't.'

'I don't like to say it,' Victor offered gruffly, 'but I think you're cutting off your nose to spite your face.'

Ottilie turned to him. 'How do you mean?'

'You like Thimblebury, don't you?'

'Yes.'

'And you like working with the doctor and Lavender?'

'Yes.'

'And we've got a fix for your house, so I don't see the problem. Nobody wants money off you, if that's what you're worried about.'

'No,' Ottilie said. 'I didn't think that... and you'd deserve to be paid for your work – that's partly the problem. I feel awful having everyone do all that for me for nothing.'

'It's not for nothing,' Victor said. 'It's because we all want you to stay.'

Ottilie looked from Corrine's hopeful face to Victor's more pragmatic expectation, and then gave in. Why was this even a question? Of course she wanted to stay. She didn't want to go back to Manchester or some industrial town in Cheshire or Staffordshire where she didn't know anyone and she'd have to give up the glorious landscape she woke up to every morning.

'OK,' she said finally. 'But you must let me pay you some rent for staying here.'

'You can try,' Corrine said with a smile. 'But you'll find it back in your purse again if you do. So that's that. Come on – eat your cake. There's plenty more where that came from.'

Victor leaped down from the cab of his tractor with far more agility than a man of his age ought to have. Ottilie almost burst out laughing at the sight of it.

'I didn't realise you were bringing the heavy artillery,' she called as she closed the back door of Daffodil Farm behind her and went to join him. Corrine had made them both a packed lunch, which Ottilie had in her bag. She'd moved into their guest room the previous day with enough of her belongings to do the few weeks they'd anticipated she might be there, but had been due on shift at the surgery, and so this was the first oppor-

tunity they'd had to start work on her house. Fliss had granted
her some annual leave and brought a locum nurse in to enable
Ottilie to get stuck in – anything, she'd said pointedly, if it
meant not having to recruit another new nurse.

Ottilie had been reluctant to do this, even sceptical about
what anyone could achieve on the little money she had spare,
but now she was excited. It felt good to be doing something
positive and she couldn't wait to get her hands dirty with the
rest of the wonderful people who had volunteered their time. It
was like that DIY programme on the TV where an entire
community helped to do up someone's house – a programme
that had often reduced Ottilie to tears, and in the past much to
Josh's amusement – only this time she was the unbelievably
lucky recipient of all that kindness and goodwill.

'Tractor will be ideal to do the heavy lifting. No point in
having it stood there in the barn if I can't put it to good use now
and then. All right getting up there?' he added, nodding at
the cab.

It was then that she noticed a passenger seat. 'We're both
going down in the tractor?'

'Don't see why not. Better than walking, isn't it?'

Ottilie started to laugh. 'I didn't see this coming when I
woke up today. Yes, I should be able to get up there – just
about.'

Victor opened the door for her but let her climb up by
herself. It took more effort than she'd imagined, and once she
was up there it felt as if she was on top of a house.

'This is the first time I've ever been in a tractor,' she said,
grinning as Victor got in beside her. 'I feel like a kid!'

'Buckled up?' he asked.

'Yes.'

'Right then.'

Victor turned the key and the engine roared into life. Deep
and loud, it reverberated through Ottilie's chest. The child in

her was well and truly woken, and it was a welcome distraction from all that awaited at her house as the vehicle started to rattle across the fields, its vast wheels churning up mud at either side.

'I bet your daughters loved this when they were little!' Ottilie shouted over the engine.

Victor nodded. 'When they were small, but they soon got bored of it. Was a time I thought neither of them would take to farming and they might move away.'

'From the Lakes?'

He nodded again.

Ottilie's thoughts went to Chloe, who told anyone who would listen how desperate she was to get away from Thimblebury. Photos and dreamy footage of places like this on the television had often prompted conversations between her and Josh about whether it was the sort of place they'd like to bring up children in. It had never been a serious question, merely idle speculation, and starting a family had always been a thing they'd pushed back because their lives were too busy, or they didn't have enough money, or their careers were at critical junctures. They'd both always said they wanted children, but the time had never seemed right to try.

Now she was here, she felt that – at least while they were little – it would be an amazing place to bring up a family, but she was beginning to see that what seemed idyllic to her might not be to a youngster who needed more excitement than Thimblebury could offer. She could name a handful of people just off the top of her head who'd witnessed loved ones moving away. She thought about all the plans she'd been making for projects like the mother and baby group before disaster had struck the village. All on hold for the time being, but would they make any difference to people like Chloe in the end? Would something like that make Chloe feel less isolated, less cut off from the wider world? Ottilie would never say it to Stacey, but she could see a day when Chloe would leave, baby or not, and perhaps, to a certain extent, she understood it.

'It's a good day for it,' Victor said.

Ottilie looked at the sky through the mud-splattered windscreen of the tractor. Blue as the day she'd first arrived but warmer, the sun higher. She wondered if the heatwave that had caused the downpour would return. It would dry things out, as long as it didn't bring another storm.

'Don't you worry,' he added, perhaps sensing her misgivings. 'We'll have you sorted and back at home in no time.'

Magnus and Geoff were waiting outside Wordsworth Cottage, having arrived way before anyone else was due.

Ottilie frowned as she climbed down from the tractor.

'Who's minding the shop?'

'Chloe,' Geoff said. 'She wanted a bit of ready cash and we wanted to be here, so it was a win-win.'

'It might be the first time she's ever wanted to look after the shop for us,' Magnus said, laughing. 'She must be desperate.'

'Or she just really likes you,' Geoff said. 'I know with Chloe, it's not always obvious.'

Silently, Ottilie agreed. Chloe was a pretty closed book for the most part, but whatever her motives for agreeing to look after the shop, she was grateful to have Magnus and Geoff here. Every extra hand would make a huge difference. The fact that they'd trusted Chloe with the shop also spoke volumes of their desire to somehow make things right with Ottilie. It didn't matter how many times she told him otherwise, Magnus still blamed himself for the fact that so much damage had been done to Ottilie's house during the storm.

'Thank you,' Ottilie said.

'What for?' Geoff asked. 'We haven't done anything yet.'

'And you haven't seen his DIY skills – or lack of them,' Magnus said, hooking a thumb at Geoff.

'Don't need DIY skills to rip out some rotten old floorboards,' Victor said cheerfully as he pocketed the keys to the tractor and joined them. 'A bit of elbow grease will do the trick.'

'He hasn't got any of that either,' Magnus said, and Geoff nudged him with mock affront, but then grinned.

'Well I'm happy you're here,' Ottilie said. 'Extra hands are appreciated. I don't know what I would have done if everyone hadn't been so kind.'

'We do,' Victor said. 'You'd have buggered off.'

Magnus nodded. 'So we all get something out of it, because it means you're staying in Thimblebury.'

Ottilie still wasn't used to this kind of affection from people who, really, she barely knew, and it constantly surprised her, but it filled her with warmth just the same. She could never have imagined when she'd packed up her house in Manchester to come here that there could be such an incredible, welcoming community waiting for her. She'd never imagined a community like this could exist anywhere except cosy afternoon films or romance novels, and yet, here it was. People said the world was harder these days, people more selfish and self-absorbed, and perhaps that was true, but Thimblebury showed that it wasn't quite that bad everywhere.

'Good morning!'

They all turned to see Fliss's husband, Charles, walking the lane towards them. Ottilie had only met him once, briefly. He worked long hours for an accountancy firm, and as he didn't live with Fliss was often missing whenever Ottilie called round to her house. He was quite handsome, in a nerdy-older-man sort of way, rocking up in a strange combination of overalls and smart tweed jacket, his grey hair short everywhere apart from one long section at the front that he swept back and gelled in place.

'Is this where I sign up for hard labour?' he asked.

'You've come to help?' Ottilie asked.

'I haven't come to stand around watching,' Charles replied with a chuckle. 'Although that might be entertaining. Fliss told me your predicament and I have a few hours to spare this morning, so here I am. I'm quite looking forward to flexing my muscles – it'll make me feel all manly. It might make Fliss think I'm all manly too, and after thirty-five years of marriage I'm all for new ways of impressing her. She's a very hard woman to impress, you know.'

Victor grinned. 'I'll bet. The best always are. We're glad to have any hours you can spare.'

'I don't know what to say.' Ottilie gave him a warm smile. 'Thank you.'

Victor turned to look up the road, and Ottilie was suddenly aware of a rumbling sound. A few seconds later, the outline of another tractor was visible, making its way down the narrow lane towards them.

'This'll be our Leon,' he said as the tractor drew closer.

Ottilie racked her brain for a moment, trying to place Leon. Most likely it was the husband of one of Victor's daughters, but as yet the opportunities to get to know them had been fewer than they had with others, so she'd only met them once or twice, as she had Fliss's husband. They'd seemed agreeable enough on the occasions that she had, but both Penny and Melanie and their husbands kept their own company up on their own farmhouses on Victor's land and rarely came down to socialise in the village.

'What time do you call this?' Victor hailed him as he got down from his tractor cab, and Ottilie wondered whether they'd have to open a new tractor park outside her house, and how anyone with a car was going to get past.

'Dog got out again,' Leon said, nodding at everyone else. 'Penny was busy with the kids, so I had to chase him down. Daft as a brush, that one – found him trying to get in with your girls.

I think that breeder was lying when he told us he was a sheep-dog; no intention of herding anything, just wants to play.'

'At least you got him,' Victor said.

As they all caught up on pleasantries, Victor's other son-in-law, Damien, arrived, and then Stacey – much to Ottilie's surprise and delight – and then, just as they were all about to go inside and make a start, there was one last arrival. Ottilie's sharp intake of breath was almost audible as he found a space to park his car and got out.

'I'm not late, am I?'

'Well, well…' Victor went over to clap him on the back. 'Heath Reynolds, as I live and breathe! How are you? Haven't seen you in donkey's!'

'Yeah, I know,' Heath said, glancing Ottilie's way for the briefest instant before turning back to Victor. 'How's everything at the farm? I heard about Corrine. I'm sorry—'

'No need!' Victor said. 'Corrine will be right as rain in no time, thanks to Ottilie here catching it early.'

'I didn't—' Ottilie began, but Victor put a hand up.

'Stop with that modesty. Everyone knows if you hadn't told her to go straight down to Dr Cheadle things could have been a whole lot worse. Now then, are we all going to stand around here like a Sunday school meeting or are we going to get cracking on that there house?'

There was a murmur of approval before Victor – who seemed to have been unofficially designated site foreman – began to direct people to equipment and to delegate tasks. Ottilie looked Heath's way, and found he was paying close attention to her. In the silliest, most guilty way, both looked hurriedly away again.

'I'd have thought you'd have had enough of my house,' she said once she got a moment to speak to him.

'Gran told me all about the plan, and, well, she's fond of you and you've been very good to her. She was upset that you might have to leave. She asked me if I could come, and of course I said yes.'

Ottilie gave him a grateful smile, though it was tinged with bemusement. 'It's nice that you're doing this for her.'

'Not just her,' he said briskly, striding off clutching a claw hammer before Ottilie had the chance to ask what he meant.

CHAPTER TWENTY-TWO

Ottilie was settling into life at Daffodil Farm so quickly that she wondered if she might not want to go back home when the work on her cottage was done. She'd only arrived the evening before, but Corrine and Victor were so welcoming and so easy to get along with that the worries she'd had about feeling like a stranger in their house were a million miles from her mind as she sank into their worn but comfortable sofa and allowed her eyes to close for a moment. Corrine bustled in the kitchen making supper and Victor had gone off to see to his alpaca. Ottilie had tried to offer assistance, but they'd both been adamant that they didn't need it and that she should take the opportunity to rest. So she'd washed quickly and changed into comfy clothes and, despite a niggling sense of guilt – inactivity didn't sit well with her when others were busy – she was enjoying the moment of peace.

The first day of work on her house had been messy, loud and dirty, but nobody had expected anything else. The old saying about breaking eggs to make omelette came to mind, and there was definitely some egg-breaking going on. There was probably a few more days of that to come too, and Ottilie had to keep reminding herself that, horrific as the gaping holes where her floors ought to be and the smashed-off plaster and missing skirting boards looked, things wouldn't be that way forever. She forced herself to think beyond that, to visualise a time when everything was back to normal, only better – new and improved. After all, she'd wanted to redecorate, and if she hadn't been forced to do it in such a way, she had so much else going on that it would have taken her months, maybe even years, to get round to it.

The first day had also been characterised by high spirits and heaps of enthusiasm. There was a wonderful, palpable sense of camaraderie, of a common goal that had everyone getting along, tolerant and cheery and fond of each other. Ottilie had especially loved that and she hoped it continued. She'd hate to see a day, perhaps not that far off, where reality set in enough to make people miserable and impatient, wishing they'd never agreed to help after all.

The biggest surprise of the day had been Heath's arrival, but now that Ottilie considered it, she wondered why she'd been surprised at all. She'd already seen plenty of evidence that he'd bend over backwards for his gran, and he'd been to help Ottilie before at Flo's behest, so why not this time? And she'd been pleased to see him too. Not only because of the extra pair of hands he brought with him, but because...

Ottilie opened her eyes and drew in a sharp breath as a realisation hit her. It was uncomfortable, unwelcome, and yet she couldn't deny it. She'd been pleased to see him because...

No. Absolutely not. She would not allow herself to think about him that way. It was too soon – for both of them as far as she could tell. They both came with masses of baggage; it couldn't end well, even if she was willing to give it a try, which she was not. Besides, there was no reason to suppose that he felt the same.

Her thoughts wandered to small moments, where she'd

catch his eye, where she'd overhear a snippet of conversation between him and someone else that made her smile, where she'd see him working and be unable to take her eyes off him for what was perhaps the most inappropriate length of time, and then he'd look up, sensing her attention, and she'd look away feeling unfathomably guilty. And he'd said to her when he'd first arrived that he wasn't only helping because his gran had asked him to. On a practical level it meant exactly what she'd assumed it had meant – that he was helping someone in need. But was there more to it than that? And why did the answer matter so much to her?

Corrine popped her head around the living-room door, a welcome distraction from thoughts that were tying Ottilie up in knots, thoughts she'd rather avoid having to deal with.

'Supper's ready,' she said. 'I thought I might find you asleep in here, you've been so quiet.'

'You nearly did,' Ottilie said, pushing a bright smile across her face as she stood up. 'Another half hour and I'd have been gone.'

'I'm not surprised. After supper you can have a nice long bath and then to bed if you like. I've got some lovely bath salts that will send you straight off.'

'I don't think I'll need bath salts for that,' Ottilie said as she followed her into the kitchen, where the aroma of herbs and warm bread reached her and set her stomach gurgling. She hadn't realised how hungry she was until she'd smelled the food. 'I'm sure I'll go off as soon as my head hits the pillow – I'm shattered. Where's Victor? He's not eating with us?'

'Oh, he'll be down in a few minutes – just doing something at our Penny's place.'

'Surely not more manual work?' To her shame, Ottilie could never remember whether Penny was Corrine and Victor's older or younger daughter. She didn't know either Penny or Melanie all that well. Feeling as if she ought to know and that it might be rude to ask, she simply sat at the table and stared at Corrine. 'Surely he hasn't got a scrap of energy left for anything else after the day we've had?'

'He's used to hard work – it's nothing to him. He works hard and sleeps well with a good honest day behind him – that's what his dad always taught him to do and that's what he taught our girls too. That's the farming life and he wouldn't have it any other way.'

Ottilie noticed that Corrine wasn't sitting down with her. Instead, she was back and forth tidying the kitchen.

'You're not eating?' she asked.

Corrine gave her hand a vague wave. 'Not hungry.'

'Have you eaten?' Ottilie asked more deliberately.

'Yes, yes...'

Corrine turned on the hot-water tap, but she didn't look round as she gave her reply, and Ottilie knew from long experience of dealing with patients that she was lying. She hadn't eaten and she had no intention of doing so. Her treatment hadn't yet started and so she hadn't lost her appetite through that – more likely she was worried.

'You know you really need to keep your strength up,' Ottilie said.

'I am.'

'How come I don't believe you?'

At this Corrine turned to her.

'Are you stressing?' Ottilie pressed. 'Because it's perfectly normal to feel stressed about what you're going through. And if you want to talk it through, well... you have a captive audience right here. You might as well make use of me, because I'm not going anywhere and I owe you big time anyway.'

Corrine turned off the tap and sat at the table, her shoulders slumping. 'I know there's nothing to worry about – it's been caught early and a little bit of surgery to remove it will see me right – but I can't help but think about what Victor would do if...'

Corrine's eyes misted. She sniffed loudly and shook her head. 'Ignore me,' she said. 'I'm overthinking it. I know it's going to be fine.'

'It's natural to have morbid thoughts at a time like this,' Ottilie said gently. 'You're being faced with your mortality, and though we all think about that from time to time, it's not often it's spelled out so graphically to us. Let's face it, you have a disease that could kill you. It won't, because as you say we've caught it early, but the fact remains that it *could*, and so you're bound to see beyond the immediate situation and sometimes dwell on the worst-case scenario, the what ifs. You wouldn't be human if you didn't. And you're bound to worry that it might go wrong, and that you might still end up leaving loved ones behind. Don't apologise for thinking any of that – it's normal and understandable.'

'Well,' Corrine said briskly, 'that's all very well, but there are people a lot worse off than me.'

'Also true, but it's all relative, isn't it? There are also lots of people better off and some the same. It doesn't make any difference – your fears are your fears and your feelings are your feelings and comparing them to anyone else's achieves nothing in the end. If they matter to you, if they affect you, then they matter, regardless of whether you're worse or better off than anyone else.'

Corrine gave a wan smile. 'I get the feeling you've given that speech a few times before.'

'Not really. And I'm not talking as a nurse now but as your friend.'

Corrine stood up and went to the sink again, turning her back on Ottilie as she plunged her hands into the washing-up water. 'Eat up,' she said, her voice thick with emotion. 'You must be starving.'

Ottilie wondered whether to go and give Corrine a hug but decided against it. Sometimes it was hard to call; some liked to be left alone to compose themselves; others welcomed the contact. Ottilie wasn't sure which camp Corrine might fall into, but knowing that she was a very practical farmer's wife, perhaps she was one of the former and perhaps she'd be best left to sort herself out. Ottilie had let her know that a sympathetic ear was always on hand should Corrine need it, and hopefully that was enough.

It felt as if she'd no sooner fallen asleep than Ottilie woke to the alarm the following morning. Corrine had been right: after supper and a hot bath, Ottilie had been exhausted, falling into bed and nodding straight off. If this was the farmer's way – a good honest sleep from a good honest day's work, Ottilie had to say she was a fan. There were no jumbled dreams as there so often were normally, no restless tossing and turning, only blissful oblivion. And even though the alarm had gone off far too early for her liking, she'd felt refreshed once she'd woken.

Corrine had been quiet as she'd made breakfast and then afterwards, as she sent Ottilie and Victor off in the tractor for another day working on Wordsworth Cottage. Ottilie wondered how much that had to do with their conversation the previous evening and couldn't decide whether it was a good thing or not. She hoped she was OK. She'd never had an illness that was even vaguely life-threatening – though she'd nursed plenty who had – and so she couldn't imagine what Corrine might be thinking and feeling about it, but she did know that whether she admitted it or not, Corrine needed a good support network around her if she was going to get through this – not only physically but mentally as well. Ottilie was determined she was going to be a part of that support network – under the current circumstances it was the least she could do to repay her and Victor's kindness.

'Decent turnout again,' Victor said as he killed the tractor engine outside Ottilie's house. 'That's good – if we make as much progress as we did yesterday, we'll have you back in your home in no time.'

'Shame.' Ottilie smiled. 'I was just getting used to being looked after by you and Corrine.'

'You're welcome to stay as long as you want.'

'Ah, you say that, but we'll see how you feel this time next year when I'm still there, living like a slovenly teenager in your spare room.'

Victor chuckled as he hopped down from the cab. Ottilie followed him, taking far more care. Her gaze went over the assembled volunteers. Everyone save Fliss's husband, Charles, had come back – even, Ottilie noted, her pulse imperceptibly quickening, Heath.

'Ready for more of the same, boss?' Magnus grinned.

'I can't believe you all came back,' Ottilie said.

'Charles sends his apologies,' Geoff said. 'He used exactly those words. In a very posh voice of course,' he added, making Magnus give a saucy giggle. '*Please offer Ottilie my sincere apologies for my absence today...*' he continued in a decent impersonation of Charles, clearly delighted he'd made Magnus laugh and determined to keep it going.

Ottilie smiled. 'Oh well, I can't expect everyone to drop everything to come here. I'm grateful for any help I can get. I mean, it's already so amazing that this is happening at all – I can't thank you enough.'

'You said that about a million times yesterday,' Magnus said, shaking his head with a broad smile. 'Would you stop already?

We know we're great; you're going to give us all heads as big as Ullswater.'

As she caught his eye, Heath gave her a silent nod of acknowledgement, and to her mortification she blushed. No sir, she wasn't about to admit to herself that he looked good today, that she was happier to see him than anyone else, that she hoped to get more time to chat to him, that she found herself intrigued more each time they met, that she wanted to know everything there was to know. She wasn't going to admit it, and it wasn't going to happen. She especially wasn't going to admit – even to herself – that Flo might have been right to try and get them together, that she might have seen potential neither of them could. Perhaps in another life, but not this one, not now, not after what Ottilie had been through, not while there were so many other complications still unresolved.

'So shall we get started?' Victor asked. 'Who wants to do what? We need a couple of folks in the kitchen to get the rest of that floor up.' He looked at Stacey. 'What did you decide about the outhouse? Still think it could dry out all right in there?'

'I think so,' Stacey said uncertainly.

'I think,' Ottilie put in, 'that it's not a priority, because I don't use it all that much, and it's a tiled floor, so perhaps we can leave it for now and see how it goes.'

Victor nodded. 'Agreed. It's the wood that's the big problem – joists and such. Let's concentrate on getting the rest of that done today. If we make good time tomorrow we can start to look at replacing what's no good. I'll need a couple of chippies with me then if anyone's any good with wood.'

'I'm not too bad,' Heath said. 'I think I could turn my hand to it if someone tells me what to do.'

'That's one,' Victor said.

'And I ought to have a go, as it's my house,' Ottilie said. 'Though I can't promise it'll be up to professional standards.'

'I'll go and see Bob Hodgkins too,' Victor said. 'He's a bit slow these days, but he knows a thing or two about wood-working and he can oversee, even if he's not strong enough to do it himself. And seeing as he's always moaning how boring his retirement is...'

'I'll pop in and see him if you like,' Magnus said.

'Do we need to go and fetch some wood?' Heath asked. 'I can borrow a van if it helps.'

Victor nodded. 'Makes more sense than taking a tractor into town. If you could.'

'Tomorrow we might need it, you say?'

'Let's see how we get on this morning,' Victor replied.

'I'll make a quick call,' Heath said, 'just to be sure I can have the van tomorrow either way.'

As he pulled out his phone and moved to a quieter spot, his gaze caught Ottilie's. She aimed a grateful smile his way, and he nodded briefly. It was lucky there was so much else going on today to distract her, because those unwanted thoughts were back to plague her again.

Work had been non-stop and spirits had been high. Considering how devastated she'd been when the flood had first hit, Ottilie couldn't remember the last time she'd felt this cheery. It was good to be doing something, and now she could see progress her spirits were lifted. The radio had been playing all morning, mostly chart hits, but then the programme changed, the DJ playing musical theatre classics, and Magnus and Geoff were proving what good voices they both had by singing along.

'You ought to be on the West End,' Ottilie said.

'Oh, if only,' Magnus replied with a pleased smile.

'He's too much of a diva to be on the West End,' Geoff put in. 'They'd never cope with him.'

'And that's saying something,' Stacey put in. 'They must have some massive egos in those theatre dressing rooms.'

Ottilie laughed. 'Aww, poor Magnus.'

'Thank you,' Magnus said, grinning at Ottilie. 'At least someone's on my side.'

He and Geoff lifted a length of ruined wood between them and carried it out. Ottilie could hear them bickering about it as they went.

Which way are you going?

Not that way, that...

Are you trying to dunk us in the river?

I'm nowhere— Watch my foot!

Stacey and Ottilie exchanged a grin. As Stacey turned back to the plaster she was knocking off, Ottilie glanced round to see Heath watching her. Like lightning, he looked back to his work, forcing the claw of his hammer beneath a stubborn nail in the floorboard.

'It looks a bit stuck,' she said. 'It might help if I loosen the other end...'

Ottilie stepped onto the floorboard, unaware that Heath had freed it so that now his end was untethered. Like something from a cartoon, it flipped up and narrowly missed his groin.

He leaped back with a yelp. 'Jesus!'

'I'm so sorry!' Ottilie squeaked as the floorboard landed again with a musty thump. 'I had no idea it was going to do that!' She rushed over. 'Are you all right? It didn't hit you, did it?'

'A minor miracle considering the effort you put in,' he said, eyeing the board balefully.

Ottilie stared at him, but he looked so mortally offended that despite the fact she'd nearly castrated him, she felt a sudden urge to laugh.

'It's not funny,' he said. 'I might want children one day.'

This only made Ottilie's smirk grow, and she fought harder to keep the laughter in. But it had been a losing battle from the start, and it finally burst free.

She giggled. 'I *am* sorry!'

'You sound it. I'd hate to see what you're like when you're not sorry.'

'I can't help it... Your face...'

'You nearly swiped my face off with that board.'

'You keep your face in your pants then?' she asked, almost breathless with laughter. 'Oh my God, your face is even angrier!'

'I'm not angry,' he sulked. 'I'm traumatised. My life flashed before my eyes.'

'Stop!' Ottilie snorted. 'Oh God, please stop!'

Victor came in, directing a bemused glance from one to the other. 'Everything all right in here?'

'Yes,' Ottilie said, trying to regain her composure.

'It very nearly wasn't,' Heath said. 'My crown jewels were in mortal danger.'

Victor grinned. 'I don't think I should ask.'

'I don't think I could bring myself to talk about it if you did,' Heath replied, and though he was doing a decent job of looking outraged, Ottilie could see that he wanted to smile now too.

'This might be a good time to stop for lunch anyway,' Victor said. 'If you're not in the middle of something you might as well have a break.'

'Yes, boss.' Ottilie grinned.

Ten minutes later everyone was sitting outside on Ottilie's back lawn sharing a pile of food that she'd tipped out onto a picnic blanket so they could help themselves. There was no standing on ceremony here – it was every man for himself and manners were for days when they weren't all covered in dust and grime, fingers riddled with splinters.

Magnus and Geoff were listening to Stacey recount an incident involving Chloe and one of her infamous sulks, while Victor was on the phone to Corrine, checking she was all right. Ottilie smiled sadly as she caught bits of the conversation. He'd never let on, but he was as scared for her as she'd admitted being for him. She knew that things would turn out all right, but hoped that she wasn't wrong, because she couldn't imagine how they'd cope if not.

The situation left her sitting with Heath, and it didn't go unnoticed by him either.

'Was it something we said?' she asked.

He reached for a flask and unscrewed the cap. 'It must be. You have to wonder if it's deliberate.'

'Huh?'

'You know, we've been put together and everyone else is pretending to be too busy to sit with us.'

'Don't be daft.'

'I'm not. My gran has got form with this sort of thing and she's not above recruiting a few willing accomplices.'

'What sort of thing?'

'This...' He nodded discreetly at the gathering, and Ottilie noticed Magnus glance quickly at her, and then Geoff, and then both of them continued their conversation as if they hadn't been looking at all.

'They're all in on it,' he added.

Ottilie raised her eyebrows at him.

'Come on,' he continued, 'don't tell me you haven't seen what's going on here.'

'Tinder by stealth,' she said ruefully, and he laughed.

'There are two single people, therefore they must belong together. I think my gran might be to blame.'

'Oh, I totally blame her.' Ottilie glanced at Stacey, who was talking to Magnus and Geoff, and wondered why Flo had zeroed in on her rather than Stacey to match Heath up to. Granted, Stacey was older, but she looked younger than her years, still very attractive, and was probably in a much better place to start dating again than Ottilie was. She wondered whether Heath found Stacey attractive, and then wondered why she suddenly found herself caring about that.

'I know she's only trying to help—'

'Is she? Do we seem that desperate?'

'I think I must do,' he said. But then his smile faded. 'She's had to see too much of what I went through with my ex. I suppose she wants to see me happy – and that's not a crime, is it?'

'She's mentioned your ex, but she's never really told me anything about what went on.'

He shrugged as he poured some tea from the flask. 'I wouldn't know where to start to fill you in. It was messy, and I think that might cover it enough for you to understand?'

'I won't ask then.'

'It's not that I don't want you to ask,' he said quickly, 'it's just that I don't know how to say it without bringing it all back, and I don't want to ruin a very nice conversation.'

'We're having a nice conversation?'

'Don't you think so?'

'If you like talking about skirting boards, then yes.'

He laughed, a rich warm laugh that was new to her. She liked it. She instantly wished she didn't like it quite so much. Whatever Flo was up to, Ottilie was afraid it was working, and that scared her.

'It sounds like it was very different for you,' he said as his laughter faded. 'I heard some of what happened there. For what it's worth – probably not much – I'm sorry.'

'Thanks,' Ottilie said, the memory of Josh prompting a squirming guilt that she could be thinking of how attractive Heath was when it wasn't yet twelve months since she'd lost him.

There was an unspoken understanding that this wasn't the

time to go into detail, and so Heath asked no more and Ottilie didn't offer.

'Did you always want to be a nurse?' he asked instead.

She couldn't help but smile at this. Here she was on solid ground.

'I can't remember wanting to do anything else. I've heard some people say it's a calling, and I suppose that's the best way to describe it for me. I trained with girls who saw it as a job that they'd thought about and decided on for all sorts of reasons – pay and career prospects and stuff – but honestly, I think if I'd had to do it for free, I probably would have done.' She smiled. 'In fact, I didn't get the exams I needed at school to go into train- ing, so I had to go to night classes to try again. It didn't enter my head to do something I was more suited to – academically, I mean – because I was determined that I was meant to be a nurse. My mum says I used to pretend to nurse my teddies before I even knew what a nurse was.'

'Not many people can say they're doing what they always felt they were meant to do. And you like it? It's what you thought it would be?'

'I love it. I couldn't imagine doing anything else and I wouldn't want to. I feel very much as if I'm doing what I was put on the earth to do. I suppose that sounds corny.'

'No, I think it must be nice. I wish I could say the same.'

'You don't like your job?'

'It's all right. Pays the bills, but it certainly doesn't feel like what I was put on the earth to do. I don't think I knew what a management consultant was when I was a kid, let alone aspire to be one.'

'I don't think I know what one is now.'

'You don't want to – it's boring as hell. You'd drop off the minute I started to explain it. I sort of fell into it, truth be told. Don't get me wrong, it's been good to me, but...' He gave her a sideways look. 'I don't think it makes me anywhere near as happy as your job makes you.'

'I suppose a lot of people could say that. I know I'm lucky.'

'It's luck you sound like you deserve.'

'I don't know about that, but after the year I've had, if I hadn't got this job I don't know how I'd have got through. It's the only thing that's kept me sane.'

'You don't find it stressful ever? It's a lot of responsibility?'

'Oh God, yes. But it's also good to be thinking about how I can care for others – stops me having time to feel sorry for myself.'

'Even my gran? Don't worry – I know she must be hard work.'

'She's... *spirited*,' Ottilie said with a laugh. 'But I do like her. I think we've become sort of friends.'

'Spirited,' Heath repeated with a grin. 'Nicely done. I'll have to remember that one next time my mum and dad start complaining about her: she's not a stubborn old goat, she's just spirited.'

'Don't they all get along?'

Heath shrugged. 'Like all families, it can get complicated. Dad loves her, but they're very different people and I think they struggle to understand each other. If they weren't related, they'd have nothing in common at all.'

'And what about you?'

'Weirdly, I think I'm more like Gran than my dad is. I suppose that's why I'm the one who comes over to Thimblebury the most. And someone's got to look out for her. At the end of the day, she's an old lady who needs her family now more than ever.'

'That's how you see it?'

'Yeah.' He gave her another quizzical sideways look. 'I suppose that's why I got so offended when you told me she was lonely and nobody was coming to see her that time.'

'Is that what I actually said?' Ottilie gave a half-smile. 'I don't recall it being quite like that.'

'Not exactly, but I knew what you meant. It made me feel guilty because you were a little bit right – I'd let other things get in the way, and I hadn't been to see her as much as I ought to have done, and then I was pissed off because I felt guilty and that's not a good feeling. Especially when I couldn't argue that what you'd said wasn't true.'

'I never meant to make you feel like that, you know.'

'That almost makes it worse, because that means it definitely was true and you were only saying it as a professional, calling things how they were.'

'But you're there for her now, and that's what matters.'

'I try to be,' he said. 'I know she's not getting any younger, and sometimes I forget how little time she has left.'

'Blimey!' Ottilie broke into a laugh. 'Speaking as her nurse, I feel confident that she has decades left yet. She'll probably outlive us all.'

'She'll outlive us all by sheer force of will, she's that stubborn,' Heath said, and Ottilie's laughter grew.

'Last woman standing?'

'God, yes. You've got her worked out already.'

'Well, I think she's brilliant.'

'She thinks you're brilliant too.'

Ottilie flushed. 'She said that?'

'No, but she doesn't have to. I can tell. She never took to any of my girlfriends, and in the end she hated Mila.'

In the end? Ottilie wanted to know what had changed. In the end implied that in the beginning Flo hadn't hated Heath's ex-wife but something had happened to make her feel differently. But it didn't seem like a question he'd welcome.

'Our Flo's difficult to please then?' she said instead. 'I must be honoured.'

'You must be. I guess you've done something to earn it. You're there for her, at least.'

'Mila kept you away? Is that what happened to upset her? I don't mean to pry, but—'

'Quite the opposite,' he said, but although his tone was neutral, his expression darkened. 'She was here a lot towards the end of our marriage, sometimes without me...'

He looked as if he wanted to add something, but then he drank the last of the tea in his plastic cup and stood up. 'Can't sit here all day. Work to be done, right?'

'Um, sure. I mean, you can take as long as you want if you haven't finished your lunch. Nobody minds.'

'I've more or less finished anyway,' he said, bundling up the greaseproof paper his sandwiches had been wrapped in. 'Decent butties, by the way – compliments to the chef.'

'That was Corrine. I tried to help, but she's so fast and efficient she'd done everything by the time I'd figured out where the butter knives are kept.'

'She has butter knives? I thought everyone had one knife for everything like I do.'

Ottilie smiled, but despite his quip she detected a new tension in the air and she couldn't work out where it had come from. She'd felt she was learning about him, getting to know him, and then it was like he'd decided he'd said too much and thrown a barrier up. At least it seemed to be coming from him, but perhaps some of it was her doing too. Was she getting too close? Was she going to a place she would regret?

She'd been lonely of late, more and more understanding of Stacey's loneliness, and this was a new stage in her transition from newly bereaved to accepting widow that she didn't know how to deal with. Was her new – and now undeniable – interest in Heath just a manifestation of that? Was it loneliness driving her actions? She'd heard it said by many people that one could be surrounded by friends and yet still be lonely, but over the past few weeks she had seen for herself the truth of that statement.

Whatever else it was, logic told her it was too soon. Josh was still a constant in her thoughts and to muddy her emotional waters wouldn't be helpful at all – possibly even foolish and guaranteed not to end well. There was more to learn about Heath too, a history he was keeping back. She couldn't allow herself to get involved when there were secrets that might change everything, and it didn't seem as if he was willing to share them. She guessed it had something to do with the way his marriage had ended. She wondered whether Flo might know and if she ought to ask her, but as she watched him go back to work, she wondered whether not knowing might be better. She liked him – she could no longer deny it – and she liked where they were now, and perhaps she didn't want to ruin that with scary little things like the truth.

CHAPTER TWENTY-THREE

Ottilie's renovations had been going on for almost a week. Finally, she could see how things would look, and her mood was more positive every day. The weather had been good to them and there had been no more rain, which she'd been nervous about, even though everyone had told her there was no need.

Her help had taken it in turns to be there over the past few days. Not everyone could make every day, and Ottilie, of course, understood that perfectly well. Heath had done almost all of them though. She'd asked him how he had the time and whether he was falling behind at work, but he simply told her that he worked for himself so it was all in hand and left it at that.

Every day that she spent with him revealed a bit more of the real Heath too. Ottilie tried not to go back to Daffodil Farm thinking about him, but she always did. He was smart and quick and strong, and she admired that about him, but he was also surprisingly gentle when the moment called for it, emotionally astute and tactful. He gave little away about his marriage, but Ottilie gleaned more from what he didn't say than what he did. She could see that his ex-wife had hurt him deeply, more than he'd ever admit, and it made her sad. The Heath she was getting to know didn't deserve that.

Magnus sidled up to Ottilie as she helped Victor pack his drill at the end of another day. She'd noticed him doing the same to Heath. He'd gone over there, had a quick, quiet conversation with him, and then left him to come straight to her. She tried not to let her suspicion show as she smiled up at him.

'Everything all right, Magnus?'

'Yes. I just wanted to invite you to our movie soirée.'

'What, like film club? I thought that was next week and you hardly need to invite me; I'm in the club anyway, aren't I?'

'Of course you are. This is an extra thing. I thought it might be nice for all of us who have worked together the past few days to let our hair down.'

'Hmm. I suppose if anyone ought to be throwing a party for that, it's me.'

'But your house is hardly fit to do it. So Geoff and I thought it would be good to have it at our place.'

'Oh, right. When?'

'Can you make tomorrow night?'

Ottilie smiled. 'You know I have no social life outside film club. I'm sure I can be there. What time? You might have to make it late enough for us all to get showered and stuff. Who else is coming?'

'Not sure yet – haven't had all the RSVPs. How about eight?'

'Eight sounds fine.' She turned to Victor, who didn't seem to have been listening. 'Are you going to this film thing?'

'Oh, I don't think so.'

'But I'm sure you're welcome to this time. Magnus says it's a bonding thing for all of us – that's it, right, Magnus?'

'Yes, you're welcome to come,' Magnus said very deliberately, seeming to give Victor an odd look with it.

'Well, I'll see what Corrine says, but I expect she'll be too tired.'

'Yes, I expect so,' Magnus said in his strange way again.

Victor gave the tiniest shrug and then turned back to fitting all the components into his drill case.

'So that's eight,' Magnus said to Ottilie. 'Don't forget.'

'I'll see you tomorrow, won't I?' she asked. 'I'm sure you'd remind me if I did forget.'

'Yes, but I'm making sure you know the arrangements. We thought it might be fun to dress up a bit, so wear something a bit fancy.'

'Fancy? Really?'

'Yes, I want us to be in our Sunday best. Indulge me, won't you?'

'OK,' Ottilie said uncertainly.

Looking pleased with himself, Magnus went back to where Geoff was stacking unused timber. They had a quick word, and then Geoff looked as pleased as Magnus. The frown she'd been holding on to creased Ottilie's forehead.

If she hadn't known better, she'd have said something was being cooked up.

Ottilie had pulled out a black dress she'd bought shortly before Josh's death, had a little cry about it, and then put it back, taking out a floral one instead. It was more of a tea dress than evening wear really, but when Magnus had said to be fancy, surely he didn't expect her to turn up in a red-carpet number? And so she'd put it on, slapped on a bit of make-up and combed her hair, and hoped that would do.

Corrine was at the table finishing her tea when Ottilie went in. 'Ooh, you look nice.'

'Do you think I've overdressed? It's only Geoff's cinema after all.'

'I don't think so,' Corrine said. 'I think that looks just right. I wish I could still see where my waist was meant to be.'

'Don't be daft – you always look lovely,' Ottilie said, grabbing her handbag from the chair where she'd left it.

'You look nice,' Victor said, echoing Corrine's compliment as he came in from the front garden. 'Ready to go? I've got the engine running on the car – thought I'd better warm it up in case it didn't feel like starting.'

Ottilie nodded. 'Thanks for this. You're sure neither you want to come?'

'Oh no,' Victor said.

'There's something on telly we want to watch,' Corrine added. 'Have a lovely time and tell us all about it when you get home.'

Half an hour later, Ottilie arrived at the village shop and went round to the side gate that was always left unlocked for film club, pushed it open and then went up to the house. Through the vast windows she could see Magnus hurrying to get the door. The place seemed weirdly quiet. Usually – at least whenever film club was on – by this time the kitchen would be filled with the other members. But Ottilie couldn't see anyone else. Nor could she see any signs of the 'soirée' Magnus had promised. No food was laid out, no bottles of booze... neither could she hear any music or chatter coming from anywhere.

'Am I early?' she asked as he opened the door and swept her into a hug.

And then he held her at arm's length and gave a satisfied nod. 'You look lovely,' he said. 'Perfect. Just right.'

'OK... thank you,' Ottilie replied slowly. 'Where's everyone else?'

'In the cinema room. Come on – let's go through.'

'We don't usually go straight in there,' she said as Magnus took her hand and practically dragged her through the kitchen. 'We normally do drinks and nibbles first. Or at least have a little catch-up.'

'Yes, but that's ordinary film club. This isn't film club, is it? This is a special get-together.'

'Right...' Ottilie noticed Geoff at the door of the cinema room waiting for them, looking as shifty as Magnus was being. At least, it seemed shifty to Ottilie. To her, it seemed very much as if they were doing something they both knew they ought not to be. Not in any sinister way, but in a meddling, naughty boy sort of way.

'Magnus, what's going—'

'Come on!' Magnus said, his tone far too innocent. 'We're waiting to start.'

'You look beautiful,' Geoff said as Magnus pushed her towards him. Then he took her by the hand and led her into the cinema room, as if she'd never been there before and might not know how to get in. Or perhaps – the thought suddenly occurring to Ottilie – in case she had the notion to escape.

Inside, there was soft lighting. Not like the low lights they had just before the film began, but lighting from candles dotted all over the place. There was a table at the front row of seats, decked out with a gingham cloth, three bottles of wine and two glasses and various quite fancy-looking finger foods. There was also cheese and grapes and – ominously, as far Ottilie was concerned – a plate of oysters.

Heath stood by the screen, hands in his pockets, dressed in a soft denim shirt, looking as confused as she felt she must have done.

'Nobody else is here yet?' Ottilie asked, glancing between the three of them. And then her gaze went to the table of food. There wasn't enough there for the whole crowd Magnus and

Geoff were expecting – that much was obvious. What wasn't so obvious was what the hell was going on.

'Well,' Geoff began, 'Stacey couldn't make it because Chloe was feeling a bit under the weather. And you know Victor and Corrine were thinking about coming, but... I suppose Corrine was too tired?'

Ottilie nodded.

'And we asked Charles and Fliss, but they had something on already. And so did Lavender. And Flo said she didn't like the film, so...'

'What film is it?'

'*Shakespeare in Love.*'

'Hmm.'

'So it's just us four?' Heath asked.

'Actually' – Magnus shot a look at Geoff, and the word shifty popped into Ottilie's head again – 'we might have to leave you to it. Something's come up.'

'What?'

'Oh, something to do with our wholesaler,' Geoff said.

'At this time of night?' Ottilie asked and exchanged a look with Heath that told her he was as suspicious as she was.

'Yes, they're very busy in the day so we have to sort these things out after hours,' Magnus said. 'But don't let that stop you from enjoying the film.'

'But if no one else can make it, shouldn't we reschedule?'

'No!' Magnus and Geoff said together.

'I mean,' Magnus said, 'we've already catered for it, and you wouldn't want all the food to go to waste, would you?'

The food that only looked enough for two people? Ottilie frowned at Magnus. She couldn't help it. 'No,' she said slowly. 'I don't suppose we would. But are you sure you won't be able to join us?'

'Perhaps later,' Magnus said, ushering Geoff out of the room. 'Take a seat, relax. The film is about to start. Enjoy!'

The door closed behind them, and Ottilie looked at Heath. 'Did you know nobody else was coming?'

'No. I take it you didn't either.'

'Nope. Does this smell like a set-up to you?'

'Ever so slightly. What are we, like, twelve?'

'My thoughts exactly. So what now?'

'I suppose it'd be rude to leave after they've gone to so much trouble.'

'And the food does look good,' Ottilie said, taking a seat behind the table. The screen crackled into life as the reel began.

'It does,' Heath agreed, sitting next to her.

Ottilie reached for a grape and popped it into her mouth. And then she began to smile. 'Fancy playing them at their own game?'

'What did you have in mind?'

'Why don't we pretend to have fallen madly in love when they come in to get us at the end of the film?'

Heath opened one of the wine bottles with a grin. 'That would be hilarious. You'd have to ham it up, though. Reckon you could manage that?'

'I reckon I could.'

'Of course, we've got to watch the film first. I have to admit, it's not really my thing.'

'Not really mine either. I suppose we'll have to make the best of it. If they'd come right out with their plan and asked, I'd have given them a list of stuff I wanted to see more than *Shakespeare in Love.*'

'Well, I suppose there are worse places to be stuck,' he said, pouring a glass of wine and settling back in his seat. He shot a grin at Ottilie. 'Private cinema, good food and not a bad wine, and good company – it could be a lot worse.'

'I'm going to assume there's a compliment in there somewhere,' she returned drily.

'Oh there is,' Heath said, stuffing a pâté-covered water

biscuit into his mouth. 'Magnus and Geoff know how to put on a spread.'

'Oi!' Ottilie laughed. The sound was drowned out by the film credits beginning and she settled into her seat.

Heath poured another glass of wine and handed it to her. 'Madam...'

'Why thank you,' Ottilie said, taking it from him and sipping at it. It tasted heavy. Probably rocket fuel, she mused, part of Geoff and Magnus's master plan. Not only had she and Heath been thrown together with what those two felt was a romantic movie, there were also oysters and wine that had been selected to get them legless. Were they watching from somewhere, sniggering, hoping to see her and Heath get drunk and end up snogging?

Suddenly Ottilie bristled. This was ridiculous. She'd agreed with Heath to make the most of this, perhaps have some fun and get their own back on Magnus and Geoff for forcing this, but now she was annoyed. She glanced at Heath, who was watching the screen. She'd have expected him to be as irritated as her, but he didn't seem to be. Knowing what she did about him, that was an unexpected development. Was he actually OK with this?

She put down her glass. 'I really think we ought to go and find them and sort this out.'

He turned to her. Was that disappointment in his expression? 'I thought we were going to watch the film.'

'You said you didn't want to see this film.'

'I wouldn't have chosen it, but I don't mind watching it with you. That is, if you want to. I thought we just said we would.'

'I know but that was before...'

Ottilie let out a sigh. Magnus and Geoff clearly felt they were somehow doing a good thing for her and Heath. They were lovely people and good friends – was it really worth offending them for the sake of a couple of hours watching a film? Heath was right – they'd said they would. All she had to do was sit through this – maybe she'd even like it – and then they could go their separate ways. Magnus and Geoff would realise there'd never been any chemistry between them after all but could be happy in the fact that they'd tried, and Ottilie could get on with her life knowing that she hadn't hurt anyone's feelings.

'Just don't let me drink too much of that wine,' she said, before giving the oysters a look of misgiving. 'And as for them...'

Heath laughed as he picked up the plate and took it to another seat. 'Is that far enough away for you?'

'How anyone ever looked at one of those and thought they'd like to eat it, let alone think eating one was sexy is beyond me.'

'That's one thing we have in common then.'

'Perhaps that was secretly what Magnus and Geoff were trying to achieve.'

'They didn't mean us to eat them, just to agree that they're disgusting?' Heath retook his seat next to her and reached for his wine. 'That's a bit niche, isn't it?'

Ottilie smiled as the film's opening credits began to roll. 'I mean, if they really meant business, they should have put us in the back row.'

'I never did that,' Heath said.

Ottilie turned to him. 'You never sat in the back row of a cinema and snogged the face off someone?'

'Nope.'

'Wow. You must be the only boy in Britain who's never done that. Between the ages of sixteen and eighteen I don't think I ever saw a full movie at the cinema.'

'Well, I never felt I'd missed out until now, so thanks for that.'

'So if not that, what did you spend your teenage years doing?'

He gave a cheeky grin and she blushed.

'On second thought,' she added quickly, 'maybe I don't want to know.'

'I think it's for the best.'

Ottilie reached for a cracker and her hand brushed his. She looked to see he was reaching for the same plate. 'God, I'm sorry,' she said. 'This is going to be super awkward, isn't it?'

'It might be,' he said with a grin.

'I mean, it's like *Lady and the Tramp* or something.'

'I wouldn't know – I've never seen that film.'

She folded her arms. 'Sorry, you've never seen *Lady and the Tramp*?'

He shook his head.

'What *have* you been doing for the past thirty-odd years?'

'Clearly I've not been doing what you've been doing.'

'That was one of my favourite Disney films as a kid.'

'Never seen a Disney film.' Ottilie's mouth fell open and he laughed. 'Surely it's not that much of a shock.'

'You've never seen a Disney film? Not one?'

'Nope.'

'What did your parents do with you then? I thought it was every parent's fallback for the school holidays to stick their kid in front of a giant pile of Disney DVDs.'

'I don't know what I was doing instead. I suppose I must have been out climbing trees or hiking or something.'

'Weirdo,' Ottilie said, and the laugh that erupted from him was so loud it made her jump.

'Well,' she continued once his laughter had quietened, 'judging by the tablecloth here, I think Magnus and Geoff must have seen *Lady and the Tramp*. I'm surprised there isn't a great big bowl of spaghetti and meatballs here and no forks.'

'Oh, I've seen that bit at least.'

'Everyone's seen that bit. Have you really never seen a Disney movie?'

'Not that I can recall.'

'Not even a live action?'

'I don't know. Maybe. Is it that shocking to you I might not have?'

'I just don't know how you've avoided it. I mean, they're everywhere. You must have done.'

'Probably,' he agreed. 'I'll work on an inventory of all the films I've ever watched when this is finished, and you can tell me whether I've seen one.'

'So we're planning on staying a while, are we?'

'I'm in no rush to leave,' he said, his smile still broad but, somehow, suddenly earnest.

Ottilie blushed, grateful that he wouldn't be able to see it in the gloom. She had to admit that they hadn't watched a single second of *Shakespeare in Love* yet, they'd been so busy chatting, and she had to wonder whether Geoff and Magnus were on to something. The way they'd gone about it was misguided, but...

She shot a glance Heath's way. He was looking at the screen. She liked the Heath she was getting to know far better than the one she'd first been introduced to.

He turned and caught her eye, and she blushed again, reaching for her wine, pretending that was what she'd been doing all along.

'I thought you weren't going to drink much of that,' he said, nodding at the almost empty glass in her hand.

She hadn't noticed how fast she'd been drinking it. 'I...'

'It's good stuff, isn't it?' he said, pouring himself a top-up and then holding the bottle out for her. 'I wasn't planning on drinking that much either, but... Well, let's just say I won't be driving back to Manchester tonight.'

'Lucky you have your gran around the corner then.'

Lucky my place isn't fit to stay in too.

Ottilie allowed him to refill her glass and then took a gulp. She watched him put the bottle down and his glass up to his own lips, and it was strangely hypnotic. From nowhere, an image filled her mind, of him turning to her and kissing her. She shook it away and tried to turn her attention to the film. At this point, however, she didn't have a clue what was going on and it was hardly a distraction at all.

'It wasn't bad in the end, was it?' Heath asked as they stood outside the shop, having bid goodnight to a very smug-looking Magnus and Geoff. 'We had a laugh, didn't we?'

'The film was pretty good in the end too.'

'Was it? Not my sort of thing really, but I suppose it was all right.'

Ottilie wondered whether he'd taken in as little of the plot as she had. She'd been so busy thinking about him, acutely aware of him sitting next to her and what that was doing to her that her assertion that the film was good was a lie. She had no idea whether it had been any good or not. At least Heath seemed to be better informed on that score. Perhaps he hadn't been thinking about her in the same way. But she couldn't allow this to happen. It was better if he hadn't, and she needed to stop this silly daydreaming too. It was a fantasy, and she might have decided it was harmless if seeing him almost every day, as she did currently, wasn't such a worrying temptation.

She was feeling the effects of the wine and that wasn't helping either. As she looked up at him, it would be so easy to reach that little further and plant a kiss on those inviting lips, but that was down to the booze, wasn't it?

'Have you got to walk up to Daffodil Farm?' he asked.

Darkness had fallen, the lanes of Thimblebury ghostly silent. Ottilie glanced up at the shadow of the hills she'd have to climb to get there and was thankful that the answer to his question was no.

'Victor is going to come and get me,' she said.

'Ah. I was going to say I'd walk up there with you, but no need.'

'No, it's fine.'

'I'll wait with you until he gets here though.'

'It's Thimblebury – there's no need.'

'Still, I'd rather. There are some dodgy-looking badgers around these parts.'

Ottilie gave a warm, wine-hazed smile. God he was sexy. It had been so long since...

Her smile faded. Since Josh. *Go on, Ottilie, say it, remember it. It has been this long since you had a man because it's this long since you lost the only one that mattered.*

'I was thinking,' Heath said, interrupting her thoughts. 'I could download *Lady and the Tramp.*'

'And pop your Disney cherry.'

He smiled. 'Something like that.'

'I'm not sure that's the one for you to start with, not at your age.'

'Yeah, but I have to see it now, don't I? Considering the evening we've just had, I need to get the references.'

'I suppose there is that.'

'And I was thinking... I don't know... maybe you might come over and watch it with me?'

Ottilie's heart sank. She should have seen this coming. Stupid, stupid Ottilie; always letting her emotions get the better of her. She should have been clearer from the start. He looked so nervous, so hopeful, and she was going to smash the confidence he must have had to muster to ask this question to bits with her answer.

'Heath, I've had a great night tonight, better than I thought I would, and you're a good friend but...'

'Ah.' The physical step back he took from her was like a knife in her gut. 'Yeah, of course. It was just a thought, you know... Doesn't matter.'

'It's not that I don't think you're attractive, because I do.'

'You don't need to explain. I get it.'

'No, you don't. It's nothing to do with you—'

'I really do get it. Please, don't make it more embarrassing than it already is.'

'We'd both be rebounds for each other.'

He studied her for a moment. 'Is that what you think?'

'Isn't it right? We've both just come from relationships where...'

'I thought that was all the more reason we deserved a bit of fun. I wasn't after anything serious; I just thought we'd enjoyed each other's company tonight and it might be nice to spend more time together. It wasn't that deep; it was only company, that's all. Forget it. Clearly, it's a bigger deal for you.'

'I'm just not ready. It's not even a year—'

'Of course. I'm sorry for asking,' he said, a new stiffness to his tone that twisted the knife of guilt that little bit more. 'It was insensitive of me – I realise that now.'

'You're not! If things had been different, the timing... I don't know, maybe. I like you...'

He turned away, staring out into the darkness, and she realised she was only making it worse. Even as she tried to find words that would make it better, the sound of a clanking old Land Rover engine grew into the night air.

'This'll be Victor,' she said, relieved and frustrated in equal measure at the timing of the farmer's arrival. 'Will I see you tomorrow? At the house, I mean. I understand if you don't want to come now; I realise I don't deserve—'

'I promised my gran I'd help you, so I'll be there,' he said tersely, and then walked off in the direction of Flo's house.

CHAPTER TWENTY-FOUR

Ottilie was beginning to feel she was getting under Corrine and Victor's feet. She'd been at Daffodil Farm for six weeks, and while they'd been more than welcoming, she realised her presence was disrupting their usual routine. Every day her house was a bit closer to being ready to live in again, but it was slow going and often frustrating. Often whatever work they'd done would turn out to need redoing because of some feature or other they'd failed to take into account, or some other damage that nobody had seen until it was too late. It didn't help that they were all mostly amateurs, learning each repair on the job, watching YouTube videos or reading manuals or working it out as they looked at it. Ottilie didn't worry about the quality of the work, but she did worry that it was going to take a lot longer than anyone had anticipated, and that any enthusiasm they had was fast waning.

Some days Heath was there and some days he wasn't. He had his own job to do, of course, like most of the volunteers, and so she completely understood that. The distance between them was what was hard to bear. He was courteous, but he didn't make unnecessary conversation. On the days he turned up he worked hard and he did his best, and he smiled politely at her and said all the things he ought to say, but she knew the truth. She'd led him on and she'd hurt him and he hadn't deserved that. She'd tried to tell him that he didn't need to keep turning up, that the drive from Manchester was too much and that he didn't owe her anything, but he insisted that he'd promised Florence he'd see the project through and that he was only doing it for her.

She'd also realised that if the renovations were going to take as long as she feared, she could hardly ask Fliss to keep on a locum nurse for all that time. It was costing her boss a lot of money to pay the cover, so she'd made a call to say she was going to go back to work. With the biggest structural jobs done, Ottilie would have to somehow fit in the rest during evenings and weekends.

'I think I'll move back into Wordsworth Cottage,' she said as she sat in her uniform having breakfast with Victor and Corrine.

They exchanged an uncertain look.

'It's not finished yet,' Corrine said.

'It's fit to live in at least.' Ottilie poured herself some tea. She couldn't show it, but she was going to miss these breakfasts. It had been nice to feel like she was part of a family, rather than spending every morning eating a hurried slice of toast alone, but she also knew it couldn't last. None of them could carry on like this forever – it wasn't practical. She was also increasingly aware of the extra burden she was creating for them both, and especially with Corrine's illness, though neither of them would admit it. 'I can keep to the upstairs rooms as much as possible, and at least I have floors to walk on downstairs. It's not so bad.'

'The heating pipes aren't back in,' Victor said. 'And the nights are getting colder.'

'It's not September until next week,' Ottilie said. 'It's not that bad. Besides, it'll save on heating bills if I just put on a cardigan – it's always too tempting to put the heating on as soon as the first leaf falls from a tree anyway.'

'What about your washing and so forth?' Corrine asked.

'I'm sure I'll find a way around it. People live in worse conditions and manage all right.' She looked up from buttering a slice of toast and smiled. 'It's been lovely here, and you've been so kind, but I think I've outstayed my welcome.'

'You could never do that.'

'Besides, if I don't go home now I'm afraid I never will. And I don't know how you feel about adopting another daughter, but you're in danger of getting one whether you like it or not.'

'Whatever will I do without our chats in the evenings?' Corrine asked, looking dangerously close to tears.

'I'll visit all the time.'

'For ten minutes when you come to check on me.'

'No, proper visits, not just nurse stuff.'

'You'll be too busy. You said yourself you'll have to do your repairs at night now you're back at work in the day.'

'I promise I'll make time,' Ottilie said gently.

'I think,' Victor put in, 'what Corrine is trying to say is that having you here has been as good for us as it has been helpful to you. You've been no bother – in fact, you've helped us through a dark time. Thank you.'

'I should be saying that to you!' Ottilie said, tears burning her eyes. 'You've been brilliant. When I moved to Thimblebury I never imagined I'd make friends like you.'

Victor wafted his hand, grunted something about seeing to the girls, and then hurried out of the kitchen. Ottilie suspected a show of emotion was about to burst from him and he'd rather keep it to himself. She was sort of on the same page, but it wasn't so easy to run away from hers.

'I just have to...' Corrine began, before taking herself out of the kitchen too.

Ottilie crammed a slice of toast into her mouth and chewed

rapidly. It would stop her crying or she'd choke on it – either way the job would be done.

'Aren't you a sight for sore eyes!' Lavender was wiping down the counter of the reception desk when Ottilie arrived for her first shift for weeks.

Ottilie looked around the tiny waiting room, and a strange, unexpected affection washed over her. She never imagined she'd have missed it, and her time had been filled with a million other worries, but she realised now that she'd been away for too long. She was a nurse, first and foremost and always, and she needed to be doing what she did best – caring for others.

'Hope you've got a nice full clinic for me.'

'Be careful what you wish for,' Lavender said as she folded up the cloth and threw it into a cubbyhole beneath the desk. 'It's full, but I can't promise it will be nice. Want a preview?' she added, switching on her computer.

'It's probably a good idea,' Ottilie said, making her way around the counter to see the screen. It took Lavender a few minutes to get the page up.

Ottilie gave it a quick look and then nodded. 'Seems all right.'

'Oh, and Fliss wants to know if you can do a house call. Darryl Jones.'

Ottilie frowned. 'I haven't seen him before?'

'Perhaps not. He's on insulin. Some learning difficulties. Been no bother for the past year or so, but his mum rang to say he might be hiding his insulin so he can't take it for some unknown reason. Says his bloods are all over the place and it's the only thing she can think of. He has a history of doing random things like that. Fliss would go up there, but it might be sorted just as easily by you if you don't mind taking a look. It would save her a job.'

Ottilie wrote the name and some details down on her notepad. 'What's the address?'

'I'll print if off for you. It's a bit out of the village – Hilltop Farm – but it's only ten minutes or so in the car.'

'Brilliant. I'll go up after morning surgery.'

'I was hoping you'd say that,' Lavender said. 'That locum was all right, but she didn't half pull her face every time you asked her to do something.'

'Well we can't all be brilliant,' Ottilie said with a smile.

'You're telling me! Fliss is thrilled to have you back and so am I. At least we'll have some actual work done.'

'Is Fliss in yet?'

'Walked in two minutes before you – I don't know how you didn't see her.'

'In her office?'

'In the kitchen making coffee.' Lavender grinned. 'She went to visit Charles last night, so I expect it was a heavy one.'

Ottilie didn't need to ask what Lavender meant. She didn't think she'd ever get her head around Fliss's marital arrangements, but they seemed to work for her and Charles because they were one of the happiest couples Ottilie had ever met.

'I'll go and say good morning,' Ottilie said, leaving Lavender to continue setting up for the day.

Fliss was sitting at the kitchen table nursing a mug, though she brightened considerably as she looked up to see Ottilie coming in. 'Welcome back!'

'Thanks,' Ottilie said. 'And thank you for being so understanding about the time off.'

'Have you got everything done?'

'Not yet, but it's habitable at least. I'll get the rest done as and when.'

'And you've forgotten that silly business of leaving Thimblebury?'

Ottilie gave a sheepish smile. 'I never wanted to leave. It was the only way I could see at the time.'

'That's what happens when you don't talk to people. I hope you've learned your lesson.'

'Absolutely!' Ottilie said, glad to be back on good terms with her boss. Fliss had been so offended by Ottilie's resignation notice that she wondered if they'd ever get to this point again. Lavender had since told her that Fliss took things like that personally. One thing was certain, it wasn't an episode she wished to repeat.

'Ready to heal the sick of Thimblebury?'

'Ready as I'll ever be.'

'I couldn't agree more,' Fliss said, putting down her empty coffee cup and leaving her seat with a faint look of regret. 'I suppose we'd better go and see what Lavender has in store for us.'

CHAPTER TWENTY-FIVE

Victor had been quiet as they'd moved her belongings back into Wordsworth Cottage. Ottilie was pained to know she was the reason, but she was sure he and Corrine would be glad to get their house back.

She was surprisingly glad to be back in hers too. It was far from finished and not exactly the height of luxury, but it was hers. She'd missed its cosy, low, weirdly wallpapered ceilings, the odd angles of corners and walls that weren't straight, and door frames that seemed as if they would collapse at any moment, and the peeling paint on the windowsills and the odd clanking the cold tap upstairs made when she turned it. Victor had been right about one thing, though – as the sun went down it was chilly. With the electric back on but no radiators yet attached to the walls downstairs, Ottilie would have to get creative.

As luck would have it, Stacey had messaged her as she'd unloaded the last of her stuff from Victor's car to see whether she was settled in yet, and with her reply, Ottilie had asked whether she had a spare electric heater she could borrow.

The scent of newly sawn wood was strong as Ottilie went to get the door to find Stacey there.

'It's looking better in here,' she said, giving the new hallway floor an approving once-over.

'Isn't it?' Ottilie said.

'Heater's in the car. I could do with a hand to bring it in.'

'How did you get it in the car in the first place?' Ottilie asked as she followed Stacey back down the path.

'Chloe helped me.'

'Chloe?'

Stacey turned and gave a wry smile. 'You try telling Chloe she can't do something because she's pregnant and you'd get such a gobful it's easier to let her get on with it. It's not all that heavy with two anyway, just a bit unwieldy.'

Ottilie wasn't thrilled at the notion that Chloe had been lifting, but she understood where Stacey was coming from. Having seen first-hand Chloe's attitude to her pregnancy, she wasn't a bit surprised. Her one misgiving was that it wasn't really safe for Chloe to be overdoing things. Stacey didn't seem unduly concerned, though. Instead, she chatted as they lifted the heater from the boot of her car.

'I bet Lavender was happy to see you back at work today. Says they didn't much care for your cover. I don't think anyone did.'

'I got that impression.' Ottilie lifted her end of the heater up over the gateposts. 'It was quite nice actually. I had so many complaints about her I thought she couldn't possibly be that bad, so perhaps all the patients finally like me after all.'

Stacey laughed. 'They always liked you.'

'You didn't hear them moan that first clinic I did after Gwen had gone. You wouldn't have said that if you had.'

Between them they set the heater down in the living room.

'Got time to stay for a drink?' Ottilie asked.

'What kind of drink?'

'Any kind you like as long as it's tea. I'm clean out of booze.'

'What kind of cheap date are you? I suppose it'll have to be tea then. Although...' she continued as she followed Ottilie into the kitchen, 'Geoff says you're quite an expensive date.'

Ottilie turned to her with a wry smile. 'He still thinks his little cupid stunt worked?'

'He's convinced he's put you on the path to true love. He's a more hopeless romantic than I am, that brother of mine. Saying that, I think Magnus had more than a bit of a hand in it – bad as each other, they are.'

Ottilie shook her head as she switched on the kettle. 'I wish he had.'

'Had what?'

'Found me a bit of true love.'

When she turned back, Stacey was staring at her. 'You said... You told me it was too soon.'

'It was. I mean, it is. It's...'

Ottilie had no idea where her sudden frankness had come from. Yes, Stacey had visited a few days after the cinema debacle to share what Geoff had told her and to get Ottilie's side of the story, and Ottilie had told her in no uncertain terms that there was absolutely no way she was getting involved with Heath. Not with any man, because it was too soon. Perhaps, being here now in her empty house, despite the fact that it was good to be back home, she was reminded forcibly that home meant alone. The prospect of sleeping in a house by herself again stared her in the face and perhaps she'd had a sudden attack of nerves.

'Hmm...' Stacey was silent for a moment before she spoke again. 'Do you like him?'

'I hate to say it, but yes.'

'Why do you hate to say it?'

'Because I shouldn't be feeling that way about another man.'

'Why not? Your husband wouldn't have wanted you to be lonely, would he?'

'Of course not, but that doesn't change how *I* feel about it. It's not right; it's not proper to move on this fast, and I don't think it would be a very good idea even if I thought otherwise.'

'God, you sound like a nineteenth-century schoolmistress. Right and proper? Says who? You get to decide the timetable, no one else. You decide how you feel and what you want. It's nobody else's business if you marry twenty men next week.'

Ottilie gave a half-smile. 'Well, the law might have something to say about that.'

'But there's no law against liking another man just because you're a widow. Give it a go, one date. What harm could it do?'

'I don't—'

'Stop that! One of us ought to have a fella, and as nobody's remotely interested in me...'

'Now you can stop that!' Ottilie shot back. 'I'm sure plenty are interested – you just haven't found the right one yet.'

'I haven't found one at all. I'd go for the wrong one right now; it'd be nice just to be asked.'

'That makes you sound like a charity case and you should never feel like that. I hope you don't.'

Stacey grimaced. 'Sometimes I wonder what's wrong with me, you know? Why can't I find a nice man?'

'You live in Britain's smallest village, which hardly helps.'

Stacey laughed. 'True. I'm sure it's not Britain's smallest village but I take your point. What a pair we are.'

'There's no hope, is there?'

'There is for you if you stop being so stubborn about it for five minutes.'

'I can't.' Ottilie got two mugs out of a cupboard. 'I'm...'

'What?'

'Scared.' She let out a sigh as she looked back at Stacey.

'Scared it's too soon?'

'Scared I'm going into it for the wrong reasons. And even if I'm not, scared that I'll fall for him.'

'That's sort of the idea, isn't it?'

'I don't know. There's...' Ottilie paused. 'What do you know about him?'

'What do you mean?'

'We talked about it – we both agreed he's got trust issues.'

'And you're about the most reliable, trustworthy person I know.'

'You hardly know me.'

'I know enough. I know what my instincts tell me.'

'But what happened to make him like that? Is it too big to get past? What if he's really screwed up, like beyond-help screwed up? And I go blundering in and get involved and it's all a mess?'

'It might happen, but if anyone can help him, you can.'

'OK,' Ottilie said slowly. 'Say I could. Say I even want to – and let me tell you I have enough baggage of my own to deal with. Say we ended up... I don't know, like... happy—'

'*In love*, you mean?' Stacey raised her eyebrows.

'I'm not going to say that word because it feels like tempting fate, but what if things get good? And what if something bad happens again? What if I lose again? I don't think I can do it. I think a second time would finish me off.'

'What if something bad doesn't happen? What if it's all great? What if you turn your back on this and it ends up being the biggest mistake of your life?'

'If I did turn my back on it, I don't suppose I'd ever know either way.'

'Don't you at least want to try?'

'Yes... No...' Ottilie shook her head as if to clear it. 'I don't have a clue.'

'God, is your brain like that all the time?'

'Pretty much.'

'No wonder you're in a state then.'

'What should I do?'

'You're asking me when you know the answer I'm going to give. But it's not up to me. Only you can make that call. I know what I would do in your shoes, but we're different people, aren't we?'

Ottilie nodded slowly. She'd thought it before, but their differences were shown in sharp relief again. Stacey had been abandoned by a feckless husband and she desperately wanted to be shown love by someone who wouldn't leave her. She wanted to feel wanted. But it wasn't like that for Ottilie. She'd had that love, and it had been snatched away from her. She still felt the force of that love every single day, and she didn't think that would ever stop, not for as long as she lived. So for her, if she were to let someone new in, it was almost like one of them would have to give way for the other, and it didn't seem right that Josh's memory should be diminished, that his love should be forgotten for the sake of someone else. People could say as often as they liked that Josh wouldn't want her to be lonely, but Josh wasn't the issue – she was. She didn't want to be lonely, but she didn't want to betray her first love either, and moving on would feel like doing just that. Josh would have understood if he'd been here now. Josh would have felt the same way if she'd died and he'd been left behind. It felt like a question without answer, and she was getting sick of asking it.

'What's Flo in for?' Ottilie asked as she looked down the clinic list. She'd been back at work for a few days, back in the swing of things far quicker than she'd imagined. 'I thought all her tests had come back OK.'

'Says she needs her blood pressure checking.'

'What for? Has she got symptoms?'

'I don't know – I couldn't get any sense out of her. In the

end I thought it was easier to book her in than argue; it'll only take you a minute after all.'

'True enough. And I haven't been to visit her for a while, so it'll be useful to see how she's getting on.'

'She must be happy to be seeing so much of Heath since he's been working on your house.'

'She must,' Ottilie said carefully. Whenever Heath was mentioned these days her voice took on a careful tone. She didn't want to get drawn into anything she might regret where he was concerned.

The slot for Flo's appointment came and went, but she didn't show. Ottilie phoned her house but got no response. There wasn't time to go and see her during clinic, but after the last patient had gone, she shrugged on her coat, briefly explained to Lavender where she was going and hurried out.

Ten minutes later she was knocking on Flo's door.

'All right, all right...'

Flo's voice travelled up the hallway. At least she sounded in fairly good health. Grumpy but healthy, Ottilie thought. Pretty much business as usual.

'Oh,' she said as she opened the door. 'What have you come for?'

'You were supposed to come and see me.'

'Was I? I don't recall you asking me for tea. In fact, you've never asked me round for tea.'

'Not tea – at the surgery.'

Flo was thoughtful for a moment. 'Right,' she said finally. 'That. I did make an appointment, didn't I?'

'Yes, but you didn't keep it.'

'Well, I feel all right now.'

Ottilie tried not to frown. 'So you don't need your blood pressure checking? Because I have the reader right here if—'

'No, that's fine, but you can come in anyway.'

'I have to—'

'You can't spare a minute? You haven't been in ages.'

Ottilie let out a sigh. She supposed she hadn't been in a while, and when all was said and done she did owe Florence at least this much for how instrumental she'd been in getting Wordsworth Cottage fixed up. And she could make sure that Flo really was all right, which was the main reason she'd come.

'Just a minute,' she said.

Flo ushered her inside. 'I've got biscuits,' she said. 'Those fancy ones. You know...'

'Hmm,' Ottilie said, though she didn't know.

Flo opened the living-room door, and Ottilie had to catch the instinctive groan in her throat. How had she not seen this coming?

'Oh, you're here...'

Heath held up a hand in greeting. Ottilie had certainly seen him look more enthusiastic, but her reply wasn't much better. Flo hadn't told her he was here, and it looked as if she hadn't told him Ottilie might be calling either. And Ottilie was now quite sure Flo had been expecting her. It had to be what the bogus appointment at the surgery had been about. She must have known that when she failed to show up, Ottilie would come straight after clinic to check on her.

Clever Florence and stupid Ottilie.

'Yes,' Ottilie said, glancing at Flo briefly before turning back to him. 'Your gran didn't show for her clinic appointment. I wanted to make sure everything was all right.'

'A bit above and beyond, isn't it? Calling here, I mean? What's wrong with her? Oh, hang on – you can't tell me. But it's enough to come to her house, is it?'

Ottilie gave him a sharp look. *He* was back – that cynical, untrusting, suspicious man she'd first met in this very room.

'It's called being a nurse.'

'You're on duty then?'

'No, but that doesn't stop me from caring.'

'Sit down,' Flo instructed her.

Ottilie did as she was asked while Flo went into the kitchen.

'How have you been?' Ottilie asked Heath, more for something to break the awkwardness. She had a pretty good idea how he'd been, because she'd only seen him a few days before when he'd come to help with her radiators. That meeting had been as mortifying as this, but at least they'd had the distractions of other people and a job to do – no small talk required.

'Good,' he said with about as much conviction as a man who had no idea what the word even meant. 'How's work?'

'Like I was never away.'

'That must be good then. As you like your job so much. I mean, clearly you love it because here you are, doing it out of hours...'

'It is and I do. Is it so bad to care about people?'

Flo came back in with a cup and saucer for Ottilie, cutting short his reply – not that Ottilie particularly wanted to hear it.

'There you go.'

Heath stood up. 'I should get back. Long drive and that.'

'Already?' Florence said, and Ottilie was struck by a distinct sense of déjà vu.

Hadn't this scene played out just like this once before? Before she and Heath had got to know each other, before she'd been shown what it was she was throwing away. But it was too late now – she could see clearly that the damage was done and there was no way back. He couldn't stand to be here with her long enough to finish his tea, even if that meant upsetting his grandmother. Ottilie had hurt him and he wasn't willing to forgive, and she hardly blamed him for that. It seemed she'd triggered something in him that had almost started to heal, something to do with his past and his ex. It looked as though what Ottilie had feared as she'd discussed him with Stacey was right – he was beyond help. Whatever he'd been through had damaged him, and bringing him back was more than Ottilie could do – she had enough damage of her own to repair. Perhaps it was time to release him from all his obligations to her.

'By the way, I don't think I've really thanked you for all your help,' she began as he reached for his coat.

'It's no problem,' he said stiffly.

'I reckon we're almost done. I mean, I think what still needs doing is easy enough for me to do myself. So...'

'You don't want me to come this weekend. Got it.'

His tone was terse, and even in the midst of their current awkwardness it shocked her to hear. It was like the snarl of a wounded animal.

'I didn't mean it like that; I only meant I know you're giving up a lot of your time to come up here from Manchester, and I'm sure you'd like your weekends and evenings back.'

'That's good of you.'

And there it was again, such coldness. How could a man who'd been so warm and funny that silly night at Magnus and Geoff's cinema be so cold now? Had she really hurt him so badly? All she'd done was the sensible thing for both their sakes.

He bent to kiss Florence. 'See you next week, eh?'

Florence nodded, looking sorely put out that her plan had gone awry. In any other circumstance, Ottilie might have found it funny. Then he strode out, the sound of the front door slamming a moment later bringing that awful sense of déjà vu back again.

CHAPTER TWENTY-SIX

Her favourite part of any home improvement had always been the painting. Ottilie guessed that it was everyone's favourite bit, because this was where you finally got to see what it might look like. Plus, after the week she'd had, there was something therapeutic about being able to totally switch off and zone out, simply watching the brush go back and forth along the skirting board as the colour spread.

The front door was open, letting in a crisp breeze from the garden which carried the fumes of the paint away. On it, instead of paint, she could smell the first notes of autumn – her first one since she'd come to live in Thimblebury. Already, the leaves were turning gold and orange. In a few weeks the landscape would be alive with colour. A few months ago she'd have been terrified to leave her front door unlocked like this, but Thimblebury, despite the dramas, had been kind to her. She trusted her community completely and she felt safe. She'd been lost in all of this, content to drift, the problems of the week passing through her like all those autumn leaves carried away on a stream when the sound of a text-message alert snapped her out of it.

Putting the brush down she went to retrieve her phone from the table. Faith. She unlocked it to read the message, anxiety like a crushing weight suddenly bearing down on her once again as she readied herself for something that would inevitably stress her out in one way or another, because messages from Josh's old colleague always did.

Can you call me?

Ottilie dialled the number.

'Hey,' Faith said. She sounded tired, but perhaps that was only a reflection of how Ottilie herself was feeling. She was tired of thinking about this, tired of that shadow hanging over her life. Josh had died, but she couldn't move on, not while his murder was unresolved, not when she dreaded every phone call from his station that would rake it all up again. 'How are you doing?'

'Well, I've been better. That flooding I had has taken a few weeks to get sorted. I'm on the home stretch now, I think.'

'Oh, you mentioned it before but I didn't realise it had been so bad.'

'That's life, eh? These things happen. It's probably a good thing you didn't come to visit after all.'

'Oh, right, sorry, I did say I would, didn't I? It's just been so busy here.'

'Of course – no need to apologise. So...'

'Yes, well, I know we've been here before but I wanted to tell you we've had a breakthrough in the case. A proper one this time, Ott, at least, I hope it will be. Our guy has been brought back into custody, and this time we have a witness, one I don't think will back out. I think we might have him, Ott.'

Ottilie lowered the phone and stared at the opposite wall. She didn't have words. She didn't know how she was supposed to feel about this. She'd imagined it would be relief, but Faith was right – they'd been here before and the case had fallen apart.

'Ottilie?' Faith's voice was distant and tinny.

Ottilie put the phone back to her ear. 'Sorry... yes.'

'It's good news, isn't it?'

'Of course.'

'Are you...?' Faith stalled. 'Are you all right with this?'

'Why wouldn't I be? Like you said, if we've got a solid witness then it's going to go to trial, isn't it? And that has to be good.'

'Hold tight,' Faith said. 'The end of your nightmare might be in sight.'

'Yes. Thanks, Faith.'

'Is there anything you want to know? Anything you want to ask me?'

'I don't think so.'

'Well, you know where to find me when you change your mind. I know it's a lot to take in, and I'm sure things will occur to you when you've processed it.'

'Yes. Thanks.'

'No need,' Faith said. 'I want to catch that bastard as much as you want us to. I don't want to get your hopes up again, but I think we're going to crack it this time. I'll keep you posted.'

'Thanks,' Ottilie said again, because she had nothing else. 'Bye.'

She heard Faith's reply dimly as she ended the call. She felt... nothing. She'd imagined she'd feel relief, as she'd done the last time they'd been here, but she was numb. Perhaps because she couldn't trust this was it, she couldn't allow herself to feel anything. Surely this wasn't all she had?

As she picked up her paintbrush she tried to process it, like Faith had said. What did this mean for her? Nothing material would change, not in her world, not here in Thimblebury. And yet, she felt as if everything was about to change. Her relationship with Josh's memory would change. Did it mean she now had to move on? She would have one less reason to hold back. Did it mean that she finally had to accept he was gone and not coming back? She ought to have done that already, but somehow, this case had kept her tethered. It had been a link, a reason to hold on, and once that was gone, what then? Case closed, everyone moved on and Josh was forgotten? How could she contemplate that, and yet, she couldn't hold on forever.

As the realisation crashed in on her, numbness gave way to overwhelming sorrow, a sense of loss as great as anything she'd experienced during the first days of her mourning. When this was over, so was Josh? Was it really that simple? And what then?

Paintbrush still clutched in her hand, Ottilie sat on the floor and folded in on herself, a wave of uncontrollable emotion crashing over her. She wept, tears that came thick and fast, full-blown heaving sobs that stole her breath.

Ottilie had no idea how long she'd been crying. She hadn't heard the footsteps on the floor, but a voice made her look up, shocked and guilty, as if she'd been caught doing something she shouldn't have been. At first she couldn't quite focus through her tears, and even as she dried her eyes she was confused. Why was he here? Why now?

'Ottilie!' Heath's tone was urgent, almost panic-stricken. 'What's wrong?'

She wished she could tell him, but no words would come.

'Come here...'

Gently, he pulled her to stand and led her to a chair.

'Take your time,' he said, crouching so that he was at her level, face to face. 'And if it's something you don't want to tell me that's all right, but I'm going to stay here until you're OK.'

She stared at him. She understood the words but not what he meant. Why was he doing this? Why was he here?

'Do you need a drink? A glass of water? Something else? I can run over to Gran's – she'll have some brandy or something.'

'No.' Ottilie managed finally to utter a word. 'Don't go.'

His hand hovered over hers, uncertain. His gaze searched hers. For answers? Perhaps. She could see that he wanted to comfort her and he didn't know if he was allowed, so she instinctively reached for his hand and took it, and held it tight. He needed to comfort her and she needed to feel it. Right now she needed strength, and in that moment, she could see he was the man to give it. Whatever their differences, whatever else he might be, he was a good man.

Blindly, she reached for his other hand and pulled both of them to her face, burying herself in them.

'I'm sorry,' she whispered.

She didn't know who she was saying sorry to. To Heath, whom she'd treated so shabbily. To Josh, whom even now she felt she was betraying, simply by wanting so badly to have Heath close. To herself for denying herself the right to happiness.

He moved in and leaned his forehead on hers. She could feel his breath on her hands, could hear it coming in short bursts, and she could tell he was upset. For her? She had to suppose so, though she couldn't accept she deserved it.

'Whatever you need,' he said as she clung tighter to his hands. 'I'm here.'

She wanted him to hold her and yet hated herself for it. She wanted to be wrapped in his arms, no matter the guilt, but she had no right to ask that of him after the pain she'd caused.

But as if he'd read her thoughts, he gently pulled his hands from her grip and tipped her face up to his. She nodded in answer to his silent question, and he wrapped his arms around her and pulled her close. She buried herself in his embrace and began to cry again, and that only made him hold her closer still, as if by doing so he could absorb her sorrow and make it his own.

They stayed like that, until Ottilie had no more tears left, and then they stayed locked in silence while she listened to the beats of his heart synching with her own. And by degrees, as she returned to reality, she wondered what on earth he was making of this.

At last, she looked up at him. 'I'm sorry you had to see all that.'

'Why are you sorry? It's not your fault.'

'Still, I'm sure that was the last thing you needed.'

He shook his head. 'Doesn't matter.'

'I suppose you're wondering what could have got me in such a state.'

'Yes, but I'm not going to ask. Tell me about it if you want to, and if you don't, then don't. It's your business if you choose to keep it to yourself.'

Ottilie nodded slowly and he let go of her, pulling up a spare chair and sitting on it to face her.

'I, um...' she began. 'I just had a phone call from Josh's... my husband – from his colleague. His police colleague. I don't know if I ever told you he was in the police.'

'No, but Gran did.'

Ottilie gave a wan smile. She'd never told Flo that, but she supposed the village gossip would have done. 'Did your gran tell you how he died?'

'No.'

So that was one detail that hadn't made it round the village. At least Fliss – the only person Ottilie had confided that detail to – kept her counsel well enough.

Ottilie took a breath, ready to say it out loud, one more time. She owed Heath that much of an explanation for what he'd just seen.

'He was killed on duty by a gang member. Everyone sort of

knew who it was, but there hasn't been enough evidence to take it to court. Until now.'

'Hmm.' Heath looked down at his hands. 'So I guess it's brought that time back again? I can see why that would be distressing. Thank you.'

'For what?'

'For trusting me enough to share it with me.'

'I should be thanking you for being here.'

'I didn't do anything special; it was a lucky coincidence.'

'But still...'

'I'm glad I was. I wouldn't like to think you might have gone through that alone.' He studied her for a moment. 'Has it always been like that? That bad?'

'Sometimes,' she admitted, surprised by her own candour. 'A lot in the beginning.'

He shook his head slowly, never taking his eyes from her, so full of sympathy and pity that she could barely take the weight of it. She hated that she made him feel that way, and yet she was more grateful than she could say that he cared. 'I don't know how you get through it,' he said. 'But I understand a lot more now.'

She wondered what it was he understood, but she was too emotionally spent to ask. She was exhausted – physically as well as mentally. All she wanted to do was lie down and sleep, but there was still so much to do here and she couldn't.

'I should wrap that paintbrush before it dries out,' she began, getting up from her seat, but he waved her back down.

'I'll do it.'

'There's cling film on the table,' she said, too tired to argue. Maybe she would pack up and head to bed after all. Maybe a quick afternoon nap would see her right to starting again later.

'Did you come for something other than my breakdown?' she asked, and he turned to her with the faintest hint of a smile.

'I lost my wallet. I couldn't think where it might be and it was really only clutching at straws that I came over in case I'd dropped it here.'

'Oh, well I haven't found one. Was there a lot of money in it?'

'Not really, and I've cancelled what cards were in there, so it doesn't matter that much. The door was open... I hope you don't mind that I came in. I did shout.'

'God, don't apologise for that. I hope you find your wallet.'

'I don't really care either way. I was just in the neighbourhood and thought it was worth checking. If I don't find it, then it's only a wallet. Sometimes you need to be reminded that there are far bigger things than lost wallets.'

'True. I suppose I did that in a bit of a dramatic way,' she added ruefully.

'Sometimes...' he added slowly, almost as if talking to himself, 'you need to be reminded that no matter how bad your own pain looks, there's someone going through more.'

'Everyone's pain matters.'

'You say that but when I hear what you've been through, I don't know how you can. I feel... It doesn't matter. It's not about me now, is it?'

Ottilie wanted to tell him she was ready to listen if he needed it, but she didn't honestly feel she had the strength to spare for him at this moment, no matter how she wished she had.

'Do you want company?' he asked into the gap. 'I could stay.'

'No, it's all right. I'm sure you have things to do.'

He raised his eyebrows. 'Are you just saying that?'

'Yes,' she admitted, because she wanted him to stay more than anything. She wanted to be in his arms again where she'd felt safe and comforted and like she could face whatever came her way. She wanted to tell him how wrong she'd been, how sad she was that she'd blown her chances with him, how she realised now she'd been stupid to let him slip through her fingers, stupid to let fear and guilt stand in the way. She wanted to say that no matter what his own demons were she would help him deal with them, no matter what it took, because he was worth the effort and he was worth the risk. There might never be a right time to say those things but she still felt them. For the moment, being close was enough.

'Then I'll stay,' he said. 'Would another hug help?'

'Yes,' she said. 'I think I'd like that.'

And so he took her in his arms and she let his quiet strength flow through her.

CHAPTER TWENTY-SEVEN

Heath stayed until darkness covered the village beyond her cottage windows. Ottilie opened up to him about Josh, about her life and hopes and fears in a way she'd never done with anyone before. Once the story had been told, she couldn't quite believe it had happened that way.

'You're amazing,' he said.

Ottilie blushed. 'I don't know why you would think that.'

'What you've been through, and then to come here and start again, always thinking of others when you've had it harder than any of them.'

'It's all relative, I think. Whenever you're going through something it's hard and it doesn't feel easier just because you know someone else is going through it too. I mean, you've had your share of stress, haven't you?'

'What do you mean?'

'Your marriage. I...' Ottilie's sentence tailed off. She could tell by his face that she'd said too much, that perhaps she wasn't meant to know what she did.

'Sorry,' she added quickly. 'I didn't mean to pry – forget it.'

His expression cleared. 'Fair's fair. You've shared your story with me, so I suppose I ought to explain why I'm such a miserable git.'

Ottilie gave a small smile. 'But I don't want you to feel pressured.'

'It will probably do me good.'

'It will,' she said, knowing from recent experience that it was true.

'The thing about Mila,' he said slowly, 'is that...' He sighed and shook his head. 'I don't know where to start. I was an idiot, and when I think about how stupid I was I'm ashamed. The things that happened to me – to me and my family – a smarter man would have seen it coming, but I didn't. And I always assumed I was a smart man. But she was so convincing. Gaslighting, I think we call it, don't we?'

'That's the thing about gaslighting,' Ottilie said gently. 'The people who do it are good at it – that's why they so often get away with it. I can't tell you how many times I've come across victims of it in my job. You don't have to tell me if it's painful. I only asked because you'd listened to me and I thought... well, it's obvious to me that something's gone on and whatever it was hurt you. I wondered if you might want to talk, but I don't want to push it.'

'I never wanted to tell anyone before because I felt so stupid. But if I was going to tell anyone, then it would be you.'

'I'm glad about that. The offer will always be open if you change your mind. How long have you been split up?'

'It depends on your definition of splitting up,' he said ruefully. 'We'd been back and forth a few times over the past three years. She'd do something that didn't seem right but then she'd always have a good cover story. And I loved her... God, I loved her. I wanted to believe her every time, and I ignored what was in front of my face. The final straw was at the end of last year.'

'And you haven't been tempted to go back to her this time?'

'No. She went too far, even for me. Besides, she's got a new bloke now.'

'How do you feel about that?'

'I wish him luck – he's going to need it. He's going to need deep pockets too.'

Ottilie frowned, but she didn't follow the last bit of his statement up. If he wanted to elaborate then he would. He'd given her space to tell her story, so she had to do the same for him.

'Do you miss her? I know you say she did awful things but you also said you'd loved her.'

'I wonder now whether I was just infatuated rather than in love. How could I love someone who did stuff like she did? It's crazy though – until a few months ago I'd have probably taken her back if she'd tried hard enough to convince me. I ought to thank the new guy – he saved my bacon. Makes me a mug, doesn't it?'

'I don't think so. Love is love – you can't help it.'

'But you can choose to get out of its way when it's bad for you.'

'I'm not sure love is that simple either.'

'Listen to me...' He shook his head. 'At least I have a choice; I should be thankful.'

'It doesn't work like that.'

They needed more light, and Ottilie got up to flick a lamp on. The new sofa and armchairs she'd ordered to replace the water-damaged ones still hadn't arrived, so they were sitting on dining chairs. It was hardly comfortable and relaxed, and a good therapist would always choose a chaise longue, but what they were doing felt like therapy all the same. If they could help each other here tonight, then everything until this point would have been worth it, despite the missed opportunities and crossed wires. Finally, she knew this man, and finally, he was someone she wanted in her life, no matter how. If they were to remain friends, then that would be enough. If they were to become something more... well, she wouldn't – couldn't – push it, but she was content to trust in the future.

'I think I've kept you long enough,' he said as she sat back down.

Ottilie looked at her watch and was shocked to see it was gone eleven. 'Where did that go?' she asked with a little laugh. 'Must have been intense.'

'I think it must have been,' he said, smiling too. 'I hope in some small way it helped.'

'I could say the same to you.'

'It did,' he said. 'If you ever retrain as a psychiatrist, put me down for a session or two.'

Ottilie's laughter grew. Her eyes were still swollen and nose still hot and bunged up from her sobbing, but her thoughts were clearer than they had been in some time and she felt lighter. She had Heath to thank for that, there at the right place and the right time, like a knight on a horse coming to rescue her.

'Thank you,' she said.

He nodded, his eyes warmer than his cautious smile. 'I'll see you around, maybe?'

'You'd better. We're friends now, right?'

'I thought we were already.'

'Proper friends now.'

'Right.'

They stood facing each other for a moment. Ottilie wondered whether she ought to reach for a hug. It was funny, they'd held on to one another for some time during the evening, but now she felt shy and uncertain, and she suspected he did too. They were leaving the evening as friends, but was that all they were? What level of friends? Because there was always more than one.

In the end, he broke the deadlock by giving a good-natured nod. 'Goodnight. I hope you manage to get some sleep.'

'Yeah. Drive safe... please.'

And then he was gone, and Ottilie was alone with her thoughts again.

CHAPTER TWENTY-EIGHT

Two months since she'd first been asked to check in on a young patient at Hilltop Farm her visits were now a near daily occurrence. To save eating into clinic time, she'd made a habit of driving up there before work, just to pop her head around the door and make certain Darryl – her patient – was keeping up with his medication and his mum, Ann, was coping.

Ottilie had learned that Darryl could be challenging and sometimes didn't understand what was being asked of him, and poor Ann was alone trying to manage him and to stop the farm being repossessed by the bank. Ann's husband had died two years previously and left her trying to run everything. She was struggling with that and, as a consequence, wasn't making enough money to keep everything ticking along, and with her son's demands on top of that, Ottilie was worried she might go under. In some ways, Ann needed more help than Darryl, but Ottilie had learned that she'd never admit it. It was funny, but Ottilie could see a lot of herself in Ann in that respect. Her own battle with anxiety and badly timed panic attacks felt like one she'd started to win, but that didn't mean that she wasn't sometimes still crippled by doubts on a regular basis. But life was settling and so was she.

As she pulled the handbrake on outside the farmhouse, she was struck – not for the first time – by how bleak it was compared to Daffodil Farm where Victor and Corrine lived. One of the downstairs windows was still boarded up, even though it had been broken since Ottilie's first visit. Ann had told her she didn't know how it had been smashed, but it was obvious to Ottilie that Darryl had done it. She'd seen his frustrated temper tantrums for herself, and he was a big twenty-year-old and certainly capable. The garden was overgrown and the gate missing a few screws so that it swung crazily on its hinges. Ann's old yellow-eyed tabby was sitting on the step staring at Ottilie's car as a November sun struggled through low clouds.

Ottilie's mood had been melancholy and quiet for the past few days. The anniversary of Josh's death was close, and although she was glad to have finally moved on from that raw early grief, the old guilt was back, the sense that she ought to be sadder than she was. She still missed him of course, but it almost seemed the goal she'd set herself to start a new life had been achieved with too much success. She was constantly busy, constantly surrounded by friends and neighbours, loved and needed by her community, and moments of introspection, to remember her life with Josh, were fewer and fewer as the weeks and months went by.

As she was collecting her bits, her phone bleeped the arrival of a message.

Don't forget the party on Saturday!

Magnus. She smiled despite herself. He'd been harping on about the party he was throwing for Geoff's sixtieth for weeks and reminding everyone almost every day. This was definitely a party for him rather than his husband, and he was much more excited about it. Geoff had been content to let him get on with it.

And thank goodness they both seemed to have given up on their plan to get Ottilie and Heath together. They had perhaps realised their elaborate set-up at the cinema room hadn't worked and had taken that as a sign that their attempts had been misguided, and that was the last Ottilie had heard of it. Nobody mentioned it, as if everyone involved was a bit embarrassed now that they'd had time to reflect on it, and that suited Ottilie just fine.

As for the birthday party, she'd tried to think of ways to get out of it. Josh would be on her mind and she'd only bring the mood down. But they had another reason to celebrate – Corrine had been given the all-clear by her oncologist, so Magnus and Geoff had turned the party into a joint celebration for her too, and that made it far more difficult to get out of. Corrine and Victor had become something like surrogate parents for her and she knew they'd want to see her there.

But it wasn't just a party; it was a themed fancy-dress party, and that made it all ten times worse. Magnus had told everyone to dress as a movie character. Perhaps it would be fun to see what everyone chose, but Ottilie didn't have the time or energy to dream a costume up, let alone put it together.

Putting the phone in her bag, she got out of the car and went to knock on the door of the farmhouse. The old cat skulked away in some disgust at her approach, and as she waited for someone to answer she could hear shouting from inside.

Ann came to the door looking flustered. Ottilie could hear Darryl ranting somewhere in the house.

'Perhaps you can talk some sense into him,' Ann said helplessly as she stepped back to let Ottilie in.

'I can't promise anything,' Ottilie said, following her into the kitchen. 'Is it the usual?'

'Doesn't want to do his testing.'

Darryl was standing at the sink, glowering at his mum, but the moment he saw Ottilie following her it cleared and he broke into a smile.

'Morning, Darryl,' she said briskly. 'How are you doing today?'

'Happy now,' he said.

Ottilie gestured to a chair and he sat down. 'So you want to tell me what all the fuss is about?'

'I don't like it,' he said.

'I know,' Ottilie replied gently, opening her bag, 'but sometimes we have to do things we don't like, even though we don't like them, because they're good for us. You want to be well enough to go on that youth group camping trip next week, don't you?' Ottilie shot a furtive glance at Ann, who brightened at the mention of the respite week Ottilie had managed to organise for them. Darryl would get a free holiday, and Ann would get some desperately needed rest. It didn't matter how much love there was, sometimes a break was needed too.

'I want to go camping,' Darryl said. 'There will be trains, won't there?'

'Yes, the daytrip with the steam trains. Are you still excited about that?'

He nodded eagerly, and Ottilie mimed him pulling up a shirt sleeve.

'What are you having for breakfast?' she asked as she gave an injection with so much stealth it seemed he'd barely noticed she'd done it. 'Remember the list of good things and bad things I gave you? You're going to have something from the good list, right? Because if you have anything from the bad list then you might be too ill for the trains.'

He nodded.

'That's good then.' Ottilie reached into her bag and pulled

out a large, shiny hardback book. 'I got you a present. Saw it and thought of you straight away.'

She pushed the book across the table and Darryl's whole body seemed to glow with delight as he reached for it.

'A train book!'

Without another word, he opened it up and buried his head in the pages. Ottilie glanced round to see Ann give a tired smile.

'I think you must be an actual angel,' she said.

Ottilie laughed. 'I'm sure there are plenty who would disagree with that. At least he's sorted for another day. You'll be all right now?'

'I think so.'

'Call me if you have any problems. I'll do my best to get up here as soon as I can. Have you heard from the mental health team I put you in touch with yet?'

'Not yet.'

'OK, I'll chase that up.'

'Would you like a cup of tea before you go?'

'I'd better get down to work, thanks.'

Ottilie packed her things away. 'Bye, Darryl.'

He didn't look up from his book, and she smiled. The first happy customer of the day. And then she looked at his poor mother and remembered – not for the first time – that no matter how much bad luck she felt she'd had in her life, there were many others worse off. Perhaps she ought to try harder to appreciate the good things she did have. Starting with Geoff's party.

CHAPTER TWENTY-NINE

'Morning...' Ottilie tried not to frown as she reached the front door of Thimblebury surgery, ready to start work, to find Flo standing by it. 'Are we meant to see you this morning...?'

Flo gave a mute nod, and it was then that Ottilie noticed her trembling.

'Oh, Flo!' she cried. 'What's wrong? Come inside...'

Despite Ottilie trying to usher her in, and despite her obvious distress, Flo shook her head.

'I don't want anyone to know,' she whispered.

'Know what? Flo, what's happened?'

'Can you come and sit with me a while?'

'I can't...' Ottilie hesitated. 'You know I'd always say yes if I could, but I have a clinic full of patients this morning. You don't seem well – let me get Dr Cheadle to have a look at—'

'No!' Flo's eyes widened. 'She'd think I was silly.'

'Then how can I help? At least give me a clue. Is it a medical thing? Or is it something else? I can't help until you tell me what you need.'

'It's *her*,' Flo said, in a voice so small that Ottilie could hardly tell what she'd said.

'Who?'

'Her...' Flo's voice was louder now, her tone accusing. 'That woman. Heath's woman... Don't make me say the name.'

'His ex-wife?'

Flo nodded.

'What's she done?'

'She needs money, doesn't she? She always needs money.'

'And she's tried to get it from you?'

Flo nodded. 'I have a bit. She knows I have a bit put away. Last time Heath sorted it.'

'Flo...' Ottilie paused. 'You haven't given her anything, have you?'

'No, but she said...'

'Said what? Has she been to your house?'

Flo shook her head. 'On the phone. She said she'd get Heath into trouble if I didn't give her some. I only have a bit put away, but she knows how much it is and she wants it all. Ottilie... what should I do?'

'You certainly won't give her any money!' Ottilie exclaimed. 'Listen, I know people – my husband was a policeman and I know people in Manchester who can go and talk to her. This sounds like extortion or blackmail or something, but whatever it is, it's out of order. She's scared you half to death, hasn't she?'

'But what will she do to Heath?'

Ottilie paused, her frown deepening. 'What has she said she'll do to Heath?'

'She didn't say.'

'Then I'm sure it's all bluff. Heath said...' Ottilie thought back to their conversation about his ex. He hadn't told her what Mila had done, but he'd said how good she was at gaslighting. 'It won't be anything. She's saying what she thinks will get you to hand over your savings. Let me phone Heath—'

'Don't! He'll think I'm ever so silly!'

'He'd want to protect you! He thinks the world of you, Flo!

For the love of God, please let him deal with this. He knows his ex-wife better than anyone and he'll know what to do.'

'Do I have to go home?'

'Not if you don't want to. You won't be able to sit with me because I have patients, but I'm sure Lavender won't mind if you stay with her in the reception.'

'I can't. She'll want to know why I'm there.'

Ottilie pondered for a moment. 'OK,' she said finally. 'Would you be all right if I sit you in the kitchen with a cup of tea? I'll come and see you in between patients. We'll phone Heath now and he can be here in an hour or so. How does that sound?'

Flo gave a weak nod. Ottilie had never seen the usually indomitable old lady so distressed before. Whatever Mila had said or done, she must have really meant business.

Flo had cheered dramatically sitting in the surgery kitchen with some leftover Victoria sponge and a pot of tea. Ottilie had explained to Lavender and Fliss that they shouldn't ask her what she was doing there and that she was taking care of the situation, and they'd been content to leave it at that – though both women must have been wild with curiosity. Ottilie hoped to get permission to explain it to them later, if she even got a full explanation herself, that was. There were no guarantees. If Flo didn't want to share all the details, it wasn't up to Ottilie to push it.

An hour and a half later, Heath arrived. Lavender phoned through to Ottilie's office between patients to tell her she'd sent him into the kitchen to see Flo. They were deep in a very intense conversation when Ottilie managed to get there, both turning at her entrance with faintly guilty expressions.

'I'm sorry,' she said. 'I don't want to interrupt; I only wanted to see if everything was all right, or if there's anything I can do.'

'I don't think so,' Heath said. 'I mean, I don't think we need you to do anything. Thank you for letting her sit here until I arrived.'

'It's no problem.' Ottilie hovered at the door.

Heath glanced at Flo. 'Do you want to tell Ottilie about it?' he asked his gran.

Ottilie held up a hand. 'I don't want to know if it's going to cause a problem.'

'No, but I think you deserve an explanation. You've been more than patient – with the both of us. It's only fair we're straight with you.'

'Honestly, it doesn't matter. As long as Flo is OK – that's all I care about.'

'I know,' Heath said with a tight smile. 'And that's why I know I can trust you.' He glanced at Flo again before turning back to her. 'It's been a long time since I felt like I could trust anyone.'

Ottilie went to sit at the table with them.

'But she said...' Flo began.

Heath shook his head. 'Gran, she's trying it on with you. She can't do any of the stuff she says she can.'

'Like what?' Ottilie asked, her curiosity getting the better of her. She'd vowed to stay neutral and she hadn't wanted to pry, but there was a growing part of her that needed to know what was going on here. She was convinced, more and more, that it somehow mattered to her too.

'Oh, some bull about getting me in trouble – says she'll make an anonymous phone call to the Inland Revenue for dodgy tax, or tell the police I did something or some such crap. I don't know – every word that comes out of her mouth is a fantasy. It took me a while to realise that, but I see it now. She'll do anything for money because that's all she cares about. It's not even the worst thing she's done – not by a long chalk – but still, by her standards it's desperate.'

'What's the worst thing?' Ottilie asked, afraid of the answer but unable to stop the question.

Heath looked at his gran. 'I'd better get you home.'

'Will you be all right?' Ottilie asked, almost disappointed to know she wasn't getting any more. But she supposed it was none of her business and she was only entitled to what they chose to share.

'I will be now,' Flo said. 'Thank you.'

With a brief nod, Heath got up and took Flo gently by the arm. 'Thank you, Ottilie,' he said.

They parted at the door – Heath and Flo going off to her house and Ottilie back to her patients, her brain racing with everything she'd heard.

Ottilie had spent the afternoon pondering what she knew about Mila and her attempt to extort money from Flo. She was convinced it was a police matter but also convinced Flo wouldn't want to get them involved. With the last patient seen and the treatment room cleaned and locked up, Ottilie stepped out for home to find Heath waiting at the end of the path, a bit like his gran had been earlier. But he was alone, and he was calm.

'How is she?' Ottilie asked.

'Much better. I've managed to talk her down. Thank you,' he said.

'I didn't do anything.'

'We both know that's not true. You did more than we deserve.'

'I think a lot of your gran.'

'OK, more than I deserve,' he said with a half-smile. 'It means a lot to me that she has you close by. I feel better knowing you're here for her if she needs you. Like you were today.'

'Of course. That's what friends are for. I'm glad it's sorted.'

'Can I walk you home?'

Ottilie inclined her head. 'If you want.'

They fell into step, heading towards Wordsworth Cottage. Ottilie zipped up her jacket. Autumn was at its crisp, cold end, russet leaves still littering the pavements, cemented into cracks and gutters on the twisting lanes, but the night brought frost that hardened them. A squirrel raced nimbly up the trunk of a nearby tree and settled on a branch, beady eyes watching them go by. The sun was already setting, and Ottilie's breath curled into the air as their footsteps echoed on the road.

'I think I owe you a proper explanation,' Heath said into their brief silence.

'You don't owe me anything. It's your business.'

'OK, let me start again. I want to explain to you. I feel as if... well, I want you to understand. Would you mind? I've been a... I haven't been all that fair to you, and I'd like to...'

He let out a sigh.

'I get it,' Ottilie said. 'You don't have to tell me, but if you want to then I'm happy to listen.'

He took a deep breath, and when he let it out again it unfurled into the sky where the edges were already a frosted lilac.

'So you know about the stunt Mila tried to pull today.'

Ottilie nodded. 'Quite honestly, I still think you should go to the police about that.'

'I don't think there's any point. She hasn't done anything, and she'd only deny it.'

'I think she's got a nerve,' Ottilie said, incensed as she recalled how distressed Flo had been at the surgery door that morning. 'All this time after you split up as well.'

'She has no shame and a long memory. She won't have forgotten that Gran has a bit of money put by, just like she won't have forgotten things like my weak spots, Gran's weak spots, which buttons to push for anyone she wants to manipulate. It's all stored up in that calculating brain, ready for when she needs to use it. I wonder if she's got something missing in her brain, because she doesn't seem to operate like the rest of us. If she wants something she doesn't care how she gets it.'

'Why does that scare me a bit?'

'Oh, I don't think she'd resort to violence. She doesn't need to – she's clever enough to use other tactics.'

'Like what? What else has she done?'

Heath ran a hand through his hair. 'I don't know where to start. She was always fiddling things a bit here and there when she wanted extra cash – and she bloody loved spending, so she always wanted extra cash. I didn't exactly approve but at first it seemed like harmless things – you know, like ripping off a shop or an online catalogue or something. Sometimes it even seemed funny. I suppose that makes me as bad, but I was smitten, you know?'

Ottilie nodded. 'So when did it take a turn for the worse? When did you think, *Hang on, this isn't funny*?'

'I never wanted to see at the beginning that those harmless things had never been the only things. I'd heard about stuff she was supposed to have done to the guy before me, but I put that down to sour grapes on his part. But once she'd got me hooked, things escalated with me too – credit cards in my name that I hadn't known about, that sort of thing. The clincher, the absolute sucker punch that opened my eyes, was her going to Gran and telling her our house was going to be repossessed and that I was too proud to ask for money. Said we needed it so she was asking on my behalf, to save our home. And she nearly pulled that one off too. It was only by chance I was looking for something and I came across her bank statement and saw the money in there.'

'Flo had given it to her?' Ottilie's eyes were wide. She'd always seen Flo as a canny, shrewd character, but then, she supposed, it just went to show how people could be persuaded to do anything if they thought their loved ones were in trouble. After all, Ottilie had seen it first-hand today when Flo had shown up at the surgery earlier that day, distraught once again over one of Mila's demands. 'How much?'

'Ten thousand.' Heath said grimly.

'What a bitch!'

Heath looked taken aback for a moment at Ottilie's outburst.

'Well,' Ottilie insisted, 'she is! What a horrible thing to do! What happened?'

'It was lucky Gran decided to start up a conversation about mortgage payments when I visited a few weeks later and it all came to light,' Heath said.

His tone was practical, and Ottilie could only imagine the real turmoil going on behind it. It was no wonder he hadn't trusted her at the beginning. He'd had plenty of reason never to trust anyone again.

'But that wasn't all,' he continued. 'I discovered that Gran had changed her will.'

Ottilie whipped round. 'In favour of Mila?' she asked incredulously.

'In favour of the both of us, keeping Mum and Dad out of the loop. Mila had played on Dad's difficult relationship with Gran and used it to persuade her. I still can't quite believe she pulled it off, because you know Gran's no fool. It's sad, because it's made her harder these days too.'

'Didn't Mila realise you'd find out as soon as anything happened to your gran? And the money would belong to both of you, so even if you didn't kick up a fuss you'd have a say in how it was spent? And she'd have to wait for a long time to get it.'

He shrugged. 'I don't think playing the long game bothered her. Must have thought it was worth it. And I suppose she had plans to get it all for herself at some point, but I'll never know.

That was the final straw. I couldn't bear to look at her after that, let alone stay married to her.'

Ottilie blew out a breath. 'I can't believe someone could be that conniving.'

'Welcome to my world,' Heath said with a faint smile.

Ottilie's gate came into view. Should she ask him in?

'I've taken up enough of your time,' he said, taking the question away from her. 'I want to check on Gran before I drive back. But thanks again.'

'Thank you for telling me all this. I feel as if I understand everything a lot better now.'

'I wish I did,' he said wryly. 'One thing's for sure, I'll never understand what I saw in that woman.'

CHAPTER THIRTY

The wig had arrived in the nick of time. Ottilie was sure she could have done something with her own hair, but if she was going to dress up she might as well try to do it properly. Her long white dress hung from a hook on the back of her bedroom door. That had been free, made from a spare bedsheet by Flo, who hadn't had a clue what Ottilie wanted but had got the gist pretty quickly from a photograph and done a brilliant job. She'd found white boots in a charity shop in Keswick – the first one she'd gone into – and it had almost felt like fate.

Now, she was squinting at a tiny photograph on her phone, trying to copy the make-up on her own face. It felt loud, a bit garish – the heavy eyeliner and blood-red lips – and it wasn't a colour palette she'd ever wear ordinarily.

She took a step back to examine herself in the mirror and hardly recognised the woman staring back. But perhaps it went deeper than make-up. A year since she'd lost Josh and six months in Thimblebury – she was bound to be a different woman.

As she reached for the dress she wondered if her choice was a bit uninspired and predictable. Then again, she had to admit that predictable was probably her middle name. Safe, reliable, predictable Ottilie Oakcroft. Never taking risks, never shocking anyone, always there. It wasn't a bad thing necessarily; it was just her. At least she was fairly certain that nobody else was going to wear the same costume because she'd checked with the other women who were going to be at the party, which was almost all of her new friends apart from Fliss, who'd simply laughed in her face when Ottilie had asked if she was going to go and said she could think of better ways to spend her evening than being pestered by everyone at the party about various ailments.

Ottilie slipped on her dress and wrapped a belt around her waist. The belt was a bit off, but it would have to do. People would still know who she was meant to be – the wig would take care of that, no matter how off everything else was.

She went to the window and looked out on the glistening lane outside her cottage. It had been raining, and the sparse lamps that lit the streets and alleyways of Thimblebury were reflected in their slick surfaces. At least the rain had stopped. And since the disastrous flood, there hadn't been anything anywhere near as bad. Ottilie could only hope Fliss was right about that, a once-in-a-generation event that wasn't likely to happen again. Ottilie had only just got Wordsworth Cottage straight, and it had taken a lot of work from a lot of people – far more than she deserved – and she had absolutely no money left to do it again. Even so, knowing the community here as she did, she suspected that no matter how many times they needed to do it, they'd always be there for her. Moving to Thimblebury had seemed like a random choice at the time – the right job, the right house just happening to be thrown in her path – but more and more she felt she was somehow exactly where she was always meant to be.

.   .   .

The barn where Magnus and Geoff lived was decked with so many lights Ottilie was mildly concerned that passing planes might try to land there. The eaves, the doorways, every window, the gazebo strung over the garden, the little cinema – everything was strung with bulbs and fairy lights. She'd arrived too early to be fashionable, but as she went through the side gate and into the quadrangle at the back of the shop, she found the place was already alive with chat and laughter. Magnus was dressed as Woody from *Toy Story*, standing at a record deck with head-phones on, dancing as he cued up the next track. He looked as if he was imagining himself at a rave in Ibiza, which was even funnier when you considered that he was currently playing 'Waterloo' by ABBA.

Geoff was the first to notice her arrival and he rushed over. 'May the Force be with you!' he said, giggling as he pulled her into a hug. 'You look gorgeous!'

'You look pretty cool yourself.' Ottilie smiled as she gave his outfit a once-over. 'Someone from a Roman thing?'

'I'm Maximus Decimus Meridius, commander of the armies of the north, general of the Felix legions and loyal servant to the true emperor Marcus Aurelius.'

He slammed a fist into his breastplate and stood to atten-tion, and Ottilie broke into a laugh.

'Hang on, I should know this...'

'Aw!' His face fell. 'I hope I'm not going to have to explain this all night. Magnus said I ought to get something more obvi-ous, but I thought everyone would get this. And I thought it was sexy.'

'It is,' Ottilie said. 'Who is it?'

'It's the guy from *Gladiator*! Honestly!'

Ottilie gave an apologetic shrug. 'Sorry, I've never seen it.'

'Well, that's wasted then.'

'I'm sure everyone else has. Anyway, it still looks cool so I wouldn't worry.'

'Help yourself to a drink – they're over on the table by the cinema.'

'Thanks.'

Ottilie made her way over, stopping every so often to greet someone and swap admiration for their costumes, glad of the patio heaters warming the space. The depths of winter were still more than a month away but it was cold enough at night to feel like Christmas was close.

'Hello.'

Ottilie looked up from the drink she was pouring to see Fliss's husband, Charles, smiling at her.

'I didn't realise I'd be in the presence of royalty,' he said with a deep bow. 'Your Highness.'

Ottilie laughed and gave a nod of approval at his costume. 'Who's looking after the factory while you're here, Mr Wonka?'

'Oh, I put one of the Oompa Loompas in charge. It's a bit above his pay grade, but I couldn't miss this.'

Ottilie glanced around at the gathering.

'No,' he added, seeming to read her thoughts, 'Fliss hasn't changed her mind. She said she'd rather have a lobotomy without anaesthetic. She's gone off to stay with a friend in York, just to make sure nobody goes round and tries to talk her into coming.'

'Well,' Ottilie said, 'I'm glad you're here.'

'Me too. We can report back that it was the best party ever and make her jealous.'

'I doubt that will happen.'

'Me too, but a man can dream... Ah, here's Lavender!'

Lavender and her husband were dressed as Bonnie and Clyde. She'd been telling Ottilie for weeks about her various attempts to source the right clothes for it. The moment she saw them, she hurried over.

'Where's Han Solo?' she squeaked as she looked over

Ottilie's outfit. 'Please say you've brought a sexy Han Solo with you!'

'Oi!' Lavender's husband Gary grunted.

She nudged him with a laugh. 'Come on – you know Harrison Ford is my free pass.'

'I wouldn't worry,' Ottilie said. 'I'm fairly sure Harrison Ford isn't going to turn up tonight.'

'Oh,' Charles said, nodding at the gate to the garden. 'Here's trouble.'

Everyone turned to see Stacey and Chloe come in. Chloe was her usual cheery self, dressed in a cheerleader's uniform that showed a now quite pronounced baby bump. Stacey wore a gingham dress and a plaited wig that made her look like Dorothy from *The Wizard of Oz*, though Ottilie was certain that hadn't been her original plan. She seemed to recall something about Ripley from *Alien*, but perhaps she'd decided the costume would be too difficult to do.

'Look at you all!' Stacey cried as she dashed over, Chloe following at a slower pace. 'You look amazing!'

'So do you both,' Ottilie said.

'Last-minute change of plan,' Stacey said. 'I had this in from some Halloween or other and I thought it would do.'

'Who've you come as?' Lavender asked Chloe.

'*High School Musical*,' Chloe said, as if it was the most obvious thing in the world who she was.

As Ottilie hadn't seen it, and Lavender looked as if she was clueless too, she just smiled.

'Who are you meant to be?' she asked Ottilie.

'Princess Leia,' Stacey answered for her. 'Doesn't she look spot on?'

Chloe frowned. 'Who's that?'

There was quite comical consternation amongst the group at this bombshell.

'You don't know who Princess Leia is?' Charles almost choked on his beer. 'Star Wars?'

'Star Wars? Is that a film?'

'You don't know...'

It was lucky Charles was leaning against the timbers of the cinema, because he might have fainted away if not.

'I suppose sci-fi isn't to everyone's taste,' Ottilie said.

'I don't watch sci-fi,' Lavender replied, 'but I know the Star Wars films. Everyone knows what they are, even if they haven't seen them.'

'Well I don't,' Chloe said. 'I suppose you all think I'm stupid for not knowing.'

'Not at all,' Ottilie said. 'You watch what you watch, and why would you be interested enough to take notice of something when it's not to your taste?'

'I think we all just feel really old,' Charles added. 'To know there's a generation who don't necessarily know who Luke Skywalker and Princess Leia are. Next you'll be telling me you've never heard of John Lennon.'

'Who?' Chloe looked round at them, and Ottilie tried not to laugh at the existential look of devastation on Charles's face.

Lavender giggled. 'I think you'd better sit down,' she said, putting a reassuring hand on his shoulder.

Ottilie turned to Chloe. 'How are you doing? You can't have long to go now.'

'Three weeks,' she said. 'I wish it would come sooner; I'm sick of peeing every five minutes and my fingers puffing up. I can't even do my jeans up.'

'I think she looks lovely, don't you?' Stacey asked. 'Blooming.'

'Blooming massive,' Chloe said.

Ottilie gave a grimace of sympathy. 'At least you're nearly there, and I bet you snap right back to a size eight as soon as you're out of hospital.'

'Knowing my luck, I'll be fat forever.'

'You're not fat – you're pregnant!' Stacey sighed. She looked at Ottilie. 'I keep telling her this.'

Ottilie started a reply, but then noticed Stacey was suddenly distracted by another figure at the gate. Then she looked at Ottilie with a sly grin.

'Oh.' Lavender laughed, nudging her husband again. 'Here comes my free pass!'

Not quite Harrison Ford, but someone dressed as Indiana Jones had just been welcomed by Geoff. As he glanced across at her group, he caught her eye and waved.

'Suits him,' Stacey whispered in her ear. 'Doesn't it?'

'Oh, what a shame he didn't come as Han Solo, though,' Lavender said. 'That would have been brilliant with Ottilie dressed as Princess Leia.'

Ottilie quickly decided it would have been mortifying and silently thanked whatever force of nature had intervened. People knew better than to mention it to her, but she had a sneaking suspicion that many still wanted to push her and Heath together.

After a brief word with Geoff, he made his way over.

'I hadn't expected to see you here,' Ottilie said. 'How's everything?'

'A lot better now I've sorted out our little problem. As for tonight, I wasn't sure myself if I'd make it. But Gran said I could stay over at hers, so I thought I'd come and drive back in the morning.'

'Isn't she coming?'

'She said she might come for an hour later but she's a bit tired. She likes to make out like she's still got as much energy as she had twenty years ago, but she's slowing down. If I'm honest, it might be best if she stays home tonight. I think the business with Mila might have shaken her more than she'd like to admit.'

'Don't let her hear you say that,' Ottilie warned.

'Don't worry – I won't. She'd never speak to me again.'

'I'm glad you've sorted it out. I hope that means Mila won't try anything in future?'

'With her there's no telling, but I hope so too. If there's one positive to be had, it's that I'm absolutely sure I can't stand the sight of her now, let alone want her back.'

Ottilie gave a sympathetic smile. 'I'm sorry.'

'Why? I'm not. I've been set free and its actually pretty bloody amazing!'

Their conversation was interrupted by Charles, who came to express admiration for Heath's costume.

After exchanging a few words, he left them again, and Heath turned to Ottilie and lowered his voice. 'Am I allowed to say you look incredible?'

She smiled, flushing with pleasure. 'Thank you. Why wouldn't you be allowed to say it?'

'I don't know... I didn't want to overstep the mark.'

'I think we're past that now. You look pretty cool too. Weirdly, you look a lot like Harrison Ford, you know. I mean, in real life, not just your outfit.'

'It's been said before, which is partly why I chose this. A bit vain, I know, don't say it. Thank God I didn't go for Han Solo like Gran suggested.'

Ottilie sucked in a breath and grinned. 'That little... You do know she made this dress for me? So she knew what I was going to be wearing. Are you thinking what I'm thinking?'

'Bloody hell. That woman doesn't know when to give up, does she? I'm sorry.'

'For what? It's not your doing.'

'I know, but I don't want it to make things weird between us.'

'I won't let it get weird if you don't.'

'Glad we got that out of the way. How are you doing?' he asked.

'I'm fine.'

'I mean, really. How are you doing? We said we wouldn't keep this stuff to ourselves now – remember? I haven't forgotten you told me this month was significant.'

Ottilie gave a grateful smile. He was so considerate, so mindful of her feelings that she couldn't believe how lucky she was to have him in her life, especially when she considered how easily it could have gone another way. They'd found it difficult to understand one another at first, had very nearly gone their separate ways, and yet they'd come through it to get here. Since the day he'd found her crying, they'd reached a new understanding. They'd only seen each other a few times, and some of those had been times of great stress, unlike when he'd been working on her house, and yet, they were more comfortable and communicated better during those few occasions than they ever had before. And while she still had many regrets about the day she'd rejected his offer of something more, she wasn't going to let them ruin what she had now.

'I'm beginning to make my peace with it. It feels like yesterday since it happened, and yet so much has gone on in the space between then and now it also feels like a lifetime ago. But I'm all right, I think.'

'I'm glad.' He nudged his hat back from his face and gave a lopsided grin and she burst out laughing.

'Oh my God, that was more Indiana Jones than Harrison Ford is! Now I know why you wore that outfit! You're not secretly his stunt double, are you?'

'If only I were that cool.'

'I don't know about that, but I think you're pretty cool.'

'I think you are too.'

Ottilie blushed, and to his credit he looked away, pretending not to notice.

'Want another drink?' he asked, going to the table and running a hand over the cloth.

Ottilie suddenly recognised it as the cloth that had dressed the table when Magnus and Geoff had set them up on their cinema date. He looked up at her and she could see he recognised it too. Was he recalling that night with regret? With fondness? With a combination of both as she was doing?

'What are you having? Some of Geoff's rocket-fuel wine?'

'I suppose it might be safe enough to have some of that tonight.' Ottilie joined him at the table, holding out her glass.

Any further private conversation was cut short by more arrivals and Lavender grilling Heath over his choice of outfit. Ottilie felt a bit sorry for her husband, who was clearly feeling overlooked in favour of the man who bore a remarkable resemblance to her 'free pass'.

Magnus put Boney M's 'Rasputin' on the turntable and Chloe rolled her eyes as half the garden started to sing along. Ottilie had to feel sorry for her too. She could see why Chloe got frustrated with life in Thimblebury when the height of the social calendar was a party for a middle-aged man and his mostly middle-aged guests. She was surprised, in all honestly, to see Chloe there at all. Stacey had probably nagged her, and perhaps Chloe had decided it might be the last party she could go to for a while with the baby's arrival imminent, naff or not.

By ten, the party was in full swing. Magnus and Geoff had been doing duets on a microphone that had come from nowhere, Charles had been sick in his top hat after phoning Fliss at least half a dozen times to tell her he loved her, while Lavender and Gary were dancing on a table. All was as it should be, Ottilie thought. She'd spent some time chatting to Heath, but then he'd been sidetracked by a trio of village ladies who seemed quite enamoured by his whip. Ottilie caught his eye and laughed at his look of helplessness.

'Rescue me!' he mouthed, but she only shook her head,

laughing harder still. This, right here, as she gazed on the scene, was what she'd come to Thimblebury for. She was happier than she'd been since she'd lost Josh, and she liked to think that if he could see her now, he'd be pleased for her.

She was getting another drink when there was a tap on her shoulder. She spun round to see Stacey.

'Oh, hey, I wondered where you'd got to,' she said.

Stacey slurred her reply, but even then, Ottilie could see that she was worried. 'Have you seen Chloe?'

'Not for a while, no.'

'Oh. Only I can't find her. She's not answering her phone, and nobody else has seen her in a while.'

'She might have had enough and decided to go home? She did look a bit bored.'

'I thought that, but she didn't say anything to me.'

'Maybe she didn't want you to have to go with her.'

'I suppose so. I probably should go and look.'

'Want me to come with you?'

'No, it's—'

'I'm coming with you,' Ottilie decided.

Stacey didn't argue this time.

As they pushed their way through the crowd towards the exit, Heath called over. 'Ottilie... where are you going? You're not leaving already?'

'We have to...' Ottilie put out a hand to halt Stacey. 'Have you seen Chloe?'

'No. Should I have done?'

'It's just that Stacey can't find her.'

'Nobody has seen her for at least half an hour,' Stacey added. 'So we're going to nip back to mine to see if she's gone home.'

'I'll come with you.' Heath put his drink down on the closest table.

'There's no need,' Ottilie began, but he put a hand up to

stop her.

'To be honest, I could do with a break. I'll enjoy the walk; it'll clear my head.'

Ottilie nodded. 'OK then. It shouldn't take long anyway.'

They marched quickly down Thimblebury's deserted lanes. Some of the houses had lights on in the windows, but many were in darkness, their owners at the party. None of them were exactly worried, but there was a strange sort of expectation hanging in the air between the three of them, as if they all sensed something unexpected might be waiting for them.

'She wasn't well this morning,' Stacey said into a lull. 'But she said it wasn't anything to worry about.'

'I'm sure she just got tired,' Ottilie said. 'That's understandable.'

Stacey's house was in darkness, the log burner unlit and the rooms cold.

'This is...' Stacey yanked off her wig and tossed it onto the sofa. 'Where the hell is she?'

'Maybe she never left the party,' Ottilie said.

Stacey swore under her breath and hurried out. Ottilie was about to follow when Heath stopped her.

'You hear that?'

Ottilie strained to listen and heard it too – a sort of muffled groaning cry. 'Upstairs...'

She took to the stairs and he followed her.

The top floor was in darkness just like the ground floor, but Ottilie could hear the sound more clearly now. She knocked on the door where it seemed to be coming from. 'Chloe...?'

There was no reply, only a louder groan.

Ottilie pushed open the door to find Chloe writhing in bed, clearly in pain. The curtains were open so that the light from the street was dimly illuminating her racked features. Ottilie reached for the lamp and switched it on, and Chloe seemed to finally notice she was no longer alone.

'I don't know what to do,' she sobbed.

Heath looked at Ottilie. 'Is she having the baby?'

'I think she might be. It's a bit sudden, though. Not saying labour can't be sudden, but first babies, from what little I know, don't come this quickly. Unless... Stacey said she'd been ill this morning. She might well have been in a slow labour all day and not said anything. I mean, we all know how in denial she's been over the whole thing – probably wanted to ignore the contractions and hoped they'd go away.'

'I'll go and get Stacey,' Heath said, running out of the bedroom.

Ottilie sat on the bed and smoothed Chloe's hair from her face. Wearing her cheerleader costume she looked even younger than she was, and Ottilie's heart ached for her. This was going to be hard, and she could see Chloe was suffering already.

'It's OK,' she whispered. 'Your mum's coming.'

As she waited she called an ambulance. They were a way from the hospital and it might take a while to arrive, and even as she ended the call she was preparing herself for the fact that she might have to help Chloe give birth right here.

As if to reinforce her fears, Chloe squealed. Another contraction, it had to be, and Ottilie was now convinced Chloe was closer to the birth than they'd first thought.

A moment later a breathless Heath, followed by Stacey, burst in. The colour drained from Stacey's face as she saw Chloe in the bed.

'Chloe...' Ottilie said gently, 'you're going to have to talk to me. You know about contractions, right? The midwife would have talked you through what was going to happen. So I need you to tell me how far apart they are. And you're going to have to get ready – you might have to push here. I need to look at you... Can I take the covers off and turn you over?'

'I don't want to!' Chloe wailed.

'I know, but we're going to have to.' Ottilie nodded to Stacey. 'Come and help me.'

'I should leave,' Heath said, but Ottilie stopped him.

'Could you get some things for me. Towels, a bowl of warm water, a glass of water for Chloe.'

'Some paracetamol?' he asked.

'I think we might be a bit beyond paracetamol,' Ottilie said grimly, 'but you might as well bring them if you can find them.'

She could hear Heath race down the stairs, and then opening and slamming cupboard doors while she and Stacey got Chloe propped up on her pillows and Ottilie tried to examine her.

'I'm sorry,' she said gently. 'This isn't very dignified.'

'I feel sick,' Stacey said, and Ottilie looked up, holding on to a frown. She'd had a lot to drink and she supposed this was all a bit much, but if anyone had to be strong now for Chloe, it was her mum.

'All I need you to do,' Ottilie said, 'is be there with her. You can do that. Tell me you can do that.'

There was a knock on the open door, and when Ottilie turned to look she could see Heath was there, his face turned away.

'Do you want to take this stuff from me? I don't think I ought to be in here.'

Ottilie pulled a sheet down over Chloe's legs. 'It's fine – she's decent.'

He turned with a look of profound relief as he put the supplies down on the end of the bed.

'Could I just get some air?' Stacey asked.

'A minute,' Ottilie replied, realising that if Stacey was going to be in any state to help she was going to have to sober up. And though midwifery wasn't Ottilie's strong suit, she hadn't seen anything to make her think that Chloe was going to give birth in the next few minutes. 'I'll call you if anything happens.'

'Where's Mum going?' Chloe looked panicked as Stacey left the room. She seemed a bit out of it. Pain and fear could do that, Ottilie supposed.

'She'll be back in a minute.' Ottilie reached for the glass of water still in Heath's hand and put it up to Chloe's lips. 'Take a sip; you'll feel better.'

Chloe pushed it away. 'The baby's coming, isn't it?'

'I think so.'

'It's too soon.'

'I think someone needs to tell Baby that,' Heath said, looking shell-shocked, and despite everything, Ottilie had the sudden urge to laugh at him.

Chloe started to squeal again, grabbing hold of Ottilie's hand so hard that she had to try hard not to cry out. She gestured for Heath to sit at the top of the bed where Stacey had been.

'Let her have your hand for a minute.'

Heath looked uncertain, but then Chloe grabbed it anyway. Ottilie could see the nails digging into his flesh, but he made no attempt to move away. At that moment, Ottilie didn't think she'd ever been prouder of anyone than this man who had no reason to be there, who owed none of them this and yet hadn't uttered a single word of complaint, not even when someone was trying her best to break all the bones in his hand. There was a beat of silence, something profound passing between them, and he managed a small smile which she managed to return, and her heart gave a skip before settling into its normal rhythm.

'It's coming!' Chloe cried, breaking the moment.

'I don't think...' Ottilie began, but Chloe screeched at her.

'Yes. It. Is! I want to push!'

'But you can't...'

There was no time to worry about Heath's presence. Doing

her best to keep Chloe covered from his viewpoint, she ducked down to check and sucked in a horrified breath.

'I can see the head...'

'What?' Heath yelped. 'Should I get Stacey?'

'No time,' Ottilie said with more composure than she felt. For the first time in her nursing career, she looked at a patient and wondered if she was up to the job. She'd never assisted an emergency birth before. They were in a house with no proper equipment and no medics apart from her. Whatever happened next, it was all on her, and the notion momentarily terrified her.

She reached out and gently cradled the top of the baby's head. It was warm and slippery, and she was going to struggle to keep a grip, but they were all Chloe had, so she had to step up to the plate; she had to be good enough.

'OK, Chloe,' she said, 'if you need to bear down then go for it. Remember to pant, try to take it steady – you don't want to tear.'

'Shut up!' Chloe wailed, gripping on to Heath's hand so hard that it went white.

The head emerged, and as soon as Ottilie had it in her hand, the rest of Baby followed. There was a charged silence as Chloe slumped onto the bed.

'Hand me the towels,' Ottilie commanded.

Heath passed them over and Ottilie wrapped the tiny figure up.

'Aren't they supposed to cry?' he asked, and Ottilie suddenly realised what was missing from this scene. She rubbed the towel vigorously over the little body and held her breath.

And then a second later, the cry rang through the air and she let out a sigh.

'Yes,' she said, smiling up at Heath. 'Just like that.'

'What did I get?' Chloe asked.

Ottilie placed the baby onto her chest, skin to skin, tears in her eyes. 'A little boy.'

'How much does he weigh?'

'Haven't the foggiest,' Ottilie said, laughing through her tears. 'I can't say getting the bathroom scales ready was top of my list of priorities.'

Heath stared at Ottilie, and then at the baby, and then back at Ottilie. 'That might be the most incredible thing I've ever seen.'

'Is he all right?' Chloe asked. 'Is everything there?'

'I expect the paramedics will check properly when they get here, but I think so,' Ottilie said.

At that moment Stacey burst in. 'What the...?'

'Where the hell have you been?' Chloe demanded.

Ottilie and Heath both laughed. It hadn't taken long for things to get back to normal – or whatever passed for normal these days.

'You know what's funny that we haven't even thought about,' Heath said as they sat outside to give the paramedics room to examine Chloe and the baby. Ottilie was glad of the cold air on her face. She'd hardly been stinking drunk when they'd arrived but she was definitely sober now.

'What?'

'Chloe's baby has just been delivered by Princess Leia.'

'Assisted by Indiana Jones. God, we should have taken a photo – she's going to want that one for the family album! Maybe she'll call the baby Heath.'

'Indy, more like.'

She blew out a long, tired breath, watching it curl into the night sky. 'It's at times like these I wish I smoked. I bet a cigarette is brilliant at moments like this.'

'You're incredible,' he said, and when she turned to look at him he was gazing at her with something like awe on his face. 'You were incredible in that room tonight. I've never seen anything like it. I've never met anyone like you. I thought you ought to know that before I lose the nerve to tell you.'

'You were amazing yourself.'

'No, I didn't do anything.'

'You were there when Chloe needed you. When *I* needed you. Heath, I was terrified up there. If not for you, I think I would have run away. But you were so strong and so calm it made me calm too.'

'You didn't look terrified.'

'I was. But you were there, and it was better. When you're there it's always…'

She paused. The words she'd failed to say weren't words she'd chosen; they'd come from nowhere, but she realised now that they might be the truest words she'd ever spoken. When she'd needed him he'd always been there. She might not have realised it or even welcomed it at times, but he had. That day she'd got stuck on the hillside with Flo, the day her house had been flooded and he'd driven straight over from Manchester with sandbags and a van, all the times he'd been to help fix her house, the time when he'd found her crying, tonight… and he'd never asked for anything in return. He'd simply been there.

Actually, that wasn't quite right. He had asked for one thing, once. And she'd refused him. She didn't even know now why she'd done that. She had feelings for him – she had since the day they'd first met. Complicated, yes, sometimes so muddled that she couldn't recognise them, sometimes more negative than positive, but she had them. So why was she ignoring them? Why was she denying they existed? What was there to gain? Josh would have asked the same question of her and he'd have given her the answer – there was no point in being alone when she didn't need to be, when there were feelings on both sides – at least, she hoped that Heath felt it too.

'You're cold?' he asked, draping his jacket around her shoulders.

'Thanks,' she said.

'I wonder if the party's still going. Do you think anyone's noticed we've gone?'

'If Magnus and Geoff have they're probably doing a victory lap, thinking they've finally succeeded.'

'Probably,' he said with a tired smile.

Come on, Ottilie, say it. You've been brave once tonight, just one more time.

'You know that thing you asked me that night,' she began slowly.

'What thing?'

Ottilie pulled the jacket tighter. She could smell his cologne on it. Her legs were suddenly trembling, far worse than at any other point that night. But there was a lot riding on this. Was she about to ruin their friendship? He'd once told her how fed up he'd been with his ex-wife's back and forth, wanting him and then not. Now Ottilie was doing the same thing.

'I think I might like to watch *Lady and the Tramp* with you. If you still want to, that is.'

'Oh,' he said, and nothing else, and Ottilie held in a groan. She'd blown it. Just like that she'd blown everything.

'It doesn't matter,' she said. 'We should go back inside.'

'Ottilie, no, wait...'

She turned to face him. He looked as uncertain as her.

'I just don't know what you mean by that and I don't want to get the wrong idea. I like you. Does that mean you like me too?'

'I always liked you.'

'You could have fooled me,' he said, and she couldn't help but laugh.

'OK that's probably a fair assessment. I did think you were a miserable pain in the arse when I first met you. But I realised I'd got it wrong pretty quickly.'

'I never thought that about you. I could always see you were special.'

'Really?' She raised her eyebrows, but he nodded, not laughing this time.

'I didn't want to admit it, so I found reasons to doubt you. You have to understand...' He let out a sigh. 'I'd been hurt before, I'd been messed about, I wasn't looking for...'

'For what?'

'For this. For you. I wasn't ready, and then there you were. I didn't know how to deal with it, and I think I dealt with it badly.'

'For what it's worth, I think I did too.'

'No, you gave what I deserved. You were never to blame.'

'Do you think we can put all that behind us and start again? Do you think we might be ready now?'

'Doesn't matter what I think. You're the one who matters.'

'I don't—'

'You do to me. You're the only thing that matters to me these days. You might not want to hear this, but I think about that day at Magnus and Geoff's cinema all the time, how wrong I got it, how I could have done it differently.'

'You didn't get it wrong; it was me. That's why I'm asking you this time.'

His smile was slow and unsure, but it was also full of warmth and hope. She ached to kiss him. She hadn't wanted to kiss a man like this since Josh, and though that notion caused her pain, she realised it was sort of a necessary, good pain. Josh would always be her first and she would never stop missing him, but she was beginning to see that her life didn't have to stop, that having a new love didn't wipe out the old one.

Here she was again, boring, safe, sensible old Ottilie. Why couldn't that girl just bugger off? He was giving her all the signals, and even though he was holding back, it was out of respect for safe, boring, sensible Ottilie. That Ottilie had turned him down before, but this Ottilie was sick of being alone, sick of denying that she liked this man – she might even love him if she only gave this thing a chance.

'I promise I won't mess you around,' she said.

'I never thought you would. You really mean this? I thought... once I'd learned what you've been through, I wondered if...'

'If I would ever have another man?'

'I understood why you were careful.'

'I could say the same to you.'

'What, that I might not want another man?'

She grinned and let her head fall to his shoulder. 'I'm being serious.'

'So am I – I don't want a man.'

'I do,' she said, surprising herself. 'I want you, and I'm sick of pretending I don't.'

'You mean that?'

She looked up at him. 'Yes. If you still want me.'

'God, you have no idea!'

She nudged up the brim of his hat and reached to kiss him. Her heart was thumping so loudly she wondered vaguely if the paramedics inside with Chloe might hear and rush out to her.

As he responded, folding her into his arms, it felt as if the ground might fall away from beneath her, but that wasn't scary; it was exhilarating, and in his arms she felt safe, knowing he wouldn't let her fall. A new chapter had begun; she could sense it already, one where she was allowed to start her new life properly, one where she was allowed to find happiness again. Of all the people who might have turned that page, she never imagined it would be him, but right now she was glad it was.

'*Lady and the Tramp* then?' she murmured as they parted. 'You still haven't given your answer.'

'Hmm. Next week?'

She frowned. 'Next week? You really want to wait that long?'

'No, I'm being polite. When do you want to do it?'

'There's no time like the present,' she said. 'How about tonight?'

'Tonight?' He smiled. 'I was hoping you'd say that.'

Just then, Stacey came outside. She raised her eyebrows and grinned as they broke apart, but she didn't mention what she'd seen. She looked exhausted but very happy.

'Everything's fine,' she said. 'You two were absolute legends.'

'I don't know about that,' Ottilie said, but Heath nudged her.

'You were – stop being so modest. You were bloody brilliant.'

'We all were,' Ottilie said. 'Has Chloe decided on a name?'

'Mackenzie.'

'Oh.' Ottilie laughed, nudging Heath again. 'Sorry, but it's not going to be Heath.'

'Middle name,' Stacey said with a wink, and Heath blushed in the most adorable way.

'Seriously?'

Stacey nodded.

'Seems like someone else appreciates you almost as much as I do,' Ottilie said.

'Want to come inside for a cup of tea?' Stacey asked. 'Chloe and baby are going off in the ambulance shortly, but I expect you'll be able to see them before they go.'

Instinctively, Ottilie reached for Heath's hand, savouring the contact as he wrapped it around hers. She looked up at him. 'Shall we?'

He smiled down at her. 'Ready when you are.'

And Ottilie was ready. She was ready for this, for her new life to finally begin, for another chance at love. Whatever was coming, she was ready.

With her hand in his, she led the way inside.

A LETTER FROM TILLY

I want to say a huge thank you for choosing to read *A Helping Hand for the Village Nurse.* If you did enjoy it, and want to keep up to date with all my latest releases, just sign up at the following link. Your email address will never be shared and you can unsubscribe at any time.

www.bookouture.com/tilly-tennant

I hope you enjoyed *A Helping Hand for the Village Nurse,* and if you did, I would be very grateful if you could write a review. I'd love to hear what you think, and it makes such a difference helping new readers to discover one of my books for the first time.

I love hearing from my readers – you can get in touch through social media or my website.

Thank you!

Tilly

KEEP IN TOUCH WITH TILLY

https://tillytennant.com

facebook.com/TillyTennant

x.com/TillyTenWriter

ACKNOWLEDGEMENTS

I say this every time I come to write acknowledgements for a new book, but it's true: the list of people who have offered help and encouragement on my writing journey so far really is endless and it would take a novel in itself to mention them all. I'd try to list everyone here, regardless, but I know that I'd fail miserably and miss out someone who is really very important. I just want to say that my heartfelt gratitude goes out to each and every one of you, whose involvement, whether small or large, has been invaluable and appreciated more than I can express.

I'd like to thank my good friend Paula Chell for her help in writing this book. I've always been impressed by her dedication to the nursing profession – as I am with all the nurses I know – and I've always been interested in her stories about her long career. She and others like her are an inspiration. Anyone who dedicates themselves to caring for others is special and deserves all the thanks we can give. Paula is the very best of these people – kind, compassionate, selfless, tolerant, understanding but also brilliant fun. Her love of people shines through in all things and I count myself lucky to know her. I'm also hugely lucky that she was patient enough to answer my many, many questions about nursing – and let me tell you, there were *many*!

I also want to mention all the good friends I have made and since kept at Staffordshire University. It's been ten years since I graduated with a degree in English and creative writing but hardly a day goes by when I don't think fondly of my time there.

Nowadays, I have to thank the remarkable team at Bookouture for their continued support, patience, and amazing publishing flair, particularly Lydia Vassar-Smith – my incredible and long-suffering editor – Kim Nash, Noelle Holten, Sarah Hardy, Peta Nightingale and Jessie Botterill. I know I'll have forgotten others at Bookouture who I ought to be thanking, but I hope they'll forgive me. Their belief, able assistance and encouragement mean the world to me. I truly believe I have the best team an author could ask for.

My friend Kath Hickton always gets an honourable mention for putting up with me since primary school, and Louise Coquio deserves a medal for getting me through university and suffering me ever since, likewise her lovely family.

I also have to thank Mel Sherratt, who is as generous with her time and advice as she is talented, someone who is always there to cheer on her fellow authors. She did so much to help me in the early days of my career that I don't think I'll ever be able to thank her as much as she deserves. My fellow Bookouture authors are all incredible, of course, unfailing and generous in their support of colleagues – life would be a lot duller without the gang!

I'd also like to give a special shout-out to Jaimie Admans, who is not only a brilliant author but is a brilliant friend. There's also an honourable mention for my retreat gang: Deborah, Jo, Tracy, Helen and Julie. I live for our weeks locked away in some remote house, writing, chatting, drinking and generally being daft. You are all the most brilliant women and my life is better for knowing you all.

I have to thank all the incredible and dedicated book bloggers (there are so many of you, but you know who you are!) and readers, and anyone else who has championed my work, reviewed it, shared it or simply told me that they liked it. Every one of those actions is priceless, and you are all very special people. Some of you I am even proud to call friends now – and

I'm looking at you in particular, Kerry Ann Parsons and Steph Lawrence!

Last but not least, I'd like to give a special mention to my lovely agent Hannah Todd and the incredible team at the Madeleine Milburn Literary, TV & Film Agency, especially Madeleine herself. I'm so lucky to be a part of such a dynamic agenting powerhouse!

I have to admit I have a love-hate relationship with my writing. It can be frustrating at times, isolating and thankless, but at the same time I feel like the luckiest woman alive to be doing what I do, and I can't imagine earning my living any other way. It also goes without saying that my family and friends understand better than anyone how much I need space to write, and they love me enough to enable it, even when it puts them out. I have no words to express fully how grateful and blessed that makes me feel.

And before I go, thank you, dear reader. Without you, I wouldn't be writing this, and you have no idea how happy it makes me that I am.

PUBLISHING TEAM

Turning a manuscript into a book requires the efforts of many people. The publishing team at Bookouture would like to acknowledge everyone who contributed to this publication.

Audio
Alba Proko
Sinead O'Connor
Melissa Tran

Commercial
Lauren Morrissette
Hannah Richmond
Imogen Allport

Contracts
Peta Nightingale

Cover design
Debbie Clement

Data and analysis
Mark Alder
Mohamed Bussuri